ISBN   Softcover   978-1-955531-66-5

ISBN   Hardcover   978-1-959071-48-8

ISBN   Ebook   978-1-955531-67-2

Printed in the United States of America.

Hollywood Book Reviews

The Galactic Traveler blends satirical commentary and time travel adventure for an original story and unique writing.

Embark on a journey through time with Enoch as he takes a front-row seat to human history. Starting with an opening that introduces Enoch's familial and Biblical history that gives an example of the story's tone that weaves science fiction, history, science, and humor.

At the heart of the story is the study of mankind's evolution throughout time which is framed by an original storytelling structure with character stories, scientific perspective on Biblical timelines, and time travel.

The use of time travel weaves in commentary on history through a variety of outspoken characters and their different perspectives on the world. Their experiences ground the story in humanity with an appreciation for the connections Enoch forms which are poignant as each one serves as part of the commentary that author Charles E. Anzalone captures well.

Reviewed by Ms. Liz Konkel at Hollywood Book Reviews on September 16,2022. Submitted here in its abbreviated form.

The Galactic Traveler,
The Story of Enoch

A special thanks goes to Ms. Liz Konkel at Hollywood Book Reviews for reading my entire book and casting her independent summary of its contents. She captured the essence of my novel that moves in many directions about human beings, like us, who live on another planet with the same human frailties. When the people on Planet Bethel are assigned a mission to help Earthlings, they are willing and cooperative with those that gave them their assignment.

As a parallel footnote, Mr. Russell says it all.

Bertrand Russell (1872-1970), who championed humanitarian ideas and freedom of thought, argued that the universe "is not what I chose it to be."

"If it is indifferent to human desires: if human life is a passing episode, hardly noticeable in the vastness of cosmic process; if there is no superhuman purpose, and no hope of ultimate salvation, it is better to acknowledge this truth than to endeavor, in futile self-assertion, to order the universe to be what we find comfortable."

With a Nobel Prize for literature in 1950, Russell was considered an idealist, an analytical philosopher of the 20th century. Regarding self-esteem, he said, "We are all, whatever part of the world we come from, persuaded that our own nation is superior to all others."

He explained that his life had three passions "the longing for love, the search for knowledge, and the unbearably pity for the suffering of mankind."

Author's Personal Comment

The memory of my best friend, Bill, has carried over into the main character of this book. Bill was a fun loving, socially attractive, man who loved to chase women, while he was still married. His sense of humor and likeability were the key to bedding them down, even until the age of sixty-five when he died.

The celebration with our wives for his birthday was a drag for him, but the celebration of my birthday, one month later, was delightful when he replaced his wife with his mistress. His wife didn't know about his mistresses. My wife and I knew what was going on, and it was strange, celebrating with two different women at elaborate restaurants. It was stranger, still, knowing that his mistress didn't know about the other mistress he had out-of-state, in Georgia.

"Do you think that's all?" he asked one day when we were in our mid-fifties. "I got a few more up in Wisconsin for when I visit my customers on a territorial sales call." People saw Bill as a likeable guy who could make them feel uninhibited. His success hinged on breaking down social barriers. Before he died, Bill had suffered a severe case of shingles and then a non-reversible case of cancer.

There's another chapter to Bill's life that resembled a merry-go-round with revolving beds, replacing bobbing horses. When we were both drinking at a local bar, Bill told me that both mistresses #1 and #2, Paula and Zella, knew he was married. Then he added that Zella knew about Paula, but Paula didn't know about Zella. Zella was cheating on her husband, the lieutenant who worked on the police force and carried a 38-caliber revolver.

Bill confessed that he was in a parked car in a forest preserve in Georgia with Zella, when a patrolman approached the car, recognized Zella, and said, "Hi, ma'am . . . I didn't know it was you. Sorry."

Bill told me that a 38-bullet had his name on it. He thought he could end his escapades faster by painting a bull's eye on his back and giving each of the three women a gun after telling them the whole truth. And then, he laughed it away as he wabbled on his bar stool, once again, and gulped down another shot of scotch and water.

My main character has the same likeable qualities, the ability to sell his ideas and to make people laugh. He also has the same problems, trying to limit his love to only one woman. He isn't as wild as my friend Bill, but he possesses the ability to be amiable with people.

Charles E. Anzalone,

(Names made up to protect the innocent.)

A quote from a book, titled _Ancient Engineers_

"The pious and learned Saint Thomas Aquinas (1225-74) spent much of his life arguing, at enormous lengths and in tiny illegible handwriting, that there was no conflict between science and religion; that all truth was one and that [in conclusion] Aristotle's logic [about science] must fit the Christian faith. In fact, Saint Thomas promoted Aristotle to a kind of pre-Christian saint.

"The pious and learned Ghazzali (1058-1111) also studied the science and philosophy of the Greeks but came to different conclusions. After mature and searching considerations, he decided that these studies were harmful, because they shook men's faith in God and undermined religion; 'they lead to loss of belief in the origin of the world and in the creator.'

"Europe followed Saint Thomas while Islam followed Ghazzali. For example, in 1150 the Khalifah of the moment proved his piety by burning books of a philosophical library of Bagdad. As a result of these diverging trends, science and technology flowered in Europe so richly and advanced so swiftly that the rest of the world is still breathlessly trying to catch up. On the other hand, science in Islam withered away.

"The real irony is that Ghazzali was right and Saint Thomas wrong. Science _does_ shake men's faith in God and undermine religion."

The Ancient Engineers by L. Sprague De Camp, p. 285

A belief in both science and religion, _is_ why I write this book.

The Author

Contents

The Galactic TRAVELER,

The Story of Enoch

"To travel across Orion's Highway, to teach man how to fly among the stars, to return the ancient history that he lost at the time of the Great Flood, to return the knowledge that he had for building the Sphinx and the Great Pyramid, to improve man's plight, to give him hope . . . one person at a time. That was my mission."

Enoch, the Galactic Traveler
AD 987 — AD 2087

By

Charles E. Anzalone

— Hollywood Book Reviews —
"The Galactic Traveler blends satirical commentary and time travel adventure for an original story and unique writing. Human history is shaped through a science fiction lens with specific language to draw you into a unique world . . . (with) commentary that the author captures well."

The Galactic Traveler, The Story of Enoch

You're traveling through the galaxy at twenty-five times the speed of light. You're moving through physical objects like they were never there. You're traveling in a dimension called imaginary time, where stars and planets are visible, and yet nonexistent. Imaginary time is that dimension where magnetic bubbles, traversing semi-metallic sheets, are moving through swirling electrostatic fields. You're not worried about the pilot, Charlie, up in the cockpit, dodging space debris because he's been flying W-25's for more than one thousand Earth years, and there's no need to set an alternate course around distant objects ahead. Lying across the console of the spaceship is a thick manuscript, flipped open as though Charlie had been reading about the exploits of his friend who was a Custodian with multiple visits to Earth—Earth, the same planet where Charlie is headed.

Charlie is thinking, —— *I have known Enoch since the time we would exercise in the gym, as young men, where he silently told a friend that I was a scrawny nerd. I may have lacked the physical physique he had, but I was the best galactic space pilot he had ever seen. If Enoch understood the psychology of people, I understood the mechanics of warp space flight. Even though our personalities differed, we became the best of friends. That is why I'm transporting his manuscript back to Earth for publication, at his request. His manuscript awaits my curiosity——a curiosity longing to open the cover and start reading.*

As the sole occupant of my W-25 spaceship, I can accelerate forward at twenty-five times the speed of light with thoughts from my brain, translated through my helmet. My ship is a light-sail, not to unlike a sailboat.

Everyone on our plant lives to a ripe old age of 1200-years, unless they have an accident or a heart attack. It was deemed so by our creator: the same God who created the Earthlings, our distant cousins. We look and sometimes act like Earthlings because we are the same descendants of Adam and Eve.

Enoch, whom I admired as a Custodian, had a convincing personality and a quality that made him the ideal Brothers' Keeper. He gave of himself so that others could make the right crucial decision at the right moment in their lives. Before I left my home planet of Bethel, Enoch handed me his manuscript, shortly before his death. His last request required that I should find a publisher on Earth. I looked at him with bewilderment and asked, "The Earth year is AD 2087! Will it make any difference who on Earth reads it?"

He replied, "Literature is the creation of order out of chaos." He believed that Earthlings were still living in chaos and that his book might help people to understand themselves and God. He gained his experience as the galactic traveler, while traveling to three different worlds: Earth, Planet Bethel, our home planet, and Geesal, where the Celestials live with advanced technology and spiritualism. The Celestials gave me this spaceship that I'm piloting.

To keep his manuscript in chronological order I've added the following calendar of events.

Charlie, his best friend.

Enoch's Age	Earth Year	Event
	2500 BC	Construction begins on Orion's Highway with the construction of Khufu's pyramid. The pyramid will generate buoys across the galaxy that serve as navigation beacons across a span of three light years. Enoch's cousins, the Sadees, (Sădĕĕs), did the initial work using Egyptians labor. Both Enoch's family and the Sadees lived on Planet Bethel until the Sadees went rogue.
0 AD	987	Enoch is Born
	1095 to 1291	The Christian Crusades; complete ended in 1313
16	1147	Enoch is sixteen years old.
20	1186	Enoch meets Steve; leaves to join Crusaders
20+1	1187	Major battle with Muslim forces under Saladin
	1385	Orion's Highway is completed across the cosmos
	1475 to 1564	Life span of Michelangelo: 89 years
	1512	Paints Sistine Chapel
52	1503	Nostradamus is born.
53+3	1513	Enoch's first visit with Nostradamus
54+5	1528	New training period for Nostradamus
	1756 to 1791	Mozart is born; Lives only 35 years!

79+7	1774	Enoch's visits Mozart at 18 years old
	1685 to 1750	Johann Sebastian Bach, the baroque-era composer
	1735 to 1782	Life span of Johann Christian Bach, son of Sebastian
	1799	Rosetta Stone discovered
	1822	Rosetta Stone deciphered
	1899 to 1975	Life span of Dr. Percy Lavon Julian
98+9	1967	Dr. Barnard's first human heart to heart transplant
	1922 to 2001	Life span of Dr. Christiaan Barnard
103+10	2020	Enoch attempts to help Edward
106+10	2052	Enoch's sentence is commuted
110+10	2087	Enoch dies in Earth year AD 2087 at:
		• Biological years: 110 years plus 10 Earth years for 120 years • In Bethel years: 1,200 years or (2087-987) + 100 Earth years.

Note: Enoch spent one-year in the Crusades; four, two, and two plus years with Nostradamus, Mozart and Dr. Barnard, respectively and one-year with Edward in the twenty-first century.

Chapter 1: Enoch Starts His Autobiography

I Am Enoch

If I was asked about a major event on our planet, Bethel, I would quickly say, "Yes, everyone knows that two thousand years ago, half of our population was ordered to leave, to evacuate, to find another home on another planet! It happened during a time-frame when a rabbi on your planet was crucified. Do you still want to hear more? Please allow this old man to explain the beginning . . . perhaps, the middle . . . or even the ending. It doesn't matter where I begin because my experiences are intertwined with traveling throughout the stars, visiting historical people on Earth, and living my own life here on Bethel, where I have lived for almost 1,200 years. My most vivid memories recall three topics: the events with the Sadees, as told by my teacher, the comments of my girlfriend, Beena, and the advanced thinking of my student, Edward."

The Sadees (Sǎ'dēēs) were ordered to leave our planet during the time period that corresponds to AD 50 on your planet. They were our cousins, our brothers, humans like ourselves, from one common ancestor namely, Enoch the First—sixth generation after Adam an

My name is also Enoch. I am a distant descendent of Enoch the First, which covers a time span of 15581 years (plus the common era), when Enoch and his small family were brought to this planet. I was born in AD 987 after the Sadees had vacated our planet, a mass migration of one-hundred thousand souls: some accepting their punishment and others protesting bitterly. To understand the Sadees, we have to talk about biological mutations on our planet and long-term physical changes on Earth. Nurture is the process caused by man; nature is evolution at work modifying man. On a time-scale, nurture takes half a million years and evolution takes millions of years. The "evolution of species" should never be confused with human mutation like the head-binding of babies' heads by the Sadees.

I speak from documented pages of our history books, spanning back to the First Book of Enoch and the five chapters of the Bible, written by Moses. Our history books record the year when Adam and Eve were born, the year when Enoch was born and his departure from Earth, the years when Gobekli Tepe and the Great Pyramid were built, the year of the Great Flood, and even, more recent in time, the year when Moses wrote about all these events. A time-frame of events is important in understanding the history we share. If we want to learn about the past, beyond Adam and Eve, we have to consult with our historians who can tell us about the evolution of man, starting around eight million years ago, when hominoids began walking across vines in trees.

Based upon the writings of my ancestor Enoch and his book titled, "The Book of Enoch," the subject of people, called Nephilim, arises. He writes about the Nephilim or the "fallen ones" who were the children of the sons of God and the women of Earth. It's all true and subject to interpretation, over and over again. Their hybrid children called the "fallen ones" and sometimes called "giants" were the start of God's chosen people before history was written on Earth.

Several thousands of years passed, and then, two species did mingle and cohabitate around fifty thousand years ago, specifically, the Neanderthals, migrating southward, and Cro-Magnon man, migrating northward into an area known today as Jerusalem, Israel. Cro-Magnon man, known as homo sapiens, prevailed over Neanderthals, replacing them throughout Europe and all remaining human-like species throughout the world. As Cro-Magnon developed and advanced, his species became known as homo sapiens-sapiens.

It would seem that God favored this species over all the other remnants of the family tree. Why is this true? Is it true because God has empathy? Does He favor the human race that is having a *rough-go-of-it*? Or more profoundly, are we another experimental race?

Introduction to the Timeline

"To turn back the clock"—is a twenty-first century phrase. It signifies—"Let's go back to the beginning." People living in 1500 BC, during the time of Moses, were as interested in their past as much as we are today. We have calendars and history books. They had only the writings of Moses in Genesis, chapter 5, to tell them about their past: a past filled with historical events, a past time-stamped as far back as Adam and Eve, generations begetting generations, great floods destroying the earth, human beings lifted from Earth—taken somewhere else, a past filled with numbers representing our ancient forefathers, their birth, their death, their age when they had their first born, when their first born died. So where is this ancient calendar of events, this documented timeline? To be brief, a timeline can be extracted from more than fifty numbers collected in chapter 5 of Genesis, a chapter devoted to ancestors "begetting" more ancestors. This is my story about my ancestor, Enoch, sixth generation after Adam, taken to live on another planet. (Genesis 5:24: "And Enoch walked with God: and he was not; for God took him") When properly decoded, the words of Moses reveal the following events:

- Adam and Eve were created in 22349 BC.
- Enoch, sixth generation after Adam, was born in 15581 BC
- The Great Flood occurred in 11382 BC

(The reader is asked to refer to Appendix 2 where the narrator is changed from Enoch to the author of this book.)

It is logical to assume several hundred years after the flood that the living conditions for both man and animal were on the cusp of extinction. Our library records indicate that Gobekli Tepe and the Egyptian Sphinx were constructed on Earth in 10735 BC and 10500 BC in an effort to save the animals exiting the Ark of the Covenant and to give the people of Egypt a purpose for continued living.

Enoch reflects, remembering his arguments with Beena:

My girlfriend, Beena, used to say, "The Holy Bible reads like a book of fascinating enigmas."

With strong objections and a raised voice, I would say, "No, it does not!"

"Well, that's what the Scouts say when they come back home and mimic the conversations of Earthlings."

Sitting in her apartment and drinking milk, while having a mild argument about the true origins of man, always aroused my own curiosity. I had to set her straight. "As you know, or don't know, Beena, according to the Torah or the Hebrew Bible, which is the equivalent of the Holy Bible, Adam had a wife named Lilith." The argument intensified because she had been reading a magazine article written by a research scientist on Earth.

She put her glass of milk down and started to read the magazine article to me, "The genus name of 'homo' represents an upright walking hominid. In their search for the missing link, paleoanthropologist named each species that resembles us as Homo Neanderthal, Homo heidelbergensis, Homo erectus, and Homo habilis. Earlier species had highbrow ridges and elongated football shaped heads whereas Cro-Magnon man had a round basketball shaped head. This physical change in shape would require millions of years of evolution, if evolution can be believed. The June issue of this magazine reports the existence of Homo sapiens, identified as Irhoud 10, living in Morocco, North Africa, 315,000 years ago." The magazine that she waved in my face was printed on Earth in the twenty-first century and delivered to our doorstep on Bethel, like so many other types of information.

"Yes, Beena," I replied, while wishing I was back in Brianna's Bar having a Scotch over ice, "the Holy Bible does not mention

Lilith but it infers that there were two Adams. Genesis, chapter 2, verse 7, says, '*And the Lord God formed man of the dust of the ground, and breathed into his nostrils the breath of life; and man became a living soul.*' The second Adam is inferred in chapter 2, verse 15: '*And the Lord God took the man and put him into the Garden of Eden.*' Neither the Bible nor the Torah indicates a timeline between the first Adam and the second Adam, specifically the time difference between verse 7 and verse 15. Let's assume the timeline is four hundred thousand years and look for the missing link during that era using the latest scientific evidence."

Beena calmly poured me another glass of milk and continued reading the magazine article, "From a statistical viewpoint, a major attribute like 'brain capacity divided by height' can be plotted into a histogram to illustrate that the curve lacks normality. Instead of a Gaussian curve (conformity) a Keratosis curve appears (non-conformity). Data for the ancient Homo species plots on an ascending curve indicating change whereas data for Homo sapiens and Homo sapiens-sapiens plots on a downward sloping curve. The two curves do not align into one. This curve proves that we are not a product of evolution as per Darwin's claim but a product of something starting with 'dust' as per the Bible. If that something, called 'dust', represents Homo sapiens like DNA consisting of 2 to 4 percent from Neanderthal, then our Earthly origins on Earth and here on Bethel are part Neanderthal."

"I think we're coming together," I replied. "If God created the remaining 96 to 98 percent, then that is how it happened some 315,000 years ago, the birth year of the first Adam."

"Yes, Enoch," she said with a smile, pronouncing my name with similar sarcasm, trying to be friendly again, and demonstrating she had won the argument, "the birth year of the 'second' Adam, who married Eve, occurred in 22349 BC, as we all know. We're taught that in grade school—the story of Adam and Eve!" She had emphasized the word *second* with a raised voice.

She dropped the magazine on the end table, and I could see the editor's graphs of data showing a linear progression of early man and a break in the transition for modern man. It was obvious that evolution was not at play here, but rather the hand of God.

While we were arguing about evolution versus creationism, I was thinking about an article I had read on one of my visits to Earth. It was an interesting magazine article, well written by an Earthling in the twenty-first century:

> *Take a moment to pay attention to your hands. It will be time well spent, because they are evolutional marvels. Hold one up. Examine it. Open and close it. Play with your fingers. Touch the tips of your four fingers with your thumb. Rotate your wrist. You should be able to turn it 180 degrees with ease. Ball your hands up into a fist until your thumb lies on top of and lends support to your index, middle and ring fingers. THAT IS SOMETHING NO APE CAN DO.*

"To your point," I replied, "the author of this twenty-first century magazine and most Earthlings still believe in evolution, without knowing that the simplest form of evolution takes tens-of-millions of years. Statistical data presented by our scientist had led me to believe that man on Earth did not evolve; He was put there. As you know, Beena, our civilization here on Bethel started in 15,581 BC, without any discontinuity in our history books. Our historians talk about evolution when they refer to our cousins, the Sadees who started binding their baby's heads to elongate their cranium, based upon their radical beliefs. After multiple years of generation to generation, head-binding the physical changes became permanent, along with their facial distortion, allowing their nose to start in the middle of their brow ridge. We lived with them in peace and harmony until their egregious evacuation from our planet happened. Why they chose to elongate their heads and why they had to leave . . . well, that's another story. My point is that human evolution on a major scale is nonexistent! Charles Darwin did not have sufficient data to draw an adequate conclusion." Beena had slipped out of the room and I could see, once again, I was talking to the wall where she had stood.

Introduction to Enoch and his People

After the Sadees left our planet, many people, like myself, speculated about the severity of their crime versus their punishment. The news and gossip about their crime was kept secret and minimized, with the exception of a few historians who had briefly noted their expulsion back in the AD 50, time-frame. More readily available were the memoirs of some Sadees who had written personal diaries, during the three periods of time when they were sent to Earth as Custodians to restore conditions after the Great Flood.

To resolve their big secret for my own benefit, I started to research the issue in AD 1167, when I was eighteen years old in post-graduate school after I had earned my degrees in psychology, medicine, and surgical operations of the heart. With an immense library, at my finger tips and a university setting for higher learning, I thought I could research the past for when three major events evolved around the Sadees. I had to know why one hundred thousand Sadees were *kicked off* our planet, so to speak.

Deep within the library shelves, I found several diaries that Sadee men had written around 10735 BC, 10500 BC, and 2,500 BC—the three periods when they were on a mission to help humankind. They were sent from our planet as Custodians, as benefactors for the descendants of Noah, living throughout the middle east and Egypt. After they were ordered to leave our planet in AD 50, they revisited planet Earth around AD 1500 on their own accord to rule as gods on a small Pacific Island. Before their demise, they had started as ambassadors and emissaries on Earth, compliant with a mandate to give comfort and hope to the survivors of the flood and to replenish the animals that had survived their journey in the Ark that Noah had built.

The first diary from a Sadee working as a Custodian, transcribed around 10735 BC, read as follows:

> After traveling through the cosmos for two years, our group landed on Earth [at Gobekli Tepe] where the animal pens had been built with a visual image of the specific animal confined to each enclosure. It resembled a zoo! We were there to keep many species from going extinct. All I heard were complaints from other Custodians, "I gave up a nice bed at home on Bethel to come here and take care of these dumb animals." The younger Custodians in our group kept making mistakes, like introducing the impalas into the same cage as the leopards. The wounded and old animals had to be put down with a drug injection, until the complainers invented guns to simply shoot the animals in the head. As they reloaded their guns, they would complain, "I've never seen so many animals. How big was the Ark?"

Another diary, transcribed around 10500 BC, read as follows:

> My group came from Bethel to build the Sphinx at Giza in Egypt. We used Egyptian labor to complete the task. The work revived the Egyptian workers by giving them a purpose, a sense of duty, a religious belief, and a self-identity. It helped their ego and their morale that had continued to deteriorate among the descendants of Noah, due to the discomforts of the new world. It was a place devastated by the flood that had inundated almost the

entire world. Vegetated gardens turned to deserts. We built the statue to give them hope, to see a man's head over the body of a lion, to say that they have dominion over all animals. And yet, there were some of us who called it a stupid statue. They didn't understand what the Earthlings needed; they lacked empathy . . . my own people, I'm sorry to say.

Another diary, transcribed around 2,500 BC, read as follows:

We are known as the Custodians of Egypt. Someday we will be the Custodians of the entire world. We wear different headgear among the workers while building their pyramid, so that they will remember us and revere us. Our headgear hides our elongated heads and allows us to physically look the same as the Egyptians. To do so otherwise, frightens them.

I stopped reading. I had read enough diaries to realize that the Sadees were becoming arrogant, carried guns, and lost their compassion for humankind. They had mentally and physically transformed themselves from being a "brother's keeper" to being god-like. Around AD 1500, the Sadees visited Easter Island with intensions of becoming more God-like. After being kicked off our planet in AD 50, they wanted to prove to our Supreme Being that the worship of false idols was okay. They became spiteful for losing their home on our planet. The natives build hundreds of statues all over the island, using the same antigravity technique the Sadees had shown to the Egyptians.

In summary, the first generation of Sadees started with purity and consideration for their cousins, the Earthlings. They understood their mission to be their brother's keeper, but successive generations lacked the good will, exhibited in the hearts of their forefathers. When they were told to terminate an animal in a humane way, they resorted to guns: little guns, big guns, pistols, elephant guns and even shot guns. In Egypt, they disrupted the cascadic rhythm of societies by introducing themselves as gods. The reason for their expulsion from our planet, Bethel, had to be a crime much worse. I couldn't find any diaries written around AD 50, telling me what had happened. I needed to talk to Father Aye, our religious leader and ambassador to the Celestials.

Explanations:

The following chart is a chronological series of events, illustrating the year when Adam, Eve, and Enoch were born per Genesis, chapter 5. After decoding all the numbers in chapter 5, a calendar merges with prehistoric dates for ancient ancestors and time-frames for when the Sadees helped humanity. It also illustrates the thousands of years that the Sadees had to alter the shape of their head permanently, by binding their baby's head year after year. Enoch II refers to the Sadees as his cousins and the people on Earth as his distant cousins.

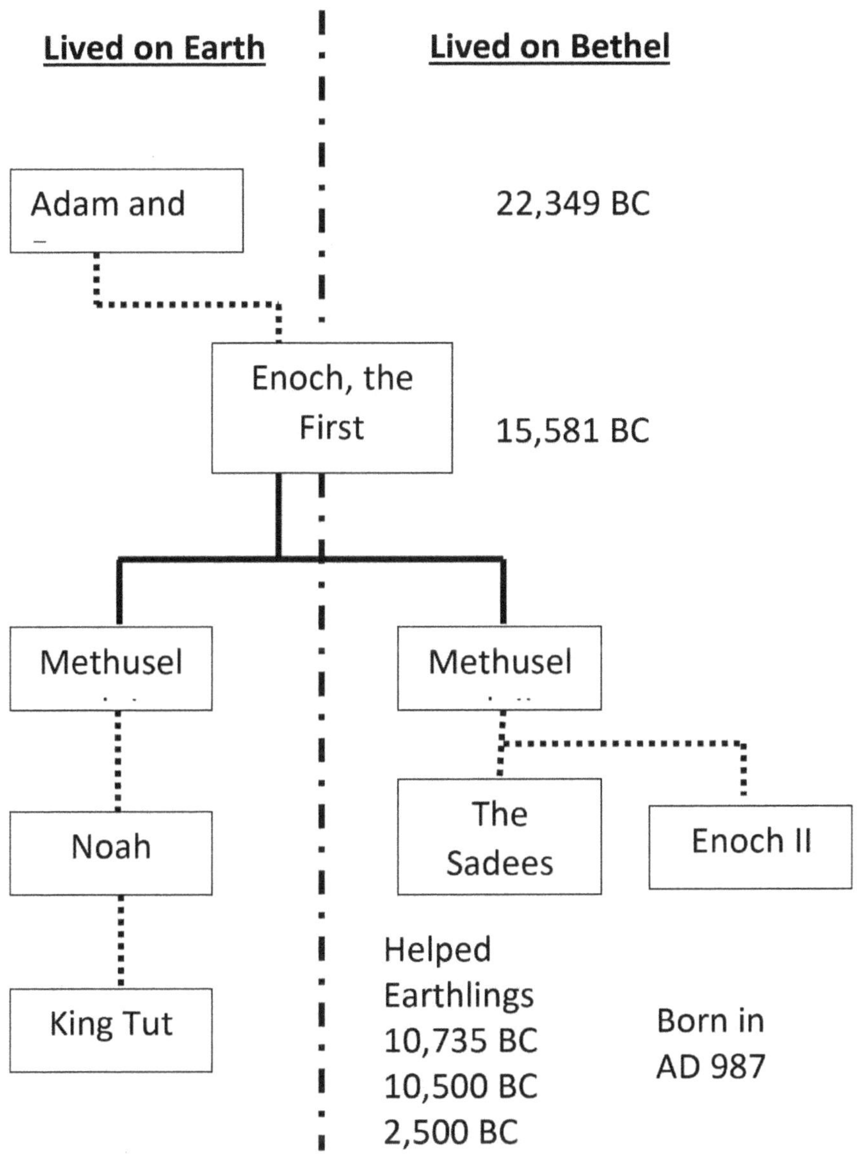

Enoch remembers Edward and his theories about galactic flight

My fourth client lived in the twenty-first century on Earth. The Scouts had arranged for our initial meeting as an accidental get together. They had studied his habits and the frequency of his visits to the local library. On the day he walked into the library, I was the librarian, fielding all questions.

"Can you please direct me toward any books related to creative writing?" he asked politely while standing on the other side of the library counter.

I would describe Edward as short and thick-set, partially bald with a residue of curly hair, inquisitive eyes behind glasses that he kept removing as he talked about his flight theories. He looked like most engineers in the twenty-first century—a nerd.

"Sure can," I said, trying to perfect my English idioms to match the twenty-first century vocabulary in America. "What's your goal?"

"I'm in the process of writing my third novel and I need some pointers."

I wasn't sure what he meant by *pointers* so I assumed it had something to do with help—help in the way of improving his sentence structure and prose. It sounded like he didn't want to win a Pulitzer Prize; he merely wanted to explain some engineering concepts with clarity. "I can help you on both accounts: finding the books and helping you with some minor editing. By the way, my name is Enoch and my nick name is Ernie, but you can call me Enoch if it doesn't sound too ancient to your ears."

"This is great," he said while packing the newly found books in his knapsack. "My name is Edward."

The following week, he returned to present me with a short article he had written after incorporating his newly found book knowledge. "Were you serious about the editing proposition?" he asked.

"I am," I replied and then started to lie, "I used to be an English professor during my younger days."

"Do you still teach?"

"No, but I like to read a lot."

"This is off the subject, but I need to know if you ever served in the military?" Edward asked.

"Yes, I did."

"Good, then you're a military man like me. I served in the Navy. Where did you serve?"

I couldn't lie about my past, anymore. With my eyes peeking over the top of my glasses, looking across the library counter, directly at him, I said, "The Crusades."

"You mean 'The Christian Crusades' like one thousand years ago?"

"Yeah," still trying to be accurate with the modern English expressions.

It's been said that the most outrageous lie or the most honest statement, presented with a look of sincerity, will always trump the actual truth.

"Yeah," he mimicked, "why not, okay, you served in the Christian Crusades." Then he continued, appearing to have totally erased from memory the last few sentences we shared. "Would you like to read one of my practice articles? It's based upon the writing instructions from the books you gave me. It's a lesson in creating master sentences or super long sentences, designed to slow down the reader."

"Sure," I said, while holding out my hand. "Does it have conflict, emotion and surprise? You need all three in a sentence, you know. Readers want a book with page-turners. They want to say, 'I started reading his book and I couldn't put it down.' I'll give you an example, 'Jones and his wife, returning from their vacation, were surprised to come home and find their house gone, their dog gone, their truck gone, their neighbor's house gone — for all of Atlantis had sunk into the sea.'"

"I get the idea." He smiled with askance. "I'll be back next week."

"I'll be here to give you my evaluation on your short article."

"Wait . . . as a matter of fact, I have the article right here — somewhere in my knapsack. Where the hell did I . . ." With his head bent downward he continued to search.

He handed me the article, and then I watched him leave the library, wondering about this type of client so different from all the others that my superiors wanted me to help. I started to read his article which really was a memoir of his earlier days when he was in the navy.

A Sailor in Prison

The prison cell, damp, musty, infested with three-inch roaches moving in the dark, was overcrowded, ten prisoners, six bunk beds, one urinal, men whispering in the shadows, others snoring in their beds, a few sleeping in a sitting position using the cell wall as a pillow.

"How did I get here?" I asked, late, as it was, three o'clock, maybe four o'clock at night; I had to get some sleep first before I could reflect on some serious answers. The bunks in the Mobile, Alabama, prison were stacked; right angle steel supports anchored to the wall, three feet, five feet and seven feet off the floor, one above the other. I had climbed into the highest bunk, uncomfortable, lumpy, and very different from my bed on the naval base back in Biloxi, Mississippi, a one-hour drive.

"How did it happen, earlier that evening, around eleven o'clock?"

Under the shadow of a ten-cent store, obscure from the moonlight, I had parked my car against the brick wall, where I slept while the police staked out the area for burglars who wanted to plunder again. Quickly, I became their suspect. A few feet from the car's front bumper, the store's brick wall, monotonous to look at, emptied random thoughts from my mind, putting me to sleep, unable to see two officers in my rear-view mirror, approaching on foot. Thoughts of having found a new girlfriend, kissing her good night only moments ago, kept me awake; the police knocking, pounding, banging on my car window also kept me awake. Visions of her shapely legs from the backside, climbing the narrow stairwell of her apartment, conflicted with visions of the cop hammering on the window, causing me to fade in-and-out of consciousness with memorable pleasure and then pain, followed by emotional repeats––pleasure, pain, . . . her legs: beautiful to see, warm to touch, the muscle in her calves fanning upward with a perfect bulge, firming with each step upward, then relaxing with softness––firm, soft, firm, soft, as she climbed the stairs.

Wearing a 1930's gangster's hat, hiding half his face, a mysterious looking man in the dark suit, banging on the car window, said in a stern voice, "Roll down your window." Then, with more emphasis in his voice, he continued, "Step out of the car, NOW." After flashing something in his hand that could have been a police officer's badge, a tin-can-top, a metal belt buckle, or a shiny pack of cigarettes, he repeated his command. "Get out of the damn car!"

I said nothing, not knowing who they were. After he repeated his command two more times, I said, "Screw you." Immediately afterward, a strong arm belonging to the second officer opened the car door and yanked me out of the driver's seat before I knew what had happened. Locked in the back of their cruiser, I was on my way to prison. They were through talking to me or trying to be nice, as nice as they could be.

To awake in the middle of the night seeing a three-inch roach crawling up the wall, inches from my face where I slept, to hear a man at the barred prison door yelling across the hall, "Thelma, I love you,", to feel put down, is an experience hard to forget. Thelma mumbled something in the woman's holding cell at the end of the distant hallway, while another man in our cell told Thelma's lover-boy to shut up, with a threatening voice, about to jump down from his seven-foot raised bunk and back up his threat.

The morning sun, shining through the barred, prison windows, splashing light on men's faces, covered with beard stubble and dried vomit, failed to bring any hope of good news. Breakfast was not forthcoming, probably thought of as a waste of time, too much effort, too much summer heat, too much bother. No one was released, Thelma's lover-boy still professing his love for her with a whispering, hoarse voice, a weaker voice, a fading voice, other men grumbling a hello as if to say, "Get out of my way, got to use the urinal [expletive deleted]." In the middle of the prison cell, sitting on a concrete stoop, one foot above the bottom floor, two men negotiated, bargaining for anything that would improve their lot.

"How many more days do you have in this hole?" said the first man.

The second man responded, "I don't know, maybe thirty."

"How would you like to trade my time for your time?"

"Why? How much time do you have left?"

"Four days! You could get out in four days instead of thirty days if we trade. Okay?"

"Why would you want to trade?" said the second man, trying to sober up and come to his senses.

"Well, I'll tell yah. My lousy mother-in-law is coming over to our house for two weeks and I don't want to be around the damn house when she's there."

Eleven o'clock and the perpendicular sunlight were approaching, what was the delay; the thought of another night in prison, without any news about my release or my dinner, reduced the volume of my subconscious voice saying, "It'll be okay. Stop worrying." It was not okay as thoughts of a captain's mass for going AWOL lingered in the back of my brain, the morning's roster list, unanswered, one voice not responding — my own voice missing rollcall.

Around twelve o'clock, Shore Patrol from my base in Biloxi came to release me. Since I was the property of the US Navy — not the Mobile police — they asked very few questions and then told me the location of my car, parked outside the police station.

Looking back sixty-plus years, when I was twenty-one years old, I realize now that I was wrong: failing to cooperate with plain-cloths police officers, resisting arrest, acting cocky. I resisted because, as the saying goes, I was empowered; I could do no wrong. My confidence on a date with a new girlfriend made me feel bold. Attitudes of feeling bold, righteous, or justified can diminish a man's perspective and his respect for authority . . . unfortunately . . . regrettably. The police had the authority to protect the ten-cent store that had been robbed the day before. They were doing their job, protecting, watching, ascending with authority, empowered, after I swore at them, owing me nothing.

Edward

On the following week, Edward returned to the library, where I greeted him and complimented him on his short memoir. "Your best sentence was eighty-four-words long! Congratulations for achieving a master sentence. Always remember, long sentences create 'style.' But be careful. They have to have logic to be effective. For a better understanding of master sentences, you should read—"

"Yes, but what did you think of the story?" Edward interrupted.

"Did she really have beautiful legs?"

"She had wonderful legs. Let's get back to the editing."

"It had depth, conflict, and more importantly a sub-plot with the drunks wanting to stay in jail. I see that you exercised the lessons of two and threes, a short burst of words sandwiched between compound, complex sentences. It resembles the writings of Virgil who wrote a book called the Aeneid. He wrote the epic poem in metrical verse, a kind of rhythmical phrases compressed into one sentence. I'm recommending that you also read *The Aeneid*. The books I gave you taught you well about creative writing, representing the art of *showing* and not *telling*. Descriptive writing allows the reader to visualize the inside of a prison cell, the strong arm of the law yanking you out of your car, your girlfriend with the beautiful legs. You did well. At a later time, we can discuss the ways to build dramatic sentences with paratactic structures, and conversely, hypotactic structures. We'll discuss sentences with a repetition of words, known as antimetabole, anaphora and polyptoton." I saw I was losing him with big words, and I had to revive his attention span. "You also narrated a story about a secret, a secret you must have carried with you for years and years. I know that —"

"That's right it was an embarrassing secret. I wanted to share it with no one," Edward said, muffling his voice, turning away into the other direction.

"I have a secret I would like to share with you. Do you remember last week when we were talking about the Crusades?"

Edward nodded as I handed him a short memoir of my experiences. We moved to a private conference room, where he started to read about my secret in the Crusades, one thousand years ago. I felt comfortable knowing that we were the only ones sitting in the library's smaller room. My writings and comments were highly confidential and intended only for him.

The Crusades

His horse bolted from a standing-still position as Steve rallied him into battle with a fierce sounding war cry, his boot heels jamming into his horse's belly, his lance under his right arm, his shield in his left hand, protecting his heart. Our two companions also let out a loud shriek, the sounds of which I never heard before. I assessed my feelings as anxious and my surroundings as an inhospitable desert, stretched to the door steps of Jerusalem. It didn't make much sense what we were doing, except that we were there to rescue the Ark of the Covenant, or even steal it if we had to.

Enoch

"Wow," Edward daydreamt. He suddenly realized I had lived centuries into the past. He thought of himself sitting on a horse, visualizing the pageantry, sharing the experience vicariously. "How do you steal an Ark?"

Needless to say, Edward was shocked to learn that I was a time traveler. He had a million questions about the Crusade, the Ark, and who I was exactly. As a Custodian, bound by our law, I was restricted from revealing too much information about space travel and Earth's historical past. He had written two books on the same genre and now he wanted to write his third book in a way that would capture people's imagination. When he was sitting in a hot tub with his sister and family, he started talking about Orion's belt and naming all the stars. His sister looked at him and asked, "Who gives a shit?"

"I'm here to make sure you're third book is a success," I said trying to get through his stary-eye look.

"What?"

"While traveling to Earth, I read both your books."

"What?" Edward knew that his questions would go unanswered if he asked Enoch about warp drive and what made a spaceship travel faster than the speed of light. How was it possible for a twenty-first century man to ask a man from the twenty-second century a question like that? He could see a fixed expression on his face and knew their conversation was terminating.

"They're too technical. Your books! People don't care about learning how to fly through the cosmos. They don't give a shit."

"What?"

And that was all Edward could say until his brain absorbed the concept of an alien visitor, who looked like any other person on Earth and spoke with a poor knowledge for English idioms. The absorption process took a full week before I saw him again.

The weeks passed. "Hey, Edward," I said when I spotted him walking into the library. "Are you up to taking an impromptu composition test."

"Sure, Enoch, what do you want me to write about?"

"Just a short story from out of the blue. Okay? You write one and I'll write a similar one about a fictional story. You know . . . as fictional as you can make it."

"You're on! This is for practice, right?"

Before Edward began to write, he asked, "I want to know something more about you, Enoch. Tell me about something you know, something Earth-shattering."

"Okay. Just this one time I can tell you something that our scientist know that is Earth-shattering. Keep in mind, our scientists do not always invent, but they do always observe. I can tell you about their latest observations regarding Earth's orbital path around your sun. Is that okay with you?"

"Yes, I'm very interested" Edward said, leaning closer across the library's conference table from where he sat.

To prevent others in adjacent rooms from hearing, Enoch began with a whispered voice, "As you already know, global warming is caused by man burning fossil fuels and deforestation, but it's also the result of the slow methodical change that occurs as the Earth orbits your sun in an elliptical path. Perihelion occurs in early January when the Earth is closest to the sun at 91.34 million miles. Aphelion occurs in early July when the Earth is farthest from your sun at 94.45 million miles. If you calculate the reduction in the radius, you get 3.29 percent.

Prior to the Great Flood, our scientist noted that this number, the radius reduction, used to be less than 1 percent. Both the radius reduction and carbon dioxide in the air have tripled since the Great Flood occurred. The change in the radius reduction hasn't changed the number of days in a year; it merely provided for hotter summers and colder winters. There was a time when the Sahara Desert was a green, lush savannah."

"Are you saying that Earth's orbital path around the sun used to be concentric and now it's elliptical?" Edward shouted.

"Yes. And it's following a path that's more elliptical."

"But why?" Edward asked with his eyes slightly wider.

"Because, it just happens that your solar system is travelling through the galaxy with Earth's orbital path polarized such that the perihelion and aphelion are directly in line with the center of the galaxy. The flat side of the orbital path always leads the way, colliding with small asteroids and meteor dust, rocks and debris."

"When you say 'flat side', are you referring the Earth's orbital path where the arc has a smaller curvature?"

"Exactly."

"What can be done about this problem? This secondary aspect of global warming, as you put it?"

"Nothing. As the flat side grows flatter, Earth's orbital path grows more elliptical. However, many things can be done to reduce global warming as you well know."

"Yea, I know," Edward agreed. "I'm ready to start a practice writing session."

"Okay," I encouraged, "write a short story about the most fictional, far-out, unimaginable thing you can think of."

While still sitting at the library's conference table, Edward began to write.

The Five Stages:
Denial, Anger, Bargaining, Depression, Acceptance

Eddie, a young bachelor, returned to his apartment on a late Friday night after a full day of work and some heavy drinking at the local bar with his buddies and coworkers. Laughing to himself and still drunk, he turned on his sixty-inch-wide screen television, only to see an unbelievable commercial with green aliens, standing in the cosmos and talking to him. "We need to speak to your leader," they said in synchronous voices. "Earth will be destroyed within five days!" Eddie simply crashed into bed, fully aware of what he had seen.

On Saturday, he remembered what he had seen on television and assumed that it was a wacky commercial. He was in complete denial until the commercial repeated itself that night. On Sunday, he was angry because he felt he had been singled out. The commercial was on all channels that night.

While sitting on the bus traveling to work, he bargained with himself, *No, this can't be true. How am I supposed to reach the President and tell him that the world will end?*

On Monday, the green aliens on the television were more emphatic in their demands, "We need to speak to your leader now." Eddie went into a state of depression.

On the next day he made up his mind that he would do something about *this world crisis* and get help. Tuesday was the day that the world ended, swallowed up by a maverick black hole randomly traveling through the galaxy.

Edward

"Off the top of your head, that sounds pretty good," I commented. "Your writing reflects your thoughts by not wanting to accept me as an alien from another planet. Is that correct?"

"Yes, you may look like us, you may talk like us, but you are different," Edward blurted out, slightly angered.

"How am I different?"

"It's your composure, your demeanor—no, not that . . . It's your tranquility like you've been saved. And it bothers me when you won't tell me about your world or what it's like being a galactic time traveler. All I know is that you're old, but you don't look any older than me."

"How old are you?"

"Eighty-ish?" Edward guessed.

"Okay," I relented, "I'll let you in on my secret. I'm one thousand and thirty years old, in Bethel years—the planet where I come from— and 103-years old, in Earth years."

"Wow. Never would have guessed. How long does your species live?"

"Our life span is fixed at 120-Earth-years, as per the Bible."

"Okay, the Bible. I'm not going there," Edward said as he pushed his chair back from the table.

"I just finished my improvising. You should read this."

Diary Entry #362 [Earth year 2022]

The big-feet people were good workers, extracting ore from the mines underneath the craters on the far side of the moon. The ore contained an element known as Moscovium that rocketed our shuttle craft, while transporting ocean water from Earth to the moon. Simple electrolysis of the water gave us the hydrogen we needed for the Moscovium fuel enhancement and the oxygen that the big-feet people needed to breathe. It was a symbiotic arrangement: we needed to monitor the Earthlings and the big-feet people needed a decent wage for working in a harsh environment under the moon's craters, where they would sweat until their long reddish fur was drenched with perspiration. They stunk so bad that we could not possibly transport them back to their home planet on our galactic cruiser. Shower water aboard our cruiser is scares! The only solution that our commander recommended was to give them a bar of soap and let them wash off the stink in a remote lake or river somewhere on Earth. We could always monitor their progress and protect them from intruders so that no one knew they existed.

Enoch

"Exceptional," Edward commented. Then he squinched his face. "Why do you title it as a diary entry?"

"Because . . . " I paused, choosing my words carefully and then continuing, "it's a totally fictious story written by an alien as a journal entry. Would you like to continue the story by adding your improvisions?"

"Okay, that's a challenge, here goes."

Diary Entry #362, Continued

Millions of years ago, the big-feet people lived on Earth. Their species, the Gigantopithecus, were becoming extinct. To propagate their species, the good aliens transported small groups to different planets in the galaxy where life was more conducive. They became physically different because they evolved in different environmental conditions.

Edward

"Very good," I said. "It needs only one correction. Don't say *good aliens* because you haven't distinguished between what is good and what is bad. Remove *good.*"

"Okay——"

"And, congratulations for spelling Gigantopithecus correctly. You have a good imagination," I said with a little eye wink.

I wanted to tell him that my composition was not fictional, but true. I suspected he knew about the ape linage because he lived in the twenty-first century. In writing a fictitious story, he subconsciously pieced together the truth. Hominids on Earth, called Big-foot, did exist! According to Father Aye, the descendants of Gigantopithecus were used by the Celestials to mine on the far-side of the moon, under the craters, for a rocket propellant that allowed them to visit Earth. Father Aye said the Celestials had a fueling depot in a geostationary orbit, miles above their mining operation. During the automation process, robots in the space-factories extracted the radio-active element and then dumped the spent ore overboard, onto the moon. I never believed him until I thought about all the mining ore, discarded in piles on the far-side, and thick moon dust deposited on the near-side of the moon, due to low gravitational settling effects.

The Celestials needed rocket fuel because they were constantly monitoring Earth for centuries—its progression, its disasters, its inventions, and its people. At altitudes beyond the range of an ordinary x7-binoculars, belonging to any Earthling, the Celestials could see Big-foot alongside Earthlings. With their huge monitor screens, they knew exactly when an Earthling was approaching them. To remove Big-foot from danger they would swoop down in their spaceship, extend their dimensional field, and scoop them up. Each country on Earth had different sightings and descriptions of Big-foot. Their physique, their hair color, and their attitude were different because they came from different worlds to work for the Celestials on the moon. Different species existed among the big-feet people because they evolved differently on their individual home planets.

It's ironic, but the big-feet people evolved with a mental capacity similar to the people on Bethel. They, like ourselves — lacked the capacity to invent. Earthlings have a gift that allows them to transition from earlier inventions like a grass bracelet, flip-flop shoes, and sewing needles to modern inventions like bicycles, automobiles, and finally nuclear bombs.

The Earthlings have the mental capacity to invent—not only material things but antiviruses, as well. So why would a ten-foot, big-foot-person work for a four-foot Celestial who's telling him where to dig down in a mine shaft under the moon's surface?

While listening to Edward as we sat in the library's conference room, thoughts about our race rambled on. Random conclusions bounced around in my brain:

Why do "we" work for the Celestials and do their bidding? It's obvious that we share the one gift that only the Celestials can give us; specifically, vaccinees and antibodies capable of destroying the so many viruses that infest the galaxy. When you think about it, there is no Lucifer, no Satan, no Beelzebub. The only anti-God particle that exists throughout the universe is the virus: a mass population killer, a non-directional, guided entity that strikes anywhere including children and the elderly. I was in Europe, centuries ago, during the spread of the Bubonic plague. I saw it decimate two-thirds of the population. And now I'm seeing it here in the twenty-first century with another virus that Edward refers to as COVID-19. It has killed almost a million people in the United States.

The big-feet people and my people know that the Celestials — working with God — can stamp out any virus with a vaccinee more potent, more lasting, ten-times faster, and more effective than any product developed by the Earthlings. It makes me wonder about Earthlings and if they are an experimental study to see how far they can go with their inventions, while maintaining a fractured society.

Even though, the people on Earth and the people on Bethel are related, the people on Earth have mentally advanced to a dangerous point where they need to be monitored by the Celestials. The Celestials advocate that the Earthlings should take a slower, steady advancement in the direction of science, the arts, and love for their fellow man. That's why I'm here on Earth again. I hope this is the last time I visit Earth. I'm getting tired and weary.

The Celestials also monitor Custodians like myself. Edward was my fourth client and I suspected the Celestials were monitoring me, as well. I'll continue with Edward's efforts to provide his views on galactic space travel in the latter part of my manuscript. I'll explain the following topics at the right time and place within my manuscript.

- Who were the Sadees and why were they forced off our planet?
- Who were the people with oblong heads and how did that get started on Earth?
- Who are the Celestials that we report to? And who do they report to?
- How are the exact dates of the Great Flood known?
- How is a calendar of ancient ancestors from Adam and Eve known?
- Why is there a time dilation between planets?
- Does Edward explain his theories about the universe, antigravity, and galactic space flight? Is he close to being right?

In the meantime, my thoughts race ahead once again:

I started my composition with memoirs in my final years, writing on a rickety old table, recalling the most memorable events in my life, the memory of Father Aye with his schooling about our planet's history, Beena with her loquacious arguments about man's origins, and Edward with his scientific theories. Then I realized that I'll have to present my credentials.

My education on Bethel had provided me with constant information about Earth's history. I had graduated as a doctor of medicine and a heart surgeon with advanced skills that I learned on planet Geesal, home of the Celestials. My travels across the galaxy gave me additional knowledge about the universe, a story that must be told.

I have to start this manuscript at the beginning, an autobiography of my life, working with Earthlings throughout the ages. As I had stated in my first few paragraphs, I could start writing from the beginning, the middle, or the ending years of my life. Perhaps, these are the memories that stand out: the Sadees with their departure from Earth, Beena with her frequent verbal debates, and Edward, lost in the woods, overwhelmed, surprised, wanting to learn more about my visit from another planet and how I traveled to Earth. If Edward had been born in Germany, France, Ethiopia or wherever, I would have learned that specific language in one day from our Scouts who update our library with its acoustical learning center, here on Bethel. Over the centuries, there were three other clients for whom I had had a successful mission; specifically, Nostradamus, Mozart, and Dr. Christiaan Barnard.

Nostradamus was a quick learner in the herbal arts of medicine and a gifted philosopher on historical predictions and potential consequences.

Mozart gave to many an appreciation for music that endeared their hearts and lightened their souls. He could take someone's music composition and replay it on a piano with small musical additions that surprised the listener and made them want more. That was the essence of Mozart, the giver.

Dr. Christian Barnard showed how we can extend our lives and appreciate the world a little bit longer. He was a pioneer in his field, a pioneer that just needed a little shove in the right direction.   . . . And now, I need to start at the very beginning of my life.

Chapter 2: My Beena: The Christian Crusades

My Early Surroundings

To be fair in the description of our planet, I have to say that we live on Bethel in a way similar to Earthlings who lived in Egypt centuries ago. Expressed in Earth years, the present time on our planet is AD 1147. I was born in AD 987 and by Earth's measurement standards, I am sixteen years old or 1147 take away 987 and divide by ten. The ten factor is a dilation in time which I'll explain later.

As I start my autobiography, I realize the need to create a visual image of our small sleepy town that exists alongside a lazy flowing river that meanders through adobe huts, lush-green palm trees and the hot summer air: . . . not too unlike the river Nile gently flowing through Egypt. Our Main Street parallels the river with a few business dwellings, a tavern at one end and a pyramid over five hundred feet tall at the other end of the street. Our pyramid was the prototype for the one that was built on the Giza

Plateau of Egypt. Everything is the same as it was in Egypt, except for our native language that translates into different names for our buildings, streets, etc., and for our metrics of time, like my age.

Overall, the view of our town resembles a lush oasis, populated with date-nut trees and fringed by the desert. Beyond the boundaries of our town, other towns exist with thousands of miles of separation and each town governed by a patriarch. The population of our world is very small, one resident for every one hundred thousand residents on Earth. Consequently, our patriarch, whom we call Father Aye, should have a job that's not too demanding as the rest of us fulfill our job assignments. Not so! We don't exactly live in a eutopia with Father Aye and the rest of us languishing about. On the contrary, everybody is busy, flying in and out of our town at the spaceport and completing their missions on Earth.

The flow of time is the biggest difference between the two planets. A man on Earth can live to eighty years of age, which is considered a very long time: whereas, the same man could live to eight-hundred years if he were on Bethel. And now, I need to create a visual of my teenage girlfriend, Beena.

Two Teenagers, Beena and Enoch

Along the banks of a lazy river, winding its way through a sleepy town filled with adobe huts, farmlands, and swaying date-nut palm trees, lies a civilization on planet Bethel, not to unlike the residents in ancient Egypt. Two teenagers following a path along the river are enjoying the afternoon sun and each other's company.

"The river walk always enlightens my spirits," Beena said. "I love to see the green grass growing under palm trees, nestled alongside a pyramid while a river flows as far as the eye can see. It takes my mind off the drudgery of learning how to be a nurse."

"It also takes my mind off learning how to be a doctor," I replied, anxious to forget about work.

As we walked along a small path away from the public, only the burbling sound of the water could be heard from the river nearby. Beena's voice was melodious, soothing, feminine and comforting as we approached the Crocodile tavern jutting out onto a pier above the river. Laughter always flowed from the tavern like a party had started. Their laughter was faint at first and then grew louder as we drew near.

"How many more years do you have until you graduate?" I asked.

"Two. And yourself?"

"One. And then I'll be able to practice being a physician. I know our society is as arcane as early Egyptians, living during the time of the pharaohs. We're almost as bad, but we do have advanced machines for X-ray diagnosis and magnetic imaging for further analysis. Up-to-date drugs make us live longer lives. Sometimes, I have difficulty with the names of drugs on our planet. I find it difficult to learn and cross-reference our vitamins with the herbs on planet Earth. Still, everyone needs a doctor. Do you plan to work in the hospital, Beena?"

"Yes. I would like to work in a big beautiful hospital that has no ugly looking appendages like that tavern hanging over a scenic river." Her voice became angry, ending with a sudden thud.

Beena was contemptuous over a broken-down tavern built on top of a pier where the population enjoyed their drinking sport. The path they followed lead into Main Street, located a few feet from the front door of the tavern where loud voices bellowed.

"Hey," I defended, "I think it looks great. That's the famous Crocodile Tavern." But, Beena continued her tirade.

"It's a disgrace. Filled with drunks and loud mouths."

"No honey. It may look run down on the outside, but the inside is quaint with soft-red stucco-walls and gas lamps. Maybe I'll go in there and celebrate when I become a doctor!"

"Yea? You'll have to . . ."

"Have to what . . ."

"Turn eighteen first! And how do you know the insides of the tavern?"

"I . . . I . . . I," I stammered, "I'm innocent." As soon as I said *innocent*, I suddenly remember the time when I was a small boy and I peeked through the open doors of the tavern and saw a blond-headed little girl, about my age, sweeping out the dirt on the floor.

The reality is that there were drunks walking out of the tavern through two different doors: the entrance door and the back door filled with a surprise. In their confusion, they walked out the back door that had no porch and immediately fell into the river . . . supposedly, filled with crocodiles.

As we continued our walk, we pass the open front door through which bellowing laughter flowed. "Disgusting," she reverberated in a voice slightly harsher than before.

When I had grown several years older, I came back from the Crusades to learn that the river didn't have any crocodiles below the tavern and that two things will quickly sober a drunk: cold river water and fear of surviving a short drop into a deep river with imaginary animals. I had had my first beer when I was a Crusader and I thought it tasted terrible until I got used to it. In addition to the decor and gas lamps, the tavern attracted me to a woman inside. I stopped acting like a boy-kid and became a man after the war. Beena never knew I had stepped into that tavern where my destiny would change.

As a boy-kid, I graduated at a very early age and became a fully certified doctor of medicine. I specialized in diseases of the heart with a minor degree in pharmacy. Beena and I took extra curriculum classes in drug medications. Pharmaceutical drugs on our planet can cure almost any disease with the exception of one: the Angio disease.

After I opened a small doctor's office a short distance from the pyramid, I treated many patients. My real goal, however, was to continue my work researching the Angio disease—a disease that limits our population growth. After Beena graduated, she treated women who could not have children and helped part-time in my laboratory. I enjoyed only a few months as a physician between the time I graduated and the time before my induction into the Crusades. I was barely getting started with a wonderful career as a physician when change came.

Excuse me for getting ahead of myself. I need to return to my teenage years and Father Dean's inspiring lectures.

Father Dean and His Lectures

Father Dean was a priest, a typical over-fed, white-robed administrator with a chubby torso, extra rolls of skin belying his robe, shaven head, blue eyes and a puffy nose. His voice reflected his character and projected his destiny—a kind, empathetic, understanding soul. He had a scientific grasp on the knowledge of Earth's ancient history and the location of our planet's library records. In reality, Father Dean was a complicated man with a list of postscripts that dangled from the innards of his mind, reminding him of things he had to do. Despite his nervousness attributed to his never ending "to-do" list, his lectures transitioned fluidly from one scientific topic to another. His students never questioned the logic of his lectures because their own theories encompassed his lectures. His wisdom pinnacled over technical details—especially over the construction of the Great Pyramid on Earth and its prototype, first-built on Bethel.

His diction was slow and methodically spoken in our native tongue that he preferred even though he could speak seven or eight Earth languages. On occasion, he would throw the class in disarray by lecturing in multiple languages: each sentence different from the preceding one. He began:

The prototype for the Great Pyramid was a practice session to refine the technology that would eventually result in a highway among the cosmos, stretching three light-years beyond Earth. It was to be and still is a navigational aid! About 3,500 years ago our people started the task. We had to build a prototype pyramid on Bethel with a sound-resonating chamber for the pharaoh and a particle-transmission chamber for the queen.

As we sat in his classroom, Beena and I had no idea what he was talking about. The origin of our pyramid was another "something" like so many other "somethings," another mystery . . . a "who cares" when you are young and growing up. We used to climb to the top of the pyramid for adventure, for fun, for excitement and for the danger because it was there. As we stood on the top, five hundred feet above the ground, we had a 360-degree panoramic view of Bethel's wonders, flushed with swaying green palms, honking geese flying in V-formation, moving pearly white clouds against a blue sky above and yellow-reddish-orange clouds in the horizon where the descending sun met the green rolling hills—the start of a Bethel sunset.

"Beena," I said, "I've read Earth's history. I've seen photos that our Scouts brought back from Earth. I believe that Bethel has a better environment because it never experienced a cataclysmic event."

"What do you mean?" she asked.

"It seems that Earth has had a long period of drought that started thirteen thousand years ago."

"That's around the time of the Great Flood."

"Exactly. Africa is a desert now, but it used to be a lush green savannah at one time. According to reports, animals grew much larger. Doesn't that make you wonder?"

"I think Father Dean is going to lecture us tomorrow on those topics."

Inside our prototype pyramid, our classroom had tapestry fans hanging from limestone ceilings, undulating in a zig-zag motion, cooling the students and Father Dean at the podium. Weaved from wool and capable of holding a fine spray of mist water, the tapestry fans provided unmatched evaporative cooling in Bethel's dry air. The ground level of the prototype pyramid was an inner core of hollowed out rooms: a complex maze of rooms for schooling, dorms, assembly halls and priests' chambers. Father Dean was about to present us with a culmination of Earth's ancient history, its catastrophes with crescendos of emanating doom and eventual salvation that restored the animals and the people on Earth.

Beena and Her Intelligence

Beena lived in the woman's dorm within the pyramid's complex rooms; I lived in the men's dorm. We grew up together. At an early age, I began to fall in love with her. Our playground was the pyramid that we climbed as kids and our bedroom was a temporary blanket in the King's Chamber where we made love.

We were kids, but our bodies were adapting to the physical strain of climbing the pyramid three and sometimes four times every month. I was getting stronger and Beena was developing more curves. On one occasion, I was precariously hanging on to a limestone about ten feet above her while she exhibited no problems with the climb until one of her breasts accidently popped out. I changed from a nonchalant boy to an observant young man.

Beena, with her reddish-brown, semi-curly hair and radiant brown eyes, had changed from a cutie to a fully developed, beautiful woman. Her hips curved out to an appropriate distance; her breasts were positioned where they should have been; and her calves flared out above her heels into a shapely manner. I guess I was a romantic with my first love. I planned nothing but witnessed everything that happened . . . even the two tongues I discovered in my mouth when she first kissed me. When we kissed, she would close her eyes and then open them with a blinking expression as if to say, "Is there more where that came from?" She was not a player and neither was I. We were experimenting teenagers about to become adults. Lying next to a lit candle in the king's chamber, we enjoyed the golden silence, outweighed by heavy breathing and a few giggles. The atmosphere intensified the sexual excitement.

We had visited the king's chamber many times even though it was an empty room void of any decorations or writings on the wall. It may have been a "nothing" room, but it was *our* nothing room. One evening a slow methodical rumbling grew in the distance as we lay on a thick blanket enjoying the afterglow. When it changed into a cacophony of sounds, we left in a hurry, never to return. The sound of shrills frequencies like screaming mixed with the sound of base frequencies rumbling like multi-note organ chords scared us.

Father Dean's Lecture

Father Dean's lecture was ground shaking because of factual events that occurred in the ancient past. Here is Father Dean:

> "I know you students paid good money for your text books. You won't need them in my class. Throw them away. If you listen carefully, you'll learn everything you need to know to pass my final exam."

"Enoch," Beena asked, "Is he serious?"

"I guess so. He is very confident of himself."

"As you know we are the descendants of Enoch, the first, along with our cousins, the Sadees, who no longer share this planet with us and the year is AD 1147, Earth-time. In all probability, you never knew that Earth's solar system was similar to our own — twin solar systems, not too unlike twin stars. Both Earth's solar system and Bethel's solar system are orbiting the same galaxy in a tangential direction at 140 miles per second with respect to the Black Hole in the center. Independent of this vector direction, Earth's solar system is also moving toward the constellation Lambda Herculis at 12 miles per second or 19 kilometers per second. Lambda Hercules is 370 light-years from Earth's sun.

"Our astronomers pushed back the millenniums of time and concluded that an asteroid landed near Earth's Yucatan Peninsula 66 million years ago. The force resounded throughout the solar system causing Earth's sun and all its planets to cross the galaxy from sector one and into sector two. When they reached the neutrino barrier in 11,382 BC, the entire solar system met catastrophes, trying to squeeze through a narrow opening in a barrier that has kept the sectors separated for eons. Without the strength of the barriers, the galaxy would simply spin down on itself. Do I hear a question?"

"What changed?" someone asked.

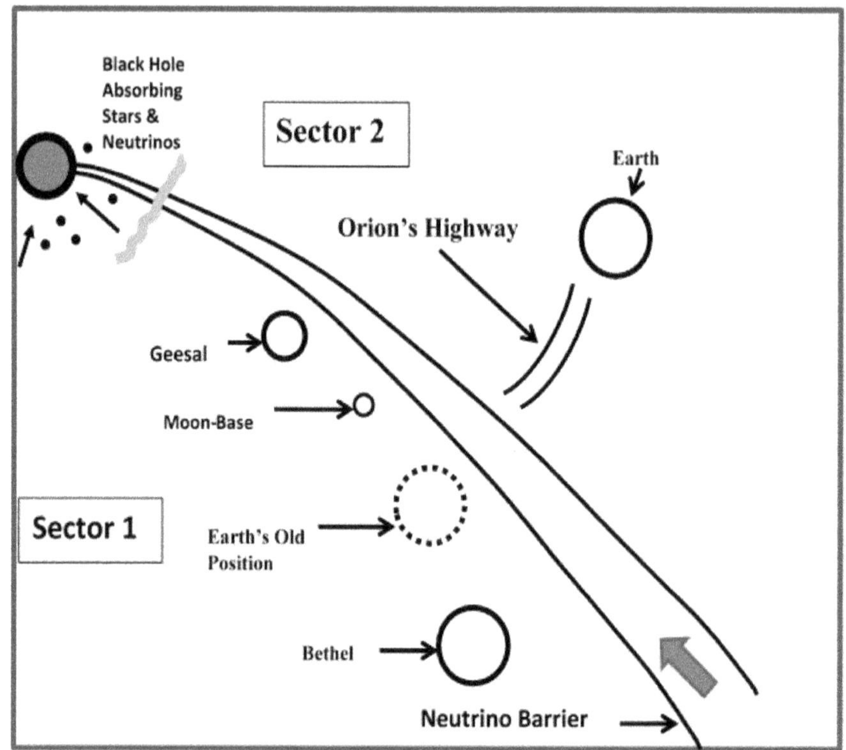

"Many things changed: the Earth's sun adopted a new rotational axis, a slight shift from the 90-degree axis, perpendicular to orbital planes that the first eight planets align with. Even Pluto adopted a forty-five-degree angle with the orbital planes. The Great Flood caused the most devastating damage when Mars gave up its water resources to Earth. The orbital paths of Mars and Earth lost their pristine, Gaussian distribution from the sun. They nearly collided! All moving objects in the galaxy develop an internal static electric force different in strength and polarization. When Mars and Earth were in proximity, lightning bolts with the same diameter as a small volcanic crater devastated both planets. And yes, many volcanos were erupting as if they were in rebellion. In 3000 BC the devastation tried to repeat itself as Mars maintained its oblong path around the sun; that is, 34 million miles closest to Earth and 63 million miles further away, using perihelion and aphelion units.

"As per the illustration, you can see the two sectors of our galaxy and the barrier that separates them; henceforth, a division of space and time, approximately, ten to one. Prior to the asteroid landing on Earth 66 million years ago, you can see where Earth's solar system resided in sector one. You can also see Orion's Highway that was created in 2500 BC and continues to build itself today after **3,647 years (2500+1147).** . . . A detail discussion will continue after lunch break. Class dismissed."

Surrounded by excited classmates, chattering about his lecture, we were left with similar thoughts, silent glances and resolute facial expressions that simultaneous said, "Let's compare notes."

Beena was the first to ask, "Enoch, what did you get out of Father Dean's lecture?"

"To be honest, I got a fist full of sand that slipped thru my fingers. But I understood the ten-to-one time difference."

"How does that work?"

"It's similar to a situation where a man sitting on a fast-moving train sees the entire landscape, but another man standing in the landscape sees a reduction in the length of the train. People on Earth are the ones in the landscape; we are the people on the train. They see a fraction of the train because their 'time' moves so fast whereas ours moves slowly. If they live to 120 years, we live to 1200 years — a ten to one ratio. If our train approached the speed of light, they would see nothing."

"I think I understand. . . . Father Dean's lecture reminds me of the time when I was a little girl. My grandmother showed me how to remove an egg from its shell without breaking the shell."

"Interesting — how so?"

"First two tiny holes are made at each end of the egg. When you blow gently into one hole, the egg and yolk exit from the other hole undamaged. If it's done too fast, the egg will tear against the sharp edges of the shell. I guess it's the same process when Earth's solar system squeezed through the neutrino barrier. The strength of a barrier compared to a solar system is probably equivalent to the strength of an eggshell compared to a fragile egg yolk. Things on Earth broke!"

"I think you are right. A dichotomy of parts."

Father Dean resumed his lecture:

> **"The prototype pyramid on our planet is exactly the same construction as the Great Pyramid on Earth. Today, our pyramid is nonfunctional, but there was a time when they both operated silently like a machine."**

Beena and I looked at each other thinking that the rumbling sound we heard while lovemaking in the king's chamber indicated that Father Dean was only partially correct about the pyramid being nonfunctional.

Father Dean continued with another illustration, demonstrating how the pyramid functioned as a machine, creating a portal, three light-years in length, for galactic travelers. Father Dean referred to the portal as Orion's Highway because of its proximity to the constellation named Orion by our people. The people of Earth learned about constellations because our earlier Custodians were there to teach them.

All students in the lecture-hall fell silent when Father Dean began to talk after pausing for a refreshing glass of water.

"The following discussions are in reference to the Great Pyramid. The King's chamber is 20 Egyptian Royal cubits (10.5 meters) east to west by 10 cubits (5.25 meters) north to south. There are two narrow shafts in the north and south chamber walls, respectively. Each shaft opens at the surface of the pyramid. Both shafts lead into the King's chamber forming a dipole antenna that moves perpendicular to the Earth's electric field. The two shafts create an electro-energy field by absorbing the geomagnetic field that surrounds the Earth. A similar product is a coil passing through a magnetic field to create a voltage and current. I'm sure you students know how an electric generator works. The pyramid is a generator creating different frequencies in different chambers.

"The northern shaft is 235 feet (72.5 meters) and the southern shaft is 160 feet (49.3 meters). When added together, they form a half wave dipole at a resonant frequency of 1.23 MHz (frequency = $3*10^8/2*(72.5 + 49.3)$ meters =1.23 MHz). A short-wave frequency at 1.23 MHz is capable of traveling around the world bouncing between the upper atmosphere and Earth's surface ground. The length of the King's Chamber is basically a quarter wave dipole equivalent to an organ pipe capable of producing a low frequency hum between the two walls at 32.4 Hz (frequency = 340m ÷ 10.5m = 32.4 Hz). As the world turns, the two shafts receive energy that is transferred to the King's Chamber to produce a low frequency hum that echoes throughout the pyramid. If the walls of the chamber were not smooth, the chamber would not resonate like a deafening organ pipe.

"The queen's chamber has its own dipole antenna—basically, two quarter wave stub antenna lines (shafts).

The northern shaft is 208 feet (64.2 meters) and the southern shaft is 177 feet (54.6 meters) beyond the chamber. Doors at the end of each shaft terminate the shafts, respectively. But each shaft has an extension beyond the doors. Using the same formula to calculate the resonance for each stub line, the frequencies are 1.37 MHz and 1.17 MHz, respectively; example, (frequency = 3x10^8/(4th Wave*54.6m) = 1.37 MHz).

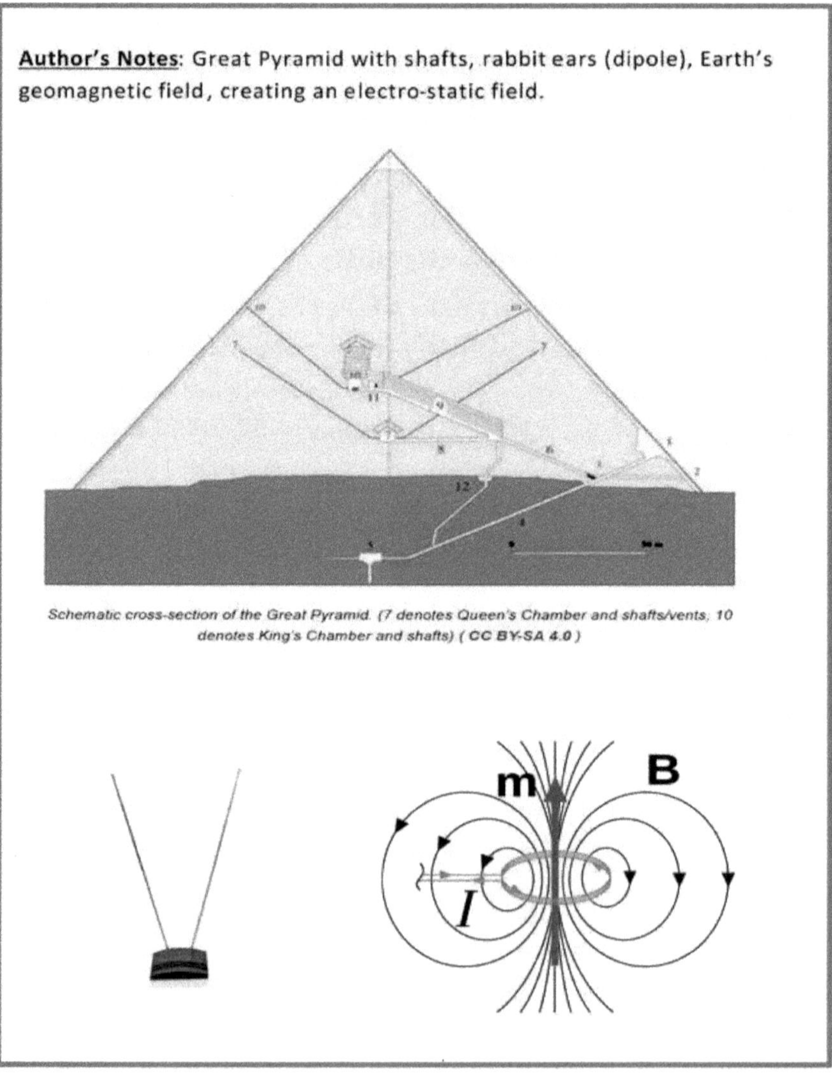

Schematic cross-section of the Great Pyramid. (7 denotes Queen's Chamber and shafts/vents; 10 denotes King's Chamber and shafts) (CC BY-SA 4.0)

"The 'ebb and flow' of the earth's magnetic field creates a 'clock', timed to the proximity of the moon, bulging the Earth at the equator and creating two tides every twenty-four hours––rhythmic events influencing the mechanics of the pyramid.

"At the top of each shaft extending from the queen's chamber are two tuning forks attached to each door. Once every twenty-four hours, current flow at the end of each terminated shaft is at its maximum value. Max current excites the tuning forks on a daily basis in sync with the geomagnetic field caused by tidal waves. The current at the shafts' end grows to its highest level once per day causing the tuning forks to emit their strongest frequency signal. On the opposite side of the pyramid, another set of tuning forks start vibrating.

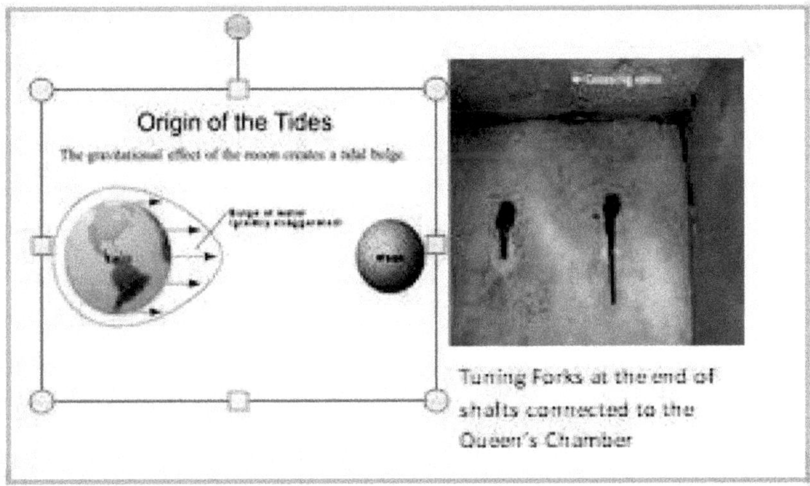

"Please refer to the overhead slid projection illustrating the tuning forks and the moon's gravitational influence on Earth. When the shafts were originally built, they were filled with magnetic beads about one inch in diameter. The beads bubbled up thru the shafts like carbon dioxide in a soda glass . . . if you're a woman or a beer if you're a man. When the beads enter the proximity of the tuning forks, they are transported into the fourth dimension and become another beacon in Orion's Highway. Every criterion is achieved for the displacement of matter through walls and into the fourth dimension—namely, sound-vibration at 32.4 Hz, small one-inch, magnetic beads and an electro-magnetic force emanating from both shafts acting as quarter wave stub lines.

"Every day two beads escape from the pyramid to start its process of floating in the wake of the solar system's trail. The vacuum of outer space expands the one-inch diameter beads into a four-inch diameter beacon, detectable by radar. As the solar system moves across the galaxy at 12 miles per second (19 km/sec), it leaves a stream of beacons in a spiral at 92 million miles on either side of the sun.

"Some of you, math experts, can calculate the number of one-inch beads needed to fill the volume of the air shafts and then calculate the length of Orion's Highway knowing one bead per shaft became a beacon every day. I'm anxious to see each math students' result because my calculations predict the completion date of Orion's Highway around AD 1385. This looks like a good math question that I can put on my final exam.

. . . Any questions?"

All the students in the assembly hall were hypnotically silent when Father Dean was talking. When he stopped, almost every student raised his or her hand with questions. Then they started asking questions among themselves as the room filled with loud existential voices. Most students had not earned a minor degree in transmission lines or fields and waves. They were the ones with the loudest voices hoping to expand their learning experience. As for Beena and I, we were mute. I walked away saying, "I'll believe it when I see it." The off-colored comment was intended for Beena's ears only. However, Father Dean was listening.

"Enoch?" he said.

"Yes, Father."

"You will see Orion's Highway during your mission to Earth, starting tomorrow. Father Aye receiver word from the Celestials requesting you and Steve start training immediately. I was going to tell you before I started my lecture, but didn't get the chance. . . . Sorry."

Beena and I looked at each other with shocked expressions. He continued his mini-lecture to us after all the other students left the room. "You and your friend, Steve, need combat training as soon as possible. You need to know how to defend yourselves with a shield, long swords, mace uniforms and weapons common to Earth's thirteenth century. The Celestials will transport you and Steve to an outpost five light-years from Earth. From there one of our own pilots will fly you and Steve to Earth with a slower warp speed spaceship. As you know, the Celestials won't loan anything that goes faster than Warp 5. They loan us the W-5s and keep the W-25s and W-50s for themselves. You can continue your martial arts on their advanced spaceships inside their accelerator pods, but after that, you'll have to endure hydro-chamber sleep on our W-5s."

Afterward, Father Dean had his own thoughts about where he stood in the religious hierarchy.

Why is it that Father Aye receives word from the Celestials before I do? I feel as though I'm always copied hours later with telepathic messages from the Celestials. I wonder if others, second in command like myself, on the other side of our planet have the same problem. I hope that someday we both receive messages at the same time. Then again, Father Aye was the one who taught me everything I know about our pyramid and how it resembles the Great

Pyramid on Earth. An Earthling visiting our planet—if there ever is one—would be shocked to see our prototype pyramid. I could ask the "all-knowing" Father Aye if Earthlings would be shocked. Or I could mentally ask the Celestials on my own. Nah, they'd never respond to my question, but they would if Father Aye asked the question.

If Father Dean was envious, no one ever knew it.

— (As he grows older, Enoch, who is now dying, thinks back about his first mission and its purpose as if he was there.) —

For the next twenty months, I will plummet across the galaxy at Warp 5, five times greater than light speed. I am on a journey in pursuit of accomplishing a mission to help mankind on Earth. Call it personal satisfaction, an obligation or perhaps a folly, or a wasted trip. This is my first endeavor. Starting with our very first ancestor called Enoch; I am the distilled essence of a culture that has survived without any wars by adhering to our form of the Ten Commandments that resembles passages of the Bible on Earth. Unable to pass these qualities to Earth's residents, I have other gifts that I can give them. From an early age, I was conditioned and trained to give humanity comfort, summed up in one word— hope.

Every child sitting at a piano, every person in a hospital, every man, woman and child will improve at what they are doing if they have hope. For over two thousand years, our group called the new Custodians have bequeath to mankind the subtlest of qualities associated with being appreciative humans—that is, complex language, abstract thinking, compassion for the arts, creation of ingenious technology, medical innovations, and appreciation for Earth's many natural beauties. Many from our planet have been working to make Earthlings advance along specific paths. Our success is attributed to our training and our ability to master new languages within days. For some unknown reason, our brains have evolved to master any language, slang, dialect or swear word in a very short time. We possess facial and body compositions identical to Earthlings.

The Sadees, our cousins, have the same ancestor who was the first human on this planet. We refer to him as Enoch, the First. On your planet, your Bible refers to him as Enoch, the sixth dynasty ancestor after Adam and Eve. The Sadees were the first Custodians that saved humanity on Earth from their own demise. They silently helped the hungry, the poor, the climate stricken, the displaced people, sleep-walking into nowhere, and the migration of masses escaping to other countries.

A quality greater than "hope" was bequeathed by the Sadees—a quality called "purpose." From 14,000 BC to 50 BC, the Sadees repurposed humanity's desire to live and prosper. They tasked them to build! Whether it was the relocation of massive stones in a circle or the assembly of limestone into pyramid shapes, the Sadees reorganized society with constructive work: the efforts of which had no payback except to the pharaohs and their priest. The Sadees replenish the animal species that were lost in the Great Flood.

As time slipped by like a spinning clock on steroids, the Sadees were instrumental at Gobekli Tepe in 10800 BC, the Sphynx in 10735 BC, Stone Hedge in 3000 BC, and the Great Pyramid in 2500 BC. The Sadees influenced the pharaoh, Akhenaten, in 1400 BC and they left artifacts in South America around 1000 BC. They helped humanity to flourish; they were the emissaries, the first Custodians, with their superior mentality, exceeding our very own. And yet, their superiority met failure when some Earthlings saw them as freaks with their elongated heads.

They Sadees chose baby-head binding; we did not. But that is another story. Simply put, the Sadees were our predecessors with the title of Custodians until we inherited the job and title. The

Sadees, our cousins, would never harm or make war on us. Their attitude is void of aggression because we originated from a control group. When Enoch the First was lifted from Earth at the command of God, he was the first member of a control group along with his immediate family. The people on Earth and our planet, Bethel, are all human beings with the same origins, namely, Adam and Eve. The only difference is that the people of Bethel are a control group with behavioral guidelines. We're similar to Earthlings in our love for God and his son Jesus. Inherently, we are do-gooders with compassion and generosity.

The people of Earth represent a free-willed, uncontrolled group with all their frailties. God gave Earth his only son to correct human frailties in hopes of improving society. Every alien, entity, and human like us was present at His birth. In my opinion, it was probably the only time within the last two millennia that God interfaced with Earthlings on a cosmic scale. The goal for every Earthling is to exceed their in-breed natural capacity and become ambassadors of the universe. Perhaps they will surpass us eventually someday: a time in the distant future if their own greed for fame, avarice, sloth, and ignorance about guns does not overtake them.

On distant planets, there is a commonality among aliens, entities and other beings set forth by the Celestials as per God's command. He wants them to conform to a "hands off" approach when visiting Earth: to walk among them as shadows, to visit their planet as unseen passersby, and more importantly, to provide no technical information that they would use to destroy themselves. The consequences would be a total loss of their religion, which is rapidly disappearing.

With too much information, Earthlings would revert to chaos: like horses running out of a burning barn only to return for some unknown reason. Advancements have to be gradual . . . over many, many centuries. Earthlings are still in the uncontrolled group—the experimental group. They can either make it or break it before judgement day, end of days, right around the corner. All the advanced members of the galaxy are watching with a "hands-off" policy; they are watching free-willed individuals and hoping they will someday fly among the stars on their own cognizance.

Chinese philosophers developed a name and a symbol representing progress and tribulations that Earthlings have to endure. They call it the "yin and the yang," two contrary forces interconnected in a natural world of "order and disorder," "the good and the bad," "progress and demise." On Earth, the concept interweaves itself into their lives. They lose a loved one and then fortitude keeps them going. Their daily humor is what saves them.

I write my manuscript with a lot of compassion and empathy for Earthlings because I have visited Earth on many occasions during my lifetime. I have witnessed their love for one another whether it is legal or out of wedlock—not too unlike our own sexual behavior. When the hormones or the estrogens kick in, the Celestials just look the other way. We talk among ourselves about the possibilities that the Celestials have no sex organs. Our people are more disciplined, more orderly with a limited free will and keenly aware of the Celestials' rules. With complete autonomy, we comply with their mission request and we visit Earth as the Sadees did to improve conditions for our Earthly cousins. We—on Bethel—are the Custodians for Earth—serving with honor and privilege. With our servitude, we always hope that someday we will be granted a few more privileges. I know this is picky, but it would be nice to travel in a modern spaceship. I would prefer the Celestials to loan us their premium spaceship like a W-25 or a premium W-50, capable of doing Warp 25 or Warp 50. I know that is asking too much. They are the ones who give us our "marching orders" because the orders come directly from God; they are the only ones who talk to Him. They also set the rules wherever we go — rules laden with punishment and hardship if we should break them.

I compose my manuscript as death approaches and I use my memoirs from the past to supplement my last sentence entries. The present year is AD 2087, the "now" year for this human being. We reference all our years in Earth's time-period. I was born in AD 987. With Earth's standards for measuring time, I have lived almost 1,200 years, one-hundred years on Bethel and twenty years on Earth. If I had lived my entire live on Earth, I would be approaching the maximum age that God set forth—120 years (Genesis 6:3).

I can write about events in the past as if they happened yesterday. Portions of my manuscript were copied from memoirs while I was making my first trip to Earth with hopes that I did not break any Celestials rules.

My first trip to Earth occurred in AD 1186 when I was a young, physically strong twenty-year-old. The Celestials drafted my good friend, Steve, and I into the Crusades. It was with honor and duty that we always served the Celestials. We had learned the English, French, and Muslim languages for that period in time. The Scouts from our planet continuously brought back phonetic language-sounds and their meaning from all the countries on Earth. I learned all three languages within two days. It took Steve three days.

(End of Enoch's reflection notes.)

Meet Steve and Charlie

Steve was an enthusiastic advocate of a gymnasium workout. He moved from one set of equipment to another like a rolling stone that gathers no moss. I complimented him with exaggerations and he complimented back by asking why I did not wear out more sleeves on my shirts with my ever expanding and bulging biceps. At a body weight of 160 pounds, Steve could bench press 400 pounds with five to nine repetitions. At a body weight of 205 pounds, I did not think about bench-pressing anything. Good times are all about having friends that boost your ego in a complimentary way or even, having friends that give you counterfeit compliments in a deliberately funny way. Steve was the latter type of friend with his fake compliments and exaggerations leading me to believe I was the best body builder he ever met. In reality, the reverse was true.

Steve was five years older. After attending tactical leadership, he became my "dedicated-thinker" person . . . and leader. He had a likeable personality. One day was devoted to exercising in the east gym with strength building machines, and the next day was devoted to combat training in the west gym with our instructor's supervision. Every time we met in the workout-gym, Steve had an exaggerated compliment that was both humorous and false. It was his way of being sociable. Every other day his compliments started with my name. I would return the fake compliments starting with his name. Here are some examples:

"Enoch, your workout abilities exceed my own because of your muscular physique?"

"Steve, are you trying to rally me?"

"Enoch, when I go home to where I live with my sister, she says that she knows whether Enoch or Charlie was in the workout-gym. When I asked her how she knew, she said, 'You come home late when Charlie is in the gym, but you come home early when Enoch is in the gym.'"

Steve was paying me another false compliment. It was fun. He made it sound like he had a physical advantage over Charlie only when they were both in the gym.

"Steve, did you know your workouts are going to cause many young women to chase you after they see bench pressing 400 pounds?"

The fake compliments stopped when we fought, mano-a-mano style, in simulated combat. Steve could out-box me with his quick jabs and punches. He was very quick and very strong. We both inflicted uncontrolled punches on each other. After the sword fighting became more serious with deeper accidental cuts, Steve said, "I think we're ready for anything." When we practiced riding a horse, Steve became so proficient, he could vault onto his horse in full armor. The irony is that we did not know what it would be like fighting dedicated, religious Muslims in the Holy Land. We may never come home!

Moreover, there was the doubtful existence of Orion's Highway. How would we get home? I had trouble believing Father Dean about a highway in the cosmos. Vast and unknown, the cosmos is a void where travelers get lost, easily. The fear of wandering the cosmos scared novice pilots—Charlie was no exception. For every traveler who lost their direction, many others had lost much more.

In the combat gym, Charlie simply watched sitting on the bench, refusing to swing a sword at an opponent or to throw a punch without reservations. With his skinny tubular frame, Charlie would have flunked every combat session. He participated in the workout sessions with only a few machines he liked. The new ones seemed to frighten him. Unbelievably, his fear of something new changed to confidence when he was at the controls of a spaceship. After earning his wings with excellent flying achievements, he accompanied us to an outpost in a Celestial's W-50 spaceship. The outpost was the place where Charlie became our new pilot, flying a W-5.

A circuitous route involving the outpost between Earth and Bethel was always a necessity. The Celestials knew how to navigate to the outpost; whereas, we lacked distant-navigation skills. Even the navigation to Earth, buried among the stars, would require skilled navigation from Charlie. As a navigational guide, Charlie brought a photograph of Mars, hoping to use it if the location of planet Mars fell along the flight path.

While in route to the outpost, Charlie and the Celestial pilot appeared to have discussed the Mars photograph. During a break period, I saw Charlie waving the photograph in front of the pilot. They looked like they were communicating, but no one on our planet understands the telepathy language of the Celestials, except for Fathers Dean and Aye. Somehow, Charlie made the transition in learning the explanation of the photograph.

After landing on the outpost, Charlie took control of a W-5 within the hanger bay of the W-50, Celestials' spaceship. We landed on the outpost, gathered supplies, and departed. Our new pilot was Charlie now.

Charlie yelled down from the cockpit, "Your break is over. It's time for your twenty days in the hydro-chambers. Good night, guys."

The hydro-chambers protected our frail human bodies, even though our race had split from the Adam-Eve gene pool after thousands of years of subtle mutations. Without a hydro-chamber, the human body can endure an acceleration of 8-gs for only a few minutes. Aboard the W-5s spaceship, traveling at five times the speed of light, the three of us required a twenty-day sleeping pod. We had to endure 17.8-gs of stress force for twenty days before we could take a twenty-four-hour break. After a mutual vote, the three of us chose twenty days in the chamber as opposed to forty days at 8.9-gs of acceleration. The comforts of a twenty-four-hour break greatly exceeded the enclosed feeling inside a chamber for twenty Earth-days. During break time, Charlie would cut back on the acceleration so that we experienced 1-g force, which is the same feeling we weighed on our home planet. It's only coincidental that a 1-g force or 32 feet/sec/sec is the same on both planets: Earth and our home planet, Bethel.

Consequently, it took five intervals of twenty days to accelerate to Warp 5 and an equal amount of time to decelerate back to Warp 0, or sub-light speed for a total of two hundred days plus recovery breaks when Charlie would set the acceleration pace at 1-g force. From the outpost to Earth on a direct path setting, the trip lasted twenty months in Earth time.

Solving for acceleration: a=v/t & converting to g-force

v=	186000	mi/sec	v=	186000	mi/sec
or v=	982080000	ft/sec	or v=	982080000	ft/sec
t=	40	days	t=	20	days
or t=	3456000	sec	or t=	1728000	sec
v/t=	284.2	ft/sec/sec	v/t=	568.3	ft/sec/sec
1_g=	32	ft/sec/sec	1_g=	32	ft/sec/sec
x_g=	8.9	g's	x_g=	17.8	g's

When I studied Earth's Bible, it seemed that many events took forty days and forty nights to complete. Could these numbers correlate to earlier space travelers hibernating in advanced space suits? The Celestials always loaned us their worst spaceship, the W-5s with uncomfortable hydro-chambers. It could have been worse; the Celestials could have loaned their first models: the W-1s with nothing more than specially designed space suits. Advanced technology has allowed the Celestials to travel with acceleration pods that eliminate any need for a space suit or hydro-chamber.

All of their spaceship traveled in the fourth dimension, but their W-25's and their W-50s have accelerator pods operating in the fifth dimension that are embedded in the fourth dimension. They walk around inside their spaceship with a controlled 1-g force, all the time. If the Celestials had loaned us a W-100, the five-light-year trip from outpost to Earth would have taken only eighteen days or 365* 5/100 without the acceleration or deceleration problems. Our trip took twenty months in Earth time because our spaceship, the W-5, did not have fifth dimension capability.

In between the warp intervals, Charlie showed us the same photograph he had shown to the Celestial pilot. Our Scouts took the photograph during their last voyage when they visited Mars. He justified the image on Mars with the following comments:

"Let's suppose you're a primitive hunter-gather with bow and arrows as your most formable weapon. You're walking thru a wooden forest and come to a wide river. On the bank of the river is a large bale of hay with a bull's-eye painted on it. When you look at the target filled with arrow holes, you realize that someone on the other side of the river had a long-distance, accurate bow that's better than yours. Here's the question: Do you venture across the river? This photo tells me that image is a warning sign for other aliens to stay away from Earth. The surface of Mars was defaced by some kind of nuclear bomb-dropping, soil-rolling, scar-devastating device. It's a warning to all other aliens that someone with a greater power than theirs is protecting Earth. Yes, Protecting!"

Steve and I looked at the photo without comment; however, the real scene of devastation on Mars frightened us. Charlie had climbed out of the cockpit and was looking at us with his eyes widely open and his mouth agape. The actual scene frightened him more than his hypothetical comments about warnings to other aliens to stay away from Earth.

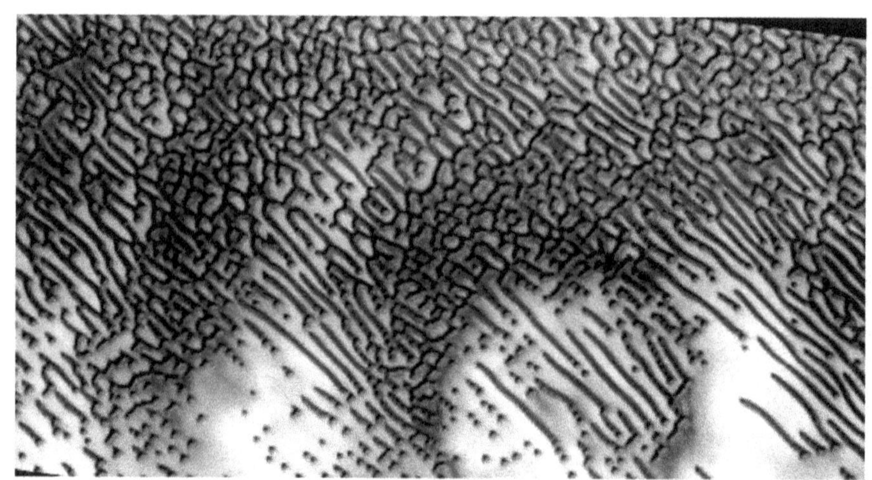

Mars with its devastated surface.

Almost halfway through the journey, Charlie gave us a one-day recovery break and then invited us into the cockpit where we could look out of the portal window and see billions of stars.

"How do you know where you're going?" Steve asked.

"I don't," Charlie replied. "I picked up a pulsar about one light-year back which is sort of helping me." Suddenly, Steve and I had a sinking feeling in our guts. We said nothing for fear of discouraging him and wondering the cosmos forever.

Charlie continued, "I triangulated our position to the pulsar and a bright star called Vega. When we're in radar distance of Orion's Highway, I'll triangulate with the pulsar and the start of the highway. The pulsar has a limited range that fades out near the highway. I need to concentrate."

Judging by the purple look on Charlie's face, Steve and I had a sinking feeling traveling to the bottom of our guts. My courage was running low, as I doubted Father Dean once again about Orion's existence. I might have been my worst enemy or just an

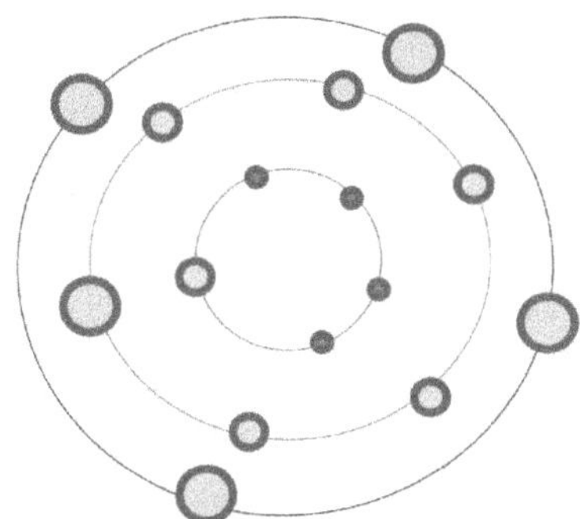

average human being. When I finally saw the highway, I began to realize that Father Dean was right and I was terribly wrong. "I'll have to apologize to him," I said softly, and then added, "if I ever see him again."

Flying though the highway was easy for Charlie. With the beacons trailing Earth at 12 miles per second, every beacon was separated by one million miles or (12mi/s*24hr/day*3600s/hr.) Similar to the treads on a wood screw, every groove was linearly separated by 365 million miles. The viewing screen captured the beacons leading to Earth's location like the inside of a wood screw spiraling to its apex. If Earth's solar system remained motionless within the galaxy like stationary horses on a merry-go-round, Orion's Highway would never have been created.

"Orion's Highway is a beautiful sight when you guys think you're lost!" Charlie said. Then he put the spaceship on autopilot. "If a star, planet, moon, or asteroid should bump into us, we're safe. We're in the fourth dimension, guys. We'll simply sail right thru them! Okay?" Now he sounded confident again.

But still, it was a sinking feeling . . . a time to forget everything except an apology to Farther Dean about my off-colored remarks . . . a time to crawl back into the hydro-chamber and . . . a time to sleep.

After the automatic pilot had decelerated the spaceship from Warp 5 to Warp 1, it awoke Charlie. The rest of the journey involved sub-light speeds from Mars and Earth. The flight path between Mars, Earth and the outpost aligned on the same solar plain as per the flight trajectory. The view of Mars in the forward port window was growing too fast. Charlie decelerated our spaceship by reversing our *sailing direction* as we approached the flow of neutrinos and reduce our speed to a tenth the speed of light (67*10^6 miles per hour/10).

Like a sailboat over any body of water, the sail can be trimmed to reduce speed. Earth was only 50 million miles away: a little less than one hour away at this speed. The immediate problem was that we had too much speed approaching Mars: We were traveling at 6.7 million miles per hour.

Charlie needed to use Mars as a braking dock to reduce our speed to a doable entry speed before we could enter Earth's atmosphere. He had trained on our home planet to decelerate a spaceship; however, our home planet compared to Mars has a different mass, gravitational pull and tangential speed around our sun. Steve and I sat upright in our cockpit seats along with Charlie hoping he had learned his lessons well. The first pass looked good.

A minor dot in a star-studded, black void of the galaxy grew larger and larger. He headed directly into the path of the on-coming Mars. The closing speeds of our spaceship and Mars added together. Suddenly, the small dot grew into a red planet without stars in the background. The planet enveloped us. The surface of Mars loomed through the port windows. Steve yelled something about crashing.

The sunlit side of Mars changed from images of craters and mountains to close-up images of sand and rock. For a moment, everything turned black. The rear cameras on our spaceship transferred images to the monitors on our consoles in front of the cockpit and to a larger monitor in the back of the cockpit. Charlie did something to cause all the seats in the cockpit to rotate 180 degrees. If we were to decelerate, we needed the protective cushion of the seats against our backs. The large monitor displayed everything; images appeared as the reverse of what we had seen: the blackout, the sand, the rocks, the mountains, the craters, and the red planet of Mars fading into a black void. We had seen the descending image toward Mars on the windward side and the floating image of Mars on the leeward side.

Charlie had sailed through Mars on the windward side in the fourth dimension and switched to third dimensional drive on the leeward side of the planet in the absence any rocket propulsion assistance. On the leeward side, the gravity of Mars reduced our ascent. Our sub-light speed decreased as the tangential speed of Mars tried to pull us along at 54,000 miles per hour. The gravitational pull was inadequate.

Suddenly, we realized we were distancing ourselves from Mars too fast as the image of Mars shrank into a bright dot. Then the gravitational pull of Mars slowly decelerated our spaceship like a rubber band stretching with Mars at one end and our spaceship at the other end. For a few hours we sat in three-dimensional space going nowhere without rocket engines that could have been effective for maneuvering; henceforth the name third dimensional drive. Gravity affects our spaceship significantly in the third dimension and it has no effect in the fourth dimension.

After letting the gravitational pull of Mars decelerate us for a while, our sub light speed reduced even more. Charlie's ability in timing relied on letting Mars decelerate us from 4 . . . to 3 . . . to 2 million miles per hour. Suddenly, we were about to crash into a three-dimensional surface on the leeward side of Mars. At an estimated two million miles per hour, we were traveling toward the surface of Mars backward. We sat, 180 degrees turned, in our padded chairs looking at the monitor on the backside of the cockpit's enclosure that would impact Mars first. If Charlie did nothing, it would have been a fatal crash resulting in a mushroom appearing cloud.

Prior to the eminent crash, Charlie quickly switched back from third dimensional drive to fourth dimensional drive. The external appearance of our spaceship on the leeward side would appear as though it had entered a large hole, opening and closing like a door.

Once again, we passed through the planet's core. Charlie said something about another round circling Mars with a pass-through and the need to approach Earth at something less than one million miles per hour. I looked at Steve. He looked back. We could not take another round of looking at the blackness of the galaxy with brightly studded lights and then seeing the very black center of Mars.

Charlie looked at our expressional faces and read our thoughts, "Wait until we travel through Earth. If it's anything like our home planet where I practiced landings, you'll see a red hot, molten core! You'll even feel the heat for about a minute." The thought made me want to puke. How much cabin heat was he talking about? I had completely misread Charlie's intensions in the gym when he looked afraid to explore new exercise equipment. With his eyebrows raised, Steve wore an expression that venerated Charlie. He may have been unskilled with gym equipment, but he certainly knew how to pilot a galactic spaceship.

Historic Note:

The era of the Crusades began in 1095 with Pope Urban II's famous speech and ended in 1291 when Acre, the last access and supply port in Palestine, was lost. St. Louis (Louis IX of France) led the seventh and last major Crusade in the years 1248 through 1250. Since the time of Constantine, Christians had gone on pilgrimages to the Holy Land. Muslims from Turkey ruled Jerusalem at the beginning of AD 638. They allowed pilgrims to cross their borders into the Holy Land. By the eleventh century, however, the situation had changed. When the number of pilgrimages to Jerusalem had peaked, the Muslim Turks took drastic control preventing any pilgrimages from entering. In reality, the Crusaders may have been concerned about wealthy travelers visiting the Holy Land, but their main goal involved exploitation and the hunt for treasures.

The Battle over Jerusalem

With a careful balance between Earth's gravitational pull and imaginary time, Charlie landed the spaceship on the outskirts of Jerusalem. The transition out of the fourth dimension had been seamless. In the fading light, Steve and I walked to the designated landmark where we observed two ominous looking men approaching in the distance. They looked over-powering. They wore chain mail body-coverings and leggings, a white surcoat with a red cross sewn on the front, a flattop helmet with a brass cross in the center, a double edged-sword, dagger, a mace, and a lance.

Steve spoke first, "Glad to see you here." He knew the men from our planet; I did not. Four white eyes in the darkness of their helmets blinked to acknowledge our presence. The fading light caught a gloved hand in a salute. Steve questioned them about the mission.

They both looked bigger and taller than we did. The biggest one spoke, "The fifth major Crusade has already started. Our Scouts report the Ark is hidden underground in a dirt chamber beneath the Dome of the Rock. My name is Derrick and my buddy is called Job."

"As you know, I'm Steve and this is Enoch. I see you brought a donkey and cart."

"Yes. We'll lead you into town."

The four of us rode the donkey-cart toward the Crusaders' campsite under an ominous looking evening sky. I should have known something bad would happen to Steve. He appeared overly confident, too energetic, too anxious as he drove the cart over bumpy paths and sharp turns.

While traveling in the cart, Derrick described the ugliness battle he had ever witnessed. "As you know, our combat training on Bethel taught us how to wound the enemy; not to kill. We easily joined the crusade effort. At the height of battle, we saw archers pick off the enemy on towers with their superior bows. During the fight, the real Crusaders cut off the heads of their enemy with a sweeping blow from their long swords. Torture by fire was not uncommon. Neither side granted mercy. Piles of heads, hands and feet lined the streets of the city. The worse fighting left corpses mingled with dead horses. The temple of Solomon was ravaged with blood up to our knees and our horses' bridal reins. We risked our lives trying not to inflict a fatal blow."

Time passed, and I, too, learned what it was like to wound a Muslim and see a Crusader next to me plunge his dagger in him, moments later. The sounds of metal crashing against emblematic shields and the clanking of cold-tempered steel swords in combat produced a frightening scene that burned its way into my memory cells. Sounds of screaming and manly grunts filled the air. The armored men hurled themselves into battle, metal crashing, screams fading, voices yelling and then fading again.

I saw Steve dismount and charge into battle with a raised shield, its emblematic, red-painted cross over canvas, covering wood, marred by successive slashes of enemy swords. Moments later, I glanced at Steve and his buddies, fighting and trying not to inflict a fatal blow. It made me sick. I felt worse when I saw Steve take a spear into his chest. The trajectory of the spear came from his flank. Sensing danger, Steve turned to face the spear in a direction where it could do the most damage — his heart! Wincing in pain, Steve summoned all his faculties and strength, trying to get up. I saw everything and felt helpless.

The Way It Happened

Derrick and Job, his buddies, saw him fall. They stood on a precipice looking down at the carnage of dead bodies, Muslims and Crusaders mixed together. Was that it: the end of a bloody battle to save the Holy Land? Or were there a few die-hards casting random arrows into the battlefield? . . . The battlefield where it all happened. Enoch didn't anticipate that one of those arrows was headed his way. The sound it made entering Steve's chest was unlike any natural sound heard on a normal day, as the metal-tipped arrow pierced his heart with a dull "thud" sound.

Derrick and Job heard Enoch confess, "I couldn't believe what happened. I saw it coming, the arrow aimed at me. Then it entered Steve's chest during its final moments of flight. Didn't they realize the battle was over—a stalemate? Why did a few die-hards, on the outskirts of the battle field, have to lob in their arrows?"

Steve had fallen down on his knee-caps with the arrow still sticking out of his chest. He beckoned his body for additional strength, while using his muscular arms to pull himself up, using Enoch as the crutch that he needed. The arrow hadn't pierced his heart, but it was deeply imbedded in his chest. Immediate heart surgery aboard their spaceship crossed their minds. They needed the confines of the medical lab aboard the ship, if only Charlie could pilot their ship to a safe ground nearby

Enoch removed the spear and quickly applied another medicated patch that he had brought from Bethel. They carried him to safety where Enoch could evaluate his condition. Steve required immediate major surgery aboard the spaceship. Enoch administered superior antibiotics from Bethel.

Under a blanket of darkness, the three men carried Steve to a remote rendezvous where they boarded their spaceship, relying upon Charlie to produce the spaceship when it was really needed. While boarding the spaceship, Enoch prepared Steve for surgery. Charlie assisted after he secured the spaceship.

Immediate Heart Surgery

During the night, Derrick and Job had told Charlie that the Ark was being relocated, and they knew where they could find it. At that point, I was more concerned about my friend, Steve, than I was about the stupid Ark. A few hours later, Charlie maneuvered the spaceship to rendezvous with Derrick and Job. They had the Ark! They had built a confidence with the leaders of the Crusaders; and now they were stealing the Ark from under their noses. They waited until the Crusaders were relocating the Ark to another hiding place. In the middle of the night, they simply walked into their camp, loaded the Ark on the donkey-cart and slipped away.

While Steve was lying on the operation table, I opened his chest, exposing his heart, and replaced the severed artery that supplies blood to the heart with a vein from his leg. I had been trained for this type of operation. I would not repeat a similar operation again on Earth for another seven hundred years. During the operation, my mind quickly raced to consider a substitution with other blood vessels. I could have removed arteries in the thorax (chest), forearm, or stomach areas; instead, I selected a vein from Steve's leg because I estimated that it would be the same size as the damaged artery. In comparison, this procedure was minimally evasive compared to the other choices and the healing process was faster. I did not know it at that time, but within another seven hundred years, I would be back on Earth helping a surgeon with his heart operations.

We left Earth's orbit and proceeded to accelerate at a rate of two g-forces. With Steve out of surgery, we had to accelerate at a slower pace. The five of us earned a good night's rest. The next day I entered the galley. I was glad to see Steve, sitting up and pouring himself a cup of refreshment. Derrick and Job had already done the same. They sat at the breakfast table comparing their three-inch, four-inch, and seven-inch wounds that I had stitched up for them.

"Good morning, men. I'm certainly glad to see you looking better, especially, you, Steve," I said as I turned to Steve with a satisfied smile. "You know, Steve, this was a close one!"

"I'm very grateful to you, Enoch," he replied and then continued, "We got the Ark! Derrick and Job stole the Ark of the

Covenant from the Crusaders who stole it from the Jewish people who acquired it from Moses."

Derrick, sitting at the galley table, put his drink down and added his version, by saying, "I'll guess that the Earthlings will continue to search its whereabouts for a thousand years."

Job started laughing to himself. He added to Derrick's comment, saying, "We should have left a false trail for them, so they would constantly be searching for the Ark in distant places like Ethiopia, Spain, or Ireland," he laughed. "Can you imagine a false documentary in the future showing people where they might find the Ark?"

Steve responded with a downward curve smile and a more authoritative voice, "Yeah, Job. That's hysterical, but right now Charlie has been signaling that break time is over, and that we have to return to our hydro chambers." I knew my operation was a success when I saw Steve giving orders again. I wrote a trip report that was transmitted across the dark empty voids of space at a thousand times the speed of light. Knowing that Fathers' Aye and Dean would have a copy before we arrived, I entered the hydro chambers for a long twenty-day, restful sleep.

The five warriors, Enoch, Steve, Derrick, Job and Charlie, slept through the twenty-day interval until their ship automatically reduced its acceleration to 1-g or normal gravity. To reach Warp 5, they would have to endure four more intervals of twenty-day, sleep-duration periods. But for now, they slept, a sleep deeper and more relaxing than they had ever dreamed, a sleep that was undisturbed by dreams. They, who had never considered sleep a luxury, slept.

Home Again

Upon our arrival, I did not anticipate a welcoming parade down the center of our town—a town that is only three blocks long! But still, we had our own little parade. Needless to say, it did not last very long as Derrick and Job wheeled Steve in a cart, past the stores that lined the street. They positioned me in front wearing my full, chain mail uniform. We marched to the sound of music right past the tailor's store, the ice cream store, the Crocodile Tavern, and all the other buildings including my old medical office until we reached the sago palm trees at the edge of the river near the end of Main Street. My medical office was just another empty adobe where a shingle had hung a few years ago stating that I was a general physician and surgeon. I remembered:

> *Not far away, between Main Street and my office door, people would gather and wait for my attention with their broken bones, scrapes, and contusions. We had no real diseases on our planet, but the people always came. The majority of my patients brought back diseases after they had visited Earth.*

For now, my old office stood empty because other physicians practiced their skills in areas they had already established. I marched past my old office building wearing a full-dressed Crusader's uniform and thinking if I would ever return from being a warrior to being a doctor once more.

Derrick, Job and Steve talked me into turning around to go back to the tavern for a celebration drink. They were enthusiastic until we reached the tavern's front door when it started to rain. Derrick and Job realized they didn't have enough money; Steve didn't want to mix alcohol with his drugs. I didn't want to debate them standing in the rain, so . . . I entered by myself.

Brianna

My first meeting with Brianna imprinted energetic events in my mind with substantial clarity, excitement and sexuality. My mind can easily replay the encounter over and over:

I saw her walking across the floor, her blond, shoulder-length hair bouncing effortlessly in the slightest breeze, her hips swaying methodically as she placed one foot directly in front of the other. There could have been rhythmic music playing, but I didn't hear anything. She moved with her shoulders pushed back and gyrating, kind of a bumpety, bump. Her torso— tall and straight—with her arms swing rhythmically. Her breast—shapely—bouncing in concert with her hair. Music was not playing, but we were feeling mutual vibrations. Her hair: creamy blond. Her torso: well proportioned. Her complexion: none was needed to enhance this woman that I saw for the first time. She approached with electric eyes that excited my passion. My eyes filled with her beauty. Her smile, a special one that overwhelmed me.

She didn't know how she walked, but then again, maybe she did. I was an observer, not a physiotherapist to evaluate something broken or bulging in the wrong direction. I stood and watched with an eighty-pound chain mail weighing me down like it wasn't there. I definitely knew she saw me too . . . or maybe she just saw the uniform covering me from head to toe.

Yes, Brianna definitely had straight blond hair. Why was I looking at her beautiful hair above her head when I should have been looking directly into her azure blue eyes? I lowered my eyes too far and then she said, "My eyes are up here." I had lowered them too much. Back from the war, the parade and all; I didn't have a chance to see Beena, my first true love. But right now,

Brianna, a vivacious woman overwhelmed by a uniform, stood in front of me.

As a bartender, Brianna was quick and efficient, alert and ready to serve her customers, but there was a slight display of boredom and anticipation for the next man that could sweep her off her feet. Brianna didn't want to be a bartender forever, bartending one customer after another with the same cordial smile and the same husky voice, which she couldn't help

"Hi," I whispered.

That was all I could say. Whether it was battle fatigue or confusion returning, I couldn't say. The man parts inside my uniform tried to crawl out, but my chain mail and my mental tardiness prevented that from happening. More words had to be spoken. I had to say more.

And then, she spoke first, with a voice a little bit on the raspy side. After all, she did own a tavern and she probably did drink some of the profits. "Are you in, what they call the army?"

I understood her point of view: she had no concept of anything militaristic because Bethel, our home planet, never had any wars. "Are you impressed?" I asked.

"Yes."

"Impressed with me or the uniform?"

"I can't see you behind your helmet. Take it off," she insisted. I took off the helmet and she added, "I'm impressed with you!"

"Is there conflict between what you see and what you say?"

"No, you appeal to me. I've seen plenty of men, plenty of drunks, and plenty of trot-heads come and go. After my parents died in a boating accident, I became the owner of this bar . . . a bar that demands a lot of work. I work hard. I work almost day and night and right now, you interest me." As she hurried from one customer's table-leftovers to another, she thought about the needs of the next customer and the needs of the tall Crusade warrior fresh from combat. "It would be nice if only . . ." she thought as another customer interrupted her thoughts asking for a beer.

She had read about the anatomy of a man's body overflowing with testosterone after physical combat and his emotions ready to fight or flee. She continued with her inner thoughts wildly gyrating, "His sexual prowess could be amazing. If he was the star of a parade down the middle of main street, I want to be a star in his eyes." There were two things she didn't know: first, he had fought in a battle over two years ago, not recently; and second, she had the Angio disease—she could never have any children with him.

Fumbling for the correct words, I inquired, "What's a trothead?" Then, I quickly added, "Sorry, that's dumb of me to ask. I'm sorry to hear about your parents."

She was too busy to stop and talk to the stranger, but that didn't prevent her from fantasizing about the cumbersome chain mail and its complicated removal. She thought about it, "How does he get in and out of it by himself or does he need someone to help with the straps?"

Brianna was a striking woman, but somehow, she turned men off. They thought of her as another barmaid, a gofer, a perpetual preteen-ager helping her parents when they were alive. In their minds, liquor always came first in a tavern, or "bar" using her terminology. I immediately liked her and her slang—slang with raspy-sounding words. I liked the sound of her voice: slowly spoken, distinct and filled with lower frequency tones. She didn't mince words. She looked a few years younger than myself. She buzzed around the tavern collecting some more empty beer bottles. Then I got a chance for another comment, "I'm interested in your work."

From the end of the bar, came the answer, "She said, 'She works hard!'" Someone was suddenly talking to me. I had another point of view from a slightly older man named Bill. Draped over the bar, head forward and shoulders hiding his drink, Bill said, "Hey you, helmet head, your sword is putting nicks in all the tables you pass. Your shield is dripping rainwater all over the floor where you came in and carelessly left it. Your clanging chain-suit needs oiling and now it's time for one more drink." Caustic comments flowed until he had realized he needed more alcohol.

"It's called chain mail," I said and then turning to Brianna, I apologized again, "Sorry for the damage. I can pay."

She replied, "You're full of apologies. Aren't you?"

My conflict with Bill started strongly aggressive but faded with additional rounds of drinks. Brianna had no conflict because her mind dwelt upon her customers. I thought about sitting on the barstool next to Bill. The conversation became a three-way talk session while Bill protected his drink with both hands inches away while Brianna darted in-and-out behind the bar. Bills sat on a barstool at the end of bar near the stairway that led up to Brianna's living quarters. I wondered if she lived alone. Then I realized my chain mail had dripped more water where I stood. With my helmet removed, I could see the water damage that I had created.

"Yeah, clunk-head. She lives upstairs," Bill said while I was looking at the stairway. "Park your chain-suit and we can have another drink together." Bill had only two nebulous thoughts mixed with mumbled comments: "My damn whisky glass is empty again and who is this guy that popped out of a tin-can helmet?"

I surveyed my surroundings as I walked back to the entrance door near the cloakroom to remove the uniform that covered my heavily padded, somewhat-ugly, street clothes. Normally, everyone had their own agenda; the appearance of an intruder, however, in their midst disrupted their thoughts. Evidently, they didn't recognize me after four years of departure. The tavern had ten other patrons: five sitting at two different tables and five more at the bar loudly discussing the results of a recent pool game. Two pool tables stood empty. Whenever someone drank their last sip of beer, Brianna dropped off another to replace it. She threw the empty beer bottles into a large metal bucket that reverberated with an irritable clanging sound that reminded me of swords hitting swords in a battle I'll never forget. I climbed on the barstool next to Bill. "Let me buy you a drink," I offered.

"Okay, my name is Bill. My friends call me just plain Bill. You can start by calling me Bill." He slurred his words a little, made sense, and then again, made no sense. But his name was definitely Bill.

"My name is Enoch. Brianna seems to already know my name. I guess the news of the parade traveled fast."

"What are you drinking?" Brianna asked with her semi-raspy voice. She delivered the drinks; gave me a wink; and rotated her eyes upstairs. Bill might have seen Brianna wink at me. I wasn't sure. He could have been her lover . . . a jealous lover — a jealous drunk at a bar could mean trouble. As the small talk between the three of us rolled on, the truth finally came out.

"I'm her uncle," Bill announced. "Her mom's younger brother. My sister asked me to watch over Brianna, and I made a promise I would keep. To get to her, you got to go throoooough me."

For a while, Bill's one-way conversation continued as he began to slur his words, pouching his lips, while saying, "throoooough me." In his stupor, he revealed that he had worked on Bethel all his life; he chased women sometimes two at the same time; and that he had recently cut his drinking in half. "I don—–don—n't use water," he proclaimed. I held back a smile; Brianna let out a giggle.

Brianna's comments echoed the flip side of Bill's comments. She took care of Uncle Bill even though she never called him uncle. She had to hire others to help her run the tavern. She was in her early twenties and she never got serious with another man. Responsibility for her parents' tavern and her mother's brother were her priorities, one and two. Unaware, I was about to become priority number three. The tavern kept her busy—away from seeing the public outside the tavern, away from meeting younger men, away from ever meeting someone in a uniform. Over the years, the tavern had become a collection of middle-aged men driven by a desire to drink and verbally show off their plumage. Like incoherent talking birds, their loud chatter resembled chopped verbal salad. In their younger days, they never went on to become Scouts or Custodians working for the benefit of people on Earth. Bill had walked a similar path into nowhere, and obviously, Brianna really needed a good friend.

I sat on the barstool sorting out the events of the homecoming and the introduction of new friends that would become my permanent friends. "Bar's closing," Brianna announced. "I'm not asking you to go home. You just can't stay." I was the only one that stayed.

I spent the night in the tavern above the bar at the request of Brianna's invitation to join her for a nightcap. I do not remember the name of the nightcap, but I do remember it was a wonderful night.

As the morning sun filtered through the bedroom windows, it found two naked bodies, still enjoying the afterglow from the pleasures of the night. Unabashed and still sleeping, Brianna and Enoch lay butt naked and spread out on a water bed. It was one of the many positions that they assumed throughout the night.

The sun danced on the ripples of the river-water, reflecting light upward to the pier that Brianna's tavern was built upon. The morning sun brought a beauty of rainbow colors except for a shadowy dark object that swam ominously beneath the pier that supported the Crocodile Tavern.

The Celestials

The people of Bethel report to the Celestials through Father Aye, a telepath and manager of his regional district. The Celestial race is very old, religious, extremely modern and they have the ability to read inner thoughts of people on Bethel, living light-years away. For example:

Look who's grumbling (their inner thoughts)

1. Father Dean—slightly envious of Father Aye—*"Why do I always have to be second in command?"*

2. Brianna—*"Work, work, work. I want some adventure. I should have been a Custodian visiting Earth."*

3. Enoch—*"It's not easy being a Custodian. As Custodians we were sent to Earth to implement a small and gradual change for a better way, and not let **their ways** change us."*

4. Bill—*"After my older sister died in a boating accident, I was supposed to be in charge of running this tavern. Why is Brianna, my niece, doing it?"*

5. Steve—*"I almost died retrieving the Ark of the Covenant for the Celestials. I'd do it all again if they asked."*

6. Charlie—"Why was I gifted with mental telepathy so that I can read the minds of the Celestials. Will I become a priest like Father Dean and Father Aye?"

7. Beena—"Regardless of how hard I work, supplying data to the Celestials, they'll never find a cure for women who can't get pregnant. When the Angio test-results come back as 'positive', they're devastated."

8. Father Aye—"There are so many things I learned from the Celestials. If I ever get the time, I should write them all down."

The morning came with the start of another workday. I reopened my physicians practice by renting the same small abode next to the river at the end of Main Street. When people heard about the success of Steve's heart surgery, they filled my office. Word traveled faster on our planet than it could have on Earth because the population ratio is one Bethel resident for every one hundred thousand Earthlings. Another difference between the two planets is biological longevity: 80 years on Earth versus 120 years on Bethel. The only difference is the faster flow of time on Earth: 120 years on Bethel are equivalent to 1,200 years measured on Earth.

I also worked part time in research where Beena assisted. The government funded research project, tried to improve the statistical rate at which our planet was losing its population. The Celestials had supplemented us with prescription drugs that would either prevent or cure most diseases. However, the "Angio disease" progressed into an incurable disease. Everyone called it a disease, but it really was a genetic mutation. Unknown to young women, mutation had destroyed their pituitary gland: a master gland secreting a hormone that influence their reproductive organs. Capable of childbearing in every other way, they lived their lives of infertility, not knowing. Time revealed that Brianna had the infliction, but Beena was exempt.

The problems of reproducing started on our planet when Enoch the First and his small band of relatives were brought to this planet. Studies have shown that Enoch's X chromosome contained a bad gene that caused some of his daughters to be barren. The Y chromosome that he passed to his sons did not affect their ability to reproduce. With the process repeating itself throughout every generation, Bethel's growth was stunned in comparison to Earth's population that blossomed despite the wars that killed so many. In essence, Bethel has only a few worrisome diseases like the one I just described. The Angio disease is incurable. Most men that want children will not marry their loved ones. Multiple pregnancy pills never help. Consequently, Celestial researchers keep trying to resolve this problem, now and since it was first discovered. The only assistance Beena and I could provide, was the categorization of infertility data. The work may have been a little boring, but then again, I got to see Beena every work day: filled with long nights . . . and then some.

Father Dean's Second Lecture

"I'm taking a course in astrophysics for extra credit and Father Dean is having a lecture tonight. Would you like to join me?" Beena asked.

"You already have your master's degree. Are you going for your PhD?"

"Yep."

"Okay. You got it. I'll see you in the lecture hall tonight," I replied.

Father Dean always amazed his classes with topics concerning our galaxy and historical references to the similarity of Earth's solar system and our own solar system. Beena and I sat side-by-side in the lecture hall.

Father Dean's Lecture on Orbital Speeds:

"Before the big change, two solar systems were very similar: that is, Earth's solar system and our own. Each solar system had planets spaced the same distance from the sun. Today, the difference is obvious. The last time some of you were here, I gave a lecture about the 'neutrino divide' within our solar system."

Father Dean looked directly at me. Obviously, he had given this lecture many times in my absence. The last lecture I attended and one he presented today were linked together. Father Dean continued,

"If you recall, previous lectures discussed Earth's solar system traveling through a neutrino barrier. Our astronomers speculate that the change was due to a maverick asteroid plowing into Earth's solar system 66 million years ago. The asteroid split into multiple parts when it passed through Jupiter's gravitational field. Large sections landed on four planets within the inner ring: Mars, Earth, Venus and Mercury, sequentially.

The momentum of the asteroid imparted its energy to the solar system causing it to drift in a different vector across the galaxy. Our solar system circles the galactic center at a rate of 144 miles per second. Millions of years ago, both solar systems had the same vector direction and speed. The asteroid impact, however, initiated a second vector at 12 miles per second causing Earth's solar system to reside close to the edge of the neutrino barrier until twenty-five thousand years ago. And then, it entered the barrier where havoc prevailed!

"If you unfold your pocket-tops, you'll see illustrations of data for nine planets whereby Earth and Mars are misaligned with the other seven planets. Based upon each planet's speed and distance around the sun, the data is incongruous with a pristine solar system. The data can be made to look pristine if Earth and Mars are repositioned further away from the sun. Our astronomers tell us that this was the situation twenty-five thousand years ago. I'll briefly explain their conclusions."

We both removed our pocket-tops simultaneously; unfolded the panels like a hankie; and saw the data he referred to.

Based upon astronomical data for Earth's solar system collected by our scientist on Bethel, Father Dean claimed that the problem occurred 66 million years ago. The solar data started to change twenty-five thousand years ago and peaked with cataclysmic destruction during the time of the great flood in 11,382 BC, a period known as the Great Flood. His charts indicate that the removal of inconsistent data produces a congruent line.

Planet	Distance from (km*10^6)	sun (mi*10^6)	One Year Rotation (days)	(mi/hr)	Planet Speed (1000*ft/sec)
Mercury	58	36	88	107055	157
Venus	108	67	224	78594	115
Earth	149	93	365	67010	97
Mars	227	141	687	53857	79
Jupiter	778	484	4332	29229	43
Saturn	1429	888	10752	21631	32
Uranus	2870	1784	30663	15229	22
Neptune	4504	2799	60140	12186	18
Pluto	5914	3675	90717	10606	16

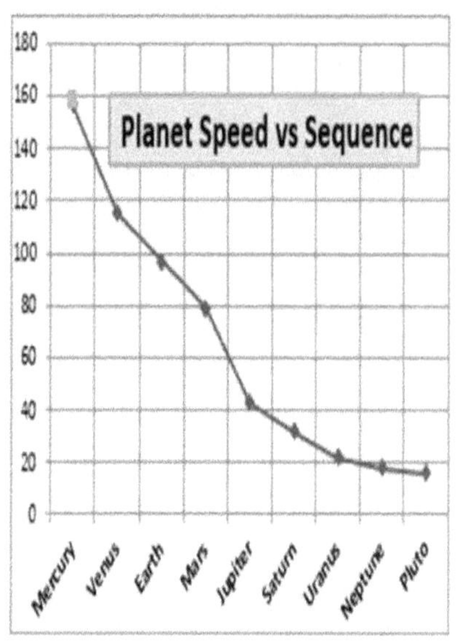

Planet	Distance from (km*10^6)	sun (mi*10^6)	One Year Rotation (days)	(mi/hr)	Planet Speed (1000*ft/sec)
Mercury	58	36	88	107055	157
Venus	108	67	224	78594	115
Earth	200	124	550	59167	87
Mars	400	249	1500	43389	64
Jupiter	778	484	4332	29229	43
Saturn	1429	888	10752	21631	32
Uranus	2870	1784	30663	15229	22
Neptune	4504	2799	60140	12186	18
Pluto	5914	3675	90717	10606	16

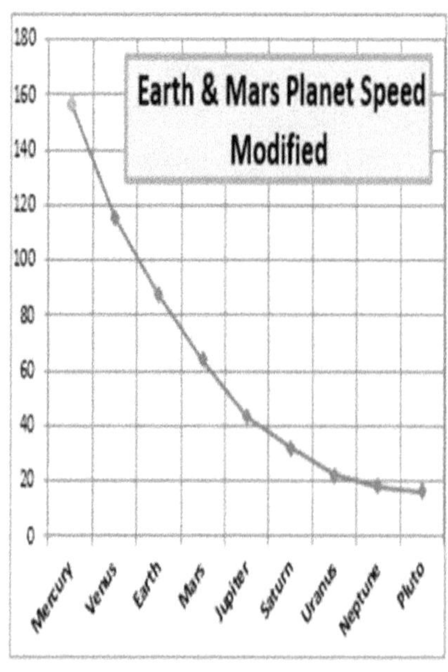

"As you can see, the circular speeds of Earth and Mars around the sun are not in unison with the other seven planets. They circle at 97 and 79 kilo-feet per second, but up until twenty-five thousand years ago, they circled at 87 and 64 kilo-feet per second, respectively. Please refer to the column on the right side of both tables. What happened? The geometric uniformity of the distance from the sun was broken. The second set of data shows the planets distance from the sun: a progression of 58, 108, 200-, 400-, 778- and 1429-kilometers times 10^6 from the sun. This progression is identical to the math expression .5, 1, 2, 4, 8 and 16. A geometric doubling! Consequently, Earth should have resided 200x10^6 kilometers from the sun a long time ago. The math expression defines a pristine solar system.

Earth had already started to cross the barrier when Adam and Eve walked in the Garden of Eden. As most of you know, our planet's history started in 15581 BC when Enoch, the First, was brought to this planet. In 11382 BC — the time of the Great Flood — Earth and Mars circled the sun in elliptical paths that converged closer and closer until Mars released its oceans of water to the gradational pull of Earth.

Yes, it did rain for forty days and forty nights due to the stronger gravitational pull of Earth, consistently increasing its influence on Mars. On Earth, people and animals either drowned or died of starvation. The oceans rose more than 400 feet until underground aquifers absorbed most of the water. Earth transitioned into a new orbital plane around the sun from 124 million miles to 93 million miles or 25 percent closer to the sun. During this transition, glaciers began melting. Thirteen thousand years ago, vegetated land turned into deserts; glaciers continued to melt; and animals grew to a smaller size. Earth adopted a centripetal orbit, centered equidistant from the sun, but Mars maintained its elliptical orbit.

Mars transformed from a vegetated landmass with an atmosphere into a sun-bleached, sterilized landmass with no atmosphere and very little remaining water that percolated underground into a super-salty liquid compound. A dying planet for millions of years, Mars suddenly lost its last vestiges of life under remaining oceans. Mars isn't much use to anyone except for when we use it as a breaking-depot during our space travels to Earth. This concludes my lecture on orbital planet speeds."

Father Dean concluded his lecture and walked out of the classroom without fielding any questions. Students, motivated to ask more questions, speculated among themselves. They wanted to know if the theories about Atlantis were true. When the collision of planets was eminent, how did the oceans of Mars travel the immense distance between the two planets? If the oceans held their form before turning to rain on Earth, what Martian sea-animals supplemented Earth's oceans? Did Mars lose any red-iron-tainted mountaintops to the gravitational pull of Earth?

Another student commented, "If Ayers rock sits on a flat surface in Australia with the same color as Mars and several crater markings, could it have originated on Mars prior to a bombardment of a meteor shower from Mars, eons ago?" There had to be an explanation for the unusual: Ayers rock in Australia, Meteor Crater in Arizona and the Coelacanths fish of Madagascar. Could a rare order of fish and other denizens of the deep survive the journey through outer space? Some students argued that living animals of the ocean could survive if Mars had approached Earth within several million miles. One student exclaimed, "Fish eggs are hardier than their parents. The same creatures swimming in Martian oceans could have populated Earth's oceans. The octopus and jelly fish don't share the characteristics of Earth's family tree of life."

Some students left the classroom while others with degrees in

Four Craters on Ayers Mountain, Australia

Earth's geography stayed. They wanted an explanation for the disappearance of Atlantis. They lacked documented evidence about Atlantis because Scouts from our planet left Earth when they saw eminent doom approaching. The only evidence is the writings of an Earthling called Plato: Born in 424 BC, student of Socrates, and teacher of Aristotle. Plato wrote about the existence of Atlantis nine thousand years before his time and a land beyond the Pillars of Hercules. Beena and I sat in the classroom listening to wild theories from these students with their advanced degrees in Earth's history, geometry and archeology.

One student used his pocket-top to present an image illustrating limestone washed by rain and resembling the pillars of Hercules. He argued that the island of Santorini could have resembled Herculean pillars. Travelers, sailing the Mediterranean between Greece and Egypt, would see them. Another student picked up on the idea claiming that the Great Flood of 11,382 BC occurred close to the period of 9,000 BC when the reporting time of witnesses is factored into Plato's documentation of time. "There may have been a volcanic eruption nine hundred years before a priest living in 600 BC wrote his report," he said. Then the student agreed to semi-factual evidence that Thera was destroyed in 1500 BC, but insisted that bigger event occurred on Thera during the Great Flood destroying the people that called their island Atlantis.

A third student was fascinated with Santorini and Meteor Crater (Arizona) residing at the same latitude and existing today as huge craters: one filled with water and the other a hollowed-out, land mass without a ridge or center mound that is typical of a real crater.

Everyone in the classroom had similar thoughts about the catastrophe of 11382 BC. Did Mars nearly crash into Earth? Did Mars give up its oceans? Or: Lose its animals, atmosphere and plant life? How close could two planets cross paths and influence a gravitational pull on each other? Five million miles? Ten million miles? Or: forty-eight million miles, the closest

The former Pillars of Hercules as per Plato on the island of Thera; now called Santorini.

they come now? They argued that the orbit of Mars was more elliptical thousands of years ago.

A fourth student summed his theory as such, "When Earth's solar system entered the neutrino barrier, cataclysmic events occurred as Father Dean explained. My theory is that Santorini Island was home for Atlanteans when it disappeared overnight in 11,382 BC. A logical explanation is that the island used to exist at the same elevation as Meteor Crater [Arizona] or approximately 5,000 feet. When Mars nearly collided with Earth, both island and . . . crater were on the same latitude closest to Mars. There is only one thing that can destroy an entire island in one day: it's not a volcano; it's not an earthquake; and certainly, it's not a tsunami. It's electricity! If you look at the Grand Canyon of Mars, Valles Martineris, you can see a cavity that extends 1,860 miles. It didn't get there with an asteroid tumbling across the surface. I believe a potential voltage difference between the two planets caused the cataclysmic sequence of events. Huge amounts of electricity can evaporate islands overnight, cut a grooved canyon in a rotating Mars and bounce back to Earth eliminating the soil in Meteor Crater. That's my theory."

The remaining students sat motionless in the classroom with faces wearing an expression of "WOW."

"Beena," I said, "I believe the last student has the correct theory about cataclysmic events."

She replied with a comment followed by a question, "I have difficulty believing that a huge meteor bombarded Earth's solar system jarring it loose from the proximity of our own solar system. Here on Bethel, our planet's axis is perpendicular to the orbital plane of the other planets rotating our sun. During daylight hours, sunlight shines from pole to pole except for areas a few degrees from each pole. Vegetation—grass, plants, and trees—grow the entire year. Our

planet has no seasons, but contrarily, Earth has seasonal climate changes because its axis is tilted by 22 degrees. Without a global tilt, Earth could have had vegetation growing from pole to pole.

"Up until 2500 BC, the Sahara Desert was a savanna, networked with rivers and crocodiles all across upper Africa. Then around 2200 BC, a drought devastated the region causing chaos and strife in Egypt. In my opinion, this is proof that Earth axis transitioned from zero axis tilt to 22-degree axis tilt. Our history books concerning Earth tell us that the Sadees were instrumental in teaching the Egyptians how to crossbreed wheat and work animals that were drought resistant. Within three hundred years, the Egyptians had learned how to survive while the rest of the world perished from hunger. There records indicate a drastic climate change from 2500 BC to 2200 BC, but the same records do not indicate the cause — or the blame — for the change in Earth's axis tilting by several degrees. A combination of many things caused Earth's climate change; namely, axis tilt, closer proximity to the sun, and atmospheric chemical changes. The Sadees, acting as the first Custodians weren't asked to document the earth's tilt or its climate changes. Their task in 2500 BC was the construction of the Great Pyramid using Egyptian labor.

Therefore, I do believe something big crashed into Earth's solar system 66 million years ago causing cataclysmic events to occur when Earth's solar system drifted across the barrier from 22,000 BC to 2200 BC. Do you think it might have been a maverick planet from a totally different solar system?"

"Possibly. The momentum of a run-away planet, the size of another Mars, could impact a planet and cause the entire solar system to move like some kind of bouncing spring. But a run-away planet? What other solar system could it have come from?" I inquired.

"I'm only guessing but I believe a run-away planet now resides within Earth's solar system as ground-up chunks of asteroids."

"Do you mean the asteroid belt?" I asked.

"Yes. There's enough space on Father Dean's first chart where the asteroid belt fits in between Mars and Jupiter. The belt's total mass is the same size as a huge run-away planet. However, Father Dean's second chart tells me that the asteroid belt never was a part of the original solar system. The sequential progression of the nine planets is uniform when planetary speed is plotted. This is why I believe that the two charts are astronomical snap shots of conditions before and after 66 million years ago!"

I showed Beena a timeline of all the major events that were discussed in the classroom. Then I added a few more events that most students had learned in different history classes.

Enoch's Personal Notes: In 11382 BC, a voltage discharge from Earth to Mars left a void between Earth's crust and its mantle. The diameter of the voltage discharge was the same diameter as the horseshoe island, called Santorini (Thera). The void slowly filled with magma over millions of years, giving rise to a volcano in the center of a horseshoe island. Then, in 1600 BC, the volcano on Santorini Island released rock, pumice and lava (13 cubic miles), leaving the initial remains of the horseshoe island with a smaller island in the center. In my mind's eye, I can envision Earthlings living on an island they called Atlantis. In 11382 BC, the voltage discharge destroyed their homes, the population and the entire island overnight. The voltage-blast spread between two worldly spheres in close proximity to each other. The electric force from Earth carved the canyons (Valles

Marineris); and the remaining oceans on Mars fell to Earth with its greater gravitational pull.

The Time-Event Calendar

Timeline	Events	Comments	2nd Comments
66 million Years ago,	Let "ESS" stand for Earth's Solar System	The dinosaurs are killed	Millions of years pass, Earth becomes very vegetated from pole to pole
22349 BC	Garden of Eden	Adam and Eve created by God	Cain kills Able: "Not my brother's keeper."
22000 BC	"ESS" is hit by run-away-planet	Earth's axis tilt is zero degrees; it's further from the sun.	Oxygen levels are ~ 35%, est. More vegetation, bigger animals.
15581 BC	Enoch, the first, relocated on Bethel	Enoch and family: 6th generation after Adam and Eve	Ordered by God to be "thy brother's keeper."
11382 BC (-)	Santorini Island releases mega voltage at Mars	Atlantis people destroyed, instantly	Top-half of island is vaporized: 5,000 feet left
11382 BC (+)	Mars loses it great oceans	Oceans travel to Earth across space.	Top-half of island is vaporized: 5,000 feet left
11382 BC	The Great Flood	The Great Flood	Cataclysmic events
10735 BC and 10500 BC	Construction of Gobekli Tepe and the Sphynx	Sadees from Bethel sent to Earth	Sadees, offspring of Enoch I, first Custodians
2500 BC	Construction of the Great Pyramid Giza Plateau, Egypt	Northern Africa is a savanna	Earth's axis is in final stage of tilting 22 degrees
2200 BC	First wave of Custodians leave earth	Northern Africa becomes a desert	Starvation problems; Egypt is taught cross-breeding

1500 BC	Moses is born	Moses writes first five chapters of Bible	Genesis is in code to reflect a calendar of events
50 BC	Sadees scar up Nazca with air strips	Sadees invite many aliens to witness birth of Christ	God is angry at the Sadees for making a spectacle; they're ordered off the planet
0 BC	Jesus is born	Only special guests are allowed to follow "Star of Bethlehem"	Remaining population on Bethel become the Custodians

The time-event calendar illustrates Beena's claim that Earth's solar system (ESS) encountered more changes with the tilting of the Earth's axis, starting in 22,000 BC and causing a gradual global warming.

Beena was smart! We had known each other for years: growing up, playing together, discovering each other's anatomy and graduating together. Thoughts of proposing marriage right in the classroom crossed my mind. The other students had left us alone in a room where I could give a long presentation on my love for her and why marriage would be the best option. I looked at her lovingly and said, "Beena . . ."

That was as far as I got when Father Dean returned to the classroom with interrupting news about a new mission back on Earth. His excitement almost rubbed off, "Enoch, the Celestials have selected you to train, educate and influence a young person on Earth into greatness. The Celestials are sending you a pocket-top with special abilities. Father Aye believes that the pocket-top can predict the future. What do you say?"

"I know I'm obligated to serve. But how can I be successful?"

Father Aye walked into the classroom and heard my comments. He looked at Father Dean, Beena and then directly at me. He said, "Try not to become a man of success but rather, try to become a man of value. Grow with integrity and it will rub off."

I returned the same honest look to Father Aye and said, "I'll remember that."

Saying Goodbye

My first Custodian adventure was about to begin. Beena became depressed when she saw me packing clothes, worn on Earth. While I was arranging my medicine bag, Beena burst out, "I want to have your baby!" The immediate silence that filled the room made us both recoil with the new idea. Beena had too many opposing goals: she wanted to raise children, she wanted to improve her acumen, and she wanted to expand her knowledge about the universe. My mission did not allow me to have more than one goal. I departed after a few more hugs and gentle words.

Brianna always looked for ways to escape ownership of her tavern: to travel the galaxy; to seek a companion with hopes she would never grow old alone. "Take me with you!" she said. "I can help you. I can cook. I can make you a drink!" She had a prodigious affinity for adventure and I was her ideal traveling companion.

I knew Father Aye would never sanction her departure. She was stuck with running a business every day, and she was burnt out. I felt sorry for her but I could do nothing. The time for departure had come. I gave her a kiss with some promising words and walked down the stairway of her home into the tavern below, and out the door. Both women had said independently that they would wait for my return. I felt like a real heal. I should have confessed that I was dating both of them and then I should have painted a bulls-eye on the back of my shirt and given each of them a Crusader's crossbow. I felt like I deserved two arrows in my back.

The First Custodian Mission and Traveling with Father Aye

Measured in Earth's timeframe of AD 1513, I was forty-three years old, well educated in medicine and traveling in a Celestial's W-50 spacecraft from Bethel, across the barrier to the outpost, and then five more light-years from the outpost to Earth. With the outpost only five light-years from Earth, we crossed the barrier in only 36 days, (or 365* 5/50 one tenth of a year while traveling fifty times the speed of light.) The spacecraft belonged to the Celestials and they controlled the trajectory while the hatch between our quarters and the cockpit was locked. Acceleration and deceleration were not a problem because the W-50 had acceleration pods that allowed us to move about the spacecraft like we were walking on our home planet with a 1 g-force.

Scouts and Custodians constantly traveled between Earth and Bethel with different job-functions. A Scout learned the language at specific places on Earth; they taught Custodians the languages, required for their mission; and they updated history books to reflect the news on Earth. Who were the new Custodians? Well . . . that was me. I quickly mastered the French language from several Scouts that accompanied Father Aye and I during the thirty-six days of travel.

Father Aye:

Father Aye was our roving ambassador traveling routinely between Earth, Bethel and Geesal where the Celestials lived. He walked through the corridors of the spacecraft like it was his first trip: unsure of which deck he was on, and forgetting the location of his berthing quarters, and yet, a person never to be underestimated. He flew the W-25s and W-50s all the time. Perhaps, he got lost because the deck layout was different on each spacecraft. He took orders from the Celestials and delivered them to Custodians with a deep authoritative voice. A tall, well-built, stately figure describes him. He resembled Father Dean, wearing a white Roman toga with a purple sash and constantly speaking in different Earthly languages. For example, he would speak in a Shakespearean language, "Bathe your hands in liquid cold," and then he would switch to modern English, "Wash your hands, guys." Without knowing what he was saying, with his arsenal of many languages, we nodded our heads and replied with a brogue response, "Aye." The nickname of Father Aye grew over the years and he didn't seem to mind. The example I gave reflects a futuristic change of the English language. The now-year was 1513; Nostradamus was born in 1503, and Shakespeare won't be born until 1564.

Father Aye's best attribute was that he learned to communicate with the Celestial in their language—mental telepathy. He may have received his instruction from the Celestials before we both started the trip. Unaware of the forthcoming news, I was asked to quickly prepare to board the same spacecraft he traveled from Geesal, the home planet of the Celestials. While traveling somewhere between the outpost and Earth, he broke the news.

"Enoch," he said, "I have another assignment for you on Earth.

The Earthlings have created a printing press. The written language will make its mark on Earth in the near future. The Scouts have discovered a ten-year old boy who shows lot of potential for being a writer someday. They have observed him as a quick learner, and his parents have scored very high in intelligence. The Scouts took sputum samples and, as you know, the (DNA) test can also be used to determine intelligence . . . along with his parents' aptitude and identification"

"Okay," I replied while wondering how the Scouts got his parents to spit in a bottle. Hundreds of years later, I learned that the Earthlings developed a similar test for parent identification, and that they called it a DNA test. The parallelism between our two worlds always fascinated me. I continued, "When do I start?"

Father Aye replied, "Soon! We'll land on Earth in a small village of France. There are two caveats that I have to give you. The first is this wristband. It has a circular pendant mounted between two straps that act as an emergency alert, sending a microwave signal to any Scout in the vicinity. Our Scouts on planet Earth outnumber the Custodians by one hundred to one. It won't be long before help arrives regardless of where you are." He handed me the wristband and continued, "Its secondary function is to allow you to identify another Custodian or Scout."

"How do I do that?"

Father Aye responded, "It's easy. When you first greet the person, use your right hand to clasp his right hand after he extends his arm. Then you need to place your left hand across his right wrist and squeeze the pendant on his wristband if he is wearing one. If the pendant moves with a metallic click, he is another person from Bethel. If the pendant has no movement, then he happens to be wearing a junk bracelet. Under no conditions are you to flex the pendant twice. That action will call a Scout as soon as possible to your rescue. Do you understand?"

"Yes." From that time forward, I always noticed whenever politicians on Earth gave each other a "two-handed" handshake. It became a signal!

"The second caveat is that you can utilize all the drugs from Bethel that you think you will need, but you are never to administer them to anyone other than your assigned person. The Celestials are very strict about this rule because they want Earthlings to progress on their own. Giving another person an antibiotic or a vaccine would extend their life and upset the balance of world development. Never leave behind any medicine on Earth and never lose the wristband. Do you understand?"

"Yes"

"Do you understand?" he repeated with his head bent downward as though I were a smaller person or child. I reassured him and then he added, "The Earth is experiencing a disease called the Black Plague. The Celestials have provided us with a vaccine that I hold in my hand. Take the bottle and use it to vaccinate yourself and the boy as soon as possible. Any questions?"

"Yes, Father. How long will I be gone?"

"Enoch, that is for you to decide. Your mission is to train the boy to be a famous writer. You'll probably need to teach him certain skills at different junctions of his life like now and again when he is a teenager, a young adult, and a mature person. In between those periods, you can come home. You are in control. The Scouts will protect you, and they will arrange for your return trips. Okay?"

Enoch Looks Forward to His Mission

Traveling at Warp 50, we crossed the barrier that separates the two spiral sectors in our galaxy, called the Milky Way. Beyond the stream of neutrinos on the other side of the barrier, I could see the multicolored beacons that our radar illuminated on the monitor screen. The green rings and yellow dots in a circular pattern outlined the entrance to Orion's Highway, a pathway that led to planet Earth. The corridor stretched three light-years across the galaxy. The beacons originated from the Great Pyramid that was built in 2500 BC by our ancestors with the help of Egyptians. For three thousand years, the pyramid released a beacon every day: henceforth, the circular pattern as the Earth circled the sun. My assignment was to help an individual become historically famous. The individual was my distant cousin, and I was about to become my Brother's Keeper.

Chapter 3: Nostradamus: The Ark

Michel Nostradamus as a Young Boy

The skill that I gave Nostradamus was the confidence to communicate ideas and to speculate outcomes based upon human nature. The latter attribute became more important than the first because he is remembered for the content of his writings and not his skills. Courses such as physiology and advanced literature that I had taken at the academy became a part of his repertoire.

I introduced myself to Nostradamus and his family when he was ten years old. The Scouts showed me where he had been playing with other boys his age. I had been silently observing him from afar when I saw him fall, bruising his kneecaps. I knew that this was my opportunity to treat his wounds and eventually, introduce myself to his family.

I rushed toward him in the playground and said, "Hi. I saw you fall. Are you alright?"

He stared at the black bag that I was caring and replied, "Are you a doctor?"

"I'm something more than a doctor. I'm a physician. I can do what a general doctor does, and I can also perform surgery. Can I look at your wounds?"

With forlorn eyes and reddened cheeks, he looked up and blushingly said, "I guess so."

If his mother were with him, he would have cried about the pain and the size of the bruise. If his father were with him, he would have kept quiet after his father pointed out how small the bruise was. A little ten-year-old girl with the same bruise would have cried regardless of who was around. Whether it is kids or adults, they all have a predictable reaction. I had to teach him how people reacted. Nostradamus had to learn predictable human nature. That is when I knew this would be a difficult mission.

As I applied an antiseptic, which was uncommon for that era, I said, "This is going to sting a little so you have to be brave."

He moaned a little, and then fearing the worse, he said, "If you're a surgeon, are you going to cut off my leg?"

"Definitely and positively not!" I quickly added as I rolled my eyes and made a funny face at him. From that point on, we had started a friendship that lasted through his tutoring and until he became a writer. Nostradamus was an exceptional child, a quick learner and well-disciplined by his parents. I understood why the Celestials had assigned me to this frail but exciting individual.

When I had left my planet to come to Earth, I brought with me a large collection of drawings that were facial expressions of my people, the Custodians. Some looked happy, some looked sad, and then there were the others expressing emotions like anger, stealth, surprise, hunger, worry, sadness, and meanness. Most Custodians are not expressive; consequently, the drawings were created with volunteer Custodians expressing different emotions that the artist insisted upon. I would either flip through the drawings on the cards or make a few faces of my own.

Nostradamus had to announce the emotion that was expressed on a person's face. After some trial and error, Nostradamus did acquire the skill of "reading people." I gave him the ability to understand people by teaching him how to recognize facial expressions at a very early age. If a writer knows people, he can anticipate events. I constantly reminded him, "Always look into a person's eyes because the eyes are the windows to the soul."

The drawings that my people had created were very artistic in resembling Earthlings, even though they were drawn with Custodians as subjects. The citizens from our planet come from one origin; that is, Enoch, the First. Whereas the people of Earth developed more facial attributes and skin color. So, it was without wonder that Nostradamus and his parents accepted me as another black-haired, brown-eyed Frenchman.

The Nostradamus Family

After meeting his parents, I learned that Nostradamus did have problems. He was unsure of himself, and at the age of ten, he was still wetting his bed. The problem did not occur every night, but over the years it had become more frequent as his father demonstrated his hopelessness with his son. I told his father that he could cure his son by carrying him to the chamber pot late at night when the boy was still sleeping. After a few weeks of fatherly dedication, his son learned subconsciously to get up and go on his own. He grew in this respect, but a small amount of insecurity remained in the following years when he became suspicious of authorities condemning his writings.

When I first met his parents, I told them that I was a physician from Vienna looking for a distant cousin named Nostradamus. As I continued to lie with an ulterior motive, I explained that I was not a Nostradamus descent, but rather a distant relative on my wife's side. To my surprise, Mrs. Nostradamus immediately accepted me into her household. She might have thought of me as a distant relative, but she cared more about the prospects of a physician tutoring her son. Then she said something in the old French language that translated as "God has given us a physician! God bless you." Now I knew that I would always be welcomed into their home because I was one of the few physicians in the entire countryside.

The days turned into weeks, and the weeks turned into months as I accomplished two goals. I rented a two-room flat with a small office where I could practice as a physician during the morning hours; and with a back room, where I could sleep at night. My immediate goal was more important: I was able to tutor Nostradamus all afternoon. The lessons, very basic during the first year, involved a little mathematics, language appreciation, science, and human psychology. He had to learn how to anticipate people in a situation if he were to become a writer. A writer is what the Celestials wanted him to be. My task was easy at first, and then it became more challenging as he grew older. I could not stay with him during his entire life. I had a life of my own to live on Bethel. The two years that I spent with him during his childhood years gave him a head start in his education and in his self-confidence. The first round of education had ended, and I was on my way home.

Advanced Cardiac Training on Planet Geesal

Fathers Aye and Dean told Steve and I that we were requested to deliver the Ark of the Covenant to the Celestials on their home planet, Geesal. Both Fathers conveyed the honor of being invited to Geesal and having two guests as an accompaniment. After Beena and Brianna heard the good news, they both wanted to go.

Brianna's mind swelled with excitement and thoughts of going to the planet where the Celestials lived. This was the moment she had been eagerly awaiting, the moment when she could step out of her work-filled tavern, the moment she would leave her planet and travel to another world, the moment she would feel like a Custodian on a mission. She looked forward to traveling with her lover, to be loved, loved for all the reasons that were so clear to her. She anticipated that Enoch would have more time to give her the attention she deserved. It was her turn, her turn to be rid of the tavern and let herself go. She deserved to have some fun, to enjoy life, to treat herself to an elevated life that was beyond what she had had imagined herself to be . . . nothing more than an elevated barmaid. And so, she thought!

From the rumors she had heard, she imagined what it would be like seeing an alien planet: the pristine landscape, the abundance of plant life and animals, the profound sunsets, and the star-filled nights. Thoughts of passionate nights raced through her head. She anticipated his muscular chest pressed against hers, the strength of his arms, and the manly groans during his moments of pleasure that turned her on. Plans swirled in her head that tonight would be "the night." She was ready for him and daydreamed about their love-making. Discretion wasn't on her mind, and it didn't bother her that she was going to a planet where the residents were very religious.

It would have been a chamfered idea with a slippery edge to invite the two women I was sleeping with; neither one had any information about my pleasures in the night that I took with the other woman. I didn't have to weigh my options too long because Steve picked Brianna and Bill. I was relieved with his quick decision. I chose Beena and Charlie. I had to pick Beena after her constant pleads to visit a mysterious planet, where planetary beauties existed, animals abounded, religion flourished, and righteousness prevailed. When both women got their wish, I almost panicked.

Beena was diametrically different than Brianna. She preferred graduate study after her post-graduation degree, schooling on top of more schooling, data-crunching to reveal the facts, science over speculation, and a glass of milk over a shot of whiskey or any alcoholic drink that quickly made her drunk.

I could blend with the character of either woman. Their differences didn't bother me because I loved them both. Beena was my enjoyable, mental challenge, and Brianna made me laugh. If accidental harm came to both women on this trip and I could physically save only one, I would have trouble choosing.

Everyone was excited because they thought of the trip as a two-week vacation — an escape to never land. Two drawbacks capped everyone's zealousness: On the second day after we arrived, the Celestials wanted Steve, Bill, Brianna and Beena to go back home; and they wanted Charlie to remain with me during my training. I learned that I would be in the surgery room the next day learning all about heart transplants. But why did they want Charlie to stay on Geesal? It was a mystery about to unfold on the Celestial's spaceship.

On the way to the Celestial's home planet, we traveled at Warp 100. Their one-of-a-kind galactic transport ship contained all amenities for comfort and ease of living. It was their best galactic spaceship for accommodating guest. Traveling within a fifth dimension, there were no acceleration or deceleration effects. The six of us were allowed to roam-about in large compartmental rooms, to watch a viewing screen with documentaries captured on Earth and to enjoy the finest cuisine common to Earth, Bethel and Geesal. However, the control room was off limits because the Celestials piloted the spaceship.

As we sat in the combination cafeteria-lounge, Charlie explained his theories on spaceflight. Most of us never thought about the "absence of time" from our home planet. Suddenly Charlie stood up in the center of the room and declared, "I can hear them talking to me!" It was a phenomenon that happened to only a few people in our society. Fathers' Aye and Dean could communicate with the Celestials, and now, Charlie could do the same!

Using mental telepathy, the Celestials had explained to Charlie that the "absence of time" is relative to the planet the person comes from. Everyone from our planet never questioned the amount of time they were absent from our planet and the amount of time they spent on a spaceship. A flight crew simply monitored the two calendar-clocks while traveling at warp speeds.

With five pairs of eyes directed at him, Charlie attempted to explain his new revelation. Charlie started by saying,

"When I was piloting our spaceship to Earth with Steve and Enoch on board, it took two years to travel a five-light-year distance. As you know, distance is a measurement of the speed of light traveling for one Earth year—not a Bethel year. The round trip took four years."

As if he were in a trance, Charlie continued, "If the passage of time is ten times faster on Earth, then our round trip should have taken forty years—not four years. Right? When we returned to Bethel with the Ark of the Covenant, we should have seen forty calendar-years pass, but we saw only four calendar years pass.

How is that possible? As my thoughts were dwelling on this question, I suddenly heard the pilot of this spaceship provide the answer."

The telepathic voice that Charlie acquired began on that day, the very moment we were all sitting in the cafeteria's lounge area, watching Charlie yacking away, while standing on a small crate, next to the crate containing the Ark of the Covenant. . . . Charlie was in communication with the Celestial piloting the ship and talking to us at the same time. We had no idea why he was acting so weird.

"Yes, go on. How did he explain it?" we asked in semi-anxious excitement.

Charlie's Explanation for Warp Speed

Charlie told us that the passage of time reverses when traveling at warp speeds. He said, "You gain what you lose." At sub-light speeds, clocks on the pilot's home planet speed up. Relatives on his home planet age faster than he does. They're older!

While Charlie carried on a two-way conversation with us and the Celestial pilot of the ship, he stopped talking to us and mentally asked the pilot, "So, do we get older or younger when we travel the cosmos?"

By now, Charlie had our complete attention because his logic was flawless and we were not sure of the answer.

Charlie continued, "It's a wash!"

"What's a 'wash'?" Steve asked with a curled lip on one side.

"With our relatives on Bethel, we do not age any faster or slower than they do. Our four-year round-trip to Earth and back advanced our calendar years on Bethel by the same amount: namely, four years. Here's the reason why: our time clocks on our spaceships slow down as we approach the speed of light; but then, our clocks speed up as we travel faster than the speed of light.

The author's theoretical definition of Charlie's statement about a "wash" is defined as a mathematical shrinkage and dilation of time whereby one negates the other. The shrinkage of time relates to Einstein's equation $t'/t = [1 - (v/c)^2]^{.5}$ where: 1) "v" is the velocity of the spaceship 2) "c" is the speed of light 3) t' is an atomic clock on the spaceship 4) t is an atomic clock in the cosmos and 5) t'/t is the shrinkage of time. If "v" exceeds "c" then Warp Speed is achieved and t'/t becomes a dilation of time. To make the formula fit the curve below, ^{2} and $^{.5}$ are replaced with undiscovered exponents, ^{x} and ^{y}. A value of $\sqrt{-1}$ is treated as imaginary time.

When plotted on log scales, the graph illustrates time changing at 1% below and above a Warp Speed of one. Since the "Past" does not exist, continuation of the original curve is transposed. A corridor with double arrows is a leap, a "wash," into hyperspace—the start of a wormhole.

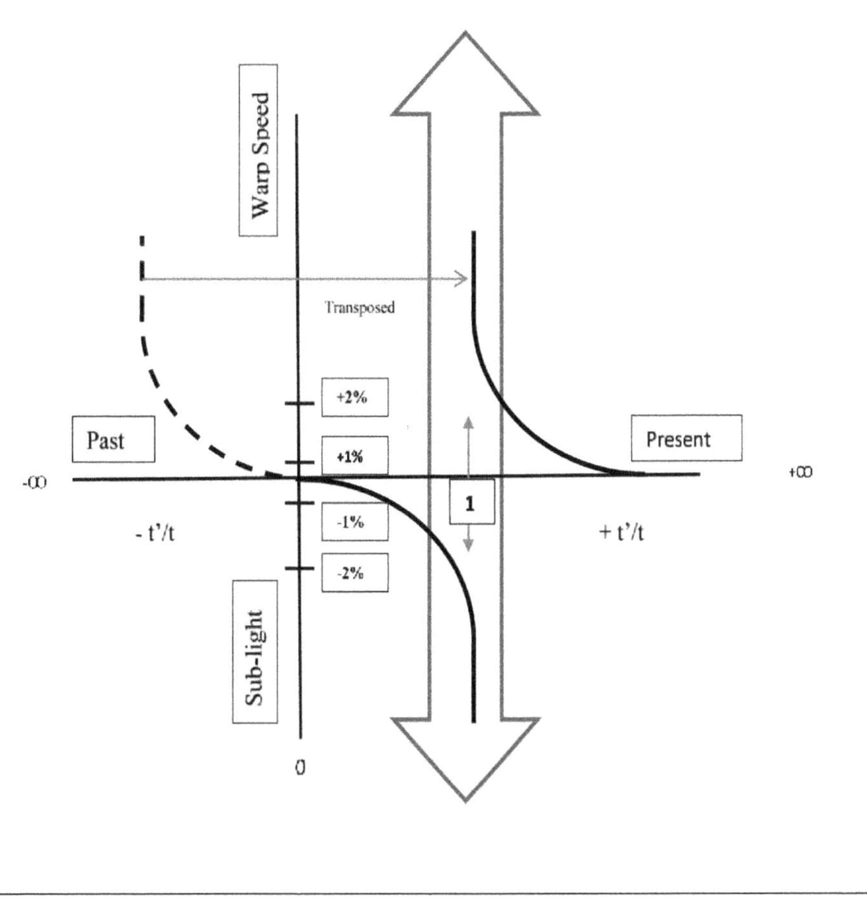

I With respect to the time passage of our home planet, the slow-down of time negates the speed-up of time. Consequently, our absence of time on Bethel took the same amount of time to complete the round trip to Earth; namely four years—not forty years."

"Of course," Steve said. "Enoch and I knew we were gone for only four years."

I followed Steve's comment by adding, "When we landed on Earth, the passage of time caused our biological clocks to age ten months for every one month and ten years for every one year, respectively, while we stayed on Earth. Our typical life span on Bethel is 1,200-years. If we had lived on Earth without any diseases, our typical life-span would have been 120-years."

"Of course," everyone agreed. Then there was a flurry of questions about Charlie's sudden ability to communicate with the Celestials using mental telepathy. The Celestials were projecting their thoughts from the cockpit across the bulkheads to the compartment where Charlie stood, next to the crate containing the Ark of the Covenant that glowed with a faint light, unseen by the passengers.

Planet Geesal

After entering Geesal's atmosphere, our pilot gave us the grand tour that everyone had waited to see. While sitting in the lounge-compartment of the spaceship, we had the option of viewing the monitors or looking out of the portholes. Hovering above the terrain, we saw tall waterfalls, lush forest and deep canyons. As our spacecraft slipped beneath the planet's ocean, we saw sea creatures swimming at various depths: Coelacanth fish resembling the same species on Earth's Ocean near Madagascar,

Mosasaurs and Plesiosaurs resembling reptiles from Earth's Mesozoic era and every animal common to present-day Earth.

The view of their city was unbelievably futuristic with tall buildings flanked by minarets resembling rocket launch sites. The Celestials had advanced beyond the age of rocket ships more than five hundred thousand years ago. Orbiting their planet, we saw satellites that controlled the weather and communication links. From a centralized office, they controlled the rain that could be directed to any place on their planet at any time. We were equally impressed with the vision of passenger vehicles traveling above the planet's surface along a laser-directed guide wire. When they came to an intersection that was common to four directions, they never collided; they merely vanished and reappeared on the other side of the intersection. Steve told me that it had something to do with imaginary time. The six of us were impressed. The Celestials were equally impressed with the return of the Ark of the Covenant. Our new discoveries on a foreign planet were only beginning.

The Night of Musical Bedrooms

Our own people from Bethel who had chosen to retire there or recover from a surgical procedure that either Celestials or Custodians had performed managed our hotel on Geesal. At the instructions of the Celestials, we were treated as royal guest lavished with fancy décor, individual bedrooms, elaborate meals and the finest spirits. Their rules stated: no wandering away from the hotel; Steve, Bill, Beena and Brianna would have to return home the next day. Charlie could stay. The hotel consisted of only Bethel personnel: Bethel workers, retired Bethel Scouts, and post-operative patients from our home planet. The Celestials never frequented the hotel they owned. Their religion prevented frivolity with us; even though, we were the ones who carried out their missions on Earth. The way I saw it, the Celestials were good guys and bad guys at the same time. Thousands of years ago they ordered every Sadee person to leave Bethel and find another planet to live on. But that's another story. We always obeyed their orders because the alternative was disobedience to God, the Supreme Being of all living souls.

While I improved my skills as a heart surgeon on Geesal, Charlie's presence remained a mystery. Yes, he had learned to communicate telepathically with the Celestial, but so did Father Aye and Father Dean. Charlie became our sole interpreter. To be honest, Charlie wore me out with his constant fact-finding, talkative, wordy, one-way conversations. He was a nerd! I had to room with him during the entire duration. He even talked in his sleep—a one-way technical jargon with the Celestials, most likely.

The evening started with an elaborate full course meal delivered to a rotating table in the center of our stationary table. The six of us could select from the center table by merely rotating the center table to the food item we wanted. We had a choice of fish, roast duck, specialty meats, vegetables and potatoes prepared as masked, baked, scalloped or fried. Our meal was followed by a constant flow of wine bottles waltzing around on the center table as our eyes and grabby hands tried to adjust to their true location.

After we finished our dinner, Steve, Charlie and Bill wandered off to explore the rest of the hotel. I sat at the dinner table with two healthy women who wanted the fun to continue throughout the night. Neither one knew I had had relations with the other woman. I was in a jam. My mind raced quickly about the idea of getting the younger woman drunk and taking the older woman to my bedroom. "Drink up," I said to Beena. The three of us had already had our fill of alcohol. Beena favored the drink she held in her hand while Brianna could have drunk a few more very easily. Brianna had an alcoholic constitution of a man. After all, she did own a tavern!

Beena didn't exactly collapse face-forward into the linen table cloth: She suddenly crashed her drink to the table and rested her head on the table. After the waiter came to help her to her bedroom, Brianna and I slipped away into my bedroom. We had barely gotten into the bed under warm blankets with our shivering naked bodies when we heard a knock outside the bedroom door. A muffled female voice said something about being cold.

"What do you want, Beena?" I replied as I motioned Brianna to jump out of bed and hide in the closet.

"I can't sleep. I'm co—co—cold," she stuttered behind the entry door.

"Brianna," I whispered, "hide inside the closet." Completely naked, she jumped out of bed and headed for the closet.

Moments later, I heard her muffle, Okay, from behind the closed closet door.

"Okay, come in," I said to Beena, still standing in the hallway.

She entered the bedroom as I got out of bed, covered my naked body with the hotel's fuzzy robe, walked to the bedroom door to greet her, and comforted her about the merits of her own bed. I found it easy to negotiate with her in her inebriated condition. I escorted her back to her bedroom and upon my return Brianna exclaimed, "WHAT Did SHE WANT?"

"I don't know. I have to talk to Bill. Can you wait for me?" I replied knowing things could only get worse.

"Yes," she pouted.

I gave up trying to find Bill. I spent time looking everywhere. When I returned a while later, I peeked into the bedroom and saw Brianna asleep. My thoughts raced to the idea that I could sleep in her bedroom if she could sleep in mine. Sex was out of the question. I had to get up and report for work within another two hours.

The Operating Room

The next day found me working in the operating room with the Celestials' renowned doctors. Charlie sat above us behind a glass dome next to a microphone that carried his words to an earpiece I wore in my ear. I wore a smaller microphone attached to my operating gown.

"Enoch," Charlie said, "can you hear me?" Then he tapped on the microphone causing a louder sound in my earpiece, blasting my eardrums.

I nodded my head. I should have known Charlie would be my personal interpreter. The Celestials had planned his stay on Geesal from the start. Charlie continued, "I'm listening to the Celestials' thoughts and they are giving you instructions through me."

"What do they want me to do?"

"They want you to learn how to remove a myxoma. The man on the operating table is a former Custodian from Bethel. He has a tumor called a myxoma growing in the left atrium of his heart. After he was examined on our home planet, he requested the operation to be performed by the Celestials," Charlie explained.

"Yes, I knew Celestials honored a Custodians request for an advanced surgical procedure. They honor both Custodians and Scouts for the work they did on Earth," I replied. "It's a token of repayment."

"This is your opportunity to learn about the human heart. Hold on . . . Wait . . . They're asking me to tell you to put insulated gloves on your hands that the nurse is giving you."

"Done," I said as Charlie continued to watch us from above.

Charlie relayed, "I can see them cutting a ten-inch incision along the length of the patient's sternum with some kind of a light-cutting machine. I can't believe what I'm seeing! Now they're separating his ribs and pulling his heart about three-inches away from his chest. They want you to hold his heart with both hands," Charlie relayed.

I held the patient's beating heart while the life-sustaining, pump-machine bypassed his heart and circulated blood into the rest of his body. I also saw the cold compacts that the nurse placed on top of his heart in attempts to lower the heart temperature to 40 degrees Fahrenheit. With cold compacts above his heart and my hands under his heart, my job was to steady the heart after it stopped beating. I thought the man would die with a non-functional heart. I had mixed feelings, mostly fear of being irresponsible.

"Enoch," Charlie said, "the doctor wants you to hold the patient's heart very steady because he's going to pass a scalpel through the right atrium, past the separating membrane, into the left atrium where the tumor is located. The surgeon is describing the tumor as a resemblance to a pear hanging by a stem on the inner wall. It's about one-inch wide and two-inches long. The surgeon is telling me the tumor interfered with the opening and closing of the heart valve. He also said that myxomas are hereditary. I hope you're not related to this Custodian on the operating table!"

As events happened, I learned the new patient was unrelated and wanted to live his new life on Geesal. I also learned about other types of operations. Celestials were so advanced they never needed a donor. They grew new body-organs as they were needed: hearts, spleens, stomachs, pancreas, gall bladder, kidney, and etc. Their secondary heart, grown in a lab, functioned as well as their original heart.

Our life expectancy at 1,200 years equates to a Celestials' life expectancy at five thousand years. When translated into Earth years, a young Celestial who monitored the construction of the Great Pyramid in 2500 BC would still be alive in AD 2500. Their history, their endeavors and their achievements had a long corporal memory that advanced their society. During the short period I lived on Geesal, I mastered the process of a heart transplant on citizens from Bethel. Post-operative patients from Bethel could anticipate a normal life expectancy of 1200-years. Post-operative Celestial patients could anticipate a normal life expectancy of five thousand years with multiple body organs grown in the laboratory.

While sitting in the observation room above the operating table, Charlie and I witnessed Celestials operating on other Celestials that needed a new organ transplant. I was shocked to see the inner organs of Celestials completely different from our own anatomy. Charlie, in a greater state of shock, could hear every word the surgeon said. Both of us saw a 4-foot-long, naked Celestial on a smaller operating table.

"Where are their sex organs?" I asked Charlie sitting next to me.

"They don't have any!" he replied.

"Are they asexual?"

"Yes. From what I can tell, they reproduce when they feel their body is ready to have a child," Charlie answered with a lonely and sunken look on his face.

With bodies that never wore out, it was understandable how the Celestials could travel thousands of light-years across the galaxy in one lifetime. If an organ wore out, it was replaced with another synthetically grown organ that came to life within their bodies. If bone rubbing on bone became a problem, the whole limb was replaced. They had a way of seeding vascular cadaver cells on mesh scaffolds and letting protein collagen replicate cells. The cadaver cells were washed away and the mesh was allowed to dissolve before they could implant the vessel, muscle or bone where it would grow into a genetic duplicate. Their medical knowledge greatly encompassed a small fraction of the heart transplant technique that I learned to perform on my own species.

There had to be a reason why I was given this technique. What was my destiny?

On the way back to our home planet, I realized that my learning experiences were more than complete. At the biological Earth-age of forty-four, I qualified to do heart transplants in an ultra-modern facility on Geesal or one that was nonexistent on Bethel. It made no sense. Heart surgeons were overly qualified on Bethel and on Earth in the year AD 1523. People on Earth were transitioning into the Dark Ages with the Black Plague lurking about. When I asked Father Aye why I was overly qualified, he said, "I don't know the future; only God does."

I persisted with my question. "If I am scheduled to revisit Nostradamus, will he need a heart transplant?"

"Again, I don't know, but you are scheduled to leave for Earth very soon. By the way, Charlie told me the Celestials are interested in you settling down and marrying either Beena or Brianna." My jaw dropped. I had no response for Father Aye. For the rest of my life, I always thought about Father Aye's last comment. Were the Celestials warning me or predicting my future? Our Bible, similar to the Bible on Earth, quotes God saying, "Be fruitful, and multiply." (Genesis 1:28)

Back to Earth

On the way back to Earth, I found myself traveling in a prestige spaceship; the best they had; a W-50 including a Celestial pilot. Travel time from the outpost to earth took 36 days (5 light-years x 12 months/W-50} or 1.2 months measured in Earth time: and 1.2 months as "absent time" on Bethel. Charlie had made it clear about the passage of time as a "wash" approaching Warp 1 from either direction. I was free to wander the spacecraft, free to observe Orion's Highway on viewing monitors, free to sleep in a bed similar to my own: a total difference from the W-5, I traveled on during my first visit to Earth. I prepared for my visit. Audio recordings prepared me for Nostradamus' native language once again.

The Earth year was AD 1528; I was forty-nine years old and Nostradamus was twenty-five years old. My second visit with the youthful Nostradamus should have had a ritualistic value, but it did not brighten his life, catch his fancy, stir his soul, or fire a brand-new passion. I felt the same way when Father Aye sent me on my first mission to help Nostradamus at ten years of age. I can still remember Father Aye, in all his wisdom, turn my thoughts around by saying, "Try not to become a man of success but rather, try to become a man of value." My path was clear. I had to teach the young Nostradamus to become a man of value: a man with integrity. A man with firm principles can understand the psychology of humanity. After I encouraged him with Father Aye's words, he adopted a purpose in life. A man of value is a person who has a visionary quest. He can weigh human tragedy, dogma, character, tenaciousness, predictability; he can put it into a quatrain that generates a futuristic view. Both author and his readers begin to think outside a framework of simple, archaic thoughts. It rejuvenates the human brain with a sense of value and prevents stagnation of thought. Thoughts always precede theory; scientific breaking thoughts and accomplishments follow in the same logical order.

My Second Visit with Nostradamus

"Michel," I said, "do you remember me when I was your teacher and doctor for two years?"

"Yes, I do. How was I to know when you would return?" he asked.

"I believe I told you I came from a home far away?" I replied.

"I remember you claiming to be an alien. . . . That was our secret."

"Did you share our secret with anyone else?"

"No, not even my parents. They both died of the Black Plague. I tried to save them with the medical drugs I learned from you; that is, poppy seeds soaked in hot water to relieve pain, skullcap seeds for headache, white spotted lungwort leaves for tuberculosis, herbal remedies and even baking flour to stop blood wounds. Lord knows, I prayed you were here. Where were you?" he declared while gritting his teeth.

"Michel," I said while looking into his wide-open eyes, "I won't lie to you. I was back on my home planet called Bethel. I had to wait until you were 'of age.'"

"'Of age' for what?"

"I had to wait until you were old enough to assume greater responsibilities. I'm sorry to hear about your parents. The Black Death is pernicious. I know you tried to save your parents and many others. I understand you. It takes courage to walk into a valley of death. But now, you are ready to start a greater career."

"A career in what? Who will hire me in this chaotic world, plagued with filth, disease and a ruling class of Spanish Inquisitors who disrupt all civility?"

"That's exactly why I'm here. To give you 'hope'; to give to you the insight that will enlighten other people around you . . . and those to come; to undo the Spanish Inquisition; to teach others, through your works, that life is more than living it; to think about life and where it is taking them, their children and grandchildren. 'Talk' is cheap. People spend 99-percent of their time talking about nonsense. They need to learn how to contemplate; how to imagine; how to think 'outside' the framework of simple, archaic thoughts."

"What will it get me?"

"Nothing . . . and everything!"

"Then why should I exert the effort?"

"Because God wants you to!"

"Thee—thee—thee God?" he stammered.

"Yes, my God and thine God, the Almighty."

In his excitement, Nostradamus switched from speaking French to speaking in Old English. Neither Michel nor Enoch realized that all the candles in the room stopped flickering and emitted a profound brightness the moment Michel grasped the idea he was special in the eyes of the lord. Shocked by the revelation, Michel subconsciously switched from his native tongue to speaking a different language and Enoch, the linguist, tracked the change immediately.

"How do you know?" Michel asked.

"He communicates through other aliens I work for."

"How do I know this is true?"

I removed the pocket-top that Father Aye had given me; placed it on the kitchen table; and allowed it to display laser light images in three dimensions about eight-inches above the table. "These images," I said, "are a gift from God to you." The holographic images appeared to dance on the kitchen table with people, futuristic automobiles, planes, trains and future events.

"Wow," he said. "From God?"

"Yes. Only the images are your gift from God. Do you still remember how to write in your native language, the way I taught you?"

"Yes," Michel said lethargically.

"Have you practiced writing?"

"No."

"That's our starting place. We'll meet early tomorrow morning. If that's okay with you."

"Okay. I want to be a part of something important."

"You will be. Believe me, you will be."

Michel's Career

Michel Nostradamus at twenty-five years old embarked on a writing career with improper sentence structure, poor punctuation marks and zero clarity of thought—everything I had "not" taught him. He had his own way of doing things because he feared the Spanish Inquisition would question his futuristic writings and then torture him. However, his interpretation of the images with matching words was uncanny. He wrote what he saw. After we had seen the same image, his interpretation of event differed than mine. Together, we saw Hitler-type leaders and the destruction of twin towers. Looking back through the years at my saved memoirs on my own pocket-top, the following quatrains are a few examples of his labors.

> **"Five and forty degrees, the sky shall burn:**
>
> **To the great new city shall the fire draw nigh,**
>
> **With vehemence the lames shall spread and churn**
>
> **When the Normans they conclusion try."**
>
> **(Century 6 Quatrain 9)**

The pocket-top required an entry date before an image appeared. We entered the number 2001 and saw Earth at an elevation higher than the clouds: a blue ball within a sea of the black cosmos. The projected, three-dimensional images zoomed in past the continents, past the clouds, past the East Coast of North America to a city called New York. Twin towers projected their loftiness above other city buildings beyond a blue ocean.

Suddenly a plane crashed into one of the tower buildings. We saw a plane descend at a steep angle and level off into the tower, turning it into a ball of flames, smoke, debris and finally white dust clouding the air.

At first, we assumed the crash was a pilot's error. Then we realized that someone had taken their own life so they could destroy the life of many others. The word *terrorist* was not in Michel's vocabulary or mine. A suicidal act made no sense and neither did their religion. However, the Normans that lived in northwestern France opposed the English people who had dual religions: namely, the Catholics and Protestants. The Normans hated England as much as the terrorist hated New York. Michel wrote the quatrain the best way he could to describe terrorist with different religion and opposable hatred.

Nostradamus had started his career. He had explained the 9/11 event in 2001 with his interpretation. While viewing the pocket-top, he became a time traveler. He could enter any year going forward or backward beyond the year he lived in. The pocket-top stayed active as long as I stayed in the house that contained my medical tools, remedies and vaccines in a black bag.

I write my autobiography with the advantage of looking back at past events in the twelfth and sixteenth to twenty-first centuries and writing them as they actually happened. With a lifespan of 1,200 years, I can reflect on my memoirs. Herein is a summary of the accomplishments of Nostradamus.

Between the dates of AD 1555 and AD 2041, I have associated actual events with his quatrains. His works are divided into 10 groups called "Centuries." Nine groups have 100 quatrains and one group has only forty-two quatrains. His very first quatrain explains his technique; for example,

<u>AD 1555, Century 1, Quatrain 1.</u>

Finally seated, at night, in secret study

At rest and alone over the bronze stool

A slender flame emerges from the wilderness

Unbelievable deeds are uttered from the wasteland.

When Nostradamus wrote this quatrain, he was referring to my pocket-top with projected holographic images above a stool where my pocket-top rested. The functionality of my pocket-top was beyond his comprehension; consequently, he referred to it as a bronze stool because the word "bronze" was an alchemical term for something unknown. The flame, of course, was the laser images of three-dimensional projections of future events.

<u>Date: 1945. Century 2, Quatrain 24</u>

With the hunger of wild beast they will cross the rivers

Most of the country will be against Hister

The great man will find himself paraded inside a cage of iron

The German child [of the Rhine] will see nothing.

<u>What Nostradamus witnessed:</u>

The Russian army crossing the Elbe and Vistula rivers

With revenge for Germany's attack on Stalingrad

His friend, Mussolini, meets his demise paraded in a cage before the   public

Hitler, born on the Danube River (Hister in Latin), sees nothing.

<u>Date: 1963, Century 6, Quatrain 37</u>

The ancient task will be completed

From on high, evil will fall on the great man

A dead innocent will be accused of the deed

The guilty one will remain hidden in the mist.

<u>What Nostradamus witnessed:</u>

The kill shot from the 6th floor of a Texas Museum,

Assassinating John F. Kennedy

Lee Harvey Oswald appeared as the dead innocent one

But the guilty one is hidden in the mist,

behind the grassy knoll

Someone associated with the Mafia accustomed to the tradition of eliminating the head of the family, the president, as per the "ancient task."

Date: 2003, Century 6, Quatrain 34

The contrivance of flying fire

Will come to trouble the besieged leader

Inside, there will be so much sedition

That the corrupt ones will despair

What Nostradamus witnessed:

He saw flaming rockets over Bagdad in the US/Iraq War

He saw Saddam Hussein losing his 24- year grip on power

When the people tore down his 23-foot statue

in Firdos Square, sedition was against

him and members of his corrupt family.

The word "contrivance" implies he was encountering problems with weapons of mass destruction.

Date: 2003, Century 6, Quatrain 97

Earthshaking, a fire from the center of the earth

Will shake the towers of the new city

As a result, two great rocks will fight a long war

Until Arethusan springs bloody the river afresh

What Nostradamus witnessed:

He sees the "two great rocks" as the divide between

Christianity and Islam faiths.

He sees an earthshaking fire as his best way to describe

aviation fuel burning in the twin towers of New York.

The Arethusan springs is a mythical name related to Ellis Island: an immigration gateway, implying new anti-immigration policies.

<u>Date: 2016, Century 1 Quatrain 16</u>
Scythes in the mill-run, joining towards Sagittarius
In it high mill-course of exaltation
Plague, famine, and death through war
The century approaches its remaking

When I saw the same images that Michel saw, I was impressed with his interpretation after reading his Century 1, Quatrain 16. I saw scythes reaping wheat and barley for the mill. I saw plenty of available food and peoples' exaltation, and then I saw it all go away with climate change.

Michel's quatrain reminded me of the Revelation of St. John the Devine who cautioned Earthlings as follows: "Unless we attempt to change our ways, the planet will be taken from us and remade in an image we find uncongenial."

As an alien visitor with interest in Earth's future as if it were my own planet, I have to say, "This quatrain is a warning about the damage to the planet and to its climate. God gave the planet as a gift. 'Sagittarius' in line one of the quatrains represents Sagittarius the archer who rides a white horse of death along with three other horsemen."

The Last Few Days of my Visit with Nostradamus

During the daytime, I worked in the adjoining room attending the sick. At night, I took the pocket-top with me, and I would go out for a smoke with my favorite pipe while Michel would write what he saw during the entire day. Michel had created nearly one thousand quatrains (four lines of verse) that he divided into ten sections or centuries. My mission was complete. I was ready to leave. I gave him all the money I had earned as a physician so he could continue his writing. He was delighted and thanked me for giving him a purpose in life.

Steve and Charlie came to pick me up and take me home. They had hitched a ride on a new Celestials' W-100 cruise ship. Charlie had the Celestials' permission to borrow a W-5 from the ship's hangar bay. He was the sole pilot and Steve was his sole passenger while they waited for me to complete my mission.

They had spent time in South America viewing the Nazca lines and ancient elongated skulls that belonged to the Sadees. They knew the history of the Sadees and their attempt to influence people in South America.

Steve would pop in every now and then with a recharged battery pack for the pocket-top and a bag of tobacco for me. I never asked, but I suspected that he used the spacecraft to charge the backup battery and asked Charlie to transport him to other parts of the world where better tobacco was available. After Steve took up pipe smoking, we would chat about countries with the best tobacco.

During the night that preceded our departure, I found myself strolling through town enjoying the aromatic aroma that emanated from my pipe. It was your typical sixteenth century scene with cobblestone streets flanked by lanterns shining from quaint little homes and their windows made of wooden shutters. In the beginning of the sixteenth century, the inhabitants were ordered to keep their lanterns burning in the windows of all houses that faced the streets. Burning lanterns increased the security for residents. Early lighting fuels consisted of olive oil, beeswax, fish oil, whale oil, sesame oil, and nut oil.

The evening mist dampened the cobbled streets causing the reflected light from the street lanterns to shimmer with muted colors across brick stones. The white stucco cottages also reflected some of the streetlight, but actually, the town's streets were dark and vacant on this ominous night.   Up in the shadows, I could see flower boxes underneath closed shutters with small vestiges of candlelight seeping through the slats. The evening was still young, and it produced sounds of laughter caught between the stop and go conversations of people talking inside their homes; but the most contagious laughter came from a tavern that looked inviting. Other sounds involved a dog barking and some stones being thrown.

As I walked down the street smoking my pipe and making casual observations, I realized that I would have enjoyed living here in this town with people who were friendly and honest. If honesty was a hallmark, then Nostradamus exemplified his people writing a report about futuristic images that he witnessed. His deep-seated goals were meant to prepare humanity for futuristic disasters. The presence of the Black Plague skipped his town and moved to adjacent towns where Nostradamus tried, after my absence, to save people with herbal medicine while wearing a breathing mask resembling the long nose of a bird.

Deep into the night, I walked down the street puffing away on my pipe when I saw another man at the opposite end of the street creating a bigger cloud of smoke. As I approached, I could see that he carried what looked like a lantern emanating a vile smell from the end of a pole. At first, I thought that he was just a farmer with a hood over his head spraying his fields with a smoking, insect repellant. Little did I know he really was a Sadee working to spread the Bubonic Plague!

I was thinking about the warning from Steve:

Steve had cautioned me about the revenge of the Sadees who wanted to destroy mankind. Earlier in their missions, they benefitted mankind when ordered by the Celestials to restore Earth's dwindling population and disappearing animals as the result of the Great Flood.

The Sadees had built the Sphynx to encourage men that they had dominion over all animals, especially the king of animals — the lion. They replenished animals lost by building Gobekli Tepe in 10500 BC. Multiple breeding pens in twenty different circular buildings contained relief images on the inside walls to indicate assigned animals that needed reproduction: all species of animal needed specialized care-giving—a monumental task and the Sadees carried out their mission as instructed.

The Sadees helped the descendants of Noah improve their spirituality and their food reserves. The buildings at Gobekli Tepe were essentially reproduction barns for all the animals of Earth.

My thoughts returned to reality as I watched a figure in the distance, resembling the grim reaper and spraying something from the lantern, high above his hooded head.

"Hey you; stop," I yelled as I ran toward the intruder while pressing my wristband two times to alert either a Scout or Steve whom I prayed would be nearby. I ran into the dark night, feeling the energy drain from my body while gasping for air.

The man in the dark, dropped the cumbersome lantern-pole and ran faster toward the edge of town. I knew that my wristband had a homing beacon for Steve to find me quickly, but he was nowhere in sight. With the last burst of energy, I threw my body forward, tackling the intruder to the ground where he fell lifeless. I had been trained to defend myself when I was a Crusader, but the energy that I had expended left me with an inability to subdue him. He started to get up. We faced each other in pugilistic formation, and just then, Steve appeared dispatching the intruder with quick results. Remembering his judo, Steve delivered a six-foot kick to his head sending him to the ground for the second time.

Moments later, two Scouts arrived from their spacecraft that channeled them down a tubular antigravity shaft. I had practiced that type of descent many times, but I preferred an actual spaceship landing. The antigravity shaft had to be used at nighttime so Earthlings would not see us descend. When I tried it in the dark; I lost my perspective, turned my body involuntarily, and descended the tubular shaft headfirst with an uncomfortable landing into the ground.

The four of us stood at the edge of town looking down at the intruder as he lifted himself into a sitting position. "What are you doing here, cousin?" Steve asked in a harsh voice. Steve knew immediately that this man with his elongated head was a descendant of Enoch the First. Over thousands of years, his species had branched off from our species due to a mutation, and yet they were our cousins: six-foot hominids like us except for their misshaped heads.

He had no answer. After a long pause, he spoke in a soft voice, "I'm on assignment."

In the dim light, the Scouts and I began to notice the intruder's elongated head: an observation that Steve had made earlier. Looking down at the intruder, sitting on the ground in the dim light, Steve instantly asked, "What's your name?"

"Milo. My name is Milo, and I desperately need the money that the Sadees are paying me," he pleaded as if we would immediately understand.

"But you're one of them! What is this goop that you're spreading in the air?"

"It's the Bubonic Plague in an aerosol spray."

There were cascading moments of silent thinking as each of us tried to recall if and when we had been vaccinated for the plague. After a self-mental-exam, we redirected our gaze from each other to this "Milo-guy" inflicting a disease in an unusual method upon Earthlings. Steve continued his diatribe with thoughts that we all shared, "You're a trader to the cause. Everyone on Bethel makes sacrifices to help the Earthlings whether they are a Custodian, a Scout, a pilot, or a worker on assignment. You come along and you're counterproductive. Don't you realize that men, women and children are suffering and dying because of you?"

"Yes. But the Sadees said that they would cure them after they found a vaccine to cure their own people. They need to extract blood serum from an individual that survived the plague so that they could create a vaccine."

Steve asked, "If you don't have the vaccine, why aren't you dead from the Bubonic Plague?"

Milo's answer made sense, "I will be!" He looked at the ground in forlornness thinking about the number of days he had left to live.

If Milo knew I had a vaccine for the plague in my black medicine bag at the house, he would have tried to steal it. Fortunately, I had treated Nostradamus with all the vaccines I possessed. As a Custodian, I was obliged to treat only my client. If I treated anyone else, I would be breaking a Celestial law that forbids treatment of another Earthling because events in the future would be altered. The Celestials favored a slow progressive destiny for Earth because its destiny was already unpredictable. Milo would be punished severely for genocide and breaking the fifth commandment after the Scouts had transported him to Geesal.

With the thought of the plague still on my mind, I realized that the expiration date for all my vaccinations had expired. Without refrigeration for the last few years, the vaccine for the Bubonic Plague probably went dormant. But still, the Sadees could probably synthesize it. I was at a crossroad trying to decide. If I gave Milo one bottle of the vaccine, he could give it to his people and their plague would end. Thousands of Sadees would be saved. On the other hand, my mission would be altered to save them. Before I could decide anything, I saw Steve looking at me. We were both thinking the same thing.

Our parallel thoughts went like this:

"What are these Sadees doing? Are they the ones responsible for the bright lights in the night sky over Germany trying to shoot down the W-25, Celestials' spaceships? It's foolish of them to try to take down a W-25 with their own W-5 spacecraft limited to only four dimensions of travel. The W-5s have nuclear tipped missiles, but the W-25s' have a more destructive weapon that extends their 5th dimensional grasp on a target with parametric oscillations that upset the fundamental vibration of every type of material within the W-5s' spaceship. If the Celestials wanted to take on a superior entity, they would have to go against the archangels mentioned in chapter 20 of the Book of Enoch: Michael, Gabriel, Uriel, Saraqael, Raguel, Remiel, Raphael and Joel.

Archangels live in a world of pure energy as per the Supreme Equation whereby energy is equated to material things times the square of the speed of light which is a constant for different sectors of the universe. As pure energy with zero mass, they can travel across galaxies one thousand times faster than the W-25s, the W-50s and the new W-100s. Conversely, they can 'reverse the equation' and materialize anywhere. The archangels can zap out the Celestials as easily as the Celestials can zap out the Sadees."

When Steve and I were aboard the W-5 spaceship with Charlie piloting the ship, the three of us settled down in the control room to discuss the Sadees, our missing cousins we never knew.

"Where are we going?" Steve asked Charlie.

"To South America," Charlie responded, "I want to show Enoch the influence the Sadees had over the indigenous people."

While we were in route to our destination, Steve started the conversation. "The Sadees act like wayward children," Steve commented in attempts to renew our earlier conversation.

"I've seen it happen over and over again," I responded. "A group of people will fight their neighbors over riches and natural resources: coal, oil, gas, gold and gems. Then they'll fight for political control of their neighbors. The third and final step is the 'worship' phase, where they're talked into losing personal possessions unless they went to war. Basically, their ambition follows a prescribed path: to riches, to power, to glory."

"I agree," Charlie said, "I came to the same conclusion while hitching a ride with the Celestials' on their W-100 spacecraft. As you know, I can telepathically hear their thoughts and they can hear mine."

"What did you learn?" Steve asked.

"I learned the truth!" Charlie said while diverting his gaze from the ship's control panel into the direction where Steve and I sat. Charlie continued:

"Like us, the Sadees were the descendants of Enoch the First who was lifted from Earth and relocated with his family on Bethel about sixteen thousand years ago. During the next two thousand years that passed, the Sadees adopted a 'cult', a 'religion', or 'whatever' you want to call it. They started binding the heads of their babies to increase their brain capacity, as they grew older. To survive the pain, they digested herbs and vitamins to increase their skull density by 25 percent in comparison to our own. Our species chose not to follow their cult. We grew intellectually, but they grew smarter. Sexual attraction between the two species died.

"The next two thousand years brought a transformation due to mutation. They did not have to bind their baby's heads — their elongated heads became a permanent disfigurement.

"The Celestials saw the advantage in using them as the first Custodians; an opportunity for Earthlings to have a 'Brother's Keeper'; the fulfillment of God's intentions before Cāin slew Aběl.

"After the Great Flood around thirteen thousand years ago, the Sadees were committed to restoring the human population and increasing the animal numbers along with experimental crossbreeding. Many animal species had died, but conditions on Earth improved until the Anunnaki arrived. While exploring the cosmos, they accidently stumbled upon the blue planet around 4,000 BC. They found Earth rich with the resources they needed.

"The Anunnaki wanted immediate power and control over Earthlings as their slaves. The events happened the way you described it, Enoch: the path to riches to power, to glory. The Anunnaki and the Sadees, backed by the Celestials, were in conflict. The two groups above the lands that join Iraq, Iran and India waged war. The ubiquitous populous reported the aerial battles in sacred books written in a language called Sanskrit. The Anunnaki's aerial fleet was technically more advanced, but the Celestials armed the W-5s that the Sadees piloted with nuclear tipped missiles. Of course, a few missiles missed their target and accidently landed on Earthlings, wiping out whole communities. However, the Sadees won the war for the benefit of mankind. The only remnant of the Anunnaki was a revengeful promise to return.

"The Sadees tasted power and the glory of eliminating an enemy. They were still subservient to the Celestials by complying with their wish to construct the Great Pyramid which built Orion's Highway by leaving a trail of bread crumbs across the cosmos. In 2500 BC, the Sadees experienced the third phase; namely, glory. The Egyptians worshiped them as gods. And they liked it.

"Then two thousand more years passed while the Sadees experienced more wealth, power and glory. They wanted to 'grow' their own worshipers on Easter Island and certain parts of South America. They transported natives from continents to Easter Island and taught them how to worship false idols with floppy ears. In South America, they mated with female Earthlings and taught mothers how to bind their baby's head. The Sadees wanted conquest, but the real damage occurred on the Nazca plains when they disfigured the Earth for following generations to witness."

When Charlie finished talking, Steve and I had simultaneous questions. Steve wanted to know, how Charlie got all the information from the Celestials, and I wanted to know, How Earth became disfigured.

"How did they do that?" I asked

"A few decades before the birth of Jesus Christ, the Sadees invited aliens from other parts of the galaxy to witness His birth. Visitors at His manger were supposed to be a selected group of aliens. But the Sadees invited every entity to an area on the Nazca plains, that can only be described as, a huge parking lot! Spaceships of all types crisscrossed the parched ground leaving contrails among the stones, pebbles and debris as they landed and departed. Perfectly straight lines stretched for miles and miles across hills and gullies. Larger spaceships created a trapezoidal disfigurement that tapered from east to west. As the aliens hovered their larger ships above the ground, while the earth's spun at 1,000 miles per hour, their landing-approach created a much wider landing pad with the displacement of more debris."

"What happened next?" Steve asked.

"Well . . .," Charlie slowly continued, "as you know, the Sadees do not live on Bethel alongside us anymore."

"Yes, go on," said Steve.

Charlie continued with first-time-news unknown to us.

"According to the Celestials, God said, 'Enough!' First, the Celestials reminded the Sadees of God's first commandment. They explained how the commandments applied to their idols on Easter Island. Then the Celestials explained to the Sadees that Earth was meant to be a pristine world, a Garden of Eden, without alien devastation to the surrounding landscape. Anyone who destroyed God's Earth would experience His wrath! The Sadees were ordered to find their own planet to live on and never return!"

Steve drew the obvious conclusion, "That explains why Milo was ordered by his own people to spread the Bubonic Plague. If the Sadees could not have their way, then they would deliberately turn to killing Earthlings to make their point before God. Absolute power corrupts absolutely!"

Our spaceship hovered above the Nazca plains where I could see straight lines, flattened mountaintops and geoglyphs resembling whales, spiders, monkey and many other animals common on Earth.

I asked Steve, "Do you think the natives created those figures in 50 BC?"

"No," he said, "Their spaceships became the equivalent of a marking pen. It's a form of 'doodle' that one creates while waiting for something to happen. Multiple aliens visiting Earth got bored."

I had to ask what seemed obvious, "Do you mean other aliens were waiting for decades to witness the birth of the son of God?"

"Yes!" both Steve and Charlie responded in unison.

My Third Trip Home

On the way back to our home planet, the W-5 spaceship was confined to the docking bay of a W-100 with Charlie inside his W-5. Steve and I speculated that the Celestials did not want Charlie to eavesdrop on their telepathic thoughts any more. The thick metal shielding of the smaller W-5 inside the W-100 kept Charlie's thought-interventions separated. However, he had all the comforts of home, traveling in the fifth dimension provided by the W-100 cruise ship; he was able to walk freely inside the W-5 with a 1-g gravity force and sleep in a regular bed.

When I arrived on my home planet, the Earth-year was AD 1532. Brianna, Beena and I were born in Earth-year AD 987. I was a few months older than Brianna who was a few years older than Beena. Both women were forty-four and a half years old in Earth's time and 445 years old in Bethel's time. My biological clock, however, advanced at a more rapid rate when I lived on Earth during the Crusades for one year; during my first visit with Nostradamus for two years; and during my second visit with Nostradamus for another two years. My biological clock was five years older than either woman. Both women made sure I knew it.

"Enoch," Brianna said, "your white sideburns make you look older. I don't believe you had them when you left for Earth."

"You're right." I said, "I didn't have white sideburns before Father Aye sent me on my missions. It's a price I pay for visiting Earth. I grow faster than you do, but that doesn't mean I love you anything less. My nights on Earth are lonely and uneventful, and that's when I think about you the most."

"That's all right," she responded. "I like dating older men."

On the first day after my arrival, I stood in the tavern of the woman I loved and she was giving me a little dig, a little laughter, and an invitation to have another drink. She stood behind the bar serving drinks the same way she did when I first met her. Time had not diminished her beauty. She looked at me with the same loving eyes and said, "I missed you too. We both need a drink before I tell you something. What will you have?"

I didn't know what to expect next. Did her Uncle Bill drown himself in the alcohol he drank? Did Beena pass away? Were Fathers' Dean and Aye still alive? I had been gone for more than twenty Earth years, equivalent to two Bethel years. Neither Steve nor Charlie had relayed any news while in route on the way home.

"I'll have a non-anxiety drink," I said.

"Chill out," she replied. "I took the test."

"What test?"

"The one you worked on for years and years supplying the Celestials with reports. Don't you remember, dopey?"

"Oh, yes, . . . the Angio test," I finally recalled while scratching my head in attempt to anticipate what she would say next.

"I flunked the test," Brianna said with tears welling up in her eyes. "I can never have any children!" Her mood transformed from jovial, to crying, to utter breakdown.

I was speechless, not knowing how to console her, not knowing if her potential for other suitors was diminished, not knowing if she even cared to get married.

"Well," I said, "it's obvious we weren't meant to have rug-rats. You know kids! Let's drink up?"

My kidding around wasn't working. She cried more and used the bartender's towel to wipe her tears that smeared her lipstick and mascara over her face. "Brianna," I continued with a more sensitive touch, "you have your whole life ahead of you. Many wonderful thinks will happen in the years to come. So, dry the tears from your pretty blue eyes. You have many years ahead of you. When I'm on Earth, I think about you often and look forward to the wonderful things that will come into both our lives."

After a while, she dried her tears and said, "You're empty. Do you want another round?"

Life on Bethel had not changed; it crept along at a snail's pace, and yet, more than two hundred Bethel-years pass. Beena continued to increase her education and provide periodic reports to the Celestials about the Angio disease. The reports gave her a small income funneled through Father Aye. Once again, I assisted her with the same enthusiasm that drew me to her. I refused payments because I had a physician's income from a practice that I had restarted in the same small building at the edge of Main Street. Other Custodians and Scouts returned from their missions on Earth with stories to tell, but mostly, injuries they sustained and diseases they incurred; namely, the bacteria types: bubonic plague, diphtheria and E. coli; and the viral types: small pox, chicken pox, German measles, polio, ebola and COVID-19; and the insect bites: dinge fever, tsetse fly and Lime sickness. Looking back, the list of viral diseases expanded into the twenty-first century when I first started writing my memoirs.

The illnesses I have mentioned are the names of commonly known illnesses in the 21st century on Earth. The common flu known as the coronavirus prevailed throughout all the centuries during my lifetime, but the more recent devastation was the COVID-19 that killed close to 2 percent of those infected.

I was a doctor living between missions. In the mid-sixteenth century, I was a young physician, practicing medicine on Bethel. I cured Custodians and Scouts of their physical ailments with the Celestials' medication in my office, and I listened to their fantastic stories while enjoying a brew in Brianna's tavern. They talked about the success of their mission and the technical advances Earthlings were making. During the Crusades, people rode donkeys, but now I heard stories of people riding in horse-drawn, enclosed carriages. Within the first seven hundred Earth-years of my lifetime, I noted the progress that man had made. His best achievements were in warfare! Unfortunately, wars stimulated man's devious thoughts.

When the Custodians and Scouts came back from Earth, they all looked a little older, but then again, the people on Bethel could count on a life expectancy of 1200 years. As they grew older, their physical appearance remained void of facial wrinkles and bent posture, diminished brain function and white sideburns. Senior citizens retained their youthful appearance—a mystery, no doubt.

The Wisdom of Bill

As usual, Bill, the old sage and nowhere to go, appeared at the end of his niece's bar on a daily basis, hovering over his drink.

"Bill," I said, "don't the returning Custodians and Scouts look a little older for their years?"

"Only, slightly," he said, "the passage of time on Earth is like a windstorm sweeping the centuries. Maybe a few gray hairs, but we hardly change in our appearance."

"Bill," I continued, "I have a serious question to ask you. Can you help me with some advice?"

"You want me to help you"—he rubbed his forehead—"a knowledgeable Custodian? And me, the town's cynosure of wine, beer, and alcoholic drinks." He paused, thought of what he was saying, then continued, "How can I help you, Enoch?"

"Years ago—"

"Is this going to be a tough question? I can't do memory questions." He said, lifting another shot and a beer to his lips.

"This is an easy question . . . years ago, we were invited for a one night's stay on planet Geesal, home of the Celestials. Do you remember?

"Yes, I remember you living dangerously with two beautiful women sharing after-dinner drinks. I can still see the three of you laughing and sitting there in the Celestials dining room after Steve, Charlie and I had left."

"Mm-hmm, that's what I want to talk about."

"If I saw the three of you caring on, then I'm sure the Celestials saw you too."

"Did Charlie say anything to you about what he might have heard from the Celestials?"

"He did. When we got home to our planet, I stood next to Charlie while he talked to Father Aye. Charlie said that the Celestials preferred you to settle down and marry one of the two women."

"Exactly, that's what Father Aye advise me. Did you get the impression that the Celestials were making it mandatory?"

"Well, you know our population is having trouble reproducing?"

"I know."

"I'm going to tell you something very confidential, Enoch. I've known about you and your two mistresses from the get-go. I'm being impartial, and fortunately your two women don't know about each other."

"But, do I really need to choose?"

"That's up to you. The Bible does say go forth and multiply. It's God's will. The Custodians make sure everyone follows His rule. Don't you want to have little Custodians running around?"

"Brianna can't have any children!"

"What?"

"It's true. She wept when she told me."

"I'm her uncle and she never told *me*!"

After Bill took moments to reflect, I interrupted his thoughts. I started with a soft voice, "I think you helped me, Bill. Let's keep this conversation to ourselves."

"I agree. What are you going to do?

"I don't know."

At seventy-nine (and seven) years old in Earth-years, I was assigned another mission by Father Aye in the Earth-year 1774.

Chapter 4: Mozart

Mozart: A Brief Overview

A small body frame without any muscle tone or an iconic smile is the best way to describe Mozart's physique. Years of playing the piano, his only exercise, gave his hands copious strength. The muscles on each hand below the fifth finger bulged into a wider palm leaving a visual impression that a buried sixth finger added muscular strength flowing from the palm into his fingers. From the age of three, his father drilled gold-clad expressions into him, "If you can't play *well*, play *loud*. If people walk past, you want them to turn their heads and ask, 'Who is that playing?'" Exercise on his piano equated to a workout with barbells in a gymnasium where his father, an exhausting promoter, counted the number of repetitions.

Stress, imposed by his father, came with a relief valve when he started taking sexual liberties with young, impressionable women. In the evening, upon invitation, the sound of his music enraptured them. From their point of view, their hearts filled with emotions listening to cascading vibrations from his piano and watching his determination while his body gyrated on a piano stool and his face contained self-fulfilling expressions. As he expended energy, they felt the need to do the same. They were his for the taking.

Standing in front of him, I was there—not as his conscience, his therapist, nor his counselor but as a teacher representing the father who failed when he had stopped all instructions during Mozart's teenage years. My mission to make the young Mozart historically famous by replacing his father appeared next to impossible. My only advantage was an ear for music: tempo and pitch, and the instant ability to learn foreign languages.

Wolfgang Amadeus Mozart

(27 January 1756—5 December 1791):

- A prolific and influential composer of the classical era
- Best-known symphonies, concertos and operas

His audacity exceeded his pugnacious habits by only a slight margin, making him less likable and more of a genius. Politicians of the court thought of him as a radical; he thought of himself as a competent composer surrounded by jesters with bells on their toes. Following the guidance of Shakespeare's satire, Mozart truly believed the world was a stage and every person around him was playing a character role: henceforth, his loud and zealous laughter at everyone who appeared as a clown, dimwit or moron. I sympathized with him when ridiculous altercations demanded a reversal of his planned intent.

His first recital in the Duke's chateau should have been a climaxing event for every attendee, but Mozart turned his last performance into a mocked charade against other popular pianist banging away on their piano: an emotional coaster ride for his critics, and a languished gag for Mozart.

Without character restraints, novices always excel to the pinnacles of their endeavors. The task of creating music is always achieved with two brains: a left and a right hemisphere; one that boldly invents the music score and the other that quarrels with itself. Outward manifestations are a mirror of a genius's inner thoughts. If the left side of the brain is dominating, the person is right-handed with characteristics of 1) logic reasoning, 2) inclination for numbers and graphs, and 3) improved math and language skills. If the right side of the brain is dominating, the person is left-handed with characteristics of 1) artistic and visual abilities, 2) improved hearing abilities, and 3) flighty disposition mixed with emotions.

Mozart was left-handed with improved hearing abilities and perfect pitch: a gift that allowed him to create inspiring music with emotion and depth. Pitch is the ability to distinguish musical tones or frequencies along with duration, loudness and timber. Timber is a sound that makes the music sound different when the pitch and loudness are the same. Learned musicians with acquired timber are able to distinguish between two different instruments, played with the same pitch, frequency, and loudness. The right side of Mozart's brain was overdeveloped—hardwired for music.

To the best of my abilities, this describes Mozart: specifically, where he was coming from, and where he was going. His inner mind spelled music notes, entwined with jubilation, happiness, lugubriousness and sometimes depression—the entire gambit. His audience may have looked apoplectic with their dropped jaws and sunken eyes but they were enjoying every minute of his music. I could see it: motionless faces with their brains absorbing every rhythmic sound. Of course, he was the anathema of political adversaries, music competitors and people in general who disliked his looks, his voice and that hysterical tone of laughter. Initially, only esoteric music lovers appreciated his inept beginnings, but his followers grew under my tutelage. My efficacious goals were to obviate apocalyptic sounds in his music and to highlight what music lovers wanted to hear—a roar, a lambasting crescendo on the keyboard into finality.

As time passed, demands for his performance became ubiquitous in all major cities. He learned how to write a music score without erasures and nothing redacted. He had mastered the transition of music notes from the brain to the score sheet because he had learned the technique when I loaned him my pocket-top that displayed piano sounds in note format on a three-dimensional holographic projection that appeared above the pocket-top. After each stanza was composed with keyboard sounds, he merely copied the three-dimensional notes to the score sheet while looking at me for satisfaction and listening for my approval. I inept at playing a musical instrument, but I knew quality music when I heard it. And so, I became his honest friend. In reality, it was my pocket-top that launched his career. My pocket-top calculated musical errors for him as easily as a modern day, instant spell-checker. Here is what little I knew about music that I learned on my home planet prior to departure:

Dissonant: *making or involving a combination of sounds that is unpleasant to listen to*

Diatonic: *relating to or based on musical scales consisting of five tones and two semitones, e.g. a major or minor scale with no extra sharps or flats added*

Chromatic harmony: *a compositional technique interspersing the primary diatonic pitches and chords with other pitches of the chromatic scale.*

A heptatonic scale *is a musical scale that has seven pitches per octave. Examples include the major scale or minor scale; e.g., in C major: C D E F G A B C—and in the relative minor, A minor, natural minor: A B C D E F G A; the melodic minor scale, A B C D E F♯G♯A ascending, A G F E D C B A descending; the harmonic minor scale, A B C D E F G♯A; and a scale variously known as the Byzantine, and Hungarian,[1] scale, C D E♭ F♯ G A♭ B C. Indian classical theory postulates seventy-two seven-tone scale types, whereas others postulate twelve or ten (depending on the theorist) seven-tone scale types collectively called thaat.*

A pentatonic scale *is a musical scale with five notes per octave, in contrast to the more familiar heptatonic scale that has seven notes per octave (such as the major scale and minor scale.)*

Toccata (noun): *a composition for a keyboard instrument written in a free style that includes full chords and elaborate runs. Toccata sounds are intended to show off the player's technique.*

The trill *(or shake, as it was known in the sixteenth century) is a musical ornament consisting of a rapid alternation between two adjacent notes, usually a semitone or tone apart, which can be* *identified with the context of the trill (compare to mordent and tremolo). It is sometimes referred to by the German Triller, the Italian trillo, the French trille or the Spanish trino. A cadential trill is a trill associated with each cadence.*

*A **Baroque piano style** is similar to ornamental architecture; another type of trill.*

__Baroque__ as defined:

1. The baroque style of architecture and art, or its period in European history

2. Highly ornamented music of the seventeenth century written by composers such as Bach, Handel, Vivaldi, and Telemann

__Legato:__ In music performance and notation, legato ([leˈga:to]; Italian for "tied together"; French lié; German gebunden) indicates that musical notes are played or sung smoothly and connected. That is, the player makes a transition from note to note with no intervening silence. Legato technique is required for slurred performance, but unlike slurring (as that term is interpreted for some instruments), legato does not forbid re-articulation. Standard notation indicates

legato either with the word legato, or by a slur (a curved line) under notes that form one legato group. Legato, like staccato, is a kind of articulation. There is an intermediate articulation called either mezzo staccato or non-legato, sometimes referred to as "portato."

Needless to say, I had listened to all types of music movements at home on Bethel, in the spacecraft that brought me to Vienna and in music halls across Europe. Added exposure to music occurred when the Scouts introduced me to Wolfgang Amadeus Mozart and his father Leopold Mozart.

My First Introduction to Mozart family

If Amadeus was pugnacious and irritating to people, his father, Leopold Mozart, was always concerned about his son and fiercely independent of his actions: basically, a contradictive person with strong emotions. Leopold wanted to know how his son was doing, but he was too busy with his own endeavors. The Scouts had advised me to visit the father and obtain his permission to tutor his son.

Our first meeting went something like this:

"How the hell are you going to tutor my son when you can't even play an instrument?" Leopold said.

I had prepared for this conflict and had anticipated his question. I could have told him that I was a visitor from another planet, or I could have said that I was a qualified tutor suited to the task. I weighed my options. He probably would not believe me if I told him I was an alien with God given powers. In reality, I was his distant cousin with the same attributes he had. The Celestials had ordered me to take this mission, to provide Amadeus with special music skills and to use my personality to unbend the personality of a teenager who lost the goals his father intended. The worse thing I could have said to Leopold was that he should have spent more time with his son. He had given Amadeus a good start by training him to play the piano and violin at age five. At seventeen, Amadeus was engaged as a musician at the Salzburg court where he grew restless with the repetition; he had become an uncontrolled teenager and his father knew it.

"It's true. I do not know how to play an instrument," I said. I was losing the battle of wits and I needed Leopold financial support on a monthly basis if I was to curb Amadeus's spending habits. "I do know, however, that your son spends your money as quickly as his fingers roll through a fortepiano!"

"If I could only obviate his bad habits," Leopold agreed while nodding his head in a diagonal direction with a scowl on his face. "But what are your qualifications? Why should I send you his monthly allowance?"

"I'll give you three reasons why I can influence your son to become historically famous. That's your goal, isn't it?"

"Yes," he replied with a downtrodden look on his face.

"First, I am a good friend with Johann Sebastian Bach, about thirty-four years your senior. Second, I have a reputation as a music critic. Perhaps you've seen my reviews in the morning papers? And thirdly, I recently helped his son Johann Christian Bach. You can write to him in London." Leopold rolled his head in improvement because he knew the Bach family. I had won him over with a simple 1-2-3 outline of my qualifications.

"How much do I have to pay you?"

"Nothing."

"You got the job."

"Thank you. I'll send you biweekly reports."

Everything I had told Leopold was true. Many years ago, I had visited both Sebastian and Christian Bach in London. Both father and son awaited my visit and greeted me with warmth and hardy handshakes. Sabastian gave me an unusually strong handshake—a "two-handed" handshake. I was flabbergasted. Why would an Earthling be wearing a pendant from Bethel? I recalled Father Aye's caveat:

> *When you first greet a person, use your right hand*
> *to clasp his right hand after he extends his arm. Then you*
> *need to place your left hand across his right wrist and*

When we were alone, Sebastian explained that a Custodian had given a bracelet to him so that he could give it to me. He knew that the Custodian was an alien from Bethel and had helped him with his career many years ago. I had to know if his former tutor, a Custodian, had left a precious bracelet in the hands of an Earthling. The Celestials had made it clear to all Custodians that technical equipment should never be left behind. "May I see your bracelet," I asked.

"Of course," he said as he removed the bracelet and handed it to me. Upon closer examination of the bracelet, my fears were squelched. The bracelet was junk! An expensive bracelet, but still, non-technical junk. The irony is that Sebastian always kept the secret between him and a former Custodian that tutored him . . . and here I stood before him, without his knowing that I was a Custodian also.

"Christian is practicing a few cord arrangements in the drawing room. Would you mind helping him with your trained ear?" Sebastian asked.

"Certainly," I replied. Then, I listened to Christian's choices as he played the fortepiano. Christian kept asking which arrangement sounded better. It reminded me of my eye doctor back home who asked, "Is this better or worse," as he slipped different lenses across my eyes.

Amadeus

In 1781 at the age of twenty-five, Amadeus was fired from his position at the Salzburg court of musicians. I asked around and learned that Amadeus had trouble with authority figures. I caught up with him in Vienna and introduced myself as a friend to his father. He was renting a small studio apartment cluttered with a fortepiano that took up too much space and a few pieces of furniture that resided on the wrong side of an invisible dividing line between the kitchen and living room. I suspected that he even rented some of the clothes he wore. He lived in poverty, spent too much money chasing women, and gave up as a music composer. When he was playing his piano, he quickly corrected his music errors by replaying the same score; but, when he was addressing his household chores, the grass could grow under his feet. His apartment resembled a cluttered, cavernous, kaleidoscope with multiple colors for every pile of junk, every random piece of used clothing, every loose music sheet, not properly stored, filed, or catalogued. He cared more about his piano and less about his apartment. His piano, like his soul, had a music score embedded within. It had to come out. The situation was sad, but it wasn't hopeless: He had ambition in his mind and the love of music in his heart. My work was cut out for me.

"Do **you** know my father?" he asked.

"Yes. To make a long story short, he put me in charge of your monthly allowance." I commented with an honest smile.

"He did what? Now I hate him even more!" Amadeus spoke while pacing the short distance between the two walls of his apartment. He walked the distance while mumbling half a sentence and completing the rest on the return trip inside his small studio apartment.

"I understand that you even hated the superiors you worked for in Salzburg?"

"Yes. They thought of me as an independent brat and I called one of them an F-bomb."

Amadeus definitely had problems. My mission would require some psychology, some patients, some spiritual references and someone to act as his guide or the father figure he lost when he was a teenager.

"Do you believe that someone is out to get you?" I asked.

"Yes."

"Who?"

"I don't know. My mind doesn't want to play the keyboard."

"Honesty is a good place for us to start. If you're honest with me, I'll be honest with you. Okay?"

"Okay. But why did my father send you? And who are you?"

I thought about an appropriate answer and replied, "Someone with greater authority than your father . . . sent me."

"Who? My grandfather?"

"We'll talk about this tomorrow after your mind has slept on the fact that I'm in charge of your destiny. And believe me; it will grow brighter. Tomorrow morning at 6:00 AM, you will show me your music scales. Good night."

On the following morning Amadeus was still sleeping. To awaken him, I had to pound on the door yelling his name.

"Yeah, yeah, yeah. Come on in Enoch. Have you had breakfast? Can I get you something to drink?"

Evidently, Amadeus had accepted the challenge of a father figure that would control his monetary purse strings. He was remembering his manners by offering me a drink. That was good. After his breakfast, he sat at the piano and started to play one of his favorite toccatas to show off his technique with elaborate runs of the keyboard.

As I listened, I saw multiple ivory keys come to life with their gymnastic flexing to a syncopated rhythm. The sound of the notes, increasing and then decreasing in volume, filled the room with a timing that was impeccable. He had natural rhythm—a talent some argue as "learned" while others argue as "gifted" from the day of their birth. I was impressed.

I had to comment. "Do you realize that your father trained you to succeed beyond his own abilities?"

Amadeus reflected on his youth, "He started me at age five. He always yelled, 'Play loud. Play loud. If you're practicing in your room and people outside walk by and they hear you hit a wrong note, they'll ask, *'Who's playing that piano?'* That's when you're getting recognition! Always play loud. If people hear you make a mistake, why should you compound your mistake with faintness? Simply go back and replay the part correctly. When you play in a concert, you play without mistakes. 'Practice, practice, practice,' he demanded."

"Your father was right." I nodded.

"Listen to this." Amadeus coveted the piano with his shoulders directly over the keyboard. The piano came alive with sounds. His piano, with its own voice for loudness, increased beyond our speaking voices.

I suddenly understood one of his father's gold-clad expressions. "Amadeus," I asked, "could you stop playing for a moment? Your father gave you a reason to play the piano, but he did not give you a purpose to play the piano."

"What's the difference?" Amadeus asked as he started to play a softer arrangement.

"Look at it this way. When I was ready for a higher school of learning, my mother took care of me that morning and started the day by saying,   'You're ready to do your best. Get good grades for me. Okay?'"

"So?"

"Don't you see? Her first comment was a reason for me to try harder, but her second comment gave me purpose. She was in the loop waiting to see me get good grades."

Amadeus agreed, "You're right my father gave me a reason. 'Be the best at anything you do,' he would always say."

"Today I'm going to give you a purpose for continuing your work."

"How?"

"Do you have religion?"

"A little."

"Okay. Let's start with the Catholics and the Protestants." I began by reading to him some of the literature I had accumulated on my home planet:

"In the Catholic doctrine, forgiveness of sin exists and it is infused, in the Protestant doctrine; sin is merely "covered", and righteousness imputed. Catholics believe faith is active in charity and good works (fides caritate formata; i.e., faith, charity, format or works) can justify man, Protestants believe faith without works can justify man because Christ died for sinners, but that anyone who truly has faith will produce good works as a product of their faith, comparable to a good tree producing good fruit. For Lutherans justification can be lost with the loss of faith; for Catholics justification can be lost by mortal sin.

One of the thorniest textual problems any Christian can face is the apparent contradiction between Paul and James. Is a religious man justified by his faith, as Paul claimed; or by his works, as James preferred to say?

For Abraham, your ancient forefather, faith and works went hand in hand; they were two sides of the same coin. The exercising of one causes the other to grow."

When I finished reading the passage, he had stopped playing the piano. "I know about the apostles, Saint Paul and Saint James and even, Abraham my ancient Biblical forefather. But why did you not say 'our' ancient forefather?"

I responded honestly, "Because I am of a different lineage than you: a different branch of the same tree." During our conversation into the late hours, I explained our differences: the origin of our species, and the fact that I was an alien from another planet about to do God's work.

The entire morning went by with Amadeus sitting on his piano stool with a dropped jaw and his eyes focused in my direction without blinking. "I don't believe you," he said.

I removed my pocket-top from my back pocket, unfolded it into four different directions and placed it on top of the piano's mantel above the keyboard.

"Play something," I said.

As soon as Amadeus started to play, the correct music notes appeared above the pocket-top in a three-dimensional holographic presentation. The notes were clearly visible across a one-foot span and a palm's width above the pocket-top.

"What is this?" he asked.

"It's your music," I replied.

"Is it something from your home planet?"

"No. It is a gift from God."

"Can I keep it?"

"Definitely, not. It wouldn't function without a proximity start-key that my body gives it."

"It's a gift from God? The God?" he asked.

"It is. It's designed by God and built by the people I work for."

Amadeus sat at his piano, wondering about his gift, mulling the idea in his head that someone, even God, really cared about him.

Then Amadeus was lost trying to understand the ability of an electronic mechanism that caused blackish notes to appear in midair. Its holographic function even escaped me; it truly was a creation by the Almighty. I only knew that my belt talked to the pocket-top with invisible radio signals that "pinged" their presence and decoded a password; henceforth, the name proximity start-key.

"Amadeus, you have to promise me that you will tell no one about your learning exercises that I'm giving to you. My reputation would be ruined if you revealed our secret and your career would be terminated. Do you understand?"

"I do. I whole-heartedly agree."

"From this day, you now have a purpose from God: to grow your faith in Him and to create 'works' that are the fruits of your labor."

Mozart never questioned the mechanics of the pocket-top. It wrote the notes in midair where he could see them and copy them on paper without any errors. And then, one day, without cause, he asked, "If you're a Custodian, here to help me, are there other Custodians in Europe doing the same?"

"I know of one individual," I replied in honesty.

"What's his name?"

"His name is Saint Germain."

Suddenly, Mozart wanted to know more about a Custodians' life and their mission. He wanted to know what Saint Germain did. I typed in the name Saint Germain on my personal pocket-top that Father Aye gave me and learned the following:

- Count Saint Germain contributed songs to the opera, L'incostanza delusa, performed in the Haymarket Theatre in London, on April 20, 1745.

- St. Germain appeared in the French court around 1748. In 1749, he was employed by Louis XV for diplomatic missions.
- Reporters claim St. Germain spoke Italian and French with the greatest facility, but Spanish and Portuguese were his natural language.
- Reporters also claimed that the count was a man of quality, designed for the church and that the count could have been a great musician if he had not been too much of a gentleman.

I translated the information that I had read to Mozart.

"As you can see Amadeus," I started to say, "Saint Germain was helping humanity a few years before you were born. He was a diplomat with negotiation skills, an employee for Louis XV, a music composer for the London Theater, a man who spoke many languages. This is how Custodians help humanity: the same way I'm helping you."

As quick as he wanted to know about other Custodians, was the same speed at which he quickly forgot. I could never forget his reply after I had worked so hard to answer his question about other aliens visiting Earth.

"Oh. Okay," he said, while his fingers reunited with his piano keyboard and his eyes focused on the black musical notes appearing above the pocket-top.

In addition, I could not forget what I had read about Count Saint Germain. I knew he definitely was a Custodian because he was seen as a person who had an extended life. He had to have come from my home planet Bethel. Father Aye never told me what other Custodians were doing. He probably didn't know because Saint Germain was perhaps working for a different Father Aye-type of person on our planet. Of course, I didn't share my additional findings with Mozart. This is how Earthlings viewed

Custodians. I've transferred the information from my pocket-top into my memoirs:

Giacomo Casanova describes in his memoirs several meetings with the "celebrated and learned impostor." Of his first meeting, in Paris in 1757, he writes:

The most enjoyable dinner I had was with Madame de Robert Gergi, who came with the famous adventurer, known by the name of the Count de St. Germain. This individual, instead of eating, talked from the beginning of the meal to the end, and I followed his example in one respect as I did not eat, but listened to him with the greatest attention. It may safely be said that as a conversationalist he was unequalled.

St. Germain gave himself out for a marvel and always aimed at exciting amazement, which he often succeeded in doing. He was scholar, linguist, musician, and chemist, good-looking, and a perfect ladies' man. For a while he gave them paints and cosmetics; he flattered them, not that he would make them young again (which he modestly confessed was beyond him) but that their beauty would be preserved by means of a wash which, he said, cost him a lot of money, but which he gave away freely. He had contrived to gain the favour of Madame de Pompadour, who had spoken about him to the king, for whom he had made a laboratory, in which the monarch—a martyr to boredom—tried to find a little pleasure or distraction, at all events, by making dyes. The king had given him a suite of rooms at Chambord, and a hundred thousand francs for the construction of a laboratory, and according to St. Germain the dyes discovered by the king would have a materially beneficial influence on the quality of French fabrics.

This extraordinary man, intended by nature to be the king of impostors and quacks, would say in an easy, assured manner that he was three hundred years old, that he knew the secret of the Universal Medicine, that he possessed a mastery over nature, that he could melt diamonds, professing himself capable of forming, out of ten or twelve small diamonds, one large one of the finest waters without any loss of weight. All this, he said, was a mere trifle to him. Notwithstanding his boastings, his bare-faced lies, and his manifold eccentricities, I cannot say I thought him offensive. In spite of my knowledge of what he was and in spite of my own feelings, I thought him an astonishing man as he was always astonishing me.

I thought the author of this article; that is, Giacomo Casanova, was a little harsh on one of our Custodians and may have perceived him in a different light. However, Casanova did say that Saint Germain claimed to be three hundred years old and that he knew the secret of Universal Medicine! I believe that Saint Germain wasn't boasting and saying those words; it was the liquor that was talking! Custodians are just as human as Earthlings.

As the weeks passed, Amadeus started to create compositions that told a specific "story" for each individual listener. There were no musical repeats within the entire composition. Each listener could visualize a story akin to life itself—a transcendence without repetition. His music had fast notes akin to people arguing, loud notes akin to violence, soft notes akin to tranquility, and finale notes that stated, "Justice triumphs!" I had my own dream "stories" when I listened. I believe I may have subconsciously guided him when I day dreamt about the moments, I spent with Beena and Brianna. (I recalled the good times laughing with Beena as we walked along the riverfront, and at the same time, I imagined I was back in Brianna's tavern watching her torso sway among the tables where customers sat enjoying the drinks she served.)

As the months passed, I kept Amadeus healthy with all the vaccines and advanced medication I brought from my home planet. If I had stayed with him over a period of ten years, he never would have died at an early age. I would have seen his early ailments and kept him alive.

Whenever he practiced, I listened to his music, but my mind was back on my home planet. He interrupted one of my daydreams with a question. "Tell me about the place where you come from. Do they have green leaves on trees there?"

"Of course, you ninny!" I continued, "Maple trees, oak trees, elm trees and every type of vegetation you have here."

"Tell me more."

"Okay. Everything is the same with the exception of time. On our planet, most individuals live between 1,100 and 1,200 years of age. Here on Earth, most people perish before forty years of age. The answer to your question is written on your face, 'Yes, we live to a ripe old age because we have no diseases.' On the other hand, one month that I spend here on Earth ages me by ten months back home."

"I don't understand."

"Let me put it this way: the year is 1781, you are twenty-five years old, and I'm seventy-nine years old by your calendar. If I were back home, I would be 790 years old."

"You don't look more than a day over forty-nine."

"Thank you. That's a compliment. Our biological clock ages slowly and our physical appearance ages even slower."

"So, you grow ten months older for every month that you stay here."

"That's right. I'm going to have to leave soon."

I left for home soon after all of the "ripe old age" questions had been discussed. At a later date, I learned that Amadeus Mozart died at age thirty-five from rheumatic fever (strep) that he had caught twice before his death. In his short thirty-five years, Wolfgang Amadeus Mozart produced over 600 works for symphony, concert, chamber, opera and choir, including Don Giovanni, The Magic Flute, and The Marriage of Figaro. He had given a part of himself that would be enjoyed and remembered throughout the ages.

The Wisdom of Father Aye

The following memoirs are a collection of conversations I had with Father Aye as he monitored advancements on other worlds. I have pieced together the following conversation with him as time progressed on Earth from 1783 to 1945. Interlocked in our conversations were the advancements on Earth; namely, the industrial revolution and the invention of peaceful mechanisms: bicycles, automobiles and television sets; and the invention of war machines: dynamite, guns, atomic and nuclear bombs.

On our planet, we were akin to the last child in the family who got hand-me-downs. We had bicycles, automobiles and television shortly after they were invented on Earth. Greater technology came from the Celestials when they felt we were ready for advancement. They had made the mistake of giving the Sadees advanced technology like the W-5s with nuclear tipped warheads to wage war on the Anunnaki. With the Sadees holding a grudge against Celestials for thousands of years, they lived on their own planet organizing plans to cause Earthlings to bring about their own demise. As much as the Custodians were productive in advancing mankind, the Sadees were counterproductive.

"Total exhaustion" describes how I felt being home on planet Bethel. I had visited Beena and Brianna independently and nothing had changed in their daily activities or our relationships. The only person who seemed different was Father Aye. A sound of concern filled his voice when he said, "Enoch, when you get a chance, could you visit my office inside the pyramid? I have some concerns about the people on both our planets."

The next day I walked over to the pyramid that the Sadees had built 4500 years ago as a prototype for the one on Earth. Inside the layered blocks of limestone among the wooden beam supports was Father Aye's office: decrepit wooden beams and yet roomy and surprisingly cool compared to the hot semitropical climate outside. The terrain was not unlike Egyptian surroundings thousands of years ago. When he saw me enter, he greeted me with enthusiasm.

"Enoch, I'm glad you're here. I've been studying animal life on planet Earth. Did you know that the Orca, a killer whale, hunts in a pack cooperating with one another and sharing the kill? Unlike lions of wolves who also hunt in packs, they snarl at one another after the kill. But the Orca's take turns circling the dead whale and feeding sequentially. Human beings are the same way; they share their food."

"We do too," I commented.

"Yes, but the people on Earth have something additional that we don't have. Do you know what makes them special or different than us?"

"They are our distant cousins," I responded. "How are they different?"

"They have fortitude, resourcefulness and the ability to imagine. They are the innovators, the dreamers, and the inventors with perseverance. The future is theirs if they don't destroy themselves first. I read your report on Nostradamus and Mozart. I found interest in Nostradamus's ability to transpose future events into words. His last quatrain about apocalyptic events due to climate change bothers me. I look at it this way:

1. After Cāin slew Aběl, time passed and then our ancestor Enoch the First was brought to this planet so that his descendants could be his Brother's Keeper back on Earth.

2. The Sadees accomplished the task of rebuilding for thousands of years; specifically . . . saving the people and animals on Earth before the grandeur of power seized them. I also read your report on Milo.

3. We are a society dependent upon the Celestials for technology. We have no inventors or dreamers. Basically, I see three branches of human beings that evolved from Adam and Eve: The Sadees, the Earthlings, and us."

"I believe you are trying to tell me that we aren't doing so well! Is that what you're saying?"

"Yes, Enoch. I have to wonder why we don't have inventors. Milo's intent to destroy Earth also bothers me. The Sadees are vengeful; they will give Earthlings advanced technology even when animosity exists between the superpowers. First, they will visibly fly their W-5s in Earth's atmosphere to let people know 'they are not alone.' It will destroy the vestiges of any religion people have. Then they will let on to proprietary technology: circuit boards, optic cables for greater transmission, a fighter's helmet that controls the plane with his thoughts, multiple attack drones that think on their own and in concert with other drones. The list goes on."

Father Aye paused for a breath and then continued, "They'll try to destroy mankind as we try to help them. It's called the 'yin and the yang': inseparable and contradicting goals. The Celestials want the people of Earth to advance, but at a slower pace. The people have to learn how to get along first; how to recognize bad leaders and how to correct anarchy. Our society thrives peacefully but it does not grow. That's what bothers me." He looked glum, casting his eyes at the floor.

As a counterpoint, I responded, "Yes, we lack the ability to invent, but we have the innate ability to learn multiple languages in short order. Steve and his wife have children, now. Charlie is industrious, bringing back bicycles for distribution among ourselves. He tells me that he thinks he can sell us new 1920 model cars. He talks about the sale of television sets that are on the horizon. Charlie believes we can silently procure technical devices on Earth or ask the Celestials for our other needs."

"You're making me laugh, Enoch. Don't you see that we are still living in The Golden Age? We are incapable of advancing our society and incapable of perpetuating our species. Earthlings, in contrast, are reproducing faster and creating their own demise. Our population on Bethel is only several hundred thousand people—no thanks to the Angio disease. We both know our planet has no diseases and you treat returning Custodians and Scouts for Earthly diseases. Have you ever wondered why you never treat them for any diseases like cancer?"

"Yes, I have. No one comes back from Earth with any form of cancer. Is it because our bodies are immune to cancer?"

"Yes. Partially, our resistance to cancer is because of the air we breathe on our planet. Eons ago, most of the oxygen on Earth was burned away when their solar system passed through the barrier-rib. Our cousins, the Sadees had extreme trouble breathing rarified air when they were helping the Maya civilization around 1000 BC. They had to resort to an oxygen mask. When we visit Earth, we can feel the oxygen drop from 30 percent, on our planet, to 20 percent on Earth. Don't you agree?"

"I've noticed that my visits are like climbing a high mountain."

"Exactly. That's why some Custodians and Scouts have to resort to an oxygen mask from time to time when visiting Earth. It also explains why you look dead tired when you come back from your missions. You're drained of energy. I know this is a sacrifice. For short durations, the human body can withstand 7-percent effective oxygen on tall mountains or 100-percent effective oxygen inside an oxygen mask. When you were on Earth, you may have contracted cancer viruses; namely human papillomavirus (HPV), liver cancer and non-Hodgkin's lymphoma which was recently named and identified by their scientists. On our planet, a sister planet of Earth, everyone is immune to almost all viruses because our atmosphere reduces the antigens in our bodies. Here

Mayan artifact of a Sadee alien with the bridge of his nose starting at the middle of his eyebrows.

on Bethel, air is purified by 30-percent oxygen destroying potential diseases, and sunlight shinning abundantly."

"Please explain?" I asked wanting to learn more about cancer and virial infections.

"When Enoch, our distant ancestor, was lifted from Earth in 15,581 BC, and brought to our planet the effective oxygen composition on Earth was 30-percent oxygen which is the same as our own atmosphere. Back then, people were healthier and animals grew much bigger than today. The cancer-virus was non-existent."

"Why is the cancer-virus prevalent on Earth now?"

"All cancer-viruses were dormant up until the Great Flood in 11,382 BC. Many Earthly diseases were in check. When Earth's solar system went through the barrier, Mars and Earth nearly collided. While Earth was flooded with the last remains of Mars's oceans, Earth lost most of its oxygen content into outer space during the turbulence. Its oxygen content went down from 30 to 20 percent."

"But how does that explain why cancer exists on Earth today?" I asked with my curiosity peaked.

"Cancer follows a statistical probability as per a Gaussian distribution curve that has a standard deviation of ±2 percent. Earth's cancer-virus flourishes in an atmosphere with an oxygen content between 16 and 24 percent and a mean value of 20 percent. Two standard deviations of ±4 percent represent 95 percent of the cancer population. Here on Bethel, we have an oxygen content of 30 percent, a nitrogen content of 68 percent and a carbon dioxide content of 2 percent in our atmosphere. We have an environment where viruses cannot survive. Our blood cells duplicate a photosynthesis process, combining sunlight with carbon dioxide to produce sugar and oxygen (O_2). The oxygen in our blood kills viruses whereas Earthlings dare not sunbathe for fear of contracting cancer. Our oxygen-rich blood cells deplete antigens when Custodians and Scouts visit Earth. When they return to Bethel—richer in oxygen—they recover from any residual antigens that they may have brought back with them."

"I understand"

Father Aye continued, "It is a bigger sacrifice for Earthlings living in a reduced oxygen-environment where the cancer virus can spread. However, the main issue is Earth's atmosphere with the increase in carbon dioxide causing climate change."

"What do we do about it?"

"Other Custodians are starting to influence twentieth century scholars and politicians to think about global warming."

"What do you want me to do about it?"

"I'm glad you asked, Enoch. I want you to visit a doctor on Earth who needs to make a major breakthrough in heart transplants. The Celestials had their reasons for training you in this procedure. Like Nostradamus' visions, the Celestials know what the future holds. By the way, I need you to return the pocket-top that Nostradamus and Mozart used."

"Wow, you dropped a bomb on me," I said shaking my head over the ability of Nostradamus and the Celestials to see the future. My thoughts ran rampant:

> *Should I be the one who alters Earth's history with a surgical ability the Celestials gave me? Why do they want me to change history once again? Insight into the future, filled with chaos, went beyond my comprehension. How can anyone see the future?*

"Am I going too fast for you?" Father Aye asked.

"Yes, I'm still confused."

"About what?"

"All of it! . . .The level of two different oxygens on Earth and Bethel, a planet where there are no diseases, and about the Sadees, our cousins, who had to leave our planet. I can't find any records about their mass exodus back in AD 50."

The Real Story About the Sadees Leaving Bethel

Father Aye began, "As you know the Sadees left this planet two thousand years ago."

"Who forced them to leave?"

"The Celestials."

"It's a long story that goes back to the time of the Great Flood in 11382 BC. With planet Earth devastated, animals dying, humanity losing all hope, the Sadees were asked by the Celestials to intervein and become their Brother's Keeper. It was the will of God."

"Are you talking about Gobekli Tepe where the animals were nourished, the Sphinx, and the Great Pyramid where man was given hope?"

"Yes. Exactly. You seem to know that part of their history," Father Aye said, nodding his head.

"What went wrong?"

"Absolute power corrupts, absolutely. The Sadees thought they could rule as gods. They were given a *man-purse* that signified their authority. Throughout the centuries their man-purse became their petroglyph on the pillars at Gobekli Tepe [as per the first frame].

"In their absence from Earth, the Anunnaki believe they were in charge of all humanity [as per the second frame].

"After the Sadees were removed from our planet, they revisited Earth in South America once again, displaying more petroglyphs of their authority [as per the third frame]. They even displayed their authority on the statues on Easter Island. The symbol is hidden underground, but it's there." Father Aye narrated.

"So, the man purse signifies authority?" I asked, waiting for conformation from Father Aye.

"That question is the same as the one I asked of the Celestials, a long time ago. You won't find the answer in any of our history books because I haven't revealed the answer to our historians for publication."

"Is the answer a secret?"

"Well . . ." Father Aye slowly began, "I guess it will be alright if I tell you the story about the man-purse. But first, let me ask you about your doctor's bag you had when you visited Nostradamus and Mozart. You did have one, didn't you?"

"Yes, I did. It was an alligator purse, made from the skin of the animals we have here on Bethel."

"And what did you carry inside your doctor's alligator purse?" Father Aye asked in pursuit of an idea he wished to make.

"My purse, or doctor's bag, whatever you wish to call it, contained all the herbal medicines, vitamins, and vaccinees that I needed for my clients and myself. As you know, Earth has always been polluted with many forms of viruses."

"Were the vaccinees in liquid form or pill form?"

"Most of the various vaccines that I got from the Celestials were in pill form with a moisture evaporator inside the bottle. Where are you going with this?"

"Enoch, don't you see the significance of petroglyphs with a man-purse worn by the Sadees and the Anunnaki?"

"Are you saying they wore a doctor's purse containing medication for themselves?"

"Exactly. If you had made yourself publicly known, the natives would have portrayed *you* as a figure carrying your alligator purse!"

"That's true. What about the rumors of the Anunnaki using humans as slaves for mining gold?" I pursued.

"The Anunnaki were sent to Earth to supplement the efforts of the Sadees who were instrumental in putting many Earthlings to work building pyramids throughout the globe. All the pyramids, with the exception of Khufu's pyramid, had zero functionality. It merely kept the people busy and out of war."

"But I have seen relief images of the Anunnaki using humans as slaves for mining. What was happening?"

"The Anunnaki did not need gold. They needed another element that was recently named as Moscovium. To accomplish their mission in lending a helping hand to the Earthlings, they needed a rocket propellant to travel between Earth and their temporary home-base."

"Are we talking about a time period around 2500 BC? Where was their home-base, back then?"

"The moon."

"Earth's moon?"

"Yes. The far side of the moon where they used humanoids to mine for Moscovium so that they and the Sadees could travel back and forth to Earth in their booster rocket ships."

"What humanoids are we talking about?" I asked, more than curious about the way this conversation was going.

"They used the Gigantopithecus species also known to us as the big-feet people to mine underneath the craters on the far side of the moon."

"Were the big-feet people happy or were they used as slaves."

"They were very cooperative," Father Aye said with an affirmative smile.

"So you're saying the big-feet weren't treated as slaves and ordered to work in the mines?"

"No. They were a gentle race. They tried to live in isolation, away from the viruses that the Earthlings spread on their migratory routes. The Earthlings, aggressive by nature, were a threat to the big-feet people. They always had innovative weapons. After centuries of conflict, the big-feet people bargained with the Celestials for a different planet to live on, and in return, they would work in the mines on the moon. Do you have any more questions?"

"Yes. Why were the Sadees forced to leave our planet? Our history books say nothing about wars on our planet, created by the Sadees. We have always lived in peace with our cousins, the Sadees."

"That's true. They thought of us as their brotherly cousins and the Earthlings as their slaves. They wanted influence. When they visited South America, they taught mothers how to head-bind their baby's head. It didn't take much convincing. They simply said, 'If you want smart children like us and the way we look, then bind their heads.'," Father Aye explained.

"So, the Sadees, the offspring of Enoch the First started as humanitarians and slowly turned into uninhibited monsters."

I stood mute as Father Aye continued. "Yes, monsters. About fifty years prior to the birth of Christ, the Sadees found out that Jesus would be born in Bethlehem. They broadcasted the news to every alien throughout the galaxy. Everyone on every planet, every entity, wanted to see the son of God. They brought gifts—not for baby Jesus, but for the Sadees who showed them where to park their spaceships in South America on the plains of Nazca. The visitors used Nazca as a

crude airport, blowing up dust, marring the land with lines five miles long in multiple directions. While they were waiting for the birth of Christ, the alien visitors had to doodle images of spiders, whales, and monkeys for their amusement."

Father Aye continued to explained how the Sadees were cast out of Bethel because they had invited other aliens to witness the birth of Jesus. Like the Pharisee hawking their merchandise in front of the temple and committing blasphemy against the Holy Spirit, the visitors at Nazca were marring Earth's surface. "If Jesus was angry at the Pharisee, then imagine how angry God was toward the Sadees?"

"I see."

"Think about it. Our God who created Earth and its inhabitants should not have to put up with a non-pristine world and its inhabitants, influenced with the knowledge that they are not alone." Father Aye said emphatically. "All one hundred thousand Sadees had to leave Bethel. My grandparents told me about the Sadees. They looked like refugees, leaving their homes, hiding in the mountains, while the Celestials searched for them and rooted them out."

"But they kept revisiting Earth?"

"Yes. They have a different agenda for destroying humanity and opposing the Celestials."

"Did some of them try to do any good," I asked. Father Aye proceeded to educate me about unknown history events.

"Back in Egypt, it was reported that *Tiye* was the mother of *Akhenaten. Our* history books revealed that Tiye *really was* the grandmother of Akhenaten. The Egyptian research team reported that Kiya might be the lady in tomb KV35 and the DNA-mother of Tutankhamun. We know that Kiya really was Tutankhamun's mother. Akhenaten's real mother was a foreign princess from the land of Bethel. Even Tutankhamun's mother was a foreign princess from the land of Bethel — with Bethel being the home planet of the Sadees.

"The cross-breeding of species from our planet with species on Earth, was to restore peoples' belief in the same God that Moses had talked to on Mount Sinai. Information was passed down from a Sadees woman to

her son, Akhenaten. His mother had been told about the 'coming of Christ.' The plan was that Akhenaten would lead the way by moving the capital from Luxor to Amarna where everyone would believe in one God. Small ideas have a way of growing very big. Eventually, everyone would be looking forward to the coming of Jesus Christ . . . as John the Baptist forecasted. But Akhenaten got it wrong: It was not about the 'sun-disk, Aten'; it was about Jesus, the 'son' of God.

"When King Tut died in 1323 BC, it marked the end of the 18th Dynasty, an era in which Egypt achieved the peak of its power. Several other pharaohs ruled between King Tut's death and the start of Ramesses II's grandeur. Ramesses II reigned from 1279 BC to 1213 BC with personal problems that were given to him by the elderly Moses. The records of Moses actual birth are unclear on both of our planets, but his lifespan was definitely 120 years — a lifespan that witnessed the reign of four significant pharaohs over a seventy-year period.

"In addition to a few minor pharaohs, Moses lived under the reign of Amenhotep III, Akhenaten, King Tut and Ramesses II. From Amenhotep III's final year of his reign in 1349 BC to Ramesses II's first year of his reign in 1279 BC, Moses lived during their reign: a span of seventy years. The Sadees filled our record books with voluminous events that Moses witnessed and the numerous notes that our emissaries bought back from Earth.   "According to the Sadees' records, Akhenaten tutored Moses on monotheism. Moses led his people out of Egypt when he was very old during the reign of Ramesses II. If Moses had lived until the death of Ramesses II, he would have been 136 years old (1349-1213), but he died at 120 years according to the Bible and our own records, the ones we share with the Sadees. A chronological timescale of events will always help to uncover the past. However, the relationship between Moses and four other pharaohs is another mystery without a coordinated time-line of events.

"Our research team here on Bethel have reconstructed the head of Tutankhamun to show that the bridge of his nose started between his eyebrows and that his head was elongated like the Sadees."

Father Aye's Conclusions

"So, you can see that some of the Sadees did try to do good by converting humanity to monotheism."

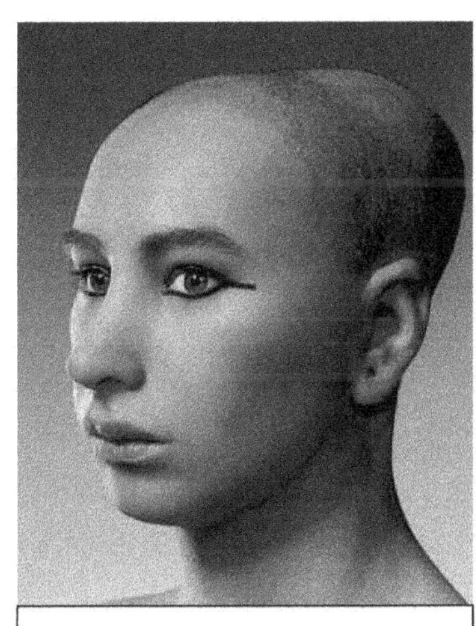

King Tutankhamun

I commented on the pictures Father Aye showed me, "It looks like King Tut, an offspring of the Sadees, had an elongated head and a typical upper bridge of the nose that starts in the middle of his eyebrows."

He blinked in the affirmative. "All the Greek gods had noses starting in the middle of their eyebrows. It makes you wonder how many societies the Sadees affected with crossbreeding and their ideas! By deforming their heads, they too had a nose bridge starting in the middle of their eyebrows."

I could see weariness in Farther Aye's face and that I needed to change the subject.

That evening, inside Father Aye's office, built into the prototype pyramid on Bethel, Father Aye explained Earth's history and its catastrophes:

- About the Great Flood back in 11382 BC, caused by an asteroid crashing into the Yucatan Peninsula, 66 million years earlier, causing the solar system to drift across the galaxy for millions of years, crossing the barrier more recently, bringing devastation to other planets as well.
- About Mars and Earth nearly colliding and Earth's drop in the supply of oxygen, which brought on more viruses and diseases.
- About the Sadees sent to rescue all the animals at Gobekli Tepe.
- About the Sadees, carrying their man-purses, filled with vaccines that they administered to the workers who helped them build the Great Pyramid of Giza.
- About the Sadees, who helped humankind, who tried to introduce a belief in one God by introducing a pharaoh that physically looked like them. And . . .
- About the Sadees who had to leave their home planet because they thought of themselves as gods.

After we had had our dinner, inside a foyer next to his office, we rested and then continued our conversation.

"Do you want back my personal pocket-top?" I asked, still wondering how Nostradamus and the Celestials could interpret the future.

"No, you can keep that. The Celestials, however, want the other pocket-top that they gave me to give to you."

"It's right here," I said as I placed it in his hands.

"You'll need your personal pocket-top when you visit Earth again to help your third client."

I could almost read Father Aye's mind about my new client. Memories flashed through my head about reasons why I was invited to Geesal, home of the Celestials.

I instantly speculated that the Celestials wanted me to perform heart-surgery on Earthlings as I had been trained on their planet, Geesal. "I can't do any heart surgery. Definitely, cannot . . . cannot! It has to be more than fifty Earth-years since I performed those operations."

"I know you did it many, many times for elderly Custodians when you lived with Charlie on Geesal, the Celestials home planet. So don't be choosy; this is your assigned mission! The Celestials know something about Earth's future that we cannot begin to imagine." Father Aye concluded by saying. "Go Enoch. Prepare and get ready." He lifted both his arms in a repeated fashion, motioning me to leave because he was exhausted from talking so much.

The Major Difference Between Two Worlds

Inside the pyramid where Father Aye's office is located, the sounds of two men were seriously talking about the difference between Earth and Bethel. Unknown to people on both planets, the truth filled the limestone office and reverberated down the chamber halls— secrets that only Father Aye knew. His  father, who was a priest during the zero-turn of the millennia, also knew the secret about procreation on Bethel. If limestone walls had ears, they would have heard his secrets.

A desk separates Father Aye and Enoch. Two chambers surround the office, an alcove for prayer and a small kitchen for the preparation of food. Two men are talking; the younger one is unsure of his next mission and needs a sense of "knowing" to bolster his confidence. Thoughts of his next mission into the twenty-first century on Earth, overwhelm him.

"Before I go, I have one more question," Enoch turned and blurted out. "How would you explain the fundamental difference between our world and theirs?"

"Do you mean the difference between our world with one-hundred-thousand inhabitants and Earth with eight-billion people? Ever since our Biblical patriarch, Enoch the First, arrived on this planet seventeen-thousand years ago, our population has paled in comparison to Earth's population growth."

"That *is* a big difference, but how do you explain their society versus our society?"

"Basically, we help them by being their Brother's Keeper, so to speak, and they help themselves in selfish ways. Never the less, do you want to hear the real difference between the two worlds?" he paused and asked again, "Summarized in just two words?"

"Yes—"

"Angio disease!" Father Aye quickly interrupted, paused, glanced at Enoch, and waited, watching for an expression on his face. Enoch got up from the desk where he was sitting, walked over to the wine cabinet where father Aye kept the sacramental wine, popped the cork and started pouring a glass of wine for himself. Father Aye calmly removed the bottle and glass from Enoch's hands, and thought, *Go out and get your own bottle of wine.*

"Do you mean the disease that prevents our women from getting pregnant? The same disease that the Celestials are working to find a cure? The same effort that Beena is making to provide the Celestials with recent data?" His voice in crescendo.

"Exactly the same," Father Aye said while calmly looking at Beena's review documents and support data.

"Our population doesn't grow! Earth's population is over producing!" Enoch replied with excitement and an elevated voice.

"There could come a day when Earth's women can't reproduce at all!" Father Aye had a look of indifference as he rubbed his forehead. "If all the women on Earth became sterile, their population would fall to zero within one century. The rest of the animal population would continue to grow as it does here on Bethel. But a full blown Angio disease would eliminate all humans on Earth! If God wills it with a virus caring the Angio disease, all humans on Earth would be eradicated by the middle of the 22nd century. It would be a solution to the problem of original sin."

Enoch fumbled in his next choice of words because he had forgotten what original sin was all about. He blinked his eye lids as if he knew and said nothing. Father Aye read his facial expression and started to speak again.

"Original sin is a Christian doctrine that says, 'everyone is born sinful.' All of us inherited original sin from Adam and Eve. It reached its second pinnacle when Cain's hands shed the innocent blood of his brother, Able. It reached its third pinnacle when Cain responded with, 'Am I my brother's keeper?'"

Enoch knew the rest of the story. "Is that why we try to atone for original sin by being our Brother's Keeper?"

"Exactly," Father Aye said, thrusting both hands forward. "As you know, each one of us is tasked with being a Scout or a Custodian, working on a mission requested by the Celestials, to improve the plight of mankind."

"So, what's the answer?"

"The Angio disease is a form of birth control," Father Aye announced as he filled his glass with water from the kitchen sink.

"Look at this glass of water. You can see that its neither half full nor half empty. The half empty metaphor would be one of our women who has the Angio disease. The half full would be a metaphor describing a woman who has one precious child by her husband."

Enoch quickly added, "Children certainly are precious on our planet."

"There you go, one of the differences. But what happens if I fill this glass with water at the top? Wouldn't you say that this represents a woman with a bunch of kids? Children that her and her husband can't properly care for?"

Enoch could see where this was going. "Hmm. The personal care and the expense increase for each child."

"Okay. What if I fill the glass with water until it spills over. What does that represent?"

"I don't know. Not good? Something in excess. Possibly a woman who had twelve kids, a different one with twelve different husbands?"

"Oh, I see you've been reading Man and Superman by George Bernard Shaw. Good for you. Then you know Shaw claims 'that when a woman wants a child, she is simply following life's natural impulses.' Every woman instinctively wants to have a child, but some don't because of timing or it's the *wrong twelve guys*."

Enoch smiled. "Okay. That's a satirical play on words. I get it."

"Here on Bethel abortion is not practiced. We never did and we never will allow for abortions. Every man and woman look forward to nurturing a child when, and if, it comes along. I'm talking about a big 'if,' here. Parents have intentions to care for that child for the rest of its life and whatever they can do to oversee its welfare when it becomes an adult."

"How is the disease transmitted?" Enoch wanted the details.

"In the first place, it's not a disease. It's a genetic mutation, passed from father to daughter. A father can also pass the mutation to his son who can have daughters that are sterile and some that are not. The mutation in our genes skips from generation to generation, capping the growth of our population——a bad thing. However, it's also a good thing because the pregnant women on our planet never think about having an abortion."

"To your point," Enoch confirmed, "I see why the Angio disease, I mean mutation, is here to stay. That *does* make a difference between the two worlds."

"It's here to stay because it's been intended to stay. It's God's intention. Based upon field reports from our Scouts, working on Earth in the twentieth century, I have concluded that poor Earthlings——a man and his wife, choosing abortion——will be less content in their marriage. However, a childless marriage here on Bethel, results in the happiness lasting longer."

"If that's the case, then why is Beena working so hard for the Celestials that are trying to find a cure? I know they can read your thoughts and that you can speak to them across the galaxy. Aren't you being counterproductive to their goals."

"That's correct, but you have to remember the Celestials are entities. They comply with God's wishes and make sure we do the same. We are different than them. We are humans with human instincts, desires, and goals. In that respect, we're not too different than our cousins on Earth."

"But why don't you explain that to the Celestials," Enoch persisted with his arm flying upward and the back of his hand trying to flap away the problem. "Why don't you ask the Celestials for permission to explain to everyone the true purpose of the Angio disease?"

"As of now, you're the only one that knows its true purpose. You must keep this a secret. I have tried explanations with the Celestials, I have argued with them, and I have also read Bernard Shaw: 'I learned long ago, never to wrestle with a pig.' And now I have to go and make an Act of Contrition. I'm deeply sorry for what I just said. I hope the Celestials aren't hearing my thoughts as we speak."

With human gestures, Father Aye disappeared in the doorway, looking up at the door's arch, his voice of apology trailing behind him through the empty limestone corridors, his head turning from side to side and watching the progress of his sandals appearing and disappearing under the white robe covering his rotund belly. He thought to himself, *I like Enoch, but I really think he doesn't truly understand the difference. I will pray for him.*

Preparing for My Next Visit to Earth

I had to take a few years; that is, Bethel years, reading my surgery notes and practicing a virtual simulation with specialized grasping tools the Celestials had given me. I had been trained with robotic hands that were an extension of my fingers. I could create stitches inside the human body with these robotic hands. Since this technology was too advanced and too prohibited on Earth, I had to retrain myself with more conventional operating tools used in the 1960s.

When Beena accidently walked into my office one day, she saw me waving a surgical knife and grasping tools over a homemade operating table where I envisioned a patient.

"What are you doing?" she asked as she approached from my backside.

"I'm operating," I said.

"On what?"

"On my patient who needs a heart transplant?"

"I don't see anyone on the table. Have you gone daft?"

"No," I replied as I turned to look at her, "but you can be my imaginary patient if you like."

"Okay, but no cutting on me," she said as she climbed onto the operating table. "I don't know what I'm getting into!"

"I can practice my old skills with your clothes on or your clothes off. Which do you prefer?"

Needless to say, there was no imaginary operation, only kissing as I looked down at her beautiful naked body resting on my operating table.

"Beena," I said with love in my voice, "your personality is always so peaceful and tranquil; not too unlike a calm valley filled with fragrant wild flowers, stalks of maze grass and their seed pods gently swaying in the wind. Through the middle of the valley, flows a gentle flowing river with a log cabin on the other side and you behind the window. So much, do I want to be behind that window with you?"

With her eyes wide open, she favored my thoughts and gave me a Mona-Lisa smile. "I would like that," she said, "but this table we're lying on is unstable."

Unaware of the problem, I continued, "My life feels like it's been dragged over a bumpy road crowded with Earthlings that are 'too-much' of everything. Their excessive vices, their unbound limitations, their unlimited desires––take them to the breaking point of their personalities. I find it difficult to visit Earth and mend broken hearts, despaired by the indifferences of their own people. Eccentric ideologies across the globe always produce wars. While at war, rapid advancements in their technology eclipse their humanity."

After a short reflection, my thoughts came back to Beena. "I had hope Father Aye did not send me on another mission because I want to be with you." Beena with her dark brown eyes made me feel I could get hopelessly lost in their depths. Her eyebrows, perfectly shaped, flared upward at first and then tapered across her beautiful eyes without a misplaced follicle. I knew I could love her more if I could only stop being me.

While I was pouring out my heart, we had to stop due to my improvised operating table starting to sway under the combined weight of our naked bodies.

My Third Mission

My trip back to Earth took place on a W-25 spaceship, piloted by Charlie, my former pilot and Celestial interpreter. Struck with amazement, I forced myself to believe that the Celestials had loaned Charlie a top-secret spaceship usually reserved for the esoteric few. While sitting in the control room, Charlie read the expression on my face and said, "This spaceship was loaned to me by the Celestials in exchange for a portion of the profits I make on my trade route. I'm sorry about the way I look with this bulky helmet on my head. I'll bet you didn't recognize me when you came aboard?"

"No. I recognized you. But right now, I'm having trouble understanding why you're piloting a top-secret spaceship. Won't the Sadees try to capture it from you?"

"Nah," he said. "The ship is equipped with threat-assessment counter-measures. All the Sadees fly in their outmoded W-5s that the Celestials gave them a long time ago. This ship can cloak itself into the 5th dimension whenever their W-5s approach. If they did steal the ship, they wouldn't know how to control it because the instructions are in the same language I speak to the Celestials. My helmet interprets the thoughts of the spaceship's central command regarding evasive maneuvers and countermeasures. So relax, Enoch. We're safe."

"Okay. Congratulations on your ability to advance from a W-5 to a W-25 pilot. I always knew you had a hidden talent. It's been a long time since you flew a W-5 to help Steve and I retrieve the Ark when we were posing as Crusaders in the twelfth century. And now here it is: the twentieth century and you're piloting a W-25. Wow."

"Yes, that was about eight hundred Earth-years ago. Or two thirds of our anticipated life span."

"So, Charlie, I heard that you're a merchant, trading Earth-manufactured bicycles and electronic goods between two worlds?"

"That's true. During my travels, I've learned a lot by rubbing elbows with Earthlings and Celestials. I've seen things you can't imagine; I've heard things that are unbelievable; and I've read the thoughts of Celestials that discuss Earth's problems."

"What problems?"

"Global warming, Enoch! They were talking about Earth's global warming," he exclaimed in a louder voice to ensure I heard him on the other side of the control room inside the W-25 he was piloting.

"The climate on Earth has been consistent over a hundred thousand years," I said.

"No, it hasn't. When Earth's solar system transgressed into the barrier, it lost its ninety-degree axis of rotation, a perpendicular alignment with respect to its orbital path around the sun."

"Yes, we learned that in our history books and the lectures from Father Dean. Go on."

"Well, the axis of rotation is about 22 degrees off the vertical, 90-degree alignment it used to have. When Earth entered the barrier thirteen thousand years ago, many catastrophic things happened: the Great Flood, the change in the axis of rotation and the repositioning of the planet closer to the sun. Twentieth century Earthlings are starting to talk about global warming due to an increase in carbon dioxide emissions, but the Celestials, in reality, are saying something totally different."

"What are they saying?"

"They're saying they tried to restore the axis of rotation and failed. They said something about Stone Hedge as a fulcrum point for slowly tilting it back with thruster-pushes over the centuries. I couldn't read their complete thoughts, and I don't have the engineering savvy to understand the mechanics. In basic terms, Earth is drying up because the seasons are more severe. If you could have seen Earth twenty or thirty thousand years ago, you would have noticed very mild winters and summers with greater atmospheric oxygen. A severe change in the axis of rotation is responsible for causing global warming over the last ten thousand years. The Celestials are anxious to tell Earthlings how to prepare for the consequences, but they don't want to 'tip their hand.'"

"I see where they're coming from."

As Charlie positioned our spaceship in the thermosphere high above Earth, I could see the northern deserts of Africa (the Sahara) on the same latitude as the jungles of Central America, in stark contrast. And I could see the southern deserts of Africa (the Kalahari) on the same latitude as the jungles of South America—another stark contrast. Over the last ten to twenty thousand years, Earth had lost its lushness due to slow and more recent accelerated global warming. Something was wrong! And this was my stop—Earth—the end of my trip.

Chapter 5: Dr. Christiaan Barnard

Dr. Christian Neethling Barnard:

November 8, 1922—September 2, 2001

• A South African cardiac surgeon who performed the world's first successful human-to-human heart transplant

• Achieved his internship and residency at the Groote Schuur hospital in Cape Town, after which he worked as a general practitioner in Ceres, a rural town in the Cape Provence In 1951, he returned to Cape Town, where he worked at the city hospital as a senior resident medical officer.

- Completed his master's degree receiving a master of medicine in 1953 from the University of Cape Town
- Performed the world's first human heart transplant operation on December 3, 1967. His first patient, Washkansky, survived the operation and lived for eighteen days. However, he succumbed to pneumonia as he was taking immunosuppressive drug.
- Continued to perform heart transplants as follows:

  1. On January 2, 1968, his patient, Philip Blaiberg, survived for nineteen months.

  2. In 1971 Dirk van Zyl received a new heart. He was the recipient who lived the longest, surviving over twenty-three years.

After his first successful heart transplant, Barnard became known as the "film star surgeon." Throughout the world, his patients loved him; he treated hundreds free of charge. Many others who were jealous of his instant success hated him. Some colleagues accused him of "stealing" their idea and their opportunity to perform the first heart transplant. Often considered spoiled with an arrogant personality, he was also regarded as kind and considerate by others. Because of his widely publicized love affairs, he became jokingly known as the "doctor of hearts," referring to the heart as an emotional symbol rather than its usual medical context.

My Third Mission

The Scouts had paved the way for my admission to Groote Schuur Hospital in Cape Town, South Africa. I was hired as a consultant in bypass surgery. The Scouts had provided the hospital with forged degrees, diplomas, and articles stating that I was an experienced heart surgeon. It was a lie, but actually, my experience, taught to me by the Celestials, exceeded the documentation they required for a heart surgeon. I met Doctor

Barnard six months before he performed his very first heart transplant in 1967.

Meeting Christiaan for the first time was a memorable experience. At forty-five years old, he had passed the formidable years unlike my previous clients, Nostradamus and Mozart—both coached, persuaded and inspired to historical renown. Christiaan's unique mind flowed into a pattern of goals, ambitions and self-inspiration. There was no need to tell him I was an alien from another planet. Even though I still carried my black satchel filled with advanced vaccines and medication, there was no need to worry about him having health problems. Except for his libido problem, he was a healthy doctor that could prescribe his own medication. Consequently, my medicine bag went along unused for my client, Dr. Barnard. I kept the medication refrigerated because I had an intuition, I may need it.

We met in the hospital cafeteria where our discussions turned to his experience transplanting hearts in animals. He believed in heterotopic procedures—"piggy back" transplants—because these experiences gave him a better success rate with animals. Then he experimented with the attachment of an animal's heart to a human heart. These double transplants or the "double pump" procedures involved the joining of a healthy monkey's heart to a human's heart. Desperately ill patients allowed desperate measures.

Biologically, I was much older than Chris—that is what I called him. According to Chris, he thought I looked fifteen years older than his own forty-five years of age. In reality, my Bethel age was 980 years and my biological age was ninety-eight-plus years. His respect for his elders and his assumption that I had more experience, allowed me to influence his decisions. He had the right idea about saving a life, but the usage of a monkey's heart as a transplant was the wrong way to go. He was sitting in the right pew; but sitting in the wrong church. A small push in the right direction would bring his fame to a point where he would lose his anonymity. My goal steered him away from the piggyback procedure to a total replacement of the human heart.

After several meetings, discussions, and drinking together in the local tavern, we became good friends. Chris, who was a handsome man, easily attracted women whether he socialized in the local tavern or worked in the hospital. He had already been married and divorced. I told him that his wild escapades were too unlikely for me because my thoughts divided between Beena and Brianna. If Bill, Brianna's uncle, was here and a lot younger, he would have made an immediate friend with Chris, drinking and consorting. They both liked the same things.

When the occasion seemed appropriate, I asked him, "Why not consider a heart-to-heart transplant on a human-to-human? It's a simple, straight forward idea!"

"No," he said, shaking his head. "There are not many people that would gladly give up the only healthy heart they possess."

"I agree. But what if they were brain dead and their heart was still active?"

"Hey, that's an idea, but I would still have trouble with infection and rejection."

"That's true, but a cross match in blood type, age, and physical size may produce better results than taking a chance with a monkey's heart."

"Good idea. You can assist with my next operation. Where do we find someone that's brain dead?" His exact words escape me, but I recall him saying something to that effect.

He invited me to assist. I succeeded in making him famous, but my problems were just beginning. The body of a woman named Denise Darvall arrived at the hospital in a brain-dead condition as the result of an accident. Dr. Barnard selected Mr. Louis Washkansky as the heart recipient. I talked to Louis who was a kind, gentle, and understanding individual. His consideration for other people manifested itself when we had lengthy conversations. The sentences between us flowed like a two-way street. When he conversed with others, he showed an interest in their life's story by asking them questions. Louis was a genuine, likeable person.

I reviewed the procedure plans with Chris by showing him on plastic models where the patient's heart should be trimmed for extraction. The Celestials had taught me how to salvage a small portion of the patient's heart and trim the donor's heart to match. Louis would receive 95 percent of a donor's heart and retain 5 percent of his own heart. The remnants of his own heart would acquire the donor's heart as a new growth. This procedure was a new learning experience for Chris.

"Chris," I said, "I recommend that you remove Louis's heart below the left atrium along the black crayon line that I'm drawing on this plastic model. The donor's heart then needs to be trimmed proportionately with the upper left atrium missing. Then, Louis's remaining heart needs to be sutured to the donor's heart. I truly believe that the operation will be a success if you save Louis's aorta and a portion of his upper left atrium."

The Celestials had taught me how to save a portion of the patient's heart because it "jump-started" the donor's heart. I had performed this operation many times on planet Geesal. Doctor Barnard, unaware of heart substitution and trimming techniques, preferred to add a monkey's heart to the patient's heart so that they worked in parallel. He listened intently and then commented, "You make it sound like it's as simple as cutting along the dotted line on your plastic model. What's missing?"

"That's a good pun," I said, laughing at his humor. "A dotted line? This will work, please trust me. Yes, think of cutting along a dotted line."

One of Chris's harder jobs, involved a confrontation with his patient prior to surgery. He had to find the right words that would assure the patient that they would survive with a monkey's heart. Our discussion of a human heart-to-heart transplant, gave him the synergy he needed for the task ahead. While his good mood prevailed, he continued with more puns. He looked at me in gratitude for my advice and said, "Thank God, at least now, I won't have to build up the patient's confidence by lying to them with comments like, 'You'll be swinging from the trees in no time.'" Then he laughed. He may have been a humorist, but he also was a brilliant steady-handed surgeon. I could only advise with verbal guidance and surgical-instrument selection because my own hands were losing their dexterity.

On the day of the operation, Chris and I worked together on Mr. Washkansky. Chris was the lead surgeon, snipping and cutting with confidence, moving his hands with the precision of a music conductor never missing a note, and believing that this man would surely live another day. Watching him operate with the plan that I had proposed became reminiscent of a maestro conducting an orchestra with many hand movements that I had witnessed during Mozart's training. The dexterity in his small hands allowed him to progress from one aspect of the procedure to the next. The quick and accurate movements of his hands and fingers resembled a video replay in fast-forward motion. I was impressed.

Upon completion, Chris looked across the operating table in my direction and said, "Thank you for helping me, Enoch."

I cannot remember if I said "You're welcome" or if I went mute with thoughts of myself: an alien with an unusual name, making history among medical pioneers.

After the patient survived the operation, I was amazed that Dr. Barnard's surgical skills had saved a life. The world was awestruck when major newspapers printed emphatic headlines. I truly believed that Chris had performed such a fine job that Mr. Washkansky could survive without advanced recovery drugs we used for our own patients; namely, steroids.

For my autobiography, I need to translate the names of all drugs and body parts that I learned from the Celestials into the names and body parts used by twentieth century Earthlings. The medical profession on our home planet adopted different nomenclature after people (like Charlie and Fathers' Dean and Aye) had read the thoughts of Celestials. Consequently, our vaccines, cures and medical procedure were advanced by centuries beyond anything the Earthlings had in the way of medication that cured all diseases and surgical procedures that healed the body. The following text is about drugs and immunization that I learned when I was a young doctor. I have translated this information into the English language to explain how I got in trouble with the Celestials.

Allow me to explain how we used recovery drugs on our home planet, known on Earth as steroids: more specifically Glucocorticoids. For clarification purposes, testosterone is one of the first steroids synthesized and manufactured by Germany after World War II. Testosterone's benefit to the human body is different from the benefits of Glucocorticoid, an anti-inflammatory and immunosuppressive drug. As a general rule, all steroid medications have names that end in "one," and they had a greater efficacy than penicillin, used on American GI's for the first time at the end of World War II.

Technical Note: The Immune System as Translated

A lymphocyte is a white blood cell that is part of the immune system in all vertebrates. Lymphocytes divide into two major categories: B-cell and T-cell lymphocytes. B-cell lymphocytes produce antibodies, a Y-shaped molecule that attacks bacterial invaders. B-cells mature in the bone marrow, thus the letter "B". T-cells lymphocytes originate in the bone marrow and mature in the thymus, thus the letter "T". They function to kill virally and parasitically infected cells.

Staying focused on B-cell lymphocytes, these cells function to produce antibodies. Antibodies resemble the letter Y. The top two points of the Y are identical to molecules on the surface of a bacterium called antigens. Antigens are the identifiers on the cell surface of molecules specific to the invading bacterial cells or pathogens. Antibodies attach to antigens in a lock-and-key fashion known as specificity, a protein's binding site. The antigen, or antibody complex is recognized by another type of white blood cell, called a neutrophil. The neutrophil comes along, engulfs the sensitized bacterium, and literally "eats" it. This process called "phagocytosis" directly translates to "cell eating."

This briefly describes the function of a normal immune system. To inhibit the immune system from attacking a foreign organ like a transplanted heart, the antibodies need to be controlled. Inhibiting the production of antibodies within the B-cell, lymphocyte is the objective.

Drugs like Glucocorticoids are also administered as post-transplantory immunosuppressants to prevent the acute transplant rejection and graft-versus-host disease: a condition whereby the lymphocytes within the transplanted tissue do not recognize the host as "self" and proceed to launch an immune response against that host. Glucocorticoid steroids (a.k.a. corticosteroids), were among the first immunosuppressive agents used in clinical transplantation, and they have remained an important component of induction, maintenance, and rejection regiments.

Three days after the operation, I could see that Mr. Washkansky was failing. His immune system tried to reject the transplanted heart. At that time, I believed that Dr. Barnard's fame would increase in proportionality to the number of days that Mr. Washkansky lived. I conveniently overlooked the warnings that Father Aye had expressed about administering Bethel's advanced drugs to Earthlings who were not clients. My client, Chris, was exempt from the administration of advanced vaccines I had brought with me, but here was his patient, Mr. Washkansky a dying man, who mentally cried out for help. I could see the anguish in his face while my compassion for his recovery grew . . . and grew. When no one was around, I injected an advanced, lifesaving drug into his potassium-chloride drip bag that hung next to his bed. The drip bag was there to replace his electrolytes. Now, it contained a lifesaving drug developed by the Celestials on Geesal. I had brought the steroid from my home planet and I had given it to Mr. Washkansky so that he could have a second chance on life.

He woke up and asked, "How are we doing?"

I responded with, "How are *you* doing?"

"I have chest pains, and I can feel my heart beating like a rabbit. Why is it doing that?"

"Louis, I probably should not tell you this, but I'm sure you will understand that this is something that is very normal."

"Okay. Hit me with it, Doc."

I proceeded to break the news as gently as I could, "When we removed the damaged heart from your chest, the vagus nerve had to be severed. There is no way of removing one without the other. Are you with me?"

"Yes. I'm following you."

"The vagus nerve carries signals to the lower half portion of your brain stem, the medulla. The brain interprets the beating signals from the heart. After cutting the vagus nerve, the brain receives no signal and the heart beats at more than one hundred beats per minute. This is normal until the healing process begins with the regeneration of nerves around the heart. You'll be as fit as a fiddle, as they say, but first I need to know that you won't run out and become a doctor with this one and only little piece of information that I know." I smiled, and he returned the smile with one that was richer.

During the following week, Mr. Washkansky rallied. Chris thought that it was due to a drug that he had added to the drip bag. He sent a sample from the contents of the drip bag to a laboratory in the United States. The steroid drug that I had brought from Geesal was in the drip bag and now, they were on their way to the Unites States. The technicians at the laboratory, named after its owner Percy Lavon Julian (April 11, 1899 to April 19, 1975), were about to analyze and then synthesize the steroid drug.

History Note

Dr. Percy Lavonn Julian, an African American born to a slave father in Montgomery, Alabama, earned his PhD in 1931 from the University of Vienna in Austria. With a doctorate in chemistry, he synthesized hormones, steroids, progesterone, and testosterone. In September of 1973, Julian applied for a U.S. patent (#3,761,469) allowing him to manufacture steroids.

Mr. Washkansky lived for eighteen days after the operation. Thesteroid medicine that I had given to him came too late. I returned to Bethel a month later, unaware that Dr. Barnard would take possession of the lifesaving drug from the Julian Laboratory and use it on another patient who lived twenty-three years after his operation. The lifesaving drug or steroid was at his disposal in any quantity that he ordered from the Julian Laboratory!

I went home thinking that I had accomplished my mission. Actually, I had. I made Dr. Barnard historically famous. Nevertheless, my compassion for a dying man resulted in the breaking of a cardinal rule. All the inhabitants on Earth now had a drug never intended for them. The steroid drug, created by the Celestials, was solely for the people on Bethel. Within the a few decades, the Earthlings would use steroids in everything imaginable: athlete's foot cream like Clotrimazole/Betamethasone, and skin ointment like Desonide. The list of steroids and synthetic steroids grew over the years.

I had altered the humanity's destiny and the Celestials held me responsible. There was no going home: no going back.

The year was 2020 and I found myself back on Earth with another client named Edward. The Scouts had arranged our accidental meeting in the local library next to where he lived. We held the majority of our meetings in the library's conference room where we could talk freely without being overheard. Edward had written two books about space travel within another dimension and now he wanted to know more about the spaceship that brought me to Earth.

I wasn't at liberty to reveal anything about our technology because Father Aye had warned me not to administer vaccines to Earthlings, other than my client, and not to transfer knowledge about our culture or the culture of the Celestials. The Celestials with their high-in-the-sky space ships were constantly monitoring the progress of Custodians like myself and the events happening throughout the world. It was tense talking to Edward because I had to weigh my words carefully and consider my reaction to his comments. I was there to help him write his third book because the Celestial wanted Earth's scientists to reevaluate fossil fuel as the appropriate propellant for a galactic spaceship. It was obvious that fuel consumption would increase exponentially as their ships approached warp speeds. They wanted humankind to break through the frontiers of outer space, but they also wanted humankind to acquire this knowledge on their own. Hopefully, Edward's third book would be an inspiration to those scientists.

The Edward and Enoch Interview:

"When did you first become interested in UFOs?" I asked, trying to break the silence and redirect his thoughts about book writing.

"In 2009, prior to the release of my second book, I traveled to Area 51 with my son-in-law and stayed at a small combination motel, bar and diner in the city of Rachel, about 10-miles from

Area-51. The town of Rachel has a greeting sign that boast a population of ninety-seven residents. It's a one-horse, two-dog, multi-wild-rabbit town in the middle of a barren desert. The largest building is a combination tavern and restaurant where rental units can be purchased for a night's sleep in a dilapidated, semi-converted trailer home minus the kitchen."

"What did you see?"

"Well . . . the usual stuff," you know. "A lot of deserts, a lot of jack rabbits that looked like they could grow horns, the road block at the entrance to Area 51 with a warning sign, saying something like 'We Shoot now, and Ask questions later.'"

"Were you guys drunk?"

"I don't drink, Enoch."

"On the way back from Area 51, we saw a mutilated cow laying alongside the road. Its head had been removed and there was a long surgical-looking cut traveling about fifteen-inches from its neck to its chest area between its shoulders. There was no blood and no head surrounding the body. It could have been dropped from the sky."

"Was your son-in-law drunk?"

"No, but he did have a couple of Scotch drinks that night."

"What did you see that night?" I asked, wanting to know more.

"We saw about two dozen lights over the town of Rachel blinking on and off. Like one second on and then three seconds off and then repeat, repeat, repeat."

"Were they big lights?"

"No, they looked the same size as stars, but closer into view."

"It could have been a thin film of moisture clouds, repeating what you saw."

"How could that be? Out in the desert? Think about it, Enoch! Moisture clouds in the desert?" Edward replied with some irritation.

"Sorry. Did your son-in-law confirm what you saw?"

"Oh yea. We talked about all the strange things we saw in the sky."

"Did you see anything else?"

"Yes, I awoke around five in the morning, went out to the porch and saw a star in the sky that started to move. It was twice as big as an ordinary star among all the other stars on that clear night. It silently traveled for about fifteen minutes from a 45 degree azimuth in the southwesterly sky to an area directly above me."

"Then what happened?" I was really interested now.

"I went back to bed, only, to listen to my son-in-law snore in the other bed. I thought this can't be happening. About five minutes later, I had to take another look."

"What came next?" I asked.

"I went to the outside porch and saw the exact same thing happening again: a star, brighter than the other stars, moving from way out in the distance to a space, directly over me, in the town of Rachel, near Area 51. It grew in brightness and size— about four times its original size."

"Did it scare you?"

"Yes. It *did* scare me. You might say this event is why I decided to finish my second book and start on my third book. I want to use what's left of my engineering education to describe how a spaceship can fly in another dimension."

After Edward told me what he had seen, my thoughts raced on:

> *I thought the people on Earth couldn't see us landing near Rachel and using Area 51 as our own spaceport, where Custodians and the Celestials could catapult their ships into galactic space. His story about the decapitated dead cow was something new. If the Sadees were back on Earth*

"Edward," I began, "we have to start with your writing composition. I checked out a few library books for you. I need you to focus on this section where the author describes twenty different types of sentence structures; namely, alliteration, anadiplosis, anaphora, antimetabole, anthesis, assonance, asyndeton, consonance. Well, . . . you can see them on this page. Personally, I like anaphora, which is a repetition of the same phrase like——'*With* malice toward none, *with* charity for all, *with* firmness in the right.'"

Edward leaned over the library's table to see where I was pointing. "I see. Do you want me to try another short story?"

"Yes. Also keep in mind the topic known as *Voice*. To be brief, Voice is the subject of the sentence in either first, second or third person and sometimes the it-person."

"I know about the different persons as in I, You, and We. What do you mean by the it-person?"

"That's when the narrator of the story is unknown as in 'Spot ran fast on his four paws.' In this case the author of the sentence is unknown: an it-person."

"I get it. 'See spot run' is in the second person because it implies '[You] see spot run.'"

"Right-on," I said, still practicing my own English idioms.

"I'll have a short draft ready for you next week," Edward replied as he exited the library's conference room.

I had exercised my duty as a Custodian by giving Edward lessons in English Composition 101, up and through 104. The contents of the library books——if he ever reads them——will give him a post graduate degree. In the following week, Edward had presented me with a documentary type of composition, titled *The Florida Guy.*

The Florida Guy

Back in 1923, a Florida man living in Miami-Dade County built Coral Castle; single handedly—a huge undertaking with the assembly of multi-ton stones. According to documentation, his neighbor reported that he saw him "praying" over a two-ton coral stones. After their eyes met, the neighbor went about his business. Then, a few minutes later, the neighbor saw the coral-stone-builder drive away with the same stone in the back of his pickup.

His name was Edward Leedskalnin (1887-1951). According to Wikipedia, "Coral Castle is noted for legends surrounding its creation that claim it was built single-handedly by Leedskalnin using reverse magnetism or supernatural abilities to move and carve numerous stones weighing many tons. Teenagers reported that he had caused the blocks of coral to move like "hydrogen filled balloons." Other reports quote Mr. Leedskalnin as saying that he had discovered the stone-moving secrets of the Egyptian, the hidden secrets past and gone, the old secrets unknown to modern man.

"That's great," I commented. "You have an amphora sentence with the word *secrets* repeated three times."

"Thank you," Edward said and quickly added. "I continued the article into something I really believe in."

"What's that," I asked, curious about his engineering abilities. As I read Edward's article, I got the impression that he was planning this section for his third book."

Time Travel

Many books and movies present the topic of time travel as a possibility. It is amazing how intuitive authors can be in expressing a simple concept of time travel as opposed to the existence of real time. We all know that real time is a "right now" situation. However, imaginary time is difficult for us to perceive, and yet, electrical engineers use the imaginary symbol j to express the reactance of a choke or a capacitor. The symbol j as in +jX or −jX represents a reactance or a form of resistance that is not real. The symbol j also has the numeric value $\sqrt{-1}$ or the square root of minus one, which cannot be reduced any further.

Engineers work with +jX in their formulas to express the reactance that current experiences as it passes through an induction coil. They also use -jX to express the reactance that voltage experiences as it passes through a capacitor. The current reactance in a coil and the voltage reactance in a capacitor are treated as diametrically opposed values; i.e., one is +jX and the other is −jX. To achieve a better picture of the events in a circuit board, engineers plot resistance on a horizontal scale from zero to a value extending to the right of zero. Resistance is treated as a property in real time. Inductive reactance, +jX, is plotted on the vertical scale in the upward direction from zero. Capacitive reactance, -jX, is plotted on the vertical scale in the downward direction from zero. Reactance is treated as a property in imaginary time.

Engineers sum up all three values into one line on the plot that represents impedance or $Z = R \pm jX$. Of course, the whole process can be summed up more easily on a Smith chart, but we will not go into that. Engineers are working with time because inductive reactance is equal to $2\pi fL$ and capacitive reactance is equal to 1/2πfC where L and C are the size of the component and f is a function of time (or t = 1/2πf). Consequently, +jX is a function of +j*t and −jX is a function of −j*t^-1 or −j/t. Both functions equate to an expression for real time. It is really very easy once a person gets in to it. The bottom line is that real time, "t," is associated with an imaginary function "j" or √-1. This association is what bridges the gap between the electrical engineering world and a *new form of physics*--a connection between imaginary time and real time. Some form of *new physics* is what we need.

We are going to hypothesize that imaginary time can be associated with gravity in a new physics world. To distinguish real time from imaginary time, we will use symbols "t" and "T," respectively. The letter "t" is used in the engineering world. We will reserve the letter "T" for a new physics world. Now, we can give imaginary time the symbol +jT and plot it as an independent variable on the horizontal axis. We will treat gravity as the dependent variable and plot it on the vertical axis. Up until now, no one has used the expressions +jT or −jT with the symbols representing imaginary time into the future or the past, respectively. The symbol +jT can represent a "time shift" or a "time warp" that is very slight with respect to real time.

Speculation implies that a forward or backward shift in time results in a visual observation of Earth tinted in slight purple or reddish color. It could explain why people in Mexico see hovering UFOs with multiple colors. If the occupants of UFOs are seeing a tinted Earth, then we are seeing them with the same color shift. It could explain why UFO occupants make crop circles to judge the passage of imaginary time by measuring the crops' deterioration in color. The occupants may have difficulty sorting out imaginary time from real time. The color shift of a crop circle over a few days tells UFO pilots their location in imaginary time with respect to real time.

Most likely, it is impossible to land on a planet in imaginary time: and only, possible to land in real time. The transmission of light in imaginary time has to be different from the way we perceive light reflection from objects in real time. Speculation would dictate that there are only two things that exists in imaginary time; namely particles with "zero mass-rest" like neutrinos and protons––which is light. Stars, planets, moons, asteroids, comets can be seen, but they are not physically there. Their existence is nothing more than a mirror's reflection with nothing on either side of the mirror. And here is the best part, "Nothing is present for a spacecraft to crash into. Space flight across the galaxy at warp speed is possible even if the pilot falls asleep at the wheel, so to speak!" The existence of warp speed dictates this logic as a necessity.

"Wow, Edward. Do you really believe in all that?" I asked.

"Yes. And if I could look under the hood of the spaceship that brought you here to Earth, I probably could tell you more."

I had to give him a partial truth. "My spaceship is not here. But continue."

Edward began, "Prior to a discussion on a new form of physics, we need to state that anything that is unknown is solvable with a hypothesis before a theory or equation finalizes the speculation. This requires an open mind on the subject. Galactic space travel by conventional means with conventional formulas cannot be achieved! Archaic thinking needs a promotion.

"Scientist at the Jet Propulsion Laboratories, or JPL, can tell you how much fuel is required to get to Mars and how the cost is astronomical. To travel even farther and quicker, we need a new hypothesis. There is no proof that one exists. Multiple hypotheses exist after noting the characteristics of unusual phenomena that eyewitnesses have reported when observing UFOs, SFOs and crop circles. These observations are a clue to another dimension that we have not experienced."

"Another dimension! You think we travel in another dimension?" I tested.

"I do. It's called imaginary time," Edward returned. "Newton's third law is about the attraction of forces, lightning and Earth's magnetic poles: specifically, charged ions in clouds attracting opposite charged ions in Earth; the Earth's magnetic poles attracting each other to produce a magnetic field. When it comes to calculating the gravitational force between heavenly spheres, Newton's equations are nonexistent. "Gravity" is an undefined variable in all modern equations. The closest expression to defining gravity is acceleration or 32 feet per second per second, a constant value here on Earth. Acceleration has different values on other planets; but the gravitational attraction between planets has no formula. The planets in our solar system are held within their orbits by centripetal force and the gravitational pull between each planet and our sun. One force off-sets the other. Einstein's equations cannot account for a gravitational force between heavenly bodies or the force between galactic bodies. Consequently, we need different equations to explain the physics of our modern world. We need a formula with a term for gravity! Newton's formula, (F=ma), lacks functionality for space travel."

"I suppose you already have a new physical type of formula for gravity?"

"I do."

We bickered back and forth. I acted like another Earth scientist with an open mind and Edward enjoyed the chance to express his views. The irony is that I had learned all this science-stuff back on my home planet when I was in the fifth grade. If he could see my face behind the mask I wore, he would see that it was saying, "Of course, we know about traveling in another dimension. You can call it 'imaginary time' if you want." My surprise intensified when Edward showed me the charts.

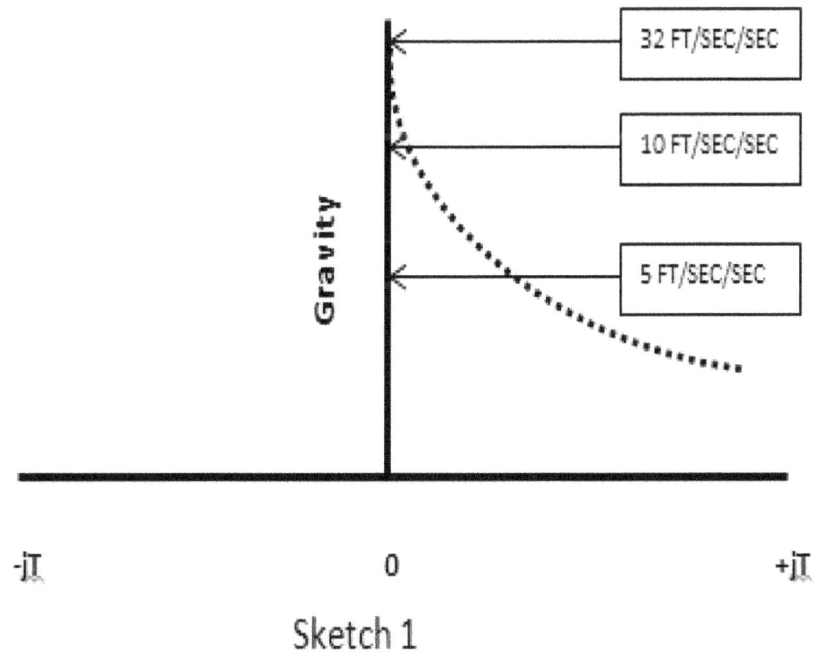

Sketch 1

"What does this chart represent?" I asked.

"It's my version of gravity versus imaginary time. I call it the GIT curve."

"Yes, but what is it saying?"

Edward slowly and methodically replied, "The curve is a fourth order, and possibly, a fifth order function where exponential factors, raised to the power of 4 and 5 are needed to write the formula. It —"

"Okay, in layman's terms, what is it saying?" I repeated.

"The chart says that gravity can be reduced while traveling further into the physical world of imaginary time. A -jT doesn't exists, but a +jT is the symbol for an object existing in another dimension."

"Can you describe an example?"

"Yes, I can. The Florida guy, that we talked about, found a way to reduce the weight of stones when he built Coral Castle. Likewise, the Egyptians in 2500 BC were capable of moving multi-ton stones in the construction of Khufu's pyramid."

Suddenly I remembered my history class in high school, on our planet, when Father Dean told us about the Sadees working in Egypt as Custodians, building a pyramid that was basically a machine, used to create a highway across the galaxy that we called *Orion's Highway*. I had to test Edward on his intuitive knowledge without letting him know that I was familiar with antigravity. "How do you suppose they lifted the stones?"

Suddenly I remembered my history class in high school, on our planet, when Father Dean told us about the Sadees working in Egypt as Custodians, building a pyramid that was basically a machine, used to create a highway across the galaxy that we called *Orion's Highway*. I had to test Edward on his intuitive knowledge without letting him know that I was familiar with antigravity. "How do you suppose they lifted the stones?"

"As an engineer, I would speculate they used several *ankhs* that produced a magnetic field in the elliptical bend and sound resonance in the cross piece at both ends of the ankh with transducers. An electrostatic field was provided by two staffs that they waved over the stone."

As he spoke, I could visualize the Sadees working the stone with their tools, the Sadees with their elongated heads and costume hats to cover their disfigurement, the Sadees deceiving the pharaoh about the need for an elaborate burial tomb, the Sadees, doing good, by giving the Egyptians employment and hope, the Sadees working to build a machine that would deposit beacons across the galaxy for other aliens to navigate by.

"Ankh" with Magnetic Coils and Audio Transducer behind Each Arm

"Do you have more on this topic?"

He pulled out a few pages from his manuscript, illustrating the procedure. He made it clear that electrical engineering was his experience, and chemical engineering was his weak suit. I looked at his writing.

A Manuscript from Edward's New Book

The aliens would start by placing a wet type of material on top of the stone block. The material could have been anything that would retain water; for example, a one-inch layer of cotton cloth, wool fiber or papyrus—anything that would soak up buckets of water. The aliens then placed several ankhs on top of the limestone block and under the saturated watery material.

The ankhs provided the magnetic force through looped induction coils and sound vibrations (greater than 20 kHz) with dual transducers at crossed ends. The

Egyptian god, Thoth, holding a Scepter and "Ankh" while wearing a breathing mask

scepter was a hand-held device that provided an electro-static field all around the limestone block as the alien waved the scepter. The ankhs had their own built-in power supply, a battery. The static field caused ions to occur among air molecules that provided a pathway for an electro-magnetic current flow.

The scepters had to be powered by a voltage generator that supplied power to RF circuits, creating the electro-magnetic force. The scepter was essentially an antenna that the alien waved around producing an electro-static field close to the stone wherever he chose. As the carbon dioxide exuded from the stone, per the equation:

$[2*(CaCO3) + H2O = Ca(OH)2 + CaO +2*(CO2)]$, the alien found it necessary to wear a headgear that acted as a breathing mask.

The picture shows the Egyptian god, Thoth, wearing a headgear, holding an ankh in his left hand and a scepter in his right hand. This ancient drawing found in the tombs of Egypt certifies the type of power aliens possessed.

The Lost Egyptian Method

Limestone is a sedimentary rock, composed mainly of skeletal fragments of marine organisms such as coral, amoeboid and mollusks. Its major materials are the minerals calcite and aragonite, which are different crystal forms of calcium carbonate ($CaCO3$). The abundance of oxygen, O3, signifies the removal from the lattice structure. Every compound has a lattice structure like infinitesimal sugar cubes with the positive and negative ions in a covalent bond at all eight corners of the cube.

The distance between each corner has an immense void compared to the size of the chemical bond that holds everything together. If limestone existed on a white dwarf star, the distance between corners compresses because a teaspoon of the white dwarf star weighs many tons. If the compressing of elements exists in the universe, the opposite process also exists, conversely—weight reduction through molecular expansion.

The best way to start is to replace the elements calcium, carbon and oxygen with different elements and eliminate carbon dioxide ($CO2$) which will permeate from the stone as a gas.

Today, chemists can heat limestone (same as calcium carbonate) to 825°C or 1517°F and produce calcium oxide and carbon dioxide as per the following equations with sequential steps:

1. $CaCO_3$ + Heat $\rightarrow$ $CaO + CO_2$

2. $CaO + H_2O \quad \rightarrow \quad Ca(OH)_2$

3. $2*(CaCO_3) + H_2O \quad \rightarrow \quad 2*(CaO) + H_2O + CO_2$

$\quad\quad\quad\quad\quad\quad\quad \rightarrow \quad Ca(OH)_2 + CaO + 2*(CO_2)$

Steps:

1. Heat causes limestone (CaC03) to change to calcium oxide (CaO) and carbon dioxide (CO2).

2. Calcium oxide (CaO) and added water (H2O) change to calcium hydroxide Ca(OH)2 .

3. Correct amounts of limestone, heat and water produce calcium hydroxide calcium oxide and carbon dioxide.

Carbon dioxide evaporates into the air, thereby reducing the weight of the quarried limestone. Limestone (calcium carbonate) and water chemically transform into calcium hydroxide and calcium oxide, both of which are a solid type of stone. The equation is valid because the number of elements on both sides of the equation is equal. Verification is as follows with the arrow sign replaced by an equal sign:

$2(Ca)+2(C)+2(H)+7(O)$

$\quad\quad\quad =1(Ca)+2(O)+2(H) +1(Ca)+1(O) +2(C)+4(O)$

$\quad\quad\quad =2(Ca) +2(C) + 2(H) + 7(O)$

The number of compounds and the number of covalent bonds for ionic compounds like Calcium Carbonate and Calcium Oxide have coequal valent electrons. The formula balances on both sides of the equal sign. It is correct, now.

The density of limestone, calcium hydroxide, calcium oxide and carbon dioxide are, respectively, 2.6, 2.2, 3.34 and 1.97 grams/centimeter cubed. The start density of limestone and the final density of calcium hydroxide and calcium oxide minus the density of carbon dioxide estimates as follows:

$$2*(CaCO_3) \rightarrow Ca(OH)_2 + CaO - 2*(CO_2)$$
$$2*(2.6) = 2.2 + 3.34 - 2*(1.97)$$
$$5.2 = 1.6 \quad \text{or a density reduction of 69.2 \% or}$$
~70%

Moving Egyptian Stones that Weighed 70% Less.

The process indicates that the density of limestone reduces by almost 70% (or the original weight times 30%, approximately). The heat-to-water treatment in steps 1 and 2 removes carbon dioxide. The process produces a 70-ton stone weighing only 21-tons. The stone retains its original volume — only the weight

changes. The boat that carried the stone from Aswan to Saqqara in ancient Egypt was 7-feet wide with a 4-foot draft and only 75 feet long as opposed to original calculations of 250 feet long. Transportation of the massive stone is now doable with a 75-foot boat, (250*30%) as opposed to a 250-foot boat!

I read his report and asked, "Doesn't the weight of the stone always stay reduced?"

"No," he said. "Read the next few pages."

His next pages were in reference to several 70-ton, underground sarcophagi, in Saqqara Egypt.

The Mystery of Stone Restoration

The Egyptians floated the 21-ton stone down a wide channel, more than 700 feet long, dug deep into the sloping ground. With the stone's edges resting on pylons, they closed off the water supplied by the Nile, disassembled the boat and allowed the sun to evaporate all the water. Then they bore deep, wide holes into the trench close to where the stone lay and along the length of the trench. They covered the stone and the bottom of the trench with a permanent stone roof and supporting walls using mud bricks. They flooded the trench once again to a level as high as the roof. The final step involved back filling of the trench, covering the roof with multiple feet of dirt and drilling deep holes from the surface down to the roof over the stone. They had provided drain holes below a tunnel and airshafts above a tunnel.

Years passed as the water in the chamber slowly drained all the while sucking air through the airshafts, laden with carbon dioxide. The air we breathe has a small percentage of carbon dioxide: approximately .04% by volume and 400 parts per million by quantity. In 2500 BC, the quantity of carbon dioxide ($CO2$) was 200 parts per million. The absorption of carbon dioxide for each sarcophagus took centuries. The process worked very slowly on the sarcophagus-stone, composed of calcium hydroxide and calcium oxide, sitting in a Nile River bed with water, evaporating up and through the underground holes, while carbon dioxide passed down through the holes, permeating the stone. The process automatically reversed itself as per the formula:

1. $Ca(OH)_2 + CaO + H_2O \rightarrow Ca(OH)_2 + Ca(OH)_2$
2. $Ca(OH)_2 + CO_2 \rightarrow CaCO_3 + H_2O$

Or

1. Calcium hydroxide and calcium oxide combined with water to produce calcium hydroxide

2. Calcium hydroxide combined with carbon dioxide within the atmosphere to produce water and calcium carbonate, the same substance as the original limestone.

After a few centuries, the 21-ton stone made from calcium hydroxide and calcium oxide increased in density as water and carbon dioxide permeate its inner core. The great grandchildren of the original laborers dedicated themselves to removing the dirt along a tunnel that led to the stone's location. The herculean task was possible only because they could work with a 21-ton stone aboard a 75-foot boat as opposed to a 70-ton stone aboard a 250-foot boat — a wonderment to this day.

Today, the stone has all the properties of a 70-ton limestone (CaCO3). In the arid desert, the lid covering the stone still sweats droplets of water underneath the bottom surface — a sign that the reversing formula is still working.

Enoch: lost listening to Edward, but still curious:

"You write about the need for *HEAT* to complete the process. Where does the *heat* come from?" I asked, looking up and then reading some more. "Oh. I see . . ."

Edward: on a roll, continuing his lengthy presentation:

"The remaining question is about the need for some kind of a heat-to-water treatment. The density of limestone in Imperial units is 162 pounds per feet cubed. So, a 70-ton stone would measure (70*2000/162) or 865 ft^3 or approximately 7'x5'x25', the same dimensions as a small bus. With this dimension in mind, the "heat-to-water treatment" is out-of-the-question. Ancient Egyptians could not have applied an 825 °C (1517 °F) heat application to a stone as big as a bus. An equivalent process was used to convert limestone into calcium oxide . . . as we shall see when we explore the properties of imaginary time. For now, the application of heat in the form of light is a possibility. A light from

The Dendera Lightbulb

an infrared bulb could have been used, a light like the Dendera Lightbulb."

Without leading him on, I asked, "Are you asking me to believe that an infrared light bulb, ten or twenty feet long, can produce the heat required for the chemical reaction to take place?"

"Yes, if it's positioned close to the stone that the Egyptians plan to move."

Edward's manuscript, although incomplete, sounded technically plausible. Major multi-ton stone-moving events took place all over his world, between four and five thousand years ago. Someone had to be teaching Earthlings how to move those stones, during a primitive stone-age era. I think I know who was responsible, but I'm not sure of their motives.

I had to see how close he was to the truth.

"What happens if that curve in your chart moves downward?" I questioned.

"Aha," he smiled, "now you're on to something."

Edward said he got his ideas, about the extension of the curve to zero gravity, from what he learned about Foo Fighters. He believed that the mysterious object, which crashed in Kecksburg, Pennsylvania, in December 9. 1965, was the same "bell-shaped"

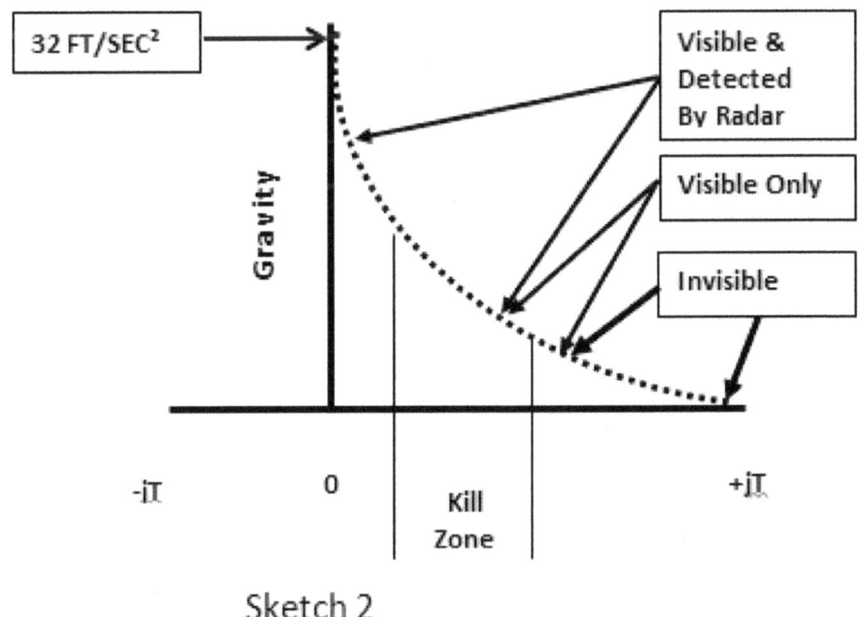

Sketch 2

object that the Germans invented, out of desperation, at the end of World War II, around 1944. He told me that he suspected that the bell or "Die Glocke" floated in outer space for 21-years, suspended in imaginary time. I copied his thoughts and conversations into my memoirs.

German scientists found the correct combination of three variables that produced two antigravity objects: the bell and Foo Fighters. They reported "high voltage," associated with the bell, produced the electromagnetic field; the rotating cylinders produced the "magnetic" field. The rotating cylinders, spinning in opposite directions, provided the variable "motion." The German scientists were successful in achieving "imaginary" time. Without previous experience, they accidently learned that objects in imaginary time drift away from Earth's orbit around the sun. Expressed another way, Earth will leave an object, suspended in imaginary time, at a rate of 67,000 miles per hour—the same speed Earth orbits the sun.

Similar to the rotating disk of the vehicle in the movie, The Time Machine, the rotating cylinders of "The Bell" imparted variables required for flight in imaginary time. Chains tied to a permanent concrete structure imbedded in the ground, harnessed the massive weight of the bell as it tried to lift above the ground. Speculation dictates that the bell broke loose from its mooring, floated in space for twenty years and landed in Pennsylvania after leaving a fiery trail across the sky. The military latched on to the bell shortly after it landed, but their chances of repeating the experiment were nil because the correct combination of the "three variables" is as remote as key-lock tumblers on a vault.

A twenty-year absence of the bell signifies that it did not leave Earth. If it merely floated in outer space, then another clue about imaginary time exists

Addition speculation states, "Foo Fighters were an emergency measure, taken by the Germans, to distract American and British bombers with their unknown weapon." The Foo Fighters had to be a miniature version of the bell: a smaller object that floats in imaginary time. Upon release at the right time of day, with small fins for guidance, their path would have an upward trajectory and their appearance would have look controlled while wind currents gave them an erratic movement. The lack of a radar return signifies that Foo Fighters were traveling away from Earth in imaginary time. The process of releasing objects into imaginary time is dangerous because the object can attempt to travel through the torso of the experimenter. Death would surely follow. And history records indicate that a few German scientists died during the laboratory project.

Hitler demanded his scientists to produce an advanced weapon for winning the war. Their discovery was so Earth shattering that they did not want to reveal their secret to the rest of the world if they lost the war. Consequently, many prisoners and many German soldiers and scientists were deliberately killed by a higher German command for a secret. The German scientists lost their lives! If Germany could not have the benefits of their secret, they did not want the rest of the world to have it either.

If the bell project had lasted several months before the end of the war thereby experimenting with imaginary time, it would have taken German scientists several more years to develop space flight with the same dedication and diligence they exhibited. As we move forward, we will see greater difficulty in developing space flight in comparison to learning about imaginary time.

Edward tried to indicate on his chart how objects in imaginary time can behave differently, when undetected by radar, deep into imaginary time and when visible at other times along the curve or the GIT curve, as he calls it.

Curious about the area he labeled as Kill Zone, I asked, "What does the mid-curve signify, where Earth's gravitational force is reduced?"

Edward explained, "I believe the German scientists discovered, accidently, during their initial experiments, that the human body cannot occupy two different dimensions at the same time. Some of their lab-tecks were killed when their Foo missile floated through space and entered their bodies. That is why they tried to weaponize their Foo missiles to bring down American bombers."

"Did it work?"

"No. According to my research, the pilots flew right through the transparent glowing objects they saw. Who's to say, if they really worked."

"How would you describe the experience aboard an object, traveling in imaginary time?" I asked.

"The best way to describe light in imaginary time is analogous to the reflection of an object in a mirror. Objects reflect their image, but they do not exist on the other side of the mirror. All objects that exist in the cosmos appear as reflection even though they do exist. This allows spaceships to pass directly through solid objects, water, dust and debris."

"What happens if your GIT curve moves lower?"

"I'm not sure," Edward commented, while studying hies third sketch. "But I can speculate that a newer physics world exists, whereby gravity behaves like magnets with positive poles and negative poles. It would signify that space travelers don't require the *pulling* force of the Earth to launch their ships; they can utilize Earth's *pushing* force."

While sitting in the library's conference room, Edward broke his concentration of the dream world he was in and asked with a sudden and cold icy stare, "So, Enoch, how did you travel to Earth from your planet?"

I knew he would eventually ask that question. Unlike Nostradamus and Mozart, they didn't care where I came from. In their minds, I came from a never-never land and I worked on a mission for someone who lived in never land. Edward, however,

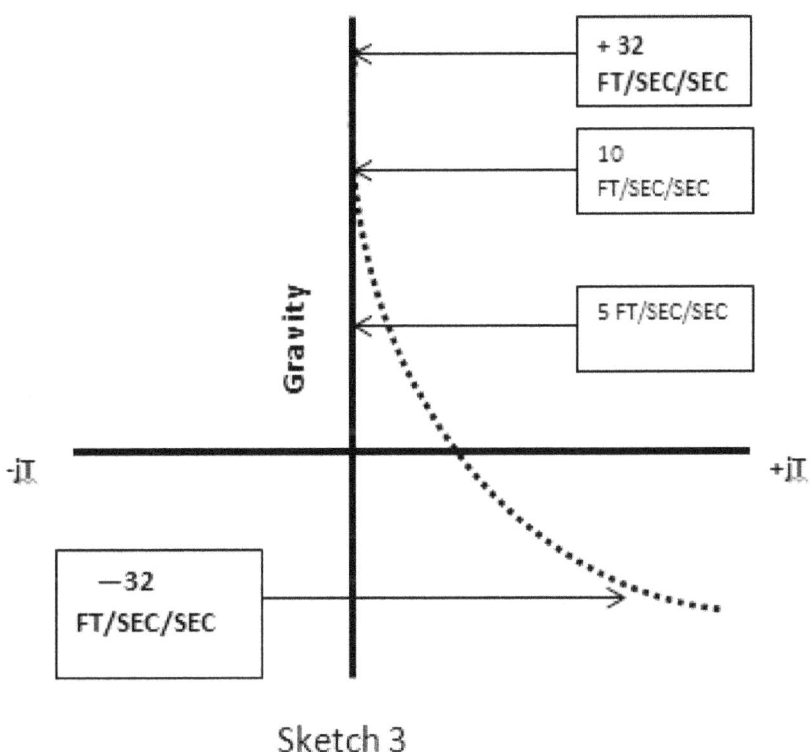

Sketch 3

was different. He had a typical, inquisitive engineering mind, born into the twentieth century.

I checked his stare, looked at him firmly, and said, "I was brought here."

"You were brought here to Earth!" he mimicked.

"Yes."

But how were you brought here? How did your ship or whatever you call it, fly through the cosmos?"

"I don't know."

"What kind of propulsion does your UFO have?"

"I don't know."

"Okay," he reasoned, appearing perturbed. "You don't know? I just explained different ways of applying antigravity, different ways of flying through space, and you don't know!"

"Let me ask you, Edward," I politely replied, "What kind of car do you drive and how many cylinders does it have?"

"I drive a 2007 Buick, Lucerne, and it has six cylinders."

"Good. What type of manifold does it have?"

"I don't know."

"Well, is the manifold a header or exhaust type?"

"I don't know," Edward echoed quietly.

"How about the induction coil that fires the spark plugs? Is it there?"

"I see where you're going with this, Enoch. I'm sorry."

"I'm sorry too. The truth of the matter is that I was brought to your planet by my friend. You can think of him as a chauffeur, who knows all about the propulsion of a galactic spaceships, He's just another human being like me, like you,"

"What's his name?"

"His name is Charlie. I've known him for almost one thousand years."

"One thousand years?"

Oh boy, I thought, here we go again. "Let's leave it there. And get on with your book writing business. Okay?"

"Okay."

On one day, out of the clear blue, Edward asked, "Are there any more Custodians, like yourself, helping individuals here in

America?" It was strange that Edward should ask the same type of question Mozart asked me many years ago.

While at home on Bethel, I had been following the news reports about musicians on Earth. Michael Jackson was one of those many musicians. I explained to Edward that a Custodian had helper Michael Jackson because one song, in particular, catapulted his fame in 1984, beyond measure. I told Edward the name of the song was *Billie Jean* and that he should lend an eye to the words of the song, I pulled up the words on my pocket-top:

Billie Jean

She was more like a beauty queen from a movie scene
I said don't mind, but what do you mean, I am the one
Who will dance on the floor in the round?
She said I am the one, who will dance on the floor in the round

She told me her name was Billie Jean, as she caused a scene
Then every head turned with eyes that dreamed of being the one
Who will dance on the floor in the round

People always told me be careful of what you do
And don't go around breaking young girls' hearts
And mother always told me be careful of who you love
And be careful of what you do 'cause the lie becomes the truth

Billie Jean is not my lover
She's just a girl who claims that I am the one
But the kid is not my son
She says I am the one, but the kid is not my son

For forty days and forty nights
The law was on her side
But who can stand when she's in demand
Her schemes and plans
'Cause we danced on the floor in the round
So take my strong advice, just remember to always think twice
(Do think twice, do think twice)

She told my baby we'd danced 'til three, then she looked at me
Then showed a photo my baby cried his eyes were like mine (oh,
no)
'Cause we danced on the floor in the round, baby

People always told me be careful of what you do
And don't go around breaking young girls' hearts
She came and stood right by me
Just the smell of sweet perfume
This happened much too soon
She called me to her room

Billie Jean is not my lover
She's just a girl who claims that I am the one
But the kid is not my son

Billie Jean is not my lover
She's just a girl who claims that I am the one
But the kid is not my son
She says I am the one, but the kid is not my son

She says I am the one, but the kid is not my son
Billie Jean is not my lover
She's just a girl who claims that I am the one

But the kid is not my son
She says I am the one, but the kid is not my son
She says I am the one
You know what you did, (she says he is my son) breaking my heart
babe
She says I am the one
Billie Jean is not my lover
Billie Jean is not my lover
Billie Jean is not my lover

Edward took his eyes off my pocket-top computer. His mind
was drifting again. "Edward," I said loudly, "you *did* want to know

about other Custodians and what they *did*? . . . Right? Don't you think the words to this song are unique?"

"In what way?"

"*In what way?*" I repeated, mocking his voice and assuming he had brain-fog.

He couldn't see that one verse, about "forty days and forty nights", didn't fit the rest of the words. I knew that one verse was the signature of a Custodian because galactic travelers know it takes forty days and forty nights to accelerate to the next warp speed at 8-gs of physical stress force. The rest of the song is a lesson about being moral — a lesson in claiming responsibility.

"Oh, Okay," he said with a shrug—the same response Mozart gave me.

I started thinking about the similarity in response between a twenty-first-century man, Edward, and an eighteenth-century man, Amadeus Mozart.

Both men, Edward and Mozart, wrapped up in their work, hell-bent on making a claim, one in science the other in music, couldn't see the forest through the trees. Jackson's song about "Billie Jean" had verbal clarity, morality and a lesson for both people, the singer and his lover. If I could speak my thoughts without insulting them, I would have said, "Look around you. It's a large world out there!"

I used my pocket-top to log into Earth's internet. Our own internet on Bethel is more precise, but I typed in the word: "Who was Count Saint Germain?" As per the internet, he was a legendary spiritual master (1710—1784) of theosophical teachings. The internet link to my own planet displayed the same information. However, the internet on Earth displayed additional information when asked specific questions, related to historical people.

History Note:

What happened to Saint Germain?

Germain claimed to have lived for over five hundred years, extending his life through his alchemical secrets. St. Germain died in 1784, at the assumed age of seventy-four, in his residence in Schleswig, a territory that would later become the border between Germany and Denmark. (As per the internet, Mar 9, 2020)

What did Saint Germain do?

Saint Germain's spiritual title is said to be Lord of Civilization, and his task is the establishment of the new civilization of the Age of Aquarius. He is said to telepathically influence people who are seen by him as being instrumental in bringing about the new civilization of the Age of Aquarius.

Additional Notes:

He was venerated as a saint in both the Catholic Church and the Eastern Orthodox Church. Abstract reports indicate that he bragged he could live forever, that he was a time traveler, and that he was seen many years after he died. He was known to have been a courtier, adventurer, inventor, alchemist, pianist, violinist, and amateur composer.

I instantly knew that Saint Germain was walking in my foot-steps; we both had an appreciation for music, we both could state we lived for hundreds of years, and we both had the same mission——to help man in his plight, and to influence civilization. The rhythm of the song had a beat that was remarkably different than Michael Jackson's other songs. "Billie Jean" was written with lyrics and a melody in a heptatonic scale. A

Edward was the type of guy who couldn't let go of his ideas about space travel. He said that he had written and published two books, titled *Galactic Travel at Warp Speed in Imaginary Time* and *Orion's Highway Across the Galaxy.* According to Edward, both his books described a technique for discovering *Imaginary Time* and for the construction of a spaceship. He claimed that the odds of discovering another dimension with his technique was something like one in nine thousand on the first try, after mixing three variables in the correct proportions, causing resonance among E-fields, H-fields and motion (or vibration).

The most interesting thing about Edward was his motivation. He believed his government was wasting their money on rocket propelled spaceships when they could have been using that money for the poor.

He told me that he had seen Mr. Elon Musk on TV appealing to scientists about their plan to colonize Mars, a planet with almost zero atmospheric pressure and traces of carbon dioxide floating in the air. Edward wrote a four-page letter to the board at Tesla, hoping they would forward the letter to Elon because his home address wasn't public information. In his letter, Edward wrote, "Dear Mr. Musk, forget about making Mars a place to live! Your number one problem is converting carbon dioxide to carbon and oxygen. If you want to do that, then why not improve the atmospheric quality here on Earth and eliminate Global Warming? If you succeed with the conversion process I'm sending you, your children and their children will be the richest people in the world with patent rights."

"Edward," I asked, "are we talking about alchemy . . . like the transformation of lead into gold? Huh?"

"Mm-hmm, something like that, Enoch. However, Gold is a noble element—nothing affects it. So, changing elements to different elements is impossible," he said. "The Egyptians had their way of resonating limestone into a lighter weight, lattice-structured stone by placing the stone into imaginary time. If they could transform stone, don't you think it's possible to transform a gas? Every property has a self-resonance where the lattice structure breaks down into something else."

"What did you write to Elon Musk?"

"I explained with a diagram how he could start with a three-foot diameter toroidal coil to induce H-fields across a gap, sliced into the circular toroid. He would have to experiment with E-fields and sound to produce the correct resonance. The product would be pure oxygen and the flaking of carbon, as soot, to be blown away from the apparatus."

"Could you sketch what the apparatus would look like?" I asked.

"Sure. In my engineering opinion, these conversion plants would save Earth from extreme seasonal changes and reverse Global Warming."

"Did you ever get a response to your letter from Mr. Elon Musk?"

"No. It's strange he would make a public request on television, not leave his forwarding address, and fail to answer my detailed four-page letter," Edward frowned.

"Oh, well."

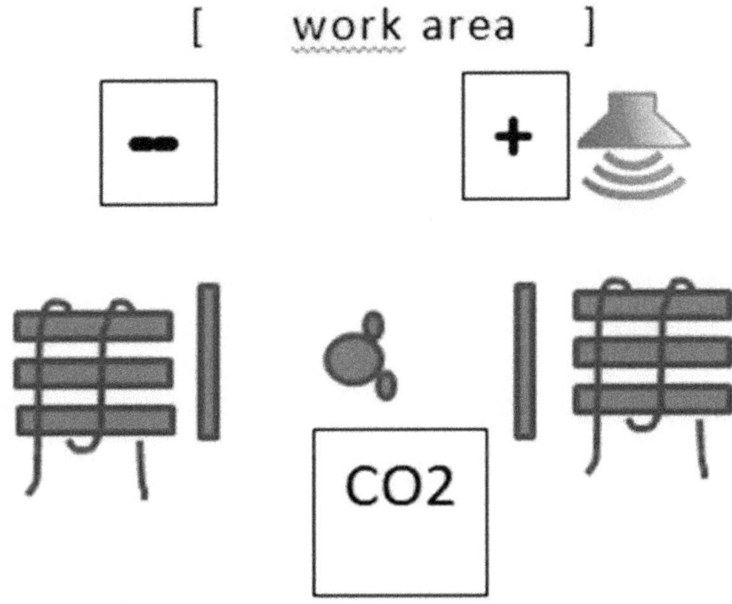

The Lord knows that Earth in the twenty-first century was having more than its share of world problems . . . and I had to get home.

Moon Base 1

I had committed a crime and after the trial, I found myself sitting on a desert-moon with an M-class rating. The moon-base had a population of one. The proceeds of the trial were too embarrassing to write down in this autobiography, but in my mind, I kept reviewing them repeatedly. I can still see myself standing in front of a high tribunal with four Celestials, sitting at their lofty benches and one Custodian, acting as their interpreter, where I stood. Father Aye walked briskly between the four judges trying to explain, "The Earthlings would have created the steroid compound within another fifty or seventy years if Enoch had not introduced it to them." Then he added, "Enoch had no other choice if he wanted the patient to live so that Doctor Barnard could become famous. To meet this goal, he was obligated to inject the steroid compound into the patient's drip bag."

The ruling came back from the four judges and an interpreter for the Celestial. Through an interpreter, they had instructed me to take care of the client and no one else. With a final coup of innuendos, the interpreter said, "Enoch you had the temerity to administer a steroid to Dr. Barnard's patient in opposition to our rules thereby, disregarding the 'acceleration of knowledge.' You have committed the same sin as Adam and Eve when they ate fruit from the tree of knowledge. Like them, you were told not to do so."

Father Aye had done his best to protect me. To become my defense attorney, he had to step down permanently as high priest. There was no going back to his former position. Steve, Bill, Charlie, Beena and Brianna — they all testified to my worth as a Custodian. After all the concluding arguments, the court found me guilty.

I was in prison now, a prison where I could roam miles and miles into either direction among the tumbleweed, saguaros, and ocotillo cactuses. My house consisted of a one-room, cinder-block abode with open windows, a bed, a sink, a toilet, a chair, a table, and a combination microwave/freezer where I kept my food. The microwave/freezer was the only device that was solar powered. My only personal possession was my pocket-top with only a few backup batteries and a solar recharger. For entertainment, I would read the manuscripts of Nostradamus that I had transferred to my personal pocket-top. When the boredom got bad, I would listen to Mozart with ear-buds. Holding an acacia twig as a baton, I orchestrated the music to entertain tall saguaro cacti and even short barrel cacti. I conducted Mozart's music with different toccatas for each plant: thunderously loud music for the tall ones and soft tender music for the short.

Then I realized that I was experiencing the same five emotions that Mozart had had when he died at an early age: denial, anger, excuses, depression, and acceptance. If I had not checked myself, I would not be writing about beautiful desert landscapes and spectacular sunsets. From that point on, I tamed my partial insanity and depression by writing my life's story on my pocket-top. I spent years writing my adventures and recalling personal and sometimes, intimate conversations with people on Earth.

THE DESERT

The orange glow from the setting desert sun, the reduced summer heat, the sweet fragrancy of desert bloom flowers piercing the evening air—all signified a change to a more tolerable day. The bittersweet flavor of being a Custodian on Earth—its trials, challenges, and joyous moments working with people that became famous—had its own psychological rewards. On Earth, I accumulated an abundance of fond memories that enumerated the lonely experiences I retain living on a desert with its own innate beauty. I was a prisoner capable of appreciating desert beauty.

I often wondered about the severity of the punishment the Sadees encountered when they had to relocate to another planet. The difficulty of living unfettered on a new planet without a rule of law imposed by the Celestials or the medical benefits they provided must have left the Sadees vindictive. I also wondered about the punishment of Milo who killed thousands of Earthlings with his bubonic aerosol. Was he justified trying to save his people by using Earthlings as guinea pigs to obtain a vaccine from a survivor? There are always two sides to a story, the yin and the yang.

My evenings watching the stars at night calmed my nerves with their brilliance more radiant than the ones seen on Earth or Bethel. If I had a gigantic telescope that would allow me to witness the events on Earth from the Moon Base where I stood, I would see people moving quickly and cars whizzing by like a movie film playing in a fast-forward motion.

I started my autobiography to introduce the reader to events that are inconceivable by Earthlings' standards. The most interesting event is the longevity of Moses—120 years. I stated that his lifespan could have been 136 years if he had lived during the full reign of Ramesses II. This is a conflict in numbers. Our historical records lack additional information on this subject. After having been a Custodian and watching my chronological years speed up living on Earth and slow down living on Bethel, I have come to believe that Moses was a special guest on Geesal, the home planet of the Celestial, where he learned the genealogy of his ancestors and also, where he really talked to God. He may have been on Geesal in God's presence before his return from Mount Sinai. He wrote the first five chapters of the Bible with historical references that only the Celestials could have given him with so many references to numbers. His presence on another planet explains how he could have lived 136 years during the end of the reign of Amenhotep III (BC 1349) to end of Ramesses' II reign (BC 1213). In reflection, my younger days took me through the Crusades in AD 1187 to my incarceration in AD 2025—a total of 838 years that passed on Earth.

For every month that passes on this moon during my incarceration, ten months transpire on Earth, but a month here truly feels like one month anywhere on Bethel or Geesal. One month here consists of thirty days. However, one day here is slightly longer than a day on Earth or Bethel. One day on this moon consists of twenty hours of sunshine without a cloud in the sky and ten hours of darkness.

Every two months, a spacecraft would land on my dusty moon with a visitor from Bethel to bring frozen food supplies. A conversation with them was limited as per Celestials' orders. Without the sound of a voice for months at a time, I was anxious to hear anyone's voice. And then one day, it was Charlie's voice.

"I'm taking you home Enoch," he said. "You've done your time. The Celestials reconsidered your case."

On the way home traveling inside his W-25 at twenty-five times the speed of light, Charlie asked, "Do you know why the Celestials commuted your sentence?"

"I don't know," I replied with a sardonic voice. "Maybe Father Aye made sculpturesque promises with visual waving of his arms to no avail. Maybe he told them what they wanted to hear: 'that I would go forth and multiply.'"

"You sound angry, Enoch."

"Perhaps I shouldn't be so reflective about the twenty-seven years I spent on a desolated moon. That's in the past now. I'm grateful the Custodians released me, but I still don't know why they commuted my life-sentence."

"Now you're sounding better. Besides, that's only 2.7 years in biological time," Charlie encouraged.

"I have a trillion questions. How is every one back home? I've written an autobiography. Can you get it published on Earth? Tell me about Brianna. Tell me about Beena."

"Well, Steve and his wife have great grandchildren now. They're helping to increase the population as per the Bible. Brianna still owns her tavern. Father Aye, Bill and Beena have passed on."

"Beena died?"

"Yes. She asked that I give you this letter."

I opened the letter and it read.

Dear Enoch,

I haven't been feeling well lately: a lot of chest pains. I had heard about your release and hoped to see you when you came home. I wanted to explain what happened the day I pretended to be your patient on the operating table. It was a beautiful moment for two bodies to bond. I will always cherish that moment and remember how much we loved each other. As a result of that union, you have a son now. I named our son after you. Please take good care of him and raise him to be a successful Custodian like yourself — to have empathy, to care for the indigent and to be a Brother's Keeper.

I have always loved you,

Beena

As I come to the end of my life span, writing my manuscript on a rickety old table holding my rusty pocket top, I realized that Beena truly loved me until the time she died many years ago. There is no going back to say: "and I love you too." All I have left is her tear-stained letter and these weakened hands typing more spelling mistakes with feeble fingers. Looking back, I gave her nothing, but she gave me a beautiful son. I raised him from a small child to a handsome young man that also became a Custodian—a wish that Beena wanted. With only a little energy left in my ability to type, I write my final chapter about events that happened in the mid-twenty-first century.

Enoch

The Earth year is 2087, as I finish writing my manuscript. I'm too old and too weary to carry on. My friend Charlie will transport it to Earth where it will be published. To some extent, the predictions of events in the twenty-first century by Nostradamus did come true. In the latter part of the century, Nostradamus predicted world famine due to an infestation by locust. Our Scouts, who continued to report events on Earth, announced the devastation, but they weren't sure how Earth was scorched. In their report, they referenced a similar event that occurred in Greek mythology, when a demigod named Phaeton drove Apollo's chariot. Phaethon asked to be allowed to drive the chariot of the sun through the heavens for a single day. The Earth froze when the horses climbed too high. When Phaeton lost control, the sun-chariot swung too low, scorching the Earth. The message is clear. Global Warming was predicted by Nostradamus as it was foretold in the mythological past as a potential catastrophe.

My first client, Nostradamus, was pliable in character and in his ability to learn from the images produced by the pocket top. My second client, Mozart, was more difficult to impress because he had grown up as an uninhibited young man with his own ideas of social convention. What is there to say about Dr. Christiaan Barnard, except that he was a terrific surgeon when he wasn't chasing women. My fourth client, was my most difficult protégé. His books and his ideas about galactic space travel faded out over time, but the short stories that he wrote for practice survived for decades on an internet tabloid titled, *I Remember*. The forerunner of the tabloid was a magazine titled, *Readers' Digest.* When I was working with Edward in 2020, he started reading library books to improve his writing skills.

Working as his Custodian, I may have impressed him with my repetitive comments, "You have to *LIVE* the experience when you write in the first-person voice or the third person voice. You can write sentences with words similar to the buds on a rose bush, but you also have to describe that beautiful red rose with additional words when it blooms. When you're writing in the first person, you have to describe your emotions. For example, 'After being told to shut up and sit down by the committee chairperson, there I stood, a clinched fist in one hand and the other hand still holding the microphone.' If you're writing in the third person, then use the same example by substituting 'I' for 'he, she or them'. Try to be as descriptive as you can with your compositions."

I've included his first composition, herein, because I like the way he stopped to describe the pear tree growing with its knurly bark. His practice stories lasted in easy-reading books over the decades, but his books with engineering advice withered because Edward had trouble with fun-to-read sentences when he wrote about scientific descriptions of atoms, particles, and galactic space.

Attached are some of his short stories here within my final chapter. Edward's stories are flashbacks during the time when he was twelve, twenty-two, and forty-seven years old. As a tribute to his effort, I prefer to include his stories within my autobiography.

I Remember Grandpa

"Chaa'lie," my grandmother would say in a soft commanding voice, "you gonna make-a the windows clean."

My grandparents migrated from Sicily at the turn of the century when they were young, energetic, and filled with dreams of a better life in Chicago. My grandmother always had a honey-do list for my grandfather, who was enjoying his retirement years and didn't want to be bothered. Born with an Italian name of Ciero, he had it Americanized to Charlie.

Europeans had a way of passing knowledge and intelligence to their offspring. The best lesson I learned from my grandfather occurred when he filled a glass of water half way at the kitchen sink and said, "This is good." As the water continued to flow out of the faucet, the water in the glass began to overflow. My grandfather said, "This is bad!—Why is this bad?"

Too young to understand his meaning, I shrugged. "I don't know why it went from good to bad. Can you do it again?"

He repeated the same process with the water flowing at a slower rate and then asked, "Why is it bad?"

"I don't know, Papa," I said in despair. "Is it bad because you're wasting water?"

"No, it's bad because *excess* in anything is never a good policy. Wine, smoking, eating food or too much candy should never be consumed in excess. As you grow older, you'll find that there so many other things you're going to want to do in excess. You'll pay for it unless you remember the water-glass lesson."

My grandparents lived in a two-flat Bungalow with a small serene back yard, enclosed by a two-foot white picket fence that enclosed tomato plants, basil shoots, and a tall lonesome-looking pear tree, surrounded by spent grass.

"Papa," I asked, "what kind of tree is this?"

"It's a pear tree," he replied, while walking in a direction further from my grandmother's voice.

"But, Papa—"

"Yes . . ." His voice cast into the other direction.

I had his attention. "If it's a pear tree, how come I don't see any tiny pears?" Then he turned to face me.

"Because it's very old."

I was only a twelve-year-old kid at the time, but I remember feeling sorry for that pear tree with its knurly bark, its severely pruned branches, its bent-over trunk—only ten feet above the ground. My grandfather was old also, but he was fun to be around. I got all my hair cuts for free because he had retired as a barber. I had secretly used his barber's chair, down in the basement, as my personal merry-go-round. Endless bottles of fragrant after-shave stood on the marble shelf below the huge mirror. I experimented with a few drops from each oddly-curved bottle, thinking it was hair oil.

"Chaa'lie," she cried out again. "When'na yu gonna—"

"Yeah, yeah, yeah," he shouted and then mumbled some more words in Italian, which had to be premium swear words. I followed behind him as he walked from the alley, past the white picket fence, and up into the gray colored wooden porch where my grandmother stood.

Together, my grandfather and I washed all the windows and even scrubbed down the ceiling above the stairway leading down into the basement. I remember my precarious climb up the six foot ladder in its folded position with two legs resting on a stair and the other two legs suspended by my grandfather who held them up in mid-air. My grandmother watched, hoping her twelve-year-old grandson wouldn't fall off the ladder and tumble down the stairs.

"Papa," I said, somewhat laughing. "A blob of soap fell off the sponge and landed on your forehead with a loud splat."

"Don't worry," he said. "It's all-ah right. Just-a keep-a going."

I remember the situation well because my grandfather looked funny with a large blob of soap suds sitting on his forehead amidst his long thinning hair and moving dangerously closer to his eyeball. If he were debilitated with soap in his eye, he still would have said, "Just-a keep-a going."

The point of this story is that all of us are coming from somewhere as we grow older. My grandfather died seven years later. I was unable to attend his funeral because the navy wouldn't release me from boot camp on my conflicting graduation day. However, I did travel home on the following day.

Looking back, I gained an epiphany by realizing that my grandfather was in his seventies when he died with his own honey-do list and that I'm in my eighties, now, with my own honey-do list. And like that bent-over pear tree, things don't come easily. If I could only remember those Italian swear words—.

The end

Edward

WV-2: Willy Victor Two

Dropping suddenly in altitude, causing our ears to pop, our airplane, called a WV-2, Super Constellation, descended rapidly as our captain announced over the PA system, "We're going down. All hands don your poop suits. I can't feather engine number four any longer."

The year was 1959; at the tender age of twenty-two years, I was in a situation, a greenhorn about poop suits, a kid complaining how my bunk above the wings, a few feet from the engine, rattled my teeth when I slept. It was my second mission, flying a circular barrier between Midway Island and Alaska. I was a third-class petty officer in charge of repairing all electronic equipment and observing Russian radar signatures on a monitor screen when the equipment wasn't breaking down. Five other sailors monitored our radar returns for intercontinental ballistic missiles.

We flew an early warning reconnaissance plane, designed to protect Americans from Russian launched ICBM missiles. The plane was built by Lockheed and designed with four reciprocating engines, two radar domes for altitude and azimuth detection, zero armament; specifically, no guns, no cannons, no bombs, only a honey bucket that the captain said we could drop on Russian ships if conditions really got bad.

"If we see a Russian sub, we'll drop the honey bucket down its periscope," said the captain with encouraging words and zero practicality. As a new crewmember, I knew my job, but the meaning of a poop suit and a honey bucket were never taught during the nine months in technician repair school that I had attended.

For eighteen hours of continuous flying between Alaska and Midway Island, two separate crews, consisting of eighteen sailors total, worked separate shifts, nine sailors sleeping, nine sailors identifying radar blips and reporting their findings to Hickam Air Force base in Hawaii, where the message was relayed to SAC in Colorado, arriving within minutes.

On one occasion during my fifth mission, I believe, our radioman errored when he accidentally reported a Dumbo airplane, traveling at 1,500 mph. I quickly learned another new word: a Dumbo is a sailor's nickname for any plane traveling less than 150 mph. Our radioman had errored by a factor of ten, causing fighter jets to scramble our area, in the middle of the Pacific, within ten minutes. With the intercom turned on, we heard the captain of the jet fighter ask our captain, "I'm here now! Where the hell is that plane doing 1500 (mph)?" Every sailor on board knew our approximate position; that is, hundreds of miles from a military base in Alaska, twenty-five thousand feet above icy cold waters, somewhere above the Pacific Ocean, in the middle of nowhere.

During my second mission, still flying as an apprentice in the middle of nowhere, there was no friendly voice from a visiting fighter pilot swearing his head off because he had been aroused from a warm bed where he slept comfortably, only moments ago. A crisis was brewing with engine number four. We were going down.

The captain had given his warning. Suddenly, eighteen sailors crammed the aisle, thirty-six elbows pushing and accidently shoving shipmates. Crewmembers scrambled through the plane's passageways looking for their poop suits, somewhere stowed in cabinets never opened before. Because this was my second trip across the Pacific, I had no idea what I was looking for—namely a poop suit: basically, a one-piece thickly padded material with only one long zipper, in front, spanning a sailor's torso. Horizontal zippers in the rear were missing. "Why do we have to wear these suits?" I asked a fellow seaman.

"Because the Pacific waters, this far north, are *so freezing cold* you wouldn't survive for more than two minutes. Donning your suit will give you an extra four minutes," he replied, hastily slipping into his own suit. He had added different swear words to describe *so freezing cold*.

In my mind, the purpose of a poop suit seemed inadequate, but the procedure of crash landing at sea—our only alternative––had been justified with practice drills, involving a twenty-man life raft deployed from the plane with sailors merging into the sea for a few minutes and swimming to their life-saving miniature boat.

A sigh of relief came when our pilot announced that he could land the plane at Adak, Alaska. Within the same breath of truth, he added a disclaimer to his expertise by saying that the landing on Adak's runway is "tricky" because he had to fly over a small mountain on his approach. He had to descend in a down-up-down direction to clear the mountain with only three engines working, each engine consisting of two rows of eight air-cooled, reciprocating cylinders. Instead of landing with sixty-four cylinders, our pilot was attempting to land with forty-eight cylinders on the other side of a mountain, blocking the runway. All crewmembers sat upright in their buckled seats, staring with chalky faces into nowhere, firmly gripping their armrest, listening to three engines roaring, visualizing a lopsided plane, flying a roller coaster path over a mountain.

I was delighted we landed safely. I remember congratulating our pilot, Lieutenant Galliger, as he calmly requested that I should take responsibility along with another seaman for emptying the "honey bucket."

"What's a honey bucket?" I asked, of my partner.

"It's that fifty-pound, shit'en toilet located in the back of the plane. The same one you and everyone else have been using." This was my second trip as an "Airedale" in the U.S. Navy, a journey that branded itself into my memory cells; the same memory cells that recall the radioman wasn't the only crewmember who made a serious mistake. Two other sailors endangered the plane as we shall see.

Adak, Alaska

Adak Island is part of the Aleutian Islands in Western Alaska. It has a rugged 275-square mile terrain of tree-less, rocky volcanic headlands. When I was there in the middle of July, 1959, I saw lumps of grass growing three feet high, a sun that looked like it would never set at midnight, fellow sailors bathing in the shower, pale and white skinned next to my golden tan that I had received days before on Midway Island.

After three weeks of logging in two hundred hours of flight time, we were ready to go home to Hawaii. Lieutenant Galliger and his officers, the copilot and navigator, had accomplished their mission. Once again, we were flying at three o'clock in the morning while our navigator sighted the stars, providing guidance to our pilot while our copilot slept. On that particular night, I couldn't sleep. I wandered into the galley for a glass of water. Then I wandered a few more feet forward into the cockpit area, where Lieutenant Galliger sat alone staring out of the window into the night's darkness. I didn't begrudge him after he had assigned me the honey bucket detail. I felt sorry for this man sitting all alone: this man, thirty-five-ish years old, tall, lean, likeable, career oriented, calm under pressure.

"Hi Captain," I said as I poked my head into the cockpit. "Do you mind if I keep you company?"

"Grab the copilot's chair," he responded.

For the next twenty minutes, or so we talked about how lonely it must get sitting in the pilot's chair doing nothing. I found agreement and learned that the most difficult task came during the procedure of "take-off and landing" a WV-2 plane, weighting 105,000 pounds and measuring 99 feet long.

With both of us looking out the plane's window while cruising at 365 mph, the navigator interrupted our conversation by announcing over the intercom that he was requesting a change in heading.

"Captain," he said, "please come to bearing 305 degrees."

Lieutenant Galliger acknowledged his request, and then turned to look at me and ask, "Would you like to fly the plane?"

"Me? Fly the plane?" I said sheepishly. I was a third-class petty officer responsible for repairing electronic equipment on the plane. I thought: flying the entire plane and all its do-dads was out of the question. The instrument panel alone looked overwhelming. And then, there was the gearshift gismo that presumably accelerated the engines.

"Look," he said, "the plane is on automatic pilot right now. All you have to do is flip this toggle switch right there. Do you see where I'm pointing?"

I looked down at a simplified, stubby toggle switch and tried to imagined how it could fly the entire plane in the up position all by itself. "Nah," I said, "I'm thirsty. I'm thinking of going back to the galley for another glass of water."

Lieutenant Galliger came back with a stronger persistence, "Flip this switch and then turn this knob here until the dial comes to 305 degrees. It's easy."

Once again, I looked down at a four-inch diameter knob, raised about a half-inch from the control panel and thought: do I turn it to the left or the right, do I turn it fast or slow?

After a full minute of studying my options, Lieutenant Galliger grabbed my hand, placed it over the four-inch diameter knob with his hand on top of mine. Judging by the speed of his action, I assumed I needed to turn the knob fast; the direction didn't matter. I turned the knob quickly in a counter clockwise direction. With the same quickness, the 105,000-pound plane went into a steep left dive. Once again, two more crewmembers had made an error. The plane was turning to the left and losing altitude as well.

I believe I saw it all—in slow motion, what seemed like ages. Galliger bolted upright in his chair, his eyes intently focused on the control panel, his eye-popping-jaw-dropping facial expression, his hands (maybe six of them), reaching, touching every knob, gearshift, gismo, steering wheel, and forcing them to compensate. Galliger reacted to the crisis for a period of time that seemed to last forever until the plane leveled off.

I was at fault; Galliger was at fault for asking me to fly the plane. In the end, it was another experience I'll always remember, especially Lieutenant Galliger's response when I told him that I was going back to the galley for a glass of water.

Looking directly into my face, eyeball to eyeball, he firmly said, "Sailor, I think you better!"

As I stood in the galley, a seaman came running up to me and asked, "What happened?" and then added, "Johnson was sleeping in his lower bunk and came rolling out into the middle of the aisle. Good thing he wasn't in the upper bunk."

Now that I'm much older, I think back and remember this experience as kind of funny . . . in its own way. I can picture Johnson, a deep sleeper, rolling out of his bunkbed at a forty-five-degree angle and continuing to sleep, fetus style, in the middle of the aisle—a true sailor, able to sleep anywhere.

These events are special, probably because I was young and everything made an impression. The fun times were as common as the scary times, like "takeoff."

The Takeoff

If you're asking, "What's it like during takeoff in a WV-2 from Midway Island", I'll tell you:

You're sitting in your strapped chair at the edge of the runway, looking at the back of the plane, and thinking, why is my chair turned around? At least I can look out the window and see a few goony birds flying over the island. The plane's interior lights are turned off. Bouncing off the engine's propellers, daylight is flickering through your window into the cabin. You're preparing for takeoff by mentally counting the passing seconds, "One thousand one, . . . one thousand two," and so on. The pilot guns the four engines and releases the brakes moments before they squeal metal against metal. The plane is still rolling, "One thousand three, . . . one thousand four." You're still counting the seconds to liftoff because you know the runway is too short for a lumbering, heavy loaded plane, trying to reach 180-miles per hour, takeoff speed. Unexpectedly, you see a goony-bird collision within the rotating propellers, sending a flurry of feathers across the wing as though the plane had crashed into a pillow—a huge pillow. A shipmate laughs, "Another damn goony bird caught waddling across the runway."

As your plane continues to accelerate, approaching the end of the runway, clearly visible in your imagination, you keep on counting, "One thousand 200, . . . one thousand 201." The plane keeps rolling on the ground . . . rolling, rolling, and rolling. You're thinking, something is wrong because the last takeoff took only 150-seconds.

Suddenly, the wheels lock into the underbelly carriage with a "clunk." You're airborne. All sins . . . forgiven.

The end

Edward

Donald

Donald was fun to watch, his beady eyes scanning his whereabouts, his short legs caring his frame with a waddle, his personality spelling "attitude", his head moving to-and-fro, looking for trouble. Donald was my pet duck, comical to look at, comical to see his beak as though attached with glue, comical to watch his tail feathers wiggling in coordination with his behavior. Donald also had a girlfriend, a cute little duck, named Daisy, that followed him with her little beady eyes wherever he chose to wander in my back yard. The neighbor's wooden fence at the back of my property, the honeysuckle bushes on the north side, the privet hedge on the south side, kept Donald from wandering away. On three different occasions, I remember looking out of our sub-basement window, seeing Donald, followed by his girlfriend, walking toward the sidewalk in front of our house. Even though they were free to wander suburban streets, they stayed self-confined in my back yard.

Donald lived to nine years, a ripe old age, considering that domestic White Pekin ducks live to an average age of seven years. His first girlfriend lived for only five years, sorry to report. Amorous lovemaking, with his weight on top of hers, broke both her legs. If they had lived in a pond when they fell in love, which was frequently, her legs and her buoyancy would have supported lover-boy. Life for them, however, was very good: eating watermelons, open-face style, raiding the vegetable garden in broad daylight, and quacking up a storm when there was nothing to quack about. Daisy had a louder quack, much louder than Donald's lower frequency, throaty, barely heard quack.

Donald's attitude gave me the impression that he thought of himself as a king, a protector, a security guard of the vegetable garden. He and his girlfriend loved to eat artichokes, thorns and all, stripping the plants bear. On a warm sunny day, while casually swimming in their five-foot wide, portable pool, a large bumblebee flew past Daisy. I couldn't believe what I saw. Daisy quickly stretched out her neck, snapped her beak at the bee with a click, and swallowed the insect, one two three, stinger and all. Donald had a very strong beak, a bite force capable of leaving welts on your ankles when you entered his garden. That's when we would have our "serious talks."

"Donald," I would say, while squatting down to his level to where his beak was next to my ear so that he could whisper his excuses, "what is your problem?"

"What did he whisper?" you ask. You may not believe that he actually talked in his low, throaty, quacking, voice, while gently nibbling on my ear. I swear! He was a pet worth having, even when he tried to escape my grasp, leaving ten-inch scars across the inside of my arms. His quarter-inch nails, three on each foot, could inflict serious pain. The scars burned for about a day and then they would completely heal after a couple of weeks. To avoid getting bit, a hand fake-out distracted his short attention span so that a comfortable grasp could be made with both hands across his wings: his wings useless for flying, but well groomed, brilliant white feathers, water-proofed with body oil from his gland and manipulated with his beak.

The Chicago winters; namely, cold, nasty, 15 degrees below freezing — was no place for warm-hearted ducks, unless they had an enclosed cage for the night. Invariably, after letting Donald and Daisy out of their cage, they would attempt to break through five inches of ice in their pool, by jumping up and down, mainly seeking drinking water. The impact of their weight wasn't enough to break through the ice and reach the fresh water that they craved. Consequently, I had to make sure their cage had fresh water and some kind of heating element to keep them warm.

Within one week's time, during the middle of winter, I had to replace five 60-watt light bulbs in their cage. Something was burning them out! The new challenge was to solve the mystery of the failing light bulbs. One night, just by luck, while sleeping with the bedroom window open, I heard a "tap-tap-tap" outside, coming from the cage where Donald slept. I got out of bed, covered my pajamas with a robe, went outside in the snow, snuck up on Donald's cage, and saw his silhouette on the cage's plastic cover and his head next to the light bulb. Donald was tapping his beak on the lightbulb, vibrating the filament to excess, simply burning out one lightbulb after another, giving me the impression, "He couldn't sleep with the lights on." I immediately installed an electrical thermal resistor under his cage. No more "tap, tap, tap," waking me up.

After daisy died, Donald moped around the backyard, pecking at his image in the basement window, thinking it was his girlfriend, acting as if he was in love with his reflection. Because he seemed so lonely, I knew I would have to get him a new girlfriend after our family relocated to my new job, 2,000 miles away, in Tucson, Arizona.

My new employer bragged about their capability to relocate all my belongings. Therefore, Donald flew to Arizona, not first class, not coach, but comfortably in his wooden cage, next to all the suitcases in the cargo hole. While in the airport, carrying Donald in his wooden cage, resting on my shoulder, a little boy, looking to see a puppy inside, said, "Look mommy, he's got a duck!" O'Hare Airport is not the place to look inconspicuous, while carrying a quacking duck through the terminal. The airlines treated Donald as though he was invisible, like just another suitcase, revolving on the conveyer belt in Tucson's baggage claim area. Everyone saw Donald quacking inside his homemade, green wooden cage, rotating on the belt alongside their suitcases.

The backyard of our new home looked like an oasis where my family could swim in a twenty-five-thousand-gallon pool, diving board included, and where Donald could swim in his own five-foot-wide portable pool surrounded by a two-foot retaining wall. Next to his pool, a spacious lawn grew close to his artichokes in the garden. At night, he had the protection of a large cage, safe from any coyotes that might jump over a six-foot wall, surrounding our backyard. You would think Donald was happy, but it was obvious he grieved for his girlfriend, Daisy.

The owner of the poultry store said, "I'm not sure I can sell you two female ducklings without knowing their gender. They're so small, only a few weeks old. It's difficult to see their sex organs." To my surprise, I was about to witness the correct procedure for learning the gender of a duckling.

The poultry owner reached into the cage of a dozen or so baby ducks scampering about, extracted one chick, turned it over in the palm of his hand, blew a puff of air from his mouth at the bird's genitals, parting the feathers, and said, "Nope, this one's a male." The next two ducks were females that I took home without any guarantee from the owner, regarding their true gender.

Fortunately, Donald got lucky. The two females grew handsomely within a couple of months, remote from Donald, sequestered, totally separated from lover-boy. Almost every morning, there were duck eggs inside the divided cage on the

The first one was a male the next two were females.

female's side. Yes, the cage was partitioned . . . because hanky-panky was not allowed in the middle of the night. We didn't want any more female ducks limping across the yard with broken legs. Their names were Daisy#2 and Daisy#3. On a few occasions, I would find a fresh egg on Donald's side of the partitioned cage. Wait a minute. Donald was incapable of laying eggs—right? The mystery deepened until I learned that fresh eggs with a soft eggshell could roll under the wooden partition because of a small gap separating the wooden divider from the contoured wire mesh that the ducks walked on. The fresh eggs rolled from Daisy#2, or Daisy#3, toward Donald, leaving me with the impression they were demanding, "Donald, you take care of the kids; we're going shopping."

When the time came to move back to the Chicago area for a better job, I had to find a new home for my three ducks. Located within the center of Tucson, is a small lake, but beautiful, surrounded by Mesquite trees, Bermuda grass, lush vegetation, and more importantly other Pekin ducks, by the hundreds.

I unloaded Donald and his two girlfriends into the lake, whereupon they swam to the center of the lake, circling each other in a five-foot diameter rotation—the same direction and the same five-foot distance they maintained in their portable pool.

Donald and his girlfriend, Daisy #1.

Why would they swim in a small lake the same way they swam in their pool? For about an hour, I watched them having fun in the middle of the lake, maybe fifty feet from where I stood. On two different occasions, I returned to the same area, never to find Donald, only to find Daisy, either 2 or 3. I could recognize my ducks from the hundreds of other ducks. My ducks had dark freckles on their beaks that I could see from a twenty-foot distance. I rented a small boat, determined to know if my ducks were safe. While rowing out into the swarm of ducks with a tin can full of duck food, all the ducks moved away stealthily, except one; it was Daisy: she came to feed from the tin can I held over the edge of the boat, all the while, wiggling her tail feathers.

In my mind, Donald could not die—I pictured him swimming underwater in five-foot circles at the bottom of the lake . . . a duck with a big heart who gave it his all.

The end

Edward

Appendix 1
The Hominin Puzzle

Like an Alfred Hitchcock movie, I have inserted myself, Charles E. Anzalone, into the character known as Charlie. Hitchcock would write his stories for television and then introduce himself as an extra actor, walking a dog in the background. I have done the same with my book. For a brief moment, I was Charlie, traveling on a W-100 space cruiser, piloted by Celestials with their telepathic communication skills, preaching to my friends, while standing on a crate, next to the crate that contained the Ark of the Covenant, talking about the feasibility of warp speed, during which the Ark was glowing its outline as a silhouette against its wooden crate.

From an engineering view-point, I never wrote how Fathers' Dean and Aye, and Charlie were able to communicate telepathically with the Celestials. So now is the time to explain that function.

The Pineal Gland:

The pineal gland is an endocrine gland that secretes hormones into the body, specifically melatonin and its precursor serotonin. Melatonin regulates sleep-awake cycles, and serotonin enhances the neurotransmission of nerve cells. The pineal gland, located at the base of the brain, contains a compound similar to a crystal that is capable of acting as a piezoelectric device, producing an electric current whenever pressure or heat is applied. Seals, walruses, and birds also have a pineal gland. The pineal gland is influenced by electromagnetic waves, which explains why birds can navigate across the world, crossing magnetic fields that surround the globe.

With these facts in mind, it is easy to see why people of Hindu faith believe the pineal gland acts as a "third eye" ––with the ability to talk to God––and why other people believe that an enriched pineal gland allows people to communicate with telepathic thoughts. Studies are underway to show that the consumption of fluoride calcifies the pineal gland, thereby, reducing the ability of the individual to *think*, making him (or her) become a "passive" person. Jewish prisoners in Hitler's concentration camps initiated these rumors.

But what if it is true? What if dental brushing with fluoride toothpaste helps teeth, but the consumption of fluoride in water destroys the brain's ability to think? Is that where we are [at] in this world? ––a far cry from having the ability to communicate telepathically? As a society, do we have the ability to think about the welfare of one another? Or, are we an experimental society, out-of-control? Is the society on Bethel, where Charlie lives, any better? Are they the off-branch of human beings, like Charlie, that tele-communicate with entities on different worlds because their pineal gland never calcifies? It makes one think!

While we're on the subject of "thinking," let us think about the cold, civil war that our United States is experiencing, as of 2021, going into 2022. But first, I need to digress.

When I was four years old, my dad was fighting in World War II and my mom was working in a factory to meet the family's financial needs. Then, at the age of five, I lived like an orphan, growing up with the daytime care of Tom, the fish store man. I was fascinated with five, maybe six, dozen, tropical-fish aquariums that contained a collage of colorful fish. Canaries, singing different songs, harmonizing with their songs, lived in multiple cages along the wall, stretching from the floor up to the nearby ceiling. I can remember catching a rabbit down in the basement and taking an afternoon nap with that rabbit on a wooden bench, that Tom had inside his store, across from the cash register. When a loud-voiced customer came into the store, I remember the rabbit jumping out of my grasp as I awoke.

When I was older, Tom told me about the comments his customers made when they saw a small boy asleep with a rabbit on a wooden bench.

Tom had a gift for seeing nature the way it could be enjoyed. Some of his customers described him as a naturalist. As a kid, and later as a teenager, I remember him as a gentle man who allowed me to see into another world with his soft-spoken words about animal behavior. He came from Poland at the age of twenty-seven; he learned the English language; and he opened one of the first tropical fish store in Chicago, around 1937.

Fascinated with the living animals inside his store, I continued to visit and revisit Tom into my teenage years and again when I introduced him to my new wife. Tom knew about animals, and one day, I asked him what he was trying to achieve with all the different fish in so many aquariums. He summed it up in one word and then continued to explain.

"Balance," he said. "It's all about balance. If you have live plants in the tank, they produce the oxygen that the fish need. If you have the right amount of sunlight, the plants grow. If the water is fresh and pure, the fish will multiply."

I had liked the colorful Siamese fighting fish and asked more questions.

Tom responded, "The Beta is a fighter! He'll get along with almost any other fish with the exception of another male Beta."

"Why?"

"He wants to have the tank to himself for when a female comes along."

"What happens if you put a female in the tank?"

"He'll kill all the other fish and then he'll raise the young in the absence of the female. Otherwise, he'll kill the female because she will try to eat the young after they hatch. The male won't eat at all, until every egg hatches."

During my pre-teenage years, I continued to visit Tom while he explained the balance of nature. In a sense, Tom was their creator. He provided the extra food and sunlight. He arranged the reproduction locations and the sheltering of young tropical fish.

From an internal viewpoint, the fish had to have their own harmony; they had to get along with one another.

Our nation, including our world, is facing a dilemma with balance and harmony. Some people smoke; some people don't. Some people own guns; some people don't. Some people want to be different; some people don't. Let's talk about industries. Some industries want profit at the expense of clean air and water; some industries don't. Other groups want to push the idea of ancient aliens, while most groups are content with their own religion. Do you see where this is going? It's going into too many directions. It's all about babble, minus the harmony . . . minus the uniformity.

After I wrote my book about the story of Enoch, I self-analyzed a situation where the story could be true if we do have a "brother's keeper" living on another world and their goal is to unify the human race in small measures. Perhaps the word "unify" is incorrect; it would be impossible to unify the Russians, the Chinese, and the Americans; it would be impossible to unify ethnic groups. Perhaps a better word that achieves harmony is the word sharing.

In thinking back, maybe that is why I picked Nostradamus, Mozart, Barnard, and Edward to share a brief moment about "a something" we all have in common. Nostradamus and Edward are about balance; Mozart and Barnard are about harmony.

Nostradamus gave us his futuristic predictions about catastrophes that we can unite against: famine, plagues, bad guys riding four horses. Edward gave us ideas about the ways we can unite our sciences. These efforts add up to balance.

Mozart gave us his music to appreciate; this is harmony. And Christiaan Barnard gave us hope so that we can live longer with a new heart, so that we can appreciate our grandchildren; this is both *love and harmony*.

Maybe it was Tom, the fish-store man, who helped me write this book by showing me how precious life is.

My goal in writing this novel was not to deceive, not to create more book royalties, not to invent a totally fictitious novel with monsters or unbelievable characters. My goal hinged on the idea of selling concepts that I believe happened in the past and could happen in the future.

In 1987, my engineering job demanded expertise in statistics. I had graduated as a "hardware" engineer with a BSEE, but my job description required that I write software with subroutines to identify semiconductors into a statistical histogram after hundreds had been transported on a conveyor belt into a test station.

In the same year, 1990, I wrote my first manuscript to prove that man's origin wasn't evolutionary. The effort involved library-type research to collect physical data for every ape and humanoid species known to scientists. The resulting histogram indicated the absence of a few species, unknown to scientists at that time. Since then, three new species of man have been discovered: Homo Naledi in South Africa, Homo Luzonensis on the island of Luzon in the Philippines, and Homo Floresiensis in Indonesia.

The crude data listed below illustrates a new histogram that *does not* have conformity. In other words, Homo Sapiens *did not* evolve from Neanderthal Man. The two species may have interbred, but our species is unique, very unique! The June 2020 issue of Discovery, page 43, reports the existence of Homo sapiens, identified as Irhoud 10, living in Morocco, North Africa, 315,000 years ago.

From a statistical viewpoint, a major attribute like "brain capacity divided by height" can be plotted into a histogram to illustrate that the curve lacks normality. Instead of a Gaussian curve (conformity) a Keratosis curve appears (non-conformity). Data for the ancient Homo species plots on an ascending curve, indicating change whereas data for Homo sapiens and Homo sapiens-sapiens species plots on a downward sloping curve. The two curves do not align into one.   This histogram proves that we are not a product of evolution as per Darwin's claim but a product of something starting with "dust" as per the Bible. [Genesis 2:7— "And the Lord God formed man *of* the dust of the ground and breathed into his nostrils the breath of life; and man became a living soul."]

If that something, called "dust," represents Homo sapiens like DNA consisting of 2 to 4% from Neanderthal, then that is believable. If God created the remaining 96 to 98%, then that is how it happened some 315,000 years ago, the birth year of the first Adam, the birth year of Irhoud 10, living in Morocco, North Africa. These facts were the start of my novel when Beena was arguing with Enoch.

Charles E. Anzalone

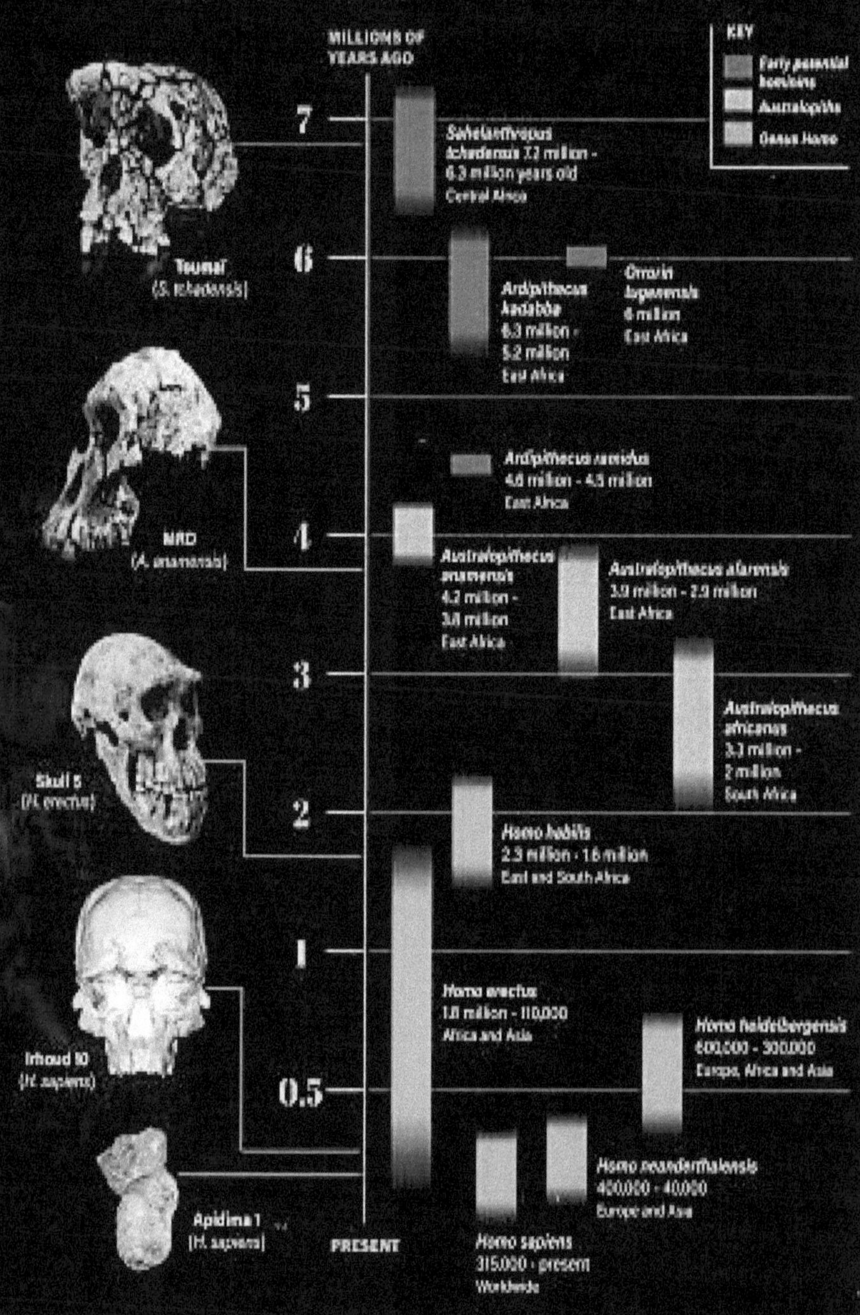
Piecing Together the Hominin Puzzle
When it comes to understanding our lineage, the more we learn,
the more paleoanthropologists want to find out.
Age ranges approximate based on current fossil record; not all hominin species shown.
MILLIONS OF YEARS AGO
KEY
Early potential hominins
Australopiths
Genus Homo
7
Sahelanthropus tchadensis 7.2 million - 6.3 million years old
Central Africa
6
Ardipithecus kadabba
6.3 million - 5.2 million
East Africa
Orrorin tugenensis
6 million
East Africa
5
Ardipithecus ramidus
4.4 million - 4.5 million
East Africa
4
Australopithecus anamensis
4.2 million - 3.8 million
East Africa
Australopithecus afarensis
3.9 million - 2.9 million
East Africa
3
Australopithecus africanus
3.3 million - 2 million
South Africa
2
Homo habilis
2.3 million - 1.6 million
East and South Africa
1
Homo erectus
1.8 million - 110,000
Africa and Asia
Homo heidelbergensis
600,000 - 300,000
Europe, Africa and Asia
0.5
Homo neanderthalensis
400,000 - 40,000
Europe and Asia
PRESENT
Homo sapiens
315,000 - present
Worldwide
Toumaï
(S. tchadensis)
MRD
(A. anamensis)
Skull 5
(H. erectus)
Irhoud 10
(H. sapiens)
Apidima 1
(H. sapiens)

		Heighth (Tall)			Weigth		Brain Size	
Index		cm	ft	in	Lbs	kg	min cc	max cc
0.9	modern humans		5	10			1270	1330
1.0	modern humans		5	7			1270	1270
1.5	Neand		5	6	183	83	1600	1600
1.7	Neand		5	5			1410	1410
2.0	H Heid	175	5	9		62	1230	1230
2.9	H erectus	185	6	1	150	68	546	1251
3.0	H erectus	146	4	9	88	40	546	973
4.0	H Hab Male		4	3	82	37	500	640
4.2	H Ergaster		6	1	139	63	803	848
4.3	H Naledi		4	9	88	39.7	465	610
4.5	H Floresiensis(Hobbit)		3	7			380	417
5.0	Aust afaren		3	11			466	466
5.5	Aust afaren		4	7			466	466
6.0	chimp		4	11	154	70	360	384

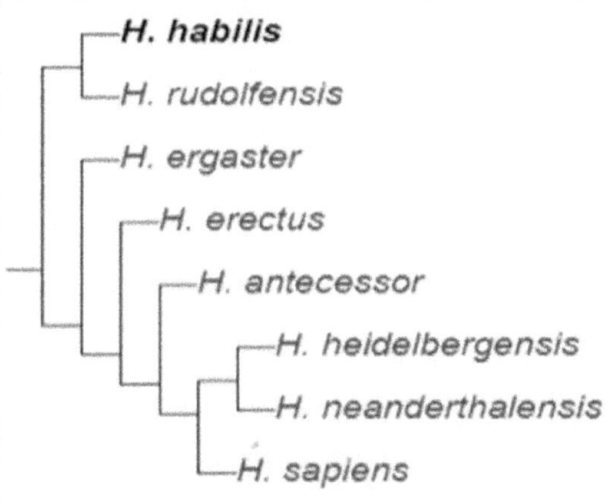

Homo family tree showing *H. habilis* and *H. rudolfensis* at the base as offshoots of the human line[18]

Log(kya)	Brain/Tall
1.0	19.0
1.5	19.0
1.8	24.2
2.3	21.7
2.6	17.8
2.9	17.1
3.0	17.1
3.3	12.5
3.3	11.6
3.4	10.7
3.5	9.7
3.5	9.9
3.5	8.5
3.7	6.5

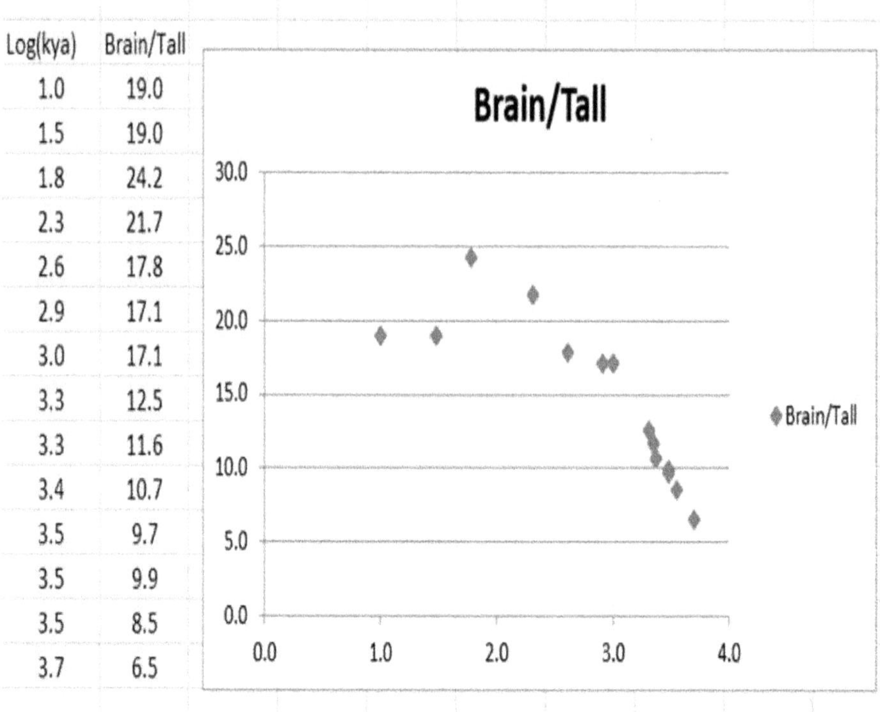

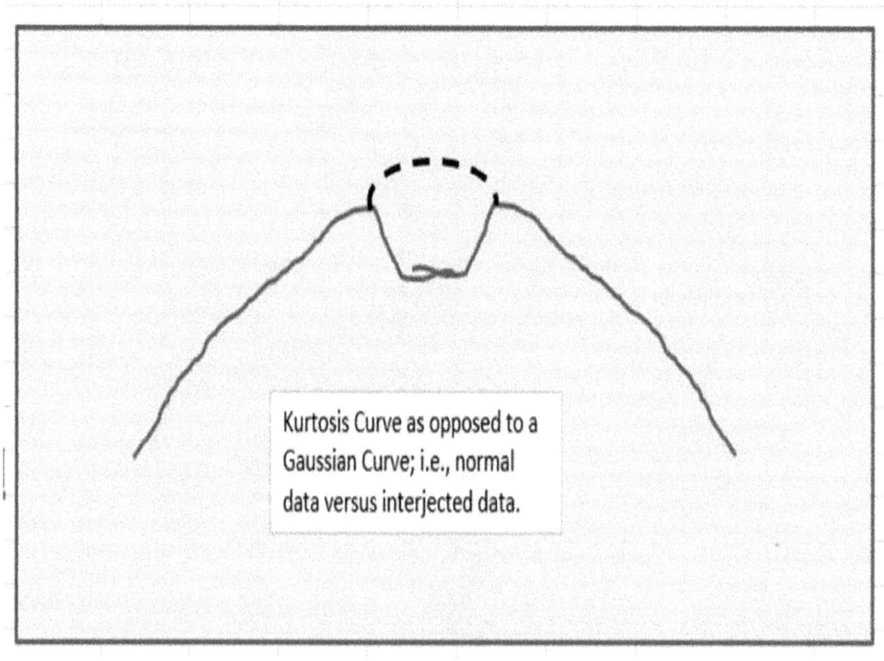

The histogram is the mirror image of the graph "Brain-Tall versus Millions of Years Ago." It shows the humanoid progression in "brain to height" ratio from a chimp at four million years ago to the hominid progression, up to two million years ago. When early man appeared, our species had a regression that didn't fall on a linear line. Both modern humans at one and a half million years ago and Homo Sapiens-Sapiens at less than a million years ago did not have a larger brain to height ratio as Neanderthal Man, who proceeded them. The result is a "Kurtosis" curve, which says that evolution from ape was not possible.

The Kurtosis curve becomes apparent after the right side of the histogram is folded (or duplicated) on the left side. Homo Sapiens-Sapiens is modern man, living 315,000 years ago in Morocco as per Discovery Magazine. The data in the histogram is explicit with the assumption that our species began independently 900,000 years ago, totally different than the homo-lineage initiated by ape.

If evolutionism and creationism are the only two choices and evolution is nonexistent, then creationism is the answer. This is scientific proof that God created our species. Yes, God created the original man. Modern man may be a cross-breed with Neanderthal, but that represents only 2 to 4 percent of our DNA.

The rest of our DNA, gives us the ability to grasp with our hands, to delicately thread a needle, to walk upright on tiny feet with a type of gyroscope-computer in our brain, to learn, to create new inventions, to produce vaccines that will fight infections, to imagine the possibilities of traveling throughout the galaxy. These God-given abilities make us different from any other animal on Earth, who can also love, procreate, and protect their love ones. All animals have the ability to provide for their progeny. However, we (us humans) are special——because we can think. At least, most of us can think! Hopefully there will be an epiphany when we don't think so differently.

Appendix 2
The Bible Decoded: The Black Hole Formula

The story of Enoch is about a fictional character who lives on another planet for 1200-years. How is that possible? How is there a *time dilation by a factor of ten?* It is my theory that human beings were meant to live for 120 biological years as per the Bible. [*Genesis 6:3—"And the Lord said, My spirit shall not always strive with man, for that he also is flesh: yet his days shall be an hundred and twenty years."*]

Human beings on Earth live to an average life span of eighty-seven years, but someday they may live to 120-years like the residents of a fictional world called Bethel. Our understanding of people living longer is understandable, but how does a person live to 1,200-years?

Historical Evidence

Historical evidence, in understanding "true" biological time, follows in two parts. The first part comes from the Bible and the second part comes from Einstein's own equation for $E = mc^2$.

Part 1

A Logical Explanation for Longevity as per Genesis, Chapter 5

When I think back to the events that prompted me to write my first book in 2007, I realize that I started the book in the middle of a series of logical justifications. My first book was titled, Galactic Travel at Warp Speed in Imaginary Time. The task was an effort to review ancient biblical ancestors and its relation to a calendar of the past. Knowledge of the past opens the doors of the future.

Initially, my thoughts flowed in a logical series of hypotheses, attempting to prove a situation and then build toward the next conclusion. My very first thoughts started with Genesis in the Holy

Bible. The Chapter about Adam and Eve and their descendants, living several hundredths of years, triggered something in my engineering mind. Ever since college graduation, I've always had a knack for tumbling numbers to derive a converging sequence. I knew, inherently, that the list of fifty-some numbers, describing the longevity of Adam—his first born, and thereafter—represented a calendar of events.

[Genesis, 5:3—"And Adam lived an [one] hundred and thirty years, and begat a son in his own likeness, after his image, and called his name Seth." Genesis, 5:4—"And the days of Adam after he had begotten Seth were eight hundred years: and he begat sons and daughters." Genesis, 5:5—"And the days that Adam lived were nine hundred and thirty years and he died."]

[Genesis, 11:24—"And Nahor lived nine and twenty years, begat Teran: Genesis, 11:25—"And Nahor lived after he begat Terah an [one] hundred and nineteen years, and he begat sons and daughters."]

The following table called "The Bible's Time Line, Decoded" was created in the following manner:

1. After Adam's name the numbers 130, 800 and 930 are entered.
2. After Nahor's name the numbers 29, 119 and 148 are entered.
3. The column labeled "Bio-years" is equal to "10" times 10*"Total (years)" divided by "After (years)." For Adam this number is 100*930/800 or 116.
4. The column labeled "Relative-years" is equal to "Bio-years" times 10.
5. Starting with Moses who was born in 1500 BC, the birth of Nahor was in 2744 BC (or 1500 + 1244).

Figure 6 The Bible's Time Line, Decoded

Name	Begat(yrs)	After(yrs)	Total(yrs)	Bio-years	Relative-yrs	Time Line(BC)
Adam&Eve	130	800	930	116	1163	-22349
Seth	105	807	912	113	1130	-21186
Enos	90	815	905	111	1110	-20056
Cainan	70	840	910	108	1083	-18946
Mahalaleel	65	830	895	108	1078	-17862
Jared	162	800	962	120	1203	-16784
Enoch	65	300	365	122	1217	-15581
Methuselah	187	782	969	124	1239	-14365
Lemech	182	595	777	131	1306	-13126

(Genesis 6:3 "The Lord said, '...his days shall be 120 years'")

Name	Begat(yrs)	After(yrs)	Total(yrs)	Bio-years	Relative-yrs	Time Line(BC)
Noah	(150 estimated)	800	950	119	1188	-11820
Flood/Noah @ 600 yrs old Genesis 10:28						-11382
Shem	100	500	600	120	1200	-10632
Arphax	35	403	438	109	1087	-9432
Salah	30	403	433	107	1074	-8345
Eber	34	430	464	108	1079	-7271
Peleg	30	209	239	114	1144	-6192
Reu	32	207	239	115	1155	-5048
Serug	30	200	230	115	1150	-3894
Nahor	29	119	148	124	1244	-2744
Terah	70	no data	205			
Abra(m)-ham	86	no data	175			
1.Ishmael						
2.Isaac						
*Jacob(Israel)						
*Joseph			110	110		
Moses			120	120		-1500

The numbers that went into the Excel chart came from the Holy Bible, Genesis, Chapters 5 and 11. The Bible refers to Adam who had his first son when he was 130 years old. He lived for another 800 years and died when he was 930 years old. To create the Excel chart, the numbers 130, 800, and 930 are entered on the first row. The numbers associated with his son, Seth, are entered on the second row. The process continues until fifty-some numbers are entered into the Excel chart. A formula was created to reflect their biological age in smaller years, typical of present-day life spans for some of our elders.

This table is unique because it shows:

1. *Enoch, Methuselah and Lemech were living longer than 120-years until God said that his days shall be 120 years.*
2. *The only exception is with Nahor who lived to 124-biological years: most likely, a copy error.*
3. *The total number of years for each Biblical ancestor decreases with time. This fact is my argument for our solar system encountering a drift across the galaxy, which has different passages of time for each sector. The "drift " was stated earlier as 12 miles per second, not to be confused with our solar system spinning through the galaxy at 144 miles per second. Our direction is a combination of the two vectors.*

Justification for the Bible Time Line, Decoded in Excel Format

The equation in the Excel chart is "justified" when a multiplier of "10" is used—not "11," not "9,"and not "8." With the multiplier of "10", it can be shown that the three ancestors of Noah: namely, Enoch, Methuselah and Lamech had bio-years of 122, 124 and 131, respectively. It was during the time of Noah when the Lord said, "His days shall be 120 years" in Genesis 6:3.

If a multiplier of "11" was used then Jered, Enoch, Methuselah and Lamech would have lived with bio-years of 132, 134, 136 and 143. If a multiplier of "8" was used, then Enoch, Methuselah and Lamech would have lived with bio-years of 97, 99 and 104. Consequently, a multiplier of "10" is justified to produce bio-years that begin to exceed 120 years. With its justification, it's also used as a multiplier of "10" in the column labeled as "Relative-yrs."

Noah could have lived longer than his father, Lamech at 131 bio-years, but his actual life span was 119 bio-years because the Lord had capped it to 120 years. Any other number than "10" would not have produced these bio-year numbers. As per the Bible:

The scriptures indicate that Noah did not resemble his father, Lamech. When Lamech confronted his grandfather, Enoch, he was told that he should accept the child because this was the work of God.

In conclusion, 120 bio-years is the maximum number of years that our species can live within any part of the galaxy, whether it's us on Earth or my fictional character, Enoch, living on his planet, Bethel.

To achieve a calendar of events, I have tumbled the numbers, starting with Moses and continued working with the longevity of his ancestors all the way back to Noah; and further back to Adam and Eve. The missing part of the equation was a number between 8 and 11. Finally, a value of "10" represented a constant for the equation of each ancestor. The Bible was reporting the "true longevity" number, and the Excel equation was calculating the biological number. In other words, the Bible was expressing an ancestor's longevity as 950 years, for example, which equated to a smaller biological year at the time of death. The bio-number for the three ancestors, preceding Noah, was greater than 120 years. According to the Bible, God said at that time that man shall live no longer than 120 years. With that information, the constant of 10 began to fit all the individual equations, associated with the data for each Biblical ancestor.

The equation, written in Excel format, illustrates that Adam's bio-years was 116 and his longevity years as expressed in the Bible was 930 years. Moses was born around 1500 BC and he lived for 120 years as per the Bible. His bio-year as per the Excel equation was 120 years. The difference is zero. The difference between Adam's reported age of 930 years and his bio-age of 116 years is greater than zero. The difference between reported age and bio-age reduces to zero as each biblical ancestor lives and dies. The difference reflects a gradient change. As the gradient grows smaller with time from one ancestor to another it signifies a global change, taking place. All the numbers in the Excel table signify a calendar of historical events and astrophysical changes. It projects the possibility of our solar system wandering about our galaxy where the measurement of time is different.

Scientist today know that our solar system is drifting through our galaxy at a speed of 12 miles per second or .005% the speed of light. There was a time when our solar system traveled faster, crashing into other solar systems, altering the orbital path of planets, and damaging the planets within. The hypothesis is feasible. The next hypothesis follows at the time of the Great Flood:

1. Our solar system migrated into another sector of the galaxy.
2. Earth and Mars nearly collided with Earth sacrificing precious oxygen into the cosmos and Mars losing its oceans.

From the second hypothesis, it is possible to say:

1. The rate of "time flow" changed whereby one year in the new sector was equivalent to ten years in the old sector.
2. If the oxygen level changed from 30% to 20%—what it is today—, then perhaps more Earthly diseases started to affect the human race. The ancient story of Pandora's Box implies the release of diseases when her curiosity prompted her to open the box.

Additional information, derived from the equation, indicates a calendar of events with the most significant being the Great Flood, during Noah's era, and the period when Adam and Eve were created. The date of the Great Flood of 11382 BC, as predicted in my book is confirmed with recent news; for example, the true age of the Sphinx and the fertile plains of Africa, that once existed, correlate in time to the Great Flood.

As stated earlier, my logic was built on these conclusions before advancing to the next hypothesis. The constant of 10 has a very significant effect on my next conclusion. The task is to let each hypothesis and conclusion lead to the feasibility of space flight. Okay?

The Excel chart, labeled "The Bible's Time Line, decoded" on page 281, has mathematical numbers that show our solar system is adrift in the galaxy because the numeric lifespan for each individual gets shorter and shorter, from 930 years starting with Adam and 120 years ending with Moses. This fact leads to a conclusion that "time" across the galaxy is a variable.

Noah &
The Great Flood
11382 BCE

MOSES
1500 BCE

<u>Part 2</u>

What is the constant "10" all about?

To reach our next conclusion, we have to use Einstein's famous equation and at the same time show that it is incorrect. Einstein proved that E=mc^2 and that the speed of light is constant throughout the galaxy and the entire universe. If we go back to the 1960's, scientists did not realize that a Black Hole exists in the center of every galaxy; or maybe, 85%, 90%, or 95% of all galaxies. We do not know the correct percentage, but we do know that the Black Hole is an "energy converter"!

It takes in mass and spits out cosmic rays. It gobbles up stars and solar systems that are nearby. It also gobbles up neutrinos emitted by every star in our galaxy.

If we think of our solar system as a spiral pie, we can postulate that each section of the pie is under a different influence by the Black Hole in the center. I believe that there are three sectors in our galaxy. It is logical to assume that material (or mass) falls into the Black Hole at a faster rate than the material from another sector. If this is true, then we have an energy labeled as E1, an E2, and an E3 in the center of our galaxy. Each "energy converter" or "E_" is peculiar to each sector. The equation representing three energy states is as follows:

The Black Hole, Energy Formula:

$E1 = E2 = E3$

$E1 = m1*c^2 = E2 = m2*c^2 = E3 = m3*c^2$ or

$E1 = m1*d^2/t^2 = E2 = m2*d^2/t^2 = E3 = m3*d^2/t^2$

The Black Hole (Energy) Equation is a model for three "energy converters" working independently of one another and thereby influencing each sector of the galaxy. We can expand the equation using the speed of light, "c," where c = d/t and "d" is distance and "t" is time. Distance is not a variable because a yardstick would be 36-inches long on this side of our galaxy as it would be on the opposite side. So that leaves "t" as a variable for each sector and the speed of light as a number that is no longer a constant throughout the galaxy—contrary to Einstein's theory.

Explained another way, each sector of our galaxy contributes different amounts of mass into the Black Hole, changing "time." **Galaxies, stars, planets and particles, as small as neutrinos, are consumed constantly by the Black Hole in the center of our galaxy.** If the energy absorption is constant for any sector, then "t," time, has to change with mass. Let us revisit the equation with some bogus numbers for "c" (speed of light, d/t) as follows:

Let c1 = .1 and c2 = 1 and c3 = 10

$E1 = m1*d^2/.1^2 = E2 = m2*d^2/1^2 = E3 = m3*d^2/10^2$

For E1 to equal E2 to equal E1, the contributing mass to the Black Hole has to have corresponding numbers like m1 equal to .01, m2 equal to 1, and m3 equal to 100.

$E1 = .01*(d^2)/.01 = E2 = 1*(d^2)/1 = E3 = 100*(d^2)/100$

Conclusion:

For a given mass of m1, m2, and m3 equal to .01, 1, and 100, the time equivalent t1, t2, and t3 equal to .1, 1, and 10.

Interpretation of the equation says, "Sector 1, contributed .01 mass units and its time sector is ".1." Sector 2, contributed one mass unit and its time sector is "1." Sector 3, contributed one hundred mass units and its time sector is "10."

The time in each sector transitions differently, a man living in Sector 1 would live .1 year; the same man living in Sector 2 would live 1 year; and again, the same man living in Sector 3 would live 10 years. The sequential ratio is the same when stretched out with a man is sector 1 living to 10 years, a man in sector 2 living to 100 years and a man in sector 3 living to 1,000 years.

Now, let's put a man living in sector 2 that we can call Earth and let's put man in sector 3 that we can call Bethel. Then we can ask what their lives are like.

We can substitute c, the speed of light, for v, velocity, because the speed of light is a velocity: i.e., [c = v].

An Allegorical Example:

The difference between Time Dilation and Universal Time is analogous to two different situations, taking place in Sector 2, Earth, and Sector 3, Bethel, the theoretical place where Enoch comes from. For example, you're living on Bethel, you're parking your car in front of a parking meter, you're planning to pick up some groceries on a small grocery list with four items. You put a silver dollar into the parking meter. The silver dollar weights 100 grams. The meter indicates you have ten minutes allotted time. You shop and return to your car with the four items of groceries, ten minutes later.

This fits the equation where:

$$E3 = m3 * c\wedge 2 \text{ or}$$

$$E3 = m3 * v\text{^}2 \text{ or}$$

$$E3 = 100 * d\text{^}2/(10\text{^}2) = d\text{^}2$$

In the second example, you're living on Earth, located in Sector 2, you're shopping for the same four, food items as before. You put a penny into the parking meter. The penny weighs one (1) gram. The meter indicates you have one minute. You're a fast shopper and you return to your car with the four, food items, one (1) minute later.

This also fits the equation

$$E2 = m2 * c\text{^}2 \text{ or}$$

$$E2 = m2 * v\text{^}2 \text{ or}$$

$$E2 = \ 1 * d\text{^}2/(1)\text{^}2 = d\text{^}2$$

And d is the same distance throughout the galaxy. Energy in the third sector equals the same energy consumed in the second sector, or E3 equals E2 as per the Black Hole Equation.

Universal Time versus Time Dilation

In this analogy Universal Time *is* one cent for every dollar and Time Dilation *is* the same accomplishment in shopping on either planet. When related to the Black Hole Equation, a silver dollar has more mass than a penny—it weighs more, maybe not one hundred times more, but it weighs more and it buys more time when fed into a parking meter. Now think of the center of our galaxy as a Black Hole, as a parking meter, pulling in massive objects like stars, planets, and solar systems, falling into a never-ending gravitational force, complying with Newton's Law that matter cannot be destroyed and somehow not breaking his law, but transforming the consumption of mass into a rate of flow in time. It stands to reason that the only byproduct that comes out of a Black Hole is time, specifically Time Dilation.

Obviously, our galaxy is uncharted and undefined, but this model is the actual representation that explains why our Biblical ancestors lived so long. Time in Sector 3 is ten times longer than it is in Sector 2 where we live.

If the speed of light is different, then light shines at a different wavelength putting a shift in the colors of the rainbow. In the above example, the speed of light in Sectors 1, 2, and 3, would be d/.1, d/1 and d/10, respectively. The wavelengths for white light (c/frequency) in Sectors 1, 2, and 3 would be long (red tint), medium (normal) and short (blue tint), respectively, in proportion to the speed of light and inversely proportional to the center frequency of the rainbow or white light. As the time changes for each sector, so does the speed of light.

Logic conclusions predict that all the rainbow-colors in another sector would be different. Our sunset is reddish-orange in color assuming that we live in Sector 2. A sunset on another planet in sector 1, would appear reddish-pink. A sunset on another planet in sector 3, would appear reddish-purple. The Elysian Fields would reside in sector 3 where a purple tint dominates as per Edith Hamilton's book.

White light from our sun is clear. Its color spectrum seen through a prism illuminates in a spectrum of red, orange, yellow, green, purple and blue with each color bar having a frequency and wavelength. Colloquial names for red and blue color bars are long wave and short wave. The color red has a lower frequency than the color blue and its wavelength is longer or stretched out compared to the wavelength of the blue color. Wavelength, measured in meters, is equal the speed of light divided by the frequency of the specific color. In Sector 1, the spectrum of colors would shift to the longer wavelength favoring the red colors because the speed of light is faster (c=d/.1). In Sector 3, the spectrum of colors would shift to the shorter wavelengths favoring the blue color because the speed of light is slower(c=d/10).

Theoretically, we live in Sector 2 where life is 100 years long and sunsets are a reddish-orange. If our solar system resided in Sector 1, we would live a full life of 1 year and the sunsets would be reddish-pink in color. If our solar system resided in Sector 3, we would live a full life of 1000 years and the sunsets would have a blue-purplish tint.

Now we have a model for Sector 3 where light shines at a different wavelength with a combination of rainbow colors that have more emphasis on the blues and the purples. This phenomenon is intriguing because Edith Hamilton describes the same event occurring in her book, Greek Mythology.

Wikipedia states, "The Greek myths were initially propagated in an oral-poetic tradition most likely by Minoan and Mycenaean singers starting in the 18th century BC." Edith Hamilton's research on ancient myths seems to correlate with the Excel chart for Bible Decoded that promotes the hypothesis that other sectors of our galaxy have a different passage of "time" and a different speed of light, based upon color hues. She references the Elysian Fields as a place where honorable men of renown go when they die . . . a place that has purplish sunsets.

The early Greeks believed—or maybe, they were taught—that the next world after death is the Elysian Fields. Edith's interesting description about the Elysian Fields is that the color of the sunlight is tinted with a shade of purple. This implies that light, composed of photons, travel at a different speed—a contradiction to Einstein's statement about the speed of light as a universal constant. Personally, I do not know where we go when we die, but we can learn as technology advances. If we do go to a place where time is different and the speed of light is different, then maybe, we are returning to where we came from! —a celestial place called home. Isn't that a wonderful thought?

The Minoan and Mycenaean people believed in the Elysian Fields with purple tinted sunsets where their spirits came to rest.

If the Speed of Light is Different, Then Time is Different

A summary of parts one and two, combined with the Black Hole "energy equation," represent the cross hairs for zeroing the concept that the passage of time is different for different sectors of our galaxy. The most significant dissertation of this hypothesis is that time is different because the speed of light is different. The measurement of your age would be different. If you had lived in sector 3, your descendants would talk about you as having lived 950 years. If you had lived in sector 2, you real age at death would be 95—a factor of "10." Your bio-age is the same regardless of where you live. Individual cells in your body will split and divide their chromosomes a fixed number of times. According to scientists, chromosomes reproduce with shorter lengths until they are too short to replicate. And then—death follows.

Let us digress for a moment. In addition to the discovery of an ancient calendar, the Bible is coded in such a way to explain the physics of the universe. Scientists know that our solar system is drifting at a specific rate within our galaxy. We can assume that our solar system crossed a detrimental barrier between time zones. According to the Excel equation, this happened back in 11,382 BC, when a multiplier of "10" is used. If a different multiplier had been used, the Great Flood would have occurred at a different time. The evidence for this appropriate date is the violent upheaval of cataclysmic events and unorthodox distribution of orbital paths of planets around our sun. The astrophysical data explains how geophysical events on Earth changed drastically around 13,000 years ago. A summarizing statement needs repeating: "It is surprising that our blue planet merged from chaos."

Additional proof for a sector barrier lies in my next dissertation about Tabby's Star; additional proof for the possibility of warp speed lies in my discussion of naturalized Gaussian distribution of neutrino speeds; and finally substantial proof in Discovery Magazine that neutrinos travel faster than light speed.

Appendix 3

Tabby's Star: Gaussian Curve

The Way it Happens

Neutrinos, those subatomic, zero-mass particles, originate in every star, travel across the galaxy, beyond light speeds, die in a Black Hole, at the center of the galaxy, move in a way similar to rain drops, splashing on roof-tops, funneling their way into the gutter, spiraling through the down-spout, moving even faster, crashing into the Black Earth that drew them there.

Basically, What Are Neutrinos?

The neutrino is so named because it is electrically neutral and because its rest mass is so small that it was long thought to be zero. Enrico Fermi (1901 – 1954) was the first person to call these particles, neutrino, because "ino" means "small" in Italian. At that time, physicist believed the atom, consisting of a nucleus and an electron, were the smallest particle. Then they discovered that the atom released an electron beyond its domain. The mass of the atom and the electron was less than their calculations predicted. Something else had to have been released! Newton's Laws, about the conservation of energy, state that matter cannot be created or destroyed. If something was missing from the atom, then that something wasn't destroyed; it merely transformed into something else—energy or another particle. The other particle turned out to be the neutrino.

As the decades passed, scientists learned, by way of extensive experiments, that the neutrino comes in three different flavors (no, not like chocolate, vanilla, and strawberry) and that it had mass, while traveling near the speed of light. If a neutrino stopped moving, it would have zero mass; henceforth, the name zero-rest mass! The latest thinking by scientists, is that our sun, a source of nuclear radiation, bombards Earth with trillions of neutrinos every second. They pass through the Earth. In addition to Newton's Law, Einstein's equations state that mass increases exponentially when approaching light speeds and that "time" slows down to a zero value.

At first, scientists thought that neutrinos couldn't oscillate (or change flavors) because they didn't have any mass. In other words, "time" will only slow down to zero with objects or particles with mass. But neutrinos do have mass! So, the question is this. If neutrinos are proven to have mass, do they really slow down as per Einstein's equation as they approach light speed?

My Claim

As a degreed electrical engineer, my claim is that neutrinos increase with mass from zero speed to light speed, to warp speeds, to multiple warp speeds. Beyond the speed of light, they keep gaining mass! I also claim that they travel much, much faster than light, constantly gaining more mass as per Einstein's equation.

If my theory is true, then man can fly across the galaxy at warp speeds within another dimension, and that dimension is imaginary time. There is no need for rocket propulsion, only a sail, a sailing mechanism that I described in my first book, *Galactic Travel Across the Galaxy in Imaginary Time,* which I wrote and published in 2007. My two earlier books contain discussions for the construction of a small round plastic ball, fitted with circuits, that can determine the three variables necessary for entering imaginary time.   Both books outline the construction of a spaceship, locked in imaginary time and collecting neutrinos like a wind-sail.

In my story about Enoch, I wrote about a fictional character, named Charlie, who gave a discussion of how it was possible to transition the light-barrier without time slowing down. Charlie said, in so many words, you gain what you lose. Listen to Charlie, once again, "You gain what you lose!" You lose time approaching the light-barrier and you gain time on the other side of the light-barrier. It has to be done very quickly.

I also claim that the passage of time has a dilation factor. Please refer to the section containing "Bible's Time Line Decoded." For example, Adam lived 930 years; his son, Seth lived 912 years, and so on. Moving along, we see that Enoch lived 365 years and his son, Methuselah, lived 969 years. When we get to the bottom of the list, we see that Moses lived to only 120 years. We know, according to modern-day scientists, that our solar system is moving across our galaxy in two different vectors, one of them with a speed of 12 miles per second. Doesn't it seem logical to conclude that the passage of time is different depending upon which sector of the galaxy you are in? If this is the case, then universal time is not a constant as Einstein predicted; universal time is a variable.

On a personal level, I also claim that the Angio disease, common on the planet of Bethel, is a real disease that childless women inherit from their fathers. My first-born daughter is childless because of a pituitary-gland problem, according to her doctors. My cousin, fathered by my father's brother, is childless. My two aunts, fathered by my grandfather, were childless. All four women had the same spouses throughout their entire lives and they couldn't have children. It's a mystery that can be explained only through gene-inheritance. I used this mystery to explain why Brianna couldn't get pregnant and how she was downtrodden when she saw the results of the test.

A Summary of My Claims

1. Neutrinos travel much faster than light and they gain mass, the faster they travel.
2. Warp speed is possible because "you gain the time that you lose" in crossing the barrier, a barrier that was disastrous for our solar system to cross.
3. There is a dilation of time across the galaxy. The passage of time is a variable. It is not a constant value. Scientists already know that atomic clocks on satellites run faster than a clock on Earth because Earth clocks are closer to a larger mass and stronger gravity.
4. The Black Hole formula exists. It shows that mass is consumed by the Black Hole at the center of our galaxy and that the byproduct is an alteration in the passage of time.
5. If neutrinos flood our galaxy, as scientist claim, then the total mass of the neutrinos is what scientist call "Dark Matter."
6. To keep our galaxy from spinning down on itself, our galaxy has to have "Barrier-ribs" made of neutrino rivers flowing into the Black Hole.
7. The Angio disease does exists within our genes.

Let's look at three topics that could bring us to a conclusion about the first three claims. Then we'll assume that warp speed is possible and imagine how it's thinkable to cross the galaxy at grater speeds by "skipping" and by traveling in a spaceship, contained within multiple dimensions, something like the Russian nesting dolls.

As an engineer, trying to help humankind, this is where I'm coming from.

Neutrino Speed: Measured and Verified

A recent article in Discovery Magazine, titled Tonight's Supernova (9/2018), discusses measurements taken for neutrinos and photons that arrived from a supernova. The article stated the following:

> "We know supernovas create neutrinos because in 1987, one went off in the Large Magellanic Cloud, a neighboring galaxy just 170,000 light-years away. Dubbed Supernova 1987A, it was the first source of neutrinos identified beyond our solar system. Three detectors, thousands of miles apart, recorded neutrinos at the exact time. What's more, the neutrinos arrived a **few hours** before visible light did. This is because neutrinos escape the collapsing core immediately, but visible light takes longer, caught up in the outer atmosphere of the exploding star."

With this information, the average speed of neutrinos, traveling as a group, can be solved. Starting with an equation developed by Hendrik Lorentz (July 1853––February 1928), we can expand upon his formula to calculate the time difference between a neutrino and a photon, both traveling at warp speeds. Lorentz's equation involves a ratio for two particles traveling close to light speeds. His equation produces a "time difference" between two travelers, one moving near to light speed and the other, stationary on Earth.

In layman terms, the Hendrick Lorentz says the following:

- Two identical-looking, twin brothers are in two different locations.
- The first brother is on Earth and the other is traveling through space at half the speed of light or .5*c. His destination is five (5) light-years away.

- Ten years go by and the first brother ages by ten (10) years and the second brother ages by 8.7 years.

The Lorentz formula for calculating the age of the second brother is equal to t' where by:

- t' = (distance/speed)*(1 - (speed/lightspeed)^2)^.5
- t' = (5 / .5) * (1 - (.5/1)^2)^.5 = 8.7 years
- And the speed ratio is %c or (.5/1) or symbolized as Wn/Wc

The uniqueness of the Lorentz formula is a "speed ratio" where (.5/1) is half the speed of light divided by the speed of light or 1 or (Wn/Wc). So, Wc is the speed of light and Wn is the speed of the second brother in his spaceship.

Let's do another example where the distance to the next star is twenty (20) light-years and the second brother is traveling at .9 times light speed:

- t' = (20 / .9) * (1 - (.9/1)^2)^.5 = 9.7 years
- and the speed ratio is %c or (.9/1)

If we let *Wn* equal the speed of the second brother's spaceship and he travels faster than the speed of light then the term (-1)^.5 will not calculate. Therefore, %c under the radical has to be flipped when working with warp speeds so that the radical doesn't have a negative number. The distance to the supernova is 170,000 light-years, as per the topic in Discovery Magazine.

Now we can work with *Wn* as the speed of a neutrino.

By extending the Lorentz equation and flipping the speed ratio (%c), we can show the time difference between two particles, a neutrino and a photon, whereby the neutrino is traveling much faster than the photon, moving at light speed.

From the Lorentz equation, we can derive my equation to calculate the difference in time between two particles traveling at warp speeds if we assume the "speed ratio" is flipped over when two particles are both traveling beyond light speeds.

When the speed ration if flipped over, we can let:

1. "t" equal to the time it takes a neutrino to travel from a distant star   where:

   $t = d/\%c$ d equals distance and %c equals the ratio of the   speed of the neutrinos divided by the speed of   light.

   Or

   $\%c = Wn/Wc$ with the warp speed of light equal to 1; that   is, (Wc =1).

   Solving for Wn, where Wn is the warp speed   of   a neutrino.

   > Then $\%c = Wn/Wc = Wn/ 1 = Wn$
   >
   > And $t = d/Wn$
   >
   > This term is the same as the Lorentz term, but the next term under the exponential is flipped instead of (speed/light speed)^2, we use (light speed/speed)^2 or (Wc/Wn)^2.

2. "t' " equal to the slower time for photons (light) coming from   a supernova.

   > The exact formula with photons on the "heels" of neutrinos leaving the supernova is difficult to formulate. Therefore, we will assume that they both leave together.

$$t' = t*(1-(\%c)^2)^{.5}$$

3. "t-t'" equal to the difference between the speeds of neutrino and photon or:

$$(t - t') = d/\%c - t*(1-(1/\%c)^2)^{.5}$$
$$= d/\%c - d/\%c*(1-(1/\%c)^2)^{.5}$$
$$= d/\%c*(1-(1*(1-\%c)^2)^{.5}$$

Since t-t' has the units of light-years, t-t', measured in hours, has to be expressed as (t-t')/(24h*365d). The speed of a group of neutrinos can be calculated if t-t' has been measured as a few hours. An equation with two unknowns can be solved in Excel format if the two unknown variable such as Wn, neutrino speed, and d, distance, are assigned a number.

Simplified:

$$(t-t')/(24*365) = Wn*(1-(1-(1/Wn)^2)^{.5}$$
$$= 365*24*(D - D*(1-(1/Wn)^2)^{0.5})$$

As an Example:

$$(t - t') = 365*24*(1700 - 1700*(1 - 1/600)^2)^{.5})$$
$$= 20.7 \text{ hours, the first line illustrated in the table.}$$

My formula can be used because it is a derivative of the Lorentz formula. As per Wikipedia, Hendrik Lorentz underpinned Einstein on his special theory of relativity. Both scientists were deriving formulas to represent object moving at light speeds and sub-light speeds. Einstein had formulas for the change in "energy" and the change in "mass" when objects approach light speeds. However, Lorentz had a formula for a change in "time." My research has led me to believe that no one has developed any new physics formulas to anticipate objects moving faster than the speed of light. Einstein's equation with the term $(-1)^{.5}$ is a road-block for newer scientist today. However, I believe an extension of the Lorentz formula, as I have proposed, does exist.

The result of the following Excel table provides interesting results, whereby "Neutrino Warp speed" or "Wn" is calculated against two randomly picked variables; namely,   "Distance to the Nova" and "t-t' delay in hours." The equation and the data table illustrate a linear regression with the exception of the last line showing that neutrinos can travel 10,000 times the speed of light with a delay of 7.4 hours. Evidently, neutrinos cannot travel that fast! At this point, I will assume that the supernova didn't explode at 170,000 light-years away but rather at 1700 light-years away.

The final results with all substitutions for calculating the speed of neutrinos is as follows:

Neutrino Warp speed	Distance to Nova	t-t' delay in hours
600	1700	20.7
800	1700	11.6
1000	1700	7.4
1200	1700	5.2
1400	1700	3.8
10,000	170000	7.4

If the measured difference was a ***few hours***, then the neutrinos could have been traveling at Warp 10,000. Not likely. Again, we do not know the time difference between the neutrinos and the photons leaving the supernova. The reporter for *Discovery Magazine* didn't relay this information from the scientists.

I know this is a lot of math. So, let's create an analogy. Let's assume there are three brothers who were born at the same time.

The first brother is living on Earth; the second brother is in a spaceship traveling at sub-light speeds; and the third brother is in a spaceship traveling at Warp 100. Let's also assume they have video-chat capabilities that take place instantly. They can see each other on a monitor screen. After **twenty years** have passed, the first brother appears with all-white hair; the second brother appears with gray hair; and the third brother has black hair, the same color as when he left Earth. The second brother looks at his brother on Earth and says, "Looks like you got a little older." The third brother agrees. Then the second brother looks at his third brother with black hair and ask, "Did you get younger, brother?"

The passage of time slows down for the person traveling at sub-light speeds, and it slows down, even more, traveling at warp speeds. This concept parallels what Charlie said, "You gain what you lose as you cross the light speed barrier." The second brother with the gray hair looked older, while the third brother with the black hair looked younger.

Sun light, composed of photons with particle mass, bounce off every hydrogen and helium atom before they leave a star. Their delay with respect to neutrinos as they leave a star lacks a method for measurement or any subsequential calculations. An analogy is two horses at the starting gate. At the sound of the bell, one horse takes off while the other stands behind the open gate. The slower horse like the photon takes off when the faster horse like the neutrino is in the home stretch. The starting delay is probably equivalent to one horse 53 feet from the finish line while the other horse is still at the starting gate, one mile away.

If the starting delay represents a one percent probability (53/5280) and the difference of time-arrival on Earth is 7.4 hours, then the group speed of neutrinos is Warp 100. Expressed in different words, groups of neutrinos leave an exploding star one hundred times faster than photons. If Discovery Magazine had published a delay between measured neutrinos arriving on Earth and light from the exploding star, they would have entered 7.4

hours. As a double check, a one percent probability of the maximum value, 170,000 light-years, equates to 1,700 light-years.

The calculations match the data for a group of neutrinos when a nova occurred in an exploding star 1,700 light-years away. To believe otherwise, is to assume that neutrinos traveled at a warp speed of 10,000 times the speed of light from a nova 170,000 light-years away.

For documentation purposes, the average speed of a group of neutrinos reduces to 100 times the speed of light. A reasonable value!

From this point, we'll assume that the ten percent rule applies. In other words, the neutrino could have been traveling at warp 1,000 and reached Earth in 7.4 hours. However, the ten percent rule allows for a delayed start of the photon, still bouncing around in the star, and provides a reasonable speed of 100 times the speed of light. In the next section, we'll illustrate a Gaussian distribution with an average speed of warp ten and an upper three sigma value of warp 20. This seems more reasonable than a warp speed of one thousand.

My story of Enoch, has the Celestials traveling at a warp speed of one hundred. Consequently, we don't know if the average warp speed of neutrinos is ten (10), one hundred (100), or one thousand (1000). But we do know that they travel faster than light. The answers can be found by our scientists when they monitor Tabby's star. I'll describe an exact method for the collection of observable data from Tabby's star and determining the average speed of neutrinos.

Imagination is required to understand how neutrinos can travel faster than the speed of light. An analogy would be a carousel (merry-go-round) spinning around at a carnival; on board, is a packet (small number) of photons and neutrinos spinning at an angular speed. Then the carousel lifts off the ground and heads for the sky at the speed of light. The force that was holding the neutrinos on the carousel breaks up. One by one, the neutrinos leave with two vector speeds: light speed and angular speed. If light speed is Warp 1 and angular speed is Warp 99, then the neutrinos are traveling at Warp 100. The photons continue to travel in packets with particle motion and wave characteristics—namely, frequency and phase (angular speed).

Similarities exist for television broadcast signals. Wave characteristics identical to a TV broadcast have three components modulating the carrier frequency; namely, FM, frequency modulation producing the sound; AM, amplitude modulation producing the picture; and PM, phase modulation producing the chroma or picture color. All electro-magnetic transmissions, including, light beams, have FM, AM and PM signatures, but proof of a light beam akin to a carousel is unmeasurable with today's scientific equipment. An imagination of fast-moving particle brings home the concept.

An additional clue to this carousel analogy is the physical construction of the hydrogen atom: one proton and one neutron dancing around each other like a fat person and a skinny person. The neutron is the smaller object in very close proximity to the proton. An electron circles the pair in an orbit much, much further away. When a hydrogen atom crashes into another hydrogen atom in the sun, nuclear fusion occurs producing helium and a small, left-over mass that converts into nuclear energy as per the equation, $E = \Delta mc^2$ whereby Δm represents a micro-fractional change in mass.

Within the proximity of the blast, radiation energy transforms a small group of stable hydrogen atoms, protons and neutrons, into photons and neutrinos that escape the gravitation pull of the sun. Small groups of both particles travel at light speeds in packets, spinning like a carousel and emitting neutrinos with its angular speed: spinning faster within the confines of the sun; and spinning slower away from the sun. A very fast angular speed causes the packet to emit "smaller" size neutrinos within the sun's plasma. As the packet leaves the sun, the angular speed slows continuing to emit "larger" neutrinos that were clinging to the packet with a greater gravitational force.

Photons remain within the confines of their packets while neutrinos of all sizes whip away with the ability to travel the galaxy, sailing through every known object until they reach their dead-end—a Black Hole. The ultra-strong gravitational pull of a Black Hole located in the center of every galaxy attracts neutrinos from every sun within its galaxy. The flow of neutrinos across the galaxy is comparable to creeks, streams and rivers of water flowing across our planet. The largest flow of neutrinos in this book is referred to as a barrier (or barrier-rib or a rib) separating our galaxy into multiple sectors. If our galaxy is 10 light-years thick, then our barrier-rib is 10 light-years thick and very, very dense in the galactic orbital plane where more and more neutrinos congregate.

To enhance the idea of a flow of neutrinos into a type of river or a barrier-rib, we will discuss the unusual phenomena of an unusual star, called Tabby's Star, with its light dimming on and off as per scientists. But first, the immediate goal is to discuss Gaussian curves and its relation to a barrier-rib within our galaxy.

The Gaussian Distribution-Curve

In the August 2001 issue, Discovery Magazine published an article about scientists who had obtained significant knowledge during their advanced research on neutrinos. They specified the significance of two important discoveries. The first was a statement that said, "More than 1,500 trillion neutrinos pass through a person's thumb nail every three seconds." The second statement on page 34 involved the usage of the word "flavor" which pertains to a report from the Kamioka Observatory.

The Kamioka Observatory is a neutrino and gravitational waves laboratory located underground in the Kamioka Mining and

Smelting Company near Hida, Japan. A set of extensive neutrino experiments had taken place at the observatory over the past two decades. All their experiments contributed substantially toward particle physics: specifically, the study of neutrino astronomy and neutrino oscillations.

According to a review of their efforts, published in Discovery Magazine, their scientist did not understand how the mass of a neutrino oscillates between being there and not being there! The Kamioka observatory also supported an even stranger idea that a given neutrino does not have one stable oscillation or one stable identity. They are quoted as saying, "As it flies along, it oscillates from one identity to another—what physicist call 'favor', which means a way of interacting with other particles." One Kamioka researcher referred to the phenomena as, "A Dr. Jekyll and Mr. Hyde sort of an affair."

Based upon earlier discussions of "Neutrino Speed," it is possible to surmise a Gaussian distribution-curve. Scientists that work with statistics, use many formulas to describe such events. The most common is a histogram whereby a random set of numbers fall into a smaller set of numbers called cells or buckets. For example, falling leaves from a maple tree characterize a histogram when their measured lengths are dropped into buckets with the smaller leaves in a bucket on the left side and the larger leaves in buckets toward the right side. Each bucket represents in a graph with cells on an x-axis and the total amount of leaves in each bucket on the y-axis. Let us assume there are three buckets for the fallen maple tree leaves. There are four leaves in the first bucket with a length between 1 to 2 inches, six leaves in the second bucket with a length between 2 to 3 inches, and four leaves in the third bucket with a length between 3 to 4 inches. A histogram with numbers 1,2,3 on the x-axis and 4,6,4 on the y-axis can be drawn to represent a Gaussian curve. Histograms have multiple shapes and corresponding names for bell-shaped curves: some lean to one side while others are flat, round or double topped. A true Gaussian curve is a histogram with symmetrical alignment on both sides as per a specific math formula.

The example using falling maple leaves is the start of a Gaussian curve. Scientists have derived formulas for Gaussian curves in the y-x-plane to define normal patterns and abnormal patterns. The formulas for a histogram can prove if the sample was contaminated. A histogram with two humps (like a Bactrian camel) would represent fallen leaves from two trees of a different type: a maple tree and an ash tree, for example.

The beauty of a Gaussian curve is that it represents "nature" and the uniform production of anything that is grown, manufactured or created in the cosmos. If a man is asked to cut a very long plank, 1 by 6 inches wide, into 4-foot lengths, some boards will measure 3.937 feet minimum while others will measure 4.0625 feet maximum 015—an error of 1/16 of an inch. Most will measure 4 feet with a perfectly square cut. Another man on the job may not achieve a perfectly square cut, and the histogram of all the cut boards will have a double hump. Consequently, we can conclude that anything that represents "natural selection" will have a Gaussian distribution-curve.

Neutrinos are "zero-rest-mass" particles; they have no weight when standing still. When they are moving, they are invisible to the eye, unavailable to the touch, and thought to increase in mass the faster they travel. They originate in the cosmos.

There are no formulas to describe the mass of a neutrino. An approximation, it would look like:

$m = m` \div (1- v^2/c^2)^{.5}$

where the real mass, m, is equal to the rest mass, m`,

at different speeds. If the "zero-rest-mass" has a small quantity, then it is divided by the square root of 1 minus the ratio of velocities squared with v equal to the actual speed of the neutrino and c equal to the speed of light. This formula is part of Einstein's predictions.

This equation illustrates the problem that scientists have in trying to believe that neutrinos travel faster than the speed of light. The theory states that nothing can travel faster than the speed of light because the mass would be astronomically large or m = m` divided by zero, when v equals c. Any number divided by zero equals infinity. However, there is a possibility that physics equations invert themselves beyond the speed of light.

Since we do not know the calculated mass of a neutrino, we can surmise a formula for neutrinos traveling faster than the speed of light as follows:

m ≈ m` * (1 + v^2/c^2)^.5

where the denominator becomes the numerator,

and as an approximation:

m ≈ m` * v/c ≈ m` * warp speed

where m` would represent the mass at Warp 1,

the speed of light, and v/c is now, warp speed.

A Gaussian distribution-curve for a group of neutrinos would look like the following:

The goal is to show galactic travel has feasibility based upon increased, particle mass of the neutrino with a Gaussian distribution as shown above. If the assumed formula for increased mass versus warp speed is correct, then the possibility of travel among the stars exists.

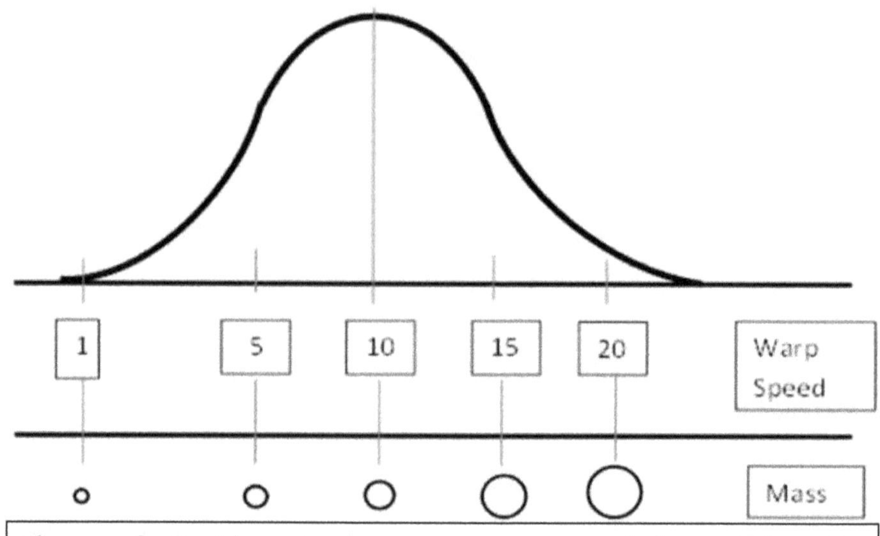

Histogram for Neutrinos, showing an average warp speed of ten, which could also be one hundred or one thousand.

Scientists are aware that neutrinos travel in dense population: something like 1,500 trillion passing through a thumbnail in three seconds. If the word *population* defines the variance in the travel of neutrinos, then a "population" represents a group's characteristics. Henceforth, speed and mass characterize the flow of neutrinos. Earlier calculations for Supernova 1987A have shown that neutrinos have an average speed of Warp 1000. For the sake of preventing an argument due to insufficient data from Discovery's magazine, we will work with a more conservative value of Warp 100 for the average speed of all neutrinos. Using a previous formula for mass increases beyond Warp 1, we can extract a linear relation between warp speed and mass. If a neutrino has a mass of 1 au (atomic unit, not to be confused with astronomical unit) at Warp 1, then its mass would be 5 au at Warp 5, and 10 au at Warp 10, etc.—a linear function.

So how does a neutrino, weighing 1 au, push a 100-ton spacecraft across the galaxy? A neutrino traveling at Warp 1 is akin to a feather with a sharp quill piercing a lacy window curtain stretched across a wooden drying frame, but a neutrino traveling at Warp 100 is akin to a water balloon breaking on impact with the window curtain. The "push" is initiated when numerous neutrinos––with larger masses, small masses, warp speeds less than Warp 100 and warp speeds greater than Warp 100––crash into the spacecraft giving it greater and greater momentum. The process is not unlike a sailboat sailing in the wind. Some sailboats can exceed the speed of the wind if the keel drag is reduced.

In 2017, I postulated the "curtain rod" theory in my journal while writing in a doctor's office, waiting for the release of my wife. Two years later as I prepared for book publication, I read in Discovery Magazine, December 2019 issue, that scientists are closer to understanding the neutrino. I will copy three statements from their magazine:

> 1. The idea of sterile neutrinos gained traction when an experiment in the 1990s recorded a strange excess of one flavor, called the electron neutrino, over the other two (now known to be muon and tau neutrinos).

> 2. Experiments revealed that neutrinos transform from one flavor to another spontaneously as they flit about the universe.

> 3. Researches have high hopes, in fact, that landing a sterile neutrino will crack the door open into a realm of new physics beyond the standard model, dramatically dubbed the dark sector.

As an optimistic author, I was delighted to read scientists will eventually associate the neutrino as a particle more common to the fourth dimension with various mass densities. The "flavors" that they define, equate to my description of a feather and a water balloon piercing a curtain hung on a curtain rod. This is the "push" needed to propel a spacecraft.

Conflict with Einstein's Equations

Einstein's Theories

In 1905, Einstein published a paper known as The Special Theory of Relativity that included the following topics and conclusions:

1. Speed of light is constant

2. Length contradiction whereby an object's length appears shorter when moving than its proper length

3. Time dilation is the difference between two observers experiencing an event.

4. Relative mass covers the laws of motion

5. Mass-energy equivalence, $E = mc^2$

6. Adoption of the Lorentz transformation equation published by a Dutch physicist in 1902 regarding the passage of time

In 1915, Einstein published another paper known as The General Theory of Relativity that included the following topics:

1. Inclusion of Newton's law of universal gravitation whereby force can be calculated as the attraction between two static particles or magnetic poles

2. The curvature of "space-time"

3. The acknowledgement of radiation emission consisting of:

- Electromagnetic waves

- Radio waves

- Microwaves

- Infrared, visible light, ultraviolet, X-rays, Gamma rays

4. Acknowledgement that energy cannot be created or destroyed

The Lorentz transformation was discussed in Appendix 3 to show how the minus sign under a radical ($\sqrt{-1}$), or $(-1)^{.5}$ produces unknown results. The conclusion in Appendix 3 was that minus sign under the radical sign does not impose a problem when traveling in imaginary time.

This appendix is an addition to Einstein's General Theory to show that the curvature of space-time defines the existence of a barrier separating sectors of our galaxy. The barrier is the flow of neutrinos traveling at multiple warp speeds and imposing the blockage of light referred to by scientists as "Tabby's Star," KIC 8462852.

Rib Theory with Images of Tabby's Star in Different Positions

The possibility of the existence of a Dyson sphere was presumed by scientists to be the culprit causing the fading and brightening of Tabby's Star in the constellation of Cygnus. For several years, scientists measured a 20 percent dimming of light from Tabby's Star. They have proposed the following explanations:

1. If a planet the size of Jupiter revolved around Tabby's Star, it would block 1-percent of the light. Therefore, the planet circling Tabby's Star would have to have a diameter twenty times larger than the diameter of Jupiter. (Conclusion: impossible.)

2. Because the blockage of light is aperiodic, scientist propose that an elliptical dust-cloud circles Tabby's Star producing dimming of light for two days followed by another dimming one-month or even one year later. (Conclusion: impossible.)

Scientists are at a loss to justify their explanations (shown above) and the possibilities of a Dyson sphere created by aliens to generate power as it surrounds the star. A more logical explanation for the dimming is due to a dust-cloud of neutrinos––not dust particles. The reader is asked to envision a river of neutrinos lumped together in high-density blocks of matter, flowing between Tabby's Star and Earth. The aperiodic randomness occurs when the river of neutrinos flows in an erratic motion between sectors of our galaxy. Like any river on Earth, the river of neutrinos between galactic sectors has *bends and turns*, giving it the characteristics of lumped matter flowing at astronomical speeds.

The strongest proof for the existence of high-speed neutrinos are measurements similar the ones Einstein used to verify his General Theory of Relativity. Calculations were made with data taken from Discovery Magazine to show that the average warp speed of a neutrino travel at Warp 1000. The data in Discovery Magazine was recorded by scientists who measured the arrival of neutrinos "a few" hours ahead of the arrival of photons from a supernova that exploded in 1987. Sequentially, a Gaussian curve was illustrated with the neutrino's average speed of Warp 10, which could also be Warp 100. Due to the possibility of measurement errors by the scientists, the most likely speed of average neutrinos is Warp 100.

If humankind is destined to fly to the stars propelled by the speed of neutrinos, it is important to collect proof in the form of astronomical data. Rib Theory is about the separation of the spiral arms of our galaxy due to fast flowing blocks of neutrinos flowing in between sectors of the spiral arms.

Tabby's Star and our solar system are on the same galactic plane that runs through the center of the galaxy. We live in a plane with half the galaxy above us and the other half below us. Rib Theory also states the flow of neutrinos in the galactic center between spiral arms is very dense. The flow of neutrinos causes the light from Tabby's Star to dim and reappear aperiodic. The following sketch shows that the dimming of light from Tabby's star is a process caused by a dense flow of neutrinos. A cyclic flow of dense blocks of neutrinos, followed by a lesser flow of neutrinos, permits light to shine through in a random order. Earlier discussions showed that photons travel in a way called packets. Both photons and neutrino share a random method of travel; namely, packets and blocks. (I have chosen the word block(s) to label a group of neutrinos packed together in high density, akin to peas in a pod.)

Measurements can be made to verify this theory as follows:

Einstein's General Theory

My "Rib Theory" (circa 2020)

Tabby's Stars Positions (1 & 2) in the Next Spiral Arm of our Galaxy

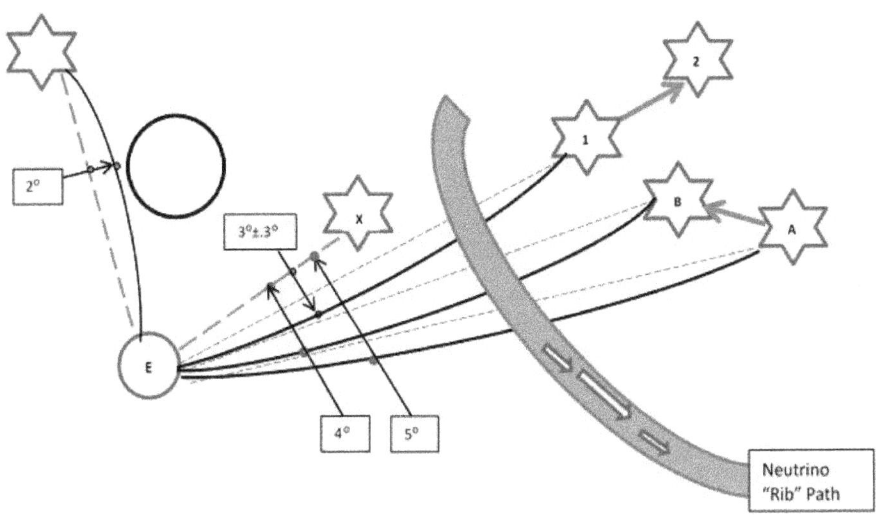

Light Beams (aka: Photons)

w/ Straight Path

w/ Actual Path

2° Arc Difference

= $\int$ mass of photon & sun speed

Neutrinos

w/ Strong Wave

w/ Weak Wave

+1° Arc Variance

= $\int$ neutrinos' mass & speed

A Logic Measurement:

1. The light difference of $3°\pm.3°$ between star, X, in Earth's sector is measured against Tabby's Star, 1, in the sector.

2. At a later date, step 1 is repeated when the light from Tabby's Star can still be seen. If the measurement is the same, then the Neutrino Rib is not influencing the data. Every star in the galaxy is constantly drifting to a new location; i.e., point 1 to point 2. Tabby's Star has a drift variance of $.3°$.

Now, let's assume Tabby's Star starts in position A.

3. When the light from Tabby's Star fades, the light difference of $5°$ between star, X, in Earth's sector is measured against Tabby's Star in position A.

4. A day or two later the measurement is repeated as the light from Tabby's Star returns. Now the light difference is $4°$ as Tabby's Star appears to be in position B. The mass of the neutrino block has simulated a shift in the star's position as if it moved from position A to position B, a shift of $+1°$ ($5°- 4°$).

Both sketch and the logic, illustrate a similar technique used to prove Einstein's General Theory. The average speed and mass of neutrinos can be determined from angular shifts, the known distance to Tabby's Star and its known mass. Several years after Einstein announced his General Theory of Relativity, scientists were able to record the difference between two light paths from the same star during a solar eclipse. In the sketch above, the polar coordinates specified in degrees represent numbers for discussion purposes. If the distance to star behind the sun is known, then the arc difference of $2°$ (degrees) can be related to the functionality of the mass of the photon and the known mass of the sun: expressed mathematically as 2^0 Arc Difference = ∫ mass of photon and sun. The gradational pull of the sun is so strong that it bends the light beam because the light beam is a series of photons with particle mass.

The same technique can be used to model information about neutrinos creating a "barrier-rib" by measuring the degree of variance in light coming from a distance star in an adjacent spiral arm.

With respect to light coming from a reference star, X, the light from Tabby's Star exhibits a polar angle shift of one degree (5^0 minus 4^0). Two conditions have to be met to obtain valid data: first, repetitive measurements have to be made over several years and secondly, the movement of the reference star has to be in the original line of sight at all times. The above image illustrates how valid data is obtained when a star appears to move from position A to Position B with an arc variance of 1^0. The variance signifies that a wave of neutrinos, with their collective masses, are blocking the reception of photons from Tabby's Star. Similar to the Einstein experiment using a solar eclipse, the 5^0 to 4^0 difference of 1^0 can be related to the mass and speed of the neutrinos: expressed mathematically as $+1^0$ Arc Variance = ∫ mass and speed of neutrinos. (Obviously, the calculations are left for the physicist because they involve integral calculus with Cartesian and Polar coordinates.)

Partial Proof for Rib Theory

On July 30, 2018, the Science Channel presented a TV documentary on a mysterious star that they nicknamed Tabby's Star. On September 14, 2015, the Kepler telescope received light data from the Tabby's Star located in the Cygnus constellation, 1500 light-years away. Additional information from Wikipedia confirms that Cygnus is located on the center plane of the Milky Way. The Science channel reported that astronomers had no explanation for the drop in light intensity over irregular periods.

During the TV documentation, astronomers considered the possibility that the massive dimming of starlight was attributed to a planet orbiting Tabby's star. Additional calculations caused the astronomers to rule out the existence of a planet for the following reasons:

- The dimming of the star's light is aperiodic.

- The massive blocking of star's light equates to an orbiting planet   twenty times the size of Jupiter. An impossibility.

If the Tabby's Star was in another spiral arm, as suggested in the above image, then its light intensity would vary as neutrinos are masking its intensity and most likely, causing a small angular degree variance. With a little information about our galaxy and a little bit of astronomical endeavor, we can visualize our solar system and Tabby's Star in two different sectors on the same galactic plane with a "barrier-rib" in between. Since our galaxy is 10 light-years thick, the barrier-rib would have the same thickness with the strongest of gravitational waves in the center plane of the galaxy.

To preempt physicist cranking out formulas, we can speculate that neutrinos have a gravitational pull of their own because they are massive and travel at speeds greater than the speed of light. Einstein's secondary equations state that the mass of an object approaches infinity as it nears the speed of light. So, what is the answer to this contradiction: specifically, the need of a spacecraft to sail with neutrinos faster than the speed of light and yet, able to handle their increase in mass?

Both options are possible when we revert to our hypothesis about neutrinos existing in imaginary time. If we are destined to sail in a galactic spacecraft without the consumption of fuel, we are going to have to believe in a new type of physics. So let us build a scenario, "Fast moving neutrinos exceeding Warp 1, grow more massive." At Warp 100, they are easily stoppable, like water balloons hitting a curtain pinned to a curtain rod: but, at Warp 1, they are unstoppable, like a pointy arrow piercing the same curtain. Consequently, the neutrinos with the higher warp speeds push the spacecraft harder. All speculation herein is derived from the arc variance of $+1^{\circ}$, mathematically producing average mass and average speed of a neutrino.

Einstein's General Relativity Theorem was proven with light from a distant sun bending around our sun. Mathematically, the proof is an integral function of the photon's mass and the mass of our sun. The same modeling technique can be mathematically resolved with an integral math function containing the neutrinos' mass and the neutrinos' average speed as it bends the light from Tabby's Star.

Previously in Appendix 3, linear equations were used to calculate the average speed of neutrinos based upon data taken from an article in Discovery Magazine that discussed the time delay of photons with respect to neutrinos coming from a super nova. The article stated that the delay was "a few hours" and that the distance to the supernova was 170,000 light-years. My math calculations indicated that the neutrinos would have travel at warp 10,000 if the delay was 7.4 hours. However, calculations with slightly altered variables, representing a "few hours," indicated that neutrino speed varies between warp 600 and warp 1400. A conclusion was made to suggest that a more reasonable speed of the average neutrino was warp 100 with a Gaussian distribution of warp 1 to warp 200 for the neutrino population.

In conclusion, I have shown the possibility of galactic flight, using neutrinos as a propulsion mechanism; written a novel about an alien visitor, named Enoch, who told you what it was like traveling at warp speeds; used fictional characters to talk about scientific ideas, and more importantly, I have a belief that the answers to many questions are buried in the Holy Bible.

As I approach the end of my book, I just want to say that this manuscript is a second revision of a ninety-seven thousand word draft. In the first draft, I explained the "Angio" disease and how it exists in female relatives. I went into great detail describing the construction of an object that could function like a Foo Fighter—and the construction of a spaceship. But a good friend who read my first draft said it was too scientific. So, I'll end my book with a fraction of that boring scientific stuff.

The following is an Excel chart that I used for my base equations. Basically, it was used to calculate the speed of an object in free-fall towards a planet with units expressed as a percentage of the speed of light. It Is intended to be read only by other engineers.

	A	B	C	D	E	F	G	H
2	**Speed of Light**	**Feet to meter**	**seconds**	**ft/mi**	**mi/sec**	**Calculated**		**Actual**
3	3.00E+08	3.25	1	5280	1.85E+05	185000	mi/sec	186000 mi/s
4	3.00E+08	3.25	3600	5280	6.65E+08	665000000	mi/hr	671*10^6mi/hr
5								
6				**Objects in free fall**				
7	**MilesFromEarth**	**feet**	**t^2=ft/a**	**t**		**velocity**		**%c**
8	12	63360	1980	44 sec		1424	ft per sec	0.000
9	25	132000	4125	64 sec		2055	ft per sec	0.000
10	200	1056000	33000	182 sec		5813	ft per sec	0.001
11	200000	1056000000	33000000	5745 sec		183826	ft per sec	0.019
12	MilesEarthToMars							0.000
13	50000000	2.64E+11	8.25E+09	90830 sec		2906544	ft per sec	0.298
14								
15		**Velocity**						
16	**mi/hr**	**ft/hr**	**ft/sec**	**Back to mi/hr**				
17	Speed entering Earth		183826		125336			0.019
18	67000	353760000	98267		67000			0.010
19	Total speed leaving Earth		282093		192336			0.029
20								
21	Final speed arriving at Mars		2906544		1981735			
22	**Speed of light**							
23	671,000,000	3.5429E+12	984133333					101
24	**Seconds**	**Hours**	**Days**			Lght Speed		
25	5745	2	0.1			3.00E+08 m/sec		100.00
26	90830	25	1.1			9.75E+08 f/sec		100.00
27								
28								

A spacecraft's speed relative to the speed of light as it approaches

$$\%c = 100* \ 183{,}826/9.75810\verb|^|8 = .183*10\verb|^|8/9.75*10\verb|^|8$$

$$= .019\%$$

The speed of the earth around the sun is equal to circumference of its orbital path divided by 365 days. The earth is 93 million miles from the sun.

$$V = 2*\pi*93*10\verb|^|6/365 = \ 67{,}000 \ mi/sec$$

When all the correct units are introduced, the speed of the earth is 67,000 miles per hour and equivalent to .01% the speed of light. If the falling object is a UFO that does not crash on Earth— —but travels through Earth——then total vector speed of the object exiting Earth is (.019% + .01% = .029%). The UFO would be traveling at .029 percent the speed of light or 192,336 mph.

There is a high probability that a UFO spacecraft is capable of switching to zero gravity in imaginary time, and then switching back to real time while gravitation takes hold, and then switching again into imaginary time and sailing through the earth's core at .029% the speed of light. As per the data table, the spacecraft is moving at 192,000 miles per hour. The earth provides a tremendous "sling-shot" effect by traveling "through it" not "around it."

Appendix 4

Space Skipping: The Eighth Dimension

The Book of Ezekiel describes itself as the words of the Ezekiel ben-Buzi, a priest living in exile in the city of Babylon between 593 and 571 BC. His book, copied into the Holy Bible, describes a vehicle traveling in the sky as a wheel within a wheel.

An ideal galactic spacecraft should have a fifth dimensional chamber imbedded within a fourth dimensional vehicle, capable of traveling at Warp 100. The chamber is reserved for travelers who don't want to experience acceleration and deceleration. The equivalent experience is riding inside an elevator without the change in gravity—the heaviness going up and the free fall going down. If the fourth dimension, or imaginary time, can be applied to the three dimensions that we know as x, y and z, then the fifth dimension can be applied to the fourth dimension and a physical object like a spaceship.

The phrase: "a wheel within a wheel" describes the fundamental construction. Initial attempts to build a spacecraft or a smaller spaceship may reveal internal mechanical stresses that limit the ship to only Warp 10. Greater emphasis on the elimination of acceleration and deceleration is more important than trying to achieve greater warp speeds.

Let's stop and ask, "How many dimensions are possible?"

In my first book, I wrote about electromagnetic waves like RF (radio frequency) signals that travel at the speed of light with E-fields and H-fields, opening, closing, and interlocking with one another. If one electromagnetic wave could be seen standing still, it would resemble a woman's necklace with one link interlocked with another link. If you can picture a necklace twisting, then you can picture an electromagnetic wave corkscrewing through space.

Therefore, in being brief, an E-field can exist with circular sides or with straight sides. The same is true for a H-field as per the drawing. The image is a snapshot of three configurations existing in the fourth, fifth, and sixth dimensions, each having a corkscrew motion, known as "phase."

Additional dimensions are theoretically possible up to the eighth dimension. Two variables for each field, curved or straight sided, with three combinations of x, y and z equate to 2^3 or 2x2x2, producing 8 variations. Each configuration of an EMF, electromagnetic field, will produce its own imaginary time zone.

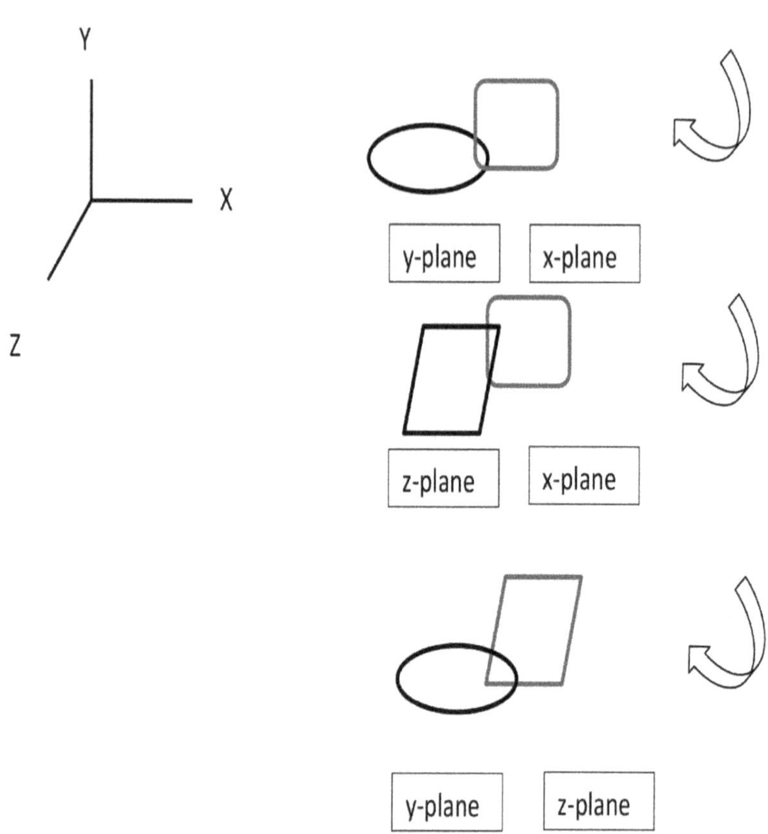

So theoretically, there are eight (8) dimensions that a spaceship can travel in. My story of Enoch starts with Enoch traveling in a W-5, a four-dimensional ship that could achieve warp 5. The story refers to the Celestials who could travel in their W-25s, their W-50s spaceships, and later on, in their W-100 space cruisers. I wrote about the Celestials having the ability to travel in the fourth and fifth dimensions, combined and not experiencing any antigravitational effects while accelerating or decelerating. The maximum speed they could achieve in their W-100 was one hundred times the speed of light.

Did I write about the Celestials traveling in the sixth dimension? No, I did not. However, the sixth dimension is easy to visualize. It's an extension of the fifth dimension that allows them to "teleport" down to their home planet!

The sixth dimension also has to have an additional advantage. If the Celestials can extend a portal into outer space, then they can theoretically use that portal to catch a neutrino wave that's moving faster. If you ever surfed in Waikiki Beach, in Hawaii, as I have, you would know what it's like to catch the top of an incoming ocean wave. When you're riding on your surfboard, you can see the wave in front of you, the one that passed you by. If you could, somehow, skip to that wave in front of you, you would be double-surfing and covering more distance.

The seventh dimension would be akin to a smooth, slick, river rock skipping across a pond of silent water—a galactic cruiser traveling at warp five-hundred without any noticeable effects on the crew while tenacious, turbulent undercurrents below impart new energy to the cruiser, a Black Hole cast into the cosmic void and pulling the travelers forward at greater speeds.

The Feasibility of Space Surfing

Einstein's theory of general relativity mathematically predicts the existence of wormholes, but none have been discovered to date. If neutrinos travel in bundles as suggested during a study of Tabby's star, then space surfing would be as common as men and women riding a surf board on ocean waves, while moving at tremendous speeds with respect to the bottom of the ocean.

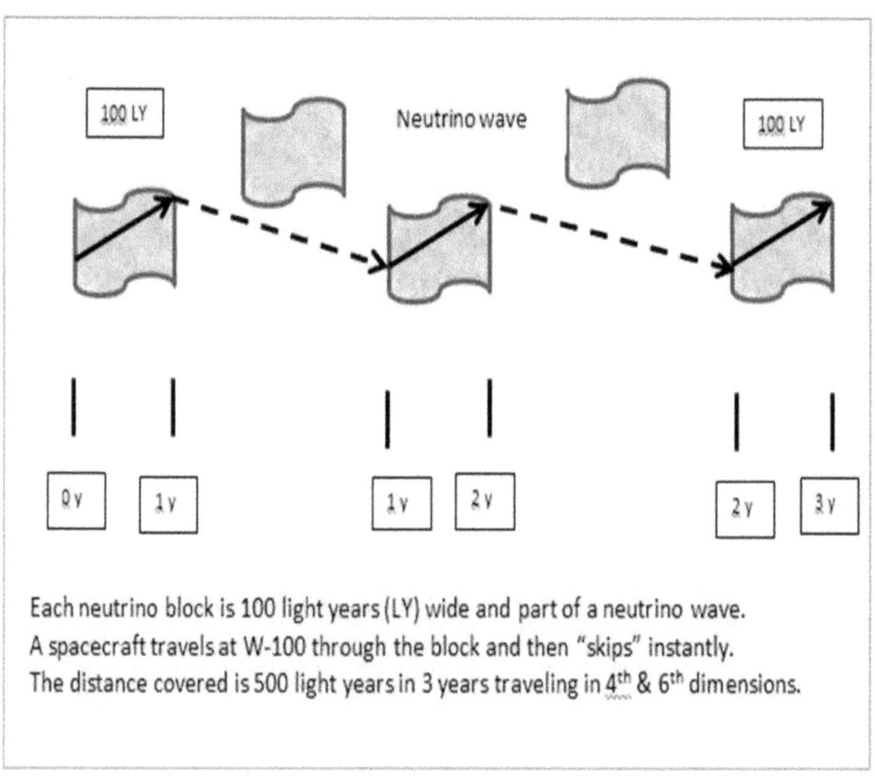

The next drawing illustrates blocks of neutrino waves like the ocean waves rolling into the coast. We have defined neutrino waves as having a dense formation when we discussed the unusual dimming of Tabby's star in Appendix 3. We have provided mathematical proof that neutrinos are traveling much faster than light speed when we quoted an article from Discovery Magazine about documented data with neutrinos arriving on Earth a ***few hours*** ahead of photons from an exploding nova.

The drawing concludes that a space craft, traveling at warp 100, can utilize the sixth dimensional *arm or portal* to grab the next *block* of neutrinos and skip across 500 light-years within three years

Actually, it is impossible for this author to imagine what it would be like traveling in the seventh dimension, casting Black Holes ahead, utilizing their gravitational pull, and traveling through them at warp-500 to absorb their energy. The idea is inconceivable because Einstein said that matter cannot be created or destroyed. Man cannot create Black Holes. But maybe Einstein was wrong? The **eighth dimension**, however, is the highest dimension of travel, possibly imaginable.

To Quote the Internet

The Higgs boson is the fundamental particle associated with the Higgs field, a field that gives mass to other fundamental particles such as electrons and quarks. The Higgs boson was proposed in 1964 by Peter Higgs, François Englert, and four other theorists to explain why certain particles have mass.

The quotation, "gives mass to particles," is Einstein's equation in reverse. Instead of $E = mc^2$, whereby mass is converted to energy, as in atomic bomb, the equation is reverse, whereby $m = E \div c^2$. The equation states that mass is created out of pure energy. This is why scientists have named the Higgs bosun particle as the God particle.

With these facts, in mind, it's easy to imagine traveling in the eighth dimension. For example, you're sitting in your living room; you see a speck of dust floating in the air next to where the floor and wall meet, along the x-axis. The speck of dust disappears. Puff. You spot the speck of dust reappear near the ceiling where the walls meet, along the z-axis.

As another example, you're sitting outside on your porch; you see a sparrow standing next to a river. The sparrow disappears. Puff, it's gone. Within the same time frame, you see the same sparrow flying up towards the mountains.

Topics Not Included in This Book

The following topics were *not included* in this book because of their lengthy, technical information.

1. The H-stones in Bolivia, South America:

- used as an early bell weather, forecasting conditions on Earth,
  - transmitted to aliens, thousands of light-years away,
  - composed of electromagnetic waves caused by lightning strikes
  - and magnetic disturbances.
2. Galactic communication techniques:
   - techniques for communicating with the home planet,
   - traveling at warp one hundred,
   - modulation of an atomic-blast frequency,
   - caused by a detonated probe sent ahead of the spaceship.
3. Navigation techniques in outer space:
   - the need for a three-dimensional guidance system,
   - Christopher Columbus sailed in only two dimensions, forward and across, with three ships from Queen Isabella and a sounding bell that rang every fifteen minutes. Longitude distances were unknown when he sailed west. So, how did Columbus know where he was going while sailing in a two-dimensional environment? Did all three ships "tack and turn" every fifteen minutes with the first two ships forming a straight line-of-view for the third ship?
4. Techniques for entering imaginary time:
   - as discussed in my first and second book with illustrations,
   - explanation of fields and waves traveling in a TEM mode,
   - or transverse electromagnetic mode.
5. Techniques for building a spaceship:
   - Again, this discussion took place in my earlier books. To be brief, illustrations show how an electromagnetic field can be combined with a magnetic field,

- and how neutrinos can be captured like a wind-sail to propel a spaceship.

Just a Few More Technical Words on Imaginary Time

If I didn't say anything more about item 4, above, it wouldn't be unfair to the reader who has come this far and wants to learn more about entering imaginary time. Here goes:

In my first two books, I draw an illustration of a plastic ball, about the size of a tennis ball, with a Colpitts oscillator inside. The function of the oscillator is controlled with built-in, photo-sensitive, steering diodes. The plastic ball is spinning in an upward wind current from an old vacuum cleaner operating in reverse, supporting the ball in midair with a controllable flow of air. Inside the center of the ball, is a *work zone or cross-section* with two air wound coils on both sides producing a magnetic field that is either constant or switched on and off. Perpendicular to the magnetic field, inside the spinning plastic ball, is an electromagnetic field that is controlled by the Colpitts oscillator to produce sinusoidal waveforms or square waveforms, richer in harmonics. If you walked into the laboratory, this is what you would see.

The technical process is to produce an electromagnetic field that "links up" with the magnetic field in the cross-section. Bessel functions are a mathematical equation to equate the amplitude of each term for the fundamental frequency and the harmonic frequencies. As an example, suppose a crude Bessel function looks like F = A*sine(x)*cosine(y) +B*sin(x)*cosine(y) +C*sine(x)*cosine(y) + et cetera with D, E, F, G and so on. The amplitudes of A and B and C are the Bessel functions. A sinusoidal wave would have "A" equal to "1", "B" equal to ".5" and "C" equal to ".25". A square wave would have "A" equal to "1", "B" equal to ".9" and "C" equal to ".8". Can you see the numeric sequence of the two different wave forms?

By trial and error, the lab-tech is trying to mate (or pair) a magnetic field that is looking for a third term Bessel function of "C" equal to ".8", a square wave. If that doesn't work, then the lab-tech tries a magnetic field looking for second term Bessel function of "B" equal to ".5", a sinusoidal wave form. The lab-tech is pulsing the plastic ball with different strobe lights. When he succeeds after an estimated combination of 9,000 trial and errors, the ball disappears into imaginary time. It will leave the proximity that the Earth occupied. It will separate from Earth at the same speed the Earth is traveling around the sun or 67,000 miles per hour, as per my working table. Now, doesn't this sound like a UFO leaving orbit at a high rate of speed?

Item 5, above, can also be described, briefly, for the scientific reader. If a small plastic, transparent ball can be launched into imaginary time, then an entire spaceship can duplicate the same procedure. As a brief example:

The design of a spaceship requires the same three basic variables; namely motion or spinning, a magnetic field, and an electromagnetic field. The only difference in technique is that the spaceship is lined with very thin, semi-metallic plates. The plates can be magnetized into "ones" and "zeros" akin to an old VHS tape recorder. The magnetic ones and zeros flow across an electromagnetic field, while the *work zone or cross-section* is spinning. And again, the spaceship will leave Earth at 67,000 miles per hour because there are no gravitational restrictions in imaginary time.

We End Where We Started

On page three of this book, I started with the beliefs of Saint Thomas and I stated my belief in both science and religion. I realize this is a very technical book. As an engineer, who reads the Bible, I have difficulty reading beyond Genesis because the words aren't plain words. They have a meaning. I believe they were written to have a special meaning, especially chapter 5, written by Moses. He had to have had some angelic help recalling specific years for the life cycles of our biblical ancestors. There are more than fifty numbers in chapter 5. I truly believe it is a calendar we were meant to interpret. Moreover, if Moses writes about seeing God, then I believe he did see God.

I could have written the story of Enoch with more emphasis on religion, with Father Aye, praying, with the people on Bethel, attending church, or with the Celestials, living closer to God. I could have, but I chose not to. We all have free choices. Isn't that why we are here . . . on this Earth and not on Bethel. And what about being our Brother's Keeper? Are we supposed to do that? I believe we are.

I wrote this arduous book, not to gain profit, not to gain notoriety, not to prove any theorems. I'm a senior citizen, and I wrote this book because I believe humanity is going in the wrong direction: a non-religious direction, a non-civilized direction, and a non-scientific direction with their wasteful rocket ships.

In conclusion, I wrote this book because I believe it is possible to travel the galaxy at warp speeds. It can be done. As a secondary benefit, I tried to explain how the atmosphere on Mars and even our own atmosphere can be depleted of carbon dioxide as per the GIT curve. Perhaps, it's more important that we solve Global Warming before we travel to the stars!

There are so many unknowns that our society faces. Within the novel section of this book, I made references to Mr. Edward Leedskalnin, the Florida guy, who claimed he had discovered the

stone-moving secrets of the Egyptians. Before I end my writings, I would like to enclose a photo of Coral Castle and dwell upon the idea that one man could move multi-ton stones.

The story about Enoch is a soft introduction for readers who are non-technical. For that matter, it could be true that there is a person of our same species, a descendant of Enoch, living on another planet, visiting Earthlings that need help.

In summary, the story of the Galactic Traveler is a proposition that:

- Einstein's formulas for the universe are incomplete,

- Charles Darwin had it all wrong,

- The Holly Bible expresses God's intent, beginning with Genesis.

To further the claim that "we are not the descendants of ape", I have written a sequenced book titled The Galactic "Time"

Traveler. The theme is similar, whereby the people on Bethel help the people on Earth, as per the request of the Celestials, who in essence live next door to God. In a way, the people of Bethel live five doors away from God, while the people of Earth, with their human frailties, live ten doors away from God. Didn't Jesus say that the kingdom of heaven has many rooms? (John 14:2 "In my father's house are many mansions.")

Personally, I believe that we are going somewhere when we die—call it the Elysian Fields or whatever. Consequently, *The Galactic **Time** Traveler* is a story about Enoch's son, born in the late twenty-first century, raised as a potential Custodian to help Earthlings, and engaged with human frailties like the rest of us. For his contrition, the Celestials give him the task of going back in time to help certain individuals on Earth. His demise is the passion he has for a woman who was born on Bethel by a human mother, Brianna, and elevated into sainthood by her father who is a religious Celestial. Enoch's son and his girlfriend travel back in time to visit different Earthlings and all the while sharing a steaming romance while performing their mission. Be sure to read my next book, slated for publication in late half of 2023.

Charles E. Anzalone

Time-Period	Name of Place And Location	What Happened?
22,349 BC	Garden of Eden	Adam and Eve walked the Earth
15,000 BC	Puma Punku, Bolivia	"H" Stones built for *Navigation* Scrubbed during re-edit
11,382 BC	Great Flood, Mt Ararat	Noah & animals disembark
10,800 BC to 10,735 BC	The Sphynx Giza Plateau, Egypt	The Sphynx is built for man to show he has dominion over all animals
10,500 BC	Gobekli Tepe, Near Mt. Ararat, Turkey	The lost animal population was restored on Earth after the flood
2,500 BC	The Great Pyramid Giza Plateau, Egypt	The Great Pyramid is built for alien *Navigation* purposes
0 BC	Nazca Lines, Peru S.A. Bethlehem, Israel	Arial landings are built in Peru Jesus is born in Bethlehem

The Author's Former Books

- *Galactic Travel at Warp Speed in Imaginary Time,* written in 2007, published the following year.
- *Orion's Highway Across the Galaxy,* written in 2011, published in 2012.

Books That Inspired the Author:

1. The Holy Bible

2. Nostradamus by Mario Reading

3. Fingerprints of the Gods by Graham Hancock

4. A Briefer History of Time by Stephen Hawking

5. The Gods of Eden by William Bramley

6. Mythology by Edith Hamilton

7. Various issues of Discovery Magazine

Literary Books That Influenced the Author:

1. *Building Great Sentences* by Professor Brooks Landon
2. *How to Write Dazzling Dialogue* by James Scott Bell
3. *Writing Creative Nonfiction* by Professor Tilar J. Mazzeo
4. *Writing Great Fiction* by Nancy Kress
5. *Conflict and Suspense* by James Scott Bell

Technical Books, Required at the University of Illinois:

1. About ten engineering books used at the University of Illinois in physics, atomic physics, thermos-dynamics, electrical engineering in fundamentals, in circuit design, in electromagnetics, in network analysis and synthesis along with a math class for every semester I attended.

Resume and Status:

1. Attended the University of Illinois for two years in Premed

2. Served in the Navy 1957 to 1961

3. Married November 24, 1962

3. Graduated from University of Illinois in 1964 with a Bachelor
   of Science degree in Electrical Engineering

4. Worked and consulted as an degreed engineer for 40-years

5. Retired and wrote two books

6. Living at home and taking care of my wonderful wife

A special thanks goes to my high school buddy and longtime friend, Bill Svetly, who showed me how to laugh and enjoy life.

I also wish to thank Ms. Lis Korkel who summarized my book and Ms. Gloria Mendez who edited my book.

Charles and Harriet Anzalone

**Prior to our 56th Anniversary, and before
my wife had a hemorrhagic stroke.**